Praise for *If Only in My Dreams*

"[A] sweet, moving love story."   —*Romantic Times*

"[W]inning romance . . . subtle, effective, and enjoyable."
—*Publishers Weekly*

"Thoroughly original and unpredictable, Markham's latest is a delight."   —*Booklist*

"[D]elivers an engaging, cinematic time-travel romance."
—Barnes & Noble

"One of the most romantic love stories of the year . . . a beautiful love story . . . refreshing and original."
—Contemporary Romance Writers

"I finished what I consider to be the best book I have read in 2006. . . . This is a book I would recommend to everyone."   —Romance Readers at Heart

"The story is poignant. . . . Wendy Markham's writing is at her best. Easily, this is her best story to date."
—Roundtable Reviews

continued . . .

If Only in My Dreams

Wendy Markham

A SIGNET ECLIPSE BOOK

SIGNET ECLIPSE
Published by New American Library, a division of
Penguin Group (USA) Inc., 375 Hudson Street,
New York, New York 10014, USA
Penguin Group (Canada), 90 Eglinton Avenue East, Suite 700, Toronto,
Ontario M4P 2Y3, Canada (a division of Pearson Penguin Canada Inc.)
Penguin Books Ltd., 80 Strand, London WC2R 0RL, England
Penguin Ireland, 25 St. Stephen's Green, Dublin 2,
Ireland (a division of Penguin Books Ltd.)
Penguin Group (Australia), 250 Camberwell Road, Camberwell, Victoria 3124,
Australia (a division of Pearson Australia Group Pty. Ltd.)
Penguin Books India Pvt. Ltd., 11 Community Centre, Panchsheel Park,
New Delhi - 110 017, India
Penguin Group (NZ), 67 Apollo Drive, Rosedale, North Shore 0632,
New Zealand (a division of Pearson New Zealand Ltd.)
Penguin Books (South Africa) (Pty.) Ltd., 24 Sturdee Avenue,
Rosebank, Johannesburg 2196, South Africa

Penguin Books Ltd., Registered Offices:
80 Strand, London WC2R 0RL, England

First published by Signet Eclipse, an imprint of New American Library,
a division of Penguin Group (USA) Inc.

First Printing, December 2006
First Printing ($4.99 Edition), November 2007
10 9 8 7 6 5 4 3 2 1

SIGNET ECLIPSE and logo are trademarks of Penguin Group (USA) Inc.

Printed in the United States of America

PUBLISHER'S NOTE
This is a work of fiction. Names, characters, places, and incidents either are
the product of the author's imagination or are used fictitiously, and any resem-
blance to actual persons, living or dead, business establishments, events, or
locales is entirely coincidental.

The publisher does not have any control over and does not assume any
responsibility for author or third-party Web sites or their content.

If you purchased this book without a cover, you should be aware that this
book is stolen property. It was reported as "unsold and destroyed" to the
publisher, and neither the author nor the publisher has received any payment
for this "stripped book."

The scanning, uploading, and distribution of this book via the Internet or via
any other means without the permission of the publisher is illegal and punish-
able by law. Please purchase only authorized electronic editions, and do not
participate in or encourage electronic piracy of copyrighted materials. Your
support of the author's rights is appreciated.

For my guys, Mark, Morgan, and Brody . . .

And in loving memory of the three beautiful women our family has lost to breast cancer: my mother, Francella Corsi; my mother-in-law, Claire Staub; and her sister, Frances Ginsberg.

Silently one by one, in the infinite meadows of heaven,
Blossomed the lovely stars, the forget-me-nots of angels.

—HENRY WADSWORTH LONGFELLOW

ACKNOWLEDGMENTS

The author acknowledges with gratitude the contributions of Mark Staub, Leonard Staub, Mark Lipton, Lisa Ginsberg, David Ginsberg, David H. Lippman, and Joel Gultz. Any historic inconsistencies are my own and quite possibly deliberate, for the sake of the plot.

Thank you also to my wonderful editor, Laura Cifelli, whose timing is exquisite; to my publicist Nancy Berland and her terrific staff; to my agents Laura Blake Peterson, Holly Frederick, and Nathan Bransford at Curtis Brown, Ltd.; and to the helpful librarians at the Katonah Village Library.

Prologue

Thanksgiving, 1941
Glenhaven Park, Westchester County, New York

"That was Glenn Miller and his Orchestra with his newest hit record, 'Chattanooga Choo Choo.' And now, before the latest news from Europe, a word from our sponsor, Lifebuoy."

Lois Landry looked up from the potato she was dicing. "Go turn that off, Doris." Her voice was sharper than the paring knife in her hand.

"But I—"

"Just do it, toots." Jed shot his kid sister a warning look.

Doris grumbled her way to the radio in the dining room, where Penny and Mary Ann were carefully setting the table with the fancy Royal Doulton wedding china.

The prized place settings had seen perhaps two dozen Thanksgiving meals in Jed's lifetime, with a few notable exceptions: 1929, in the wake of the stock market crash, when a turkey dinner was an extravagance the Landrys couldn't afford, and again a decade later, when Pop lay dying in an upstairs bedroom and a holiday meal was the last thing on anyone's mind.

Abner Landry lingered, comatose, far longer than

anyone expected, as though he were determined to see the trying decade through to its final month. Jed kept a silent, solo vigil at his father's bedside that long final night, through November's waning hours and the dawning of December.

There were no profound last words, no dramatic requests or heartfelt promises. Not aloud, anyway. Not from Pop.

But as he clutched his father's lifeless hand, Jed swore that he would come home for good. He would step into his father's shoes as head of the household and the family business.

He had kept that vow for two oppressive years now.

What matters most is that Jed is back here in Glenhaven Park, where he never expected to be, taking care of things, just like his father would have wanted.

Yes, as Jed's friend Arnold Wilkens often says, sometimes the longest way round is the nearest way home.

But I'm not going to stay any longer than I have to.

Crossing the aqua-speckled linoleum to the glass percolator on the white enamel stove top, Jed glanced at the smoky November sky beyond the glass-paned back door, then at the row of hooks on the white painted beadboard beside it.

Funny how he almost expected to see his father's brown wool jacket draped there even now. In the heat of July he finally convinced his mother to move it to the front hall closet. It hung there still, because Lois couldn't bear to give it, or any of Abner's other belongings, away.

Nor could Jed bear to ask her if he could go through the shirts and trousers and dungarees Pop left behind—much less help himself to them. Granted, at a lanky six-three, he's a full head taller than his stout father was. Still, shirt seams can be taken in, trouser hems let down . . .

If it wouldn't tear Mother apart.

But it would.

Better for Jed to keep spending whatever the household could spare on his brother Gilbert's college textbooks, or dresses and shoes each time Penny, the oldest of his three sisters, had a growth spurt. The younger girls could make do with her hand-me-downs, just as Gilbert did with Jed's. And Jed, well aware he couldn't possibly spare two dollars for a new shirt much less twenty-five for a suit, would go right on wearing his own outdated clothes.

As he poured another steaming cup of coffee, his mother set aside the potato and the knife and turned away from the sink. He noticed anew that her once luxurious dark hair was now liberally streaked with gray, and her mouth and eyes were firmly entrenched in wrinkles.

Two years of widowhood had taken a harsh toll on the woman who was once the prettiest gal in New York City, according to Pop.

Over the rim of his mug, he watched her open a white metal cabinet door and stare at the row of home-filled mason jars and store-bought cans: peaches, green beans, Spam . . .

"Did you run out of something you need?" he asked at last.

"Hmm?" she asked absently.

Jed realized she wasn't even seeing the items on the shelf. No, she was thinking about old times. Her round blue eyes—Betty Boop eyes, Pop called them—always took on that dazed expression when she thought about her late husband. Bittersweet memories were more plentiful than fallen chestnuts at this time of year, with the looming holidays and anniversary of Pop's death.

Jed repeated his question as, in the dining room, the radio abruptly went silent.

"Mother told me to do it, so there!" Doris retorted loudly over her older sisters' prompt protest. Jed pictured her scrunching up her freckled face, twisting her pink-ribboned red pigtails, sticking out her tongue.

"Aw, go chase yerself," Mary Ann shot back.

"I'm telling on you."

"For what?"

As the girls' voices became more shrill, Jed watched his mother slam the cabinet door and reach for her pack of Pall Malls on the counter.

"For being rude," Doris bellowed in the dining room.

"Go ahead and tell. I'll tell, too."

Lois thrust a cigarette between her cranberry red lipsticked mouth, then bent over the stove to light it from the gas burner.

"Do you want me to go in there and straighten things out?" Jed was compelled to offer, though doling out discipline to his siblings was his least favorite household role. The girls resented him; Gilbert defied him outright.

"No, you just sit right down and drink your coffee." Mother took a deep drag of the Pall Mall as her daughters continued to bicker. "And when you're done with your coffee, you can go next door and borrow Sarah Wenick's kitchen chairs before she leaves for her sister's house. She's loaning them to us for the day."

Both extra leaves were already in the dining room table to accommodate the assorted family members who would share the feast with Jed and his mother, siblings, and maternal grandparents, all of whom lived under this roof. Cousin Amy and her new husband were driving down from Saratoga Springs, and Uncle Elmer, Aunt Marge, and their four children were taking the train up from Brooklyn.

Everyone would do their best to make it a festive day despite their lingering grief, the looming shadow of the war in Europe, and the peacetime draft that had already claimed several of Jed's old high school pals.

So far he had been spared—a good thing considering how much he was needed here at home.

But he had yet to reconcile his long-held dreams and ambitions with reality.

From the time he was deemed academically gifted as a child, Jed knew he was destined for great things. His parents and teachers told him so; he was encouraged to study hard and strive to be the best. He graduated as valedictorian of his high school class; nobody was surprised when he won a full Ivy League scholarship.

It wasn't just giving up the potential for an important career in Boston that still stung now, two years after being forced to drop out of Harvard Law just six months shy of graduation.

It was losing Carol.

He probably shouldn't have assumed she would accept his impromptu marriage proposal.

But he brazenly had it all figured out: their summer wedding at the First Congregational Church, a honeymoon in the Catskills, the cozy newlywed nest they would create over his mother's detached garage, since Grandma and Granddad had taken over his old bedroom when he left for Harvard.

"You want me to marry you and live in a garage like . . . like a nobody?" Carol had asked in disbelief.

"Not *in* a garage. *Above* a garage."

He was still down on one knee at that point. But it didn't take him long to get up. Get up, and start walking.

Here he was, two years later, living alone over the garage of his mother's house on Chestnut Street in Glenhaven Park.

Officially a nobody.

Last he heard, Carol married some Harvard law school grad and was living in a Back Bay townhouse. A Somebody, as she always wanted to be.

Jed supposed he had a lot to be thankful for this Thanksgiving. Not marrying a self-centered social climber probably should have been one of them.

Yet he couldn't help but think he was wasting his life as a small-town bachelor, running his late father's five-and-dime, feeling like a glorified soda jerk. At one point or another he had dated most of the available gals in town and fallen in love with none of them, although several reportedly had their sights set on him.

Just yesterday, Betty Godfrey had attempted to cozy up to him over a chocolate malted and reminded him of the movie *Caught in the Draft*, which he had taken her to see after the Independence Day parade. "Remember how Bob Hope tried to avoid the service by getting married? Just think, Jed, if you were married, you wouldn't have to worry."

"I'm not worried," he told her, mopping up the countertop with a dishrag. "If I get called up, I'll serve."

"Where would that leave your mother?"

"My brother's graduating from Penn State next spring," Jed informed her. "He's planning to come back to Glenhaven Park. When he does, he'll take care of Mother and the girls and run the store."

What Jed didn't admit was that he was counting the days until Gilbert's return . . . or that he was planning to enlist the day his brother got back, anyway.

Just two years ago, FDR staunchly promised that America wouldn't fight unless attacked. Yet between the new draft, the Lend-Lease Act, and the Atlantic Charter, it was increasingly obvious that the president expected the country to be dragged into the war. And Jed would have to fight, like his father had back in 1917.

No question about it. Just as it had been his responsibility to step up as man of the house when Pop died, it would be Jed's duty to protect his country from the tyranny spreading like a malignancy overseas.

Mingling with his patriotism was an unabashed desire to see the world beyond the eastern seaboard. Yet, much to his shame, he also harbored secret doubt that he could ever harm another human being, under any circumstances.

His father always liked to tell the story of Jed's first childhood fishing expedition in the Catskills. Pop threw in his own line, landed a hefty trout—then fended off a surprise attack from his pint-sized first-born, who tore the wriggling catch from the hook and hurtled it back into the stream, shouting at Abner to pick on someone his own size.

Jed never did grow to enjoy fishing the way his father and brother did. Or, God forbid, hunting.

Not that he was a sissy. No, he lettered in three sports in high school, including football. But physical confrontation on the gridiron was one thing. Going hand-to-hand anywhere else was quite another. Unlike his volatile kid brother, he avoided schoolyard skirmishes, though when forced, he rolled up his sleeves to rescue Gilbert from the clutches of neighborhood tormentors like Waldie Smith.

Maybe if Jed thought of the Nazis as overgrown bullies, he'd be capable of violence after all. Particularly in self-defense. But he didn't like to think about that. And he didn't have to . . . not yet. Not for another six months.

Though nobody in the family knew of his intent to join, he was certain they wouldn't be surprised. His restlessness was no secret around here.

Here in the steamy, fragrant kitchen on this Thanksgiving day, watching his mother set her cigarette aside to open the oven door to check the roasting turkey, he felt a twinge of guilt for even thinking about leaving someday.

Mother needed him. They all needed him. He had been the head of the family for two years now. Two years next week.

But I need a life of my own, he told himself. *I need to get back out there. Just for a few years.*

I'll put in my time, I'll have some adventures, I'll meet a swell woman, and I'll bring her back here to settle down.

Leafy, friendly Glenhaven Park was the perfect place for a fellow to raise a family.

For Jed, it was home . . . and it probably always would be.

What he couldn't know, as he sipped his hot coffee in the comforting warmth of home on this Thanksgiving Day, was that Someday was going to come much sooner than he expected . . .

Or that his coveted ticket out of town would be only one-way.

Chapter 1

Malignant.

It's the last word Clara McCallum really comprehends, though it's far from the last one Dr. Svensen utters.

Sitting in the patients' chair, clutching the wooden arms with the tenacity of a white-knuckled flier, Clara is vaguely aware of other phrases. Phrases that are equally familiar, equally repugnant, hovering in the air like noxious fumes.

MRI and bone scan.

Lumpectomy.

Chemotherapy and radiation.

None of this is registering. None of it seems to matter.

In the wake of *malignant*, what could possibly matter?

As Dr. Svensen goes on talking in her soothing voice, Clara sits staring at the robust, foil-wrapped potted white poinsettia on her desk, regretting . . .

Well, everything.

Everything she didn't have a chance to do and now, perhaps, never will: get married, raise children, win an

Oscar or a Golden Globe or even just a Daytime Emmy, for God's sake. Is a Daytime Emmy too much to ask?

What about the rest? What about celebrating her thirtieth birthday, living somewhere other than New York City, having a baby . . .

This can't be happening.

". . . surgeon," Dr. Svensen says. ". . . hospital . . ."

It is.

It *is* happening, and Clara regrets not just things she hasn't done, but things she *did*.

Smoking cigarettes back in her Broadway days, to rev up her metabolism and keep herself audition-svelte. Ingesting all those artificial sweeteners, every day, all her adult life, right up to the ubiquitous Diet Coke she drank in the cab on the way uptown just now. Never getting enough sleep, always under so much stress . . .

And then there's Jason.

I probably shouldn't have broken the engagement after all. We came so close . . . so damned close . . .

Why did I throw away a five-year relationship on a whim, thinking something better was going to come along?

Something better never did . . . and now it never will.

"Clara . . . here." Dr. Svensen passes a box of Kleenex across her desk.

Only then does Clara realize she's crying. She accepts the box, plucks a white tissue and wipes away the tears, only to have them instantly replenished like the biological counterpart of a Hollywood rainmaking machine.

"This can't be happening to me. I have too much to do. I have a movie to make."

It sounds so incredibly lame, even to her own ears. But Dr. Svensen's sympathetic expression provides validation, so she goes on, brokenly. "Everything is finally falling into place with my career. I can't be sick. I can't *die*."

"Clara, come on. Try to breathe. Deep breaths." The doctor reaches for her hand, the one that isn't holding a soggy tissue.

Clara knows the gesture is meant to provide comfort, but it only seems to seal the raw deal. Dr. Svensen, her gynecologist since high school, is not ordinarily a touchy-feely, emotional person. Clara's prognosis must be pretty bleak if they're holding hands.

The doctor's fingers are as cool as her typical bedside manner; her grasp feels like a farewell handshake.

Clara wrenches her hand away and rakes it through her long brown hair, a longtime habit of hers.

"Clara—"

"I'm going to die." She looks into the physician's eyes, noticing that they're gray. Light gray . . . like a granite tombstone. "Right? I'm going to die."

She waits for the doctor to dispute the statement with reassurance. Or even just to put a philosophical spin on it with a bullshit line like *We're all going to die someday*.

Neither of those things happens.

Dr. Svensen squeezes Clara's hand again. "You're fortunate that we caught it early. And to be living here in Manhattan, with access to a number of fine treatment facilities."

Does she have to sound so professional, so . . . formal? Why can't she just agree that this sucks? Why can't she at least talk about miracle cures or something?

"My grandmother died of this same thing. What are my odds of surviving it?" Clara braces herself for the answer.

"Very good."

A whoosh of air escapes Clara's lungs and she slumps in her seat. "But . . . my grandmother—"

"That was decades ago." Apparently having taken a recent refresher course in McCallum family medical history via Clara's file, the doctor shakes her head. "In this day and age, a diagnosis like yours isn't the automatic death sentence it used to be."

So promise me I'm not going to die, dammit. Can't you just say that?

She can't die. She has a movie to make, her first big feature role. The kind of role that might propel a teenaged-Broadway-dancer-turned-soap-actress directly to major Hollywood player.

Why is this happening? Why now, *of all times?*

It's almost December, for God's sake. Her favorite time of year. She hasn't even started her Christmas shopping yet. She opens her mouth to tell Dr. Svensen, then clamps it quickly closed again.

Dr. Svensen won't find retail deprivation significant. She won't understand that it's not about shopping. That for Clara it's about more, so much more than that.

As a child caught in the middle of a heartbreaking divorce, Clara lived for the holidays, when her parents seemed to call an unspoken and temporary truce.

Long after he moved out, Daddy continued to come to their Central Park West apartment on Thanksgiving morning to watch the Macy's parade pass beneath their window with Clara and her mother. He even stayed to eat turkey and stuffing and the Pillsbury crescent rolls Clara always made for him because they were easy, and happened to be his favorite food in the entire world.

Daddy would eat at least six rolls and announce that he couldn't eat another bite, not even pie, though they all knew he had another dinner planned later in the day with whichever girlfriend he was seeing at the time. "I feel like the Pillsbury Doughboy," he would say, pushing back his chair from the table. That was Clara's cue to poke him in the stomach, and he would giggle, just like the Doughboy did in the commercials.

Clara loved Thanksgiving.

In December, there was Hanukkah. Daddy was half-Jewish, his mother's side. Mom was always invited to the celebration. She usually came, for Clara's sake, and because she adored latkes and applesauce and sour cream almost as much as she loved her former in-laws.

Then there was Christmas. For years after he left home, Daddy carried on the tradition of choosing a tree with Clara. They would lug it along West Sixty-eighth Street to the apartment, where Mom was waiting with hot chocolate. They decorated it as a three-some, always.

On Christmas Eve, for as long as Clara pretended to believe in Santa Claus, Daddy spent the night so he could see what Santa left her under the tree. He slept on the couch, but Clara didn't care. For one magical night of the year he was there, with her and Mom, where he belonged. For one glorious morning, the three of them woke up together, sat around together in their pajamas, just the way they used to before the divorce. Just like a real family.

"Do you have any questions, Clara?" Dr. Svensen's voice interrupts.

"Only one. But I'm assuming you can't *promise* me

that I'm not going to die of cancer, can you," Clara says flatly.

"The survival rates at your stage are increasing every year, and you have a good chance of going into full remission."

"Full remission?" Clara exhales the breath she didn't even realize she had been holding.

Full remission. That's reassuring. Still . . .

Malignant.

And no promises.

How did a routine gynecological exam lead to *this*? How is it possible that just a few hours ago, she was on the set of her new movie, running lines with her co-star? When her cell phone rang, it never even crossed her mind that it might be her doctor with the results of that routine biopsy.

After all, the lump was so small Dr. Svensen almost missed it. Clara certainly did—not that she's in the habit of self-exams, anyway.

She probably should have been, with her family history.

Probably?

For God's sake, how could you have been so lax?

Dr. Svensen didn't seem particularly worried when she found the lump, high on Clara's right breast, almost under her arm. She said she was going to test it strictly as a precaution. That it didn't feel like anything Clara should be concerned about, so she wasn't.

Nothing to be concerned about.

Hah. Famous last words.

Now her head is whirling with questions, from *Should I make a will?* to *Will I lose my hair?*

She settles on the latter, because in her line of work, it's hardly insipid.

"Possibly, depending on the chemo drug they go with," is the disconcerting reply. "But you can get a realistic-looking wig. With all the performing you've done, you're probably no stranger to wigs, are you, Clara?"

"I've never been bald underneath them," she says curtly, and her trembling fingers once again thread their way into the thick brunette mane that became her trademark back when she was on *One Life to Live*.

One Life to Live . . . ah. Talk about irony.

"I'm sorry," Dr. Svensen is saying. "I just meant that with your theatrical background, you've probably—"

"It's okay." Clara softens her tone. "I know what you meant. I'm just . . ."

She trails off, wondering how she can possibly describe what it is that she's feeling.

It would be much, much easier to describe the one thing she *isn't* feeling: *hopeful*.

After all, she can't forget that her maternal grandmother, Irene, died of breast cancer. Decades ago, as the doctor pointed out. Long before Clara was born.

The shadow of that loss hangs over her mother's life to this day, albeit not over Clara's. She has always had more of her father's breezy and upbeat disposition.

In contrast, her mother is the most skittish, fatalistic person Clara has ever known, darting through life as though the grim reaper lurks at every turn.

Jeanette Bradshaw always assumed that the cancer that took her mother and an aunt would one day claim her. She has been religious about self-exams and yearly mammograms. She's on a first-name basis with every employee at her neighborhood health food store; she supplements her diet with exotic herbs and vitamins, eats organic this and soy that, all in an effort to stave off what she considers to be the inevitable.

Wait till she finds out the old grim reaper skipped a generation, Clara thinks grimly, wondering how she's going to break the news to her mother.

Then again . . .

Why even tell her? Is sharing the burden with her mother really necessary at this stage? The last thing she wants is Mom hovering at her sickbed, helplessly wringing her hands and forcing organic sprouts down her throat.

Mom doesn't have to know until . . . well, until she *has* to know.

After all, it's not like she's going to drop by Clara's apartment anytime soon. She fled New York weeks ago, well ahead of winter's first snow. Now she's safely ensconced in a Florida condo with her new husband, Stan, whom she married last spring.

Clara is supposed to fly down for Christmas, but only for a few days because of her film's rigorous location shooting in a northern suburb.

I can always just tell her I have to work right through the holidays . . .

Yes, and then what? Spend Christmas alone . . . and bald?

There are worse things, Clara tells herself, chin up, tears dried. Far worse things than that.

Clara's block of West Eleventh Street in Greenwich Village is lined with charming nineteenth-century townhouses, their narrow frontage separated from the sidewalk by low black wrought-iron rails. Matching grillwork protects the ground-level windows and door tucked beneath the wide steps that lead to the main entrances half a story above the street.

The Federal-style facades are typically redbrick, topped by flat roofs marked by jutting deep-bracketed eaves. The distinct architectural pattern on the three main floors reminds Clara of a tic-tac-toe board: a door occupies the lower left box, while framed paned windows fill out the remainder of the grid.

Tonight, U2 is playing loudly on her iPod as she opens the low gate before her building and trudges up the steps. She initially considered choosing something more seasonal, having downloaded dozens of classic carols off the Internet just last week. Maybe Barbra Streisand's uplifting first Christmas album, or perhaps something soothing and classical: Tchaikovsky's *Nutcracker*.

But in the end, she concluded that Bono wailing familiar, angry lyrics about war and love might be the most cathartic music for her mood.

A dank breeze is blowing off the Hudson River a few blocks to the west, the unseasonably mild weather a reminder that technically, it's still autumn. Winter's inevitable chill seems months away.

Before Clara can insert her key into the lock, the front door swings open. She steps back and looks up to see Drew Becker.

The first time she met him, he was unloading a rented moving van at the curb on the fifteenth of last month.

Their eyes met above a precariously tilting stack of boxes he was carrying, and she saw a spark of recognition in his.

She wouldn't have pegged him for a soap opera fan; he must have seen her movie.

"Hi," he said, wearing the usual *Don't I know you*

from someplace? expression she's used to receiving from strangers on the street.

And for a split second, she actually thought that she might know him, too.

Then he said, "I'm Drew Becker," and she didn't recognize the name.

Nor, when she got closer and politely held the door for him, did she recognize his face after all.

She once read somewhere that four out of five people in the world have brown eyes and dark hair. Her new neighbor is among them, yet his features are anything but common. His eyes bear the translucent warmth of her father's single malt Scotch, his hair the burnished richness of her well-worn leather jacket.

But she isn't attracted to him. She might be, if she allowed herself that indulgence. But she won't. Not with him. Not with anyone.

Especially not now.

At least he didn't ask her for an autograph that first day, if indeed he did realize who she was when she introduced herself as Clara McCallum. She did find herself thinking fleetingly that she wouldn't have minded if he asked for her phone number.

But he didn't. Which was definitely for the best.

They chatted in the vestibule, but not for long. The boxes were heavy.

Just long enough for Clara to learn that Drew's from California—northern, not southern. Wine country, not Hollywood, thank God.

Maybe his flirtatious behavior on the two occasions she's run into him has nothing to do with the fact that she's an actress. Still, she's deliberately kept him at arm's length, Jason still fresh in her mind.

Now, Drew mouths something as he holds the door open for her.

She unplugs her earphones. "I'm sorry . . . what did you say?"

Drew props the door open with his shoulder. "I just asked how you are."

"Uh-oh, loaded question," she says with a bitter laugh.

"What's wrong?"

"No, nothing . . . I didn't mean to say that out loud."

"Bad day?"

"You could say that."

"Come on, no bad days allowed at Christmastime."

"It isn't Christmastime yet."

"Sure it is," he persists cheerfully.

Feeling prickly and unreasonable, she insists, "No, it isn't. Not until December. December doesn't start until Friday."

"I don't know about New York, but where I come from, Christmastime officially starts the day after Thanksgiving. Which was almost a week ago."

To her horror, she finds tears springing to her eyes.

"Well, it's not Christmas here yet," she repeats tersely. "The Rockefeller Center tree still isn't even lit."

"So that's what kicks off the holiday season in New York?"

She shrugs. Technically, it's Santa riding down Broadway at the end of the Macy's Thanksgiving Day parade, but she's not in the mood to expound on the joys of Christmas in Manhattan.

"I guess you're not big on holidays, huh?"

"Who doesn't love holidays?"

"Then you just don't celebrate Christmas?"

"No, I usually do, but this year . . ."

She shrugs again, wondering how the heck she managed to mire herself in this uncomfortable conversation.

"What are you doing this year?" asks her nosy neighbor.

"For Christmas?"

He nods.

Fighting for my life.

"Nothing."

"No family?"

"My father's going away, and I was supposed to go see my mother in Florida, but . . ." She shakes her head. "That's not going to work out."

To Drew's credit, he doesn't ask why.

"That stinks," is all he says.

"Yeah." She takes a deep breath, straightens her shoulders. "Whatever. I'll be fine. I mean, you know . . . I'm a big girl."

"Yeah, well, if you want to hang out with a big boy over the holidays, I'll be on my own, too."

"You're not going home to California?"

"Can't. No vacation time yet. I just started my job."

"What is it that you do?" she feels obligated to ask, not really caring.

"I'm an investment banker."

Just like Jason. Which promptly squashes any potential attraction she might have eventually allowed herself.

Stable, grounded, totally left-brain. Not a good match for her.

"Hey, I just realized . . . you remembered," he says cryptically.

"What you do? No, I—"

"Where I'm from."

"Oh. Right."

She's embarrassed. Why?

Because she remembered that detail from their first conversation, or because he looks so pleased?

She wants to tell him that it isn't what he thinks.

The problem is, she doesn't know *what* he thinks.

She only knows what *she* thinks, which is that it's time to go.

"Okay, well, have a good night . . ."

Drew.

But she doesn't dare tack that on. Then he'd realize she remembers his name, too.

"You, too. And hey, if you get lonely over the holidays, just knock."

"Thanks, I'll do that," she says, knowing she never will.

In her third-floor apartment, Clara flips a light switch, drops her bag just inside the door, drapes her wool coat over the nearest chair and shivers. Whoa. Is it cold in here, or is it just her?

She checks the thermostat.

It's just her.

She turns it up a few degrees to seventy-two, and hears the hiss of steam heat in the old vents. Then she moves around the room, turning on all three lamps.

There. Warmth and light. Two life-sustaining elements.

She sinks onto the couch and looks around, seeking comfort in familiar surroundings. The first time she set foot in here, she immediately concluded that it looked like a Nora Ephron movie set: the kind of place middle America would imagine an up-and-coming New York actress might live.

She's been renting the one-bedroom apartment for over two years now. Compared to her former high-rise rectangle, this place oozes charm: high ceilings, hardwoods, even a fireplace. The neighborhood is almost free of skyscrapers, allowing the sun to stream in through three southern exposure windows that overlook a flagstone courtyard tucked behind the townhouse.

Clara signed the lease—with Jason, who was her roommate until this summer—a mere month after taping her *One Life to Live* character's dramatic swan song. Her sudsy alter ego, the dastardly Arabella Saffron, was killed off at Clara's request, thus releasing her from her contract and freeing her to take her first movie role.

That was a bit part, playing Kate Hudson's friend in a romantic comedy. But she got scene-stealer reviews—not to mention an offer to pose topless in *Playboy*. Which she turned down, of course. No need to overexpose herself—literally—at this stage in her career.

The magazine people assured her agent that the offer would remain open.

Not that it matters now, Clara thinks with a pang, touching the gauze-covered scar on her right breast.

So what? You weren't going to do it anyway.

Still . . .

Stop that! Focus on the positive. You've still got a big career ahead of you as a serious actress.

Her first movie led to a slightly larger role in a critically acclaimed medical drama that unfortunately bombed at the box office. But that, in turn, opened the door to her first starring role in *The Glenhaven Park Dozen*, an ensemble period piece based on a true story.

In real life, eleven servicemen from a tiny suburban New York village perished on the beach at Normandy in the first wave of the D-Day invasion. The screenwriters have taken artistic license, making it an even twelve.

Clara plays Violet, the fictional pregnant wartime bride of Jed Landry, a doomed soldier who actually existed.

It's a juicy role. Plenty of tender, passionate moments with her heartthrob co-star Michael Marshall, a haunting monologue she gets to deliver in the fury of a staged blizzard, and a hysterical moment of truth at the climax, when she learns of her husband's fate.

Clara has devoted months of her time preparing to play Violet, immersing herself in period films, swing music, old magazines. She hired a dialect coach to help her perfect the 1940s speech style—a distinct vocal patter characteristic of the era.

She even hopped the sleek silver Metro-North train to Westchester County and spent two beautiful Indian summer afternoons up in Glenhaven Park. There, she soaked up the small-town atmosphere, chatted with old-timers, and even studied photographs and relics at the library's local history exhibit.

All because she wants to get this right, aware that it's the kind of role that can launch a career to the next level, and now . . .

Malignant.

Clara waits for the tears to begin again, but there seems to be a temporary dry spell despite the painful lump in her throat.

She looks around the living room, all hers now that Jason finally came to get the last of his possessions before Thanksgiving. There's the stack of scrapbooks that preserve sentimental childhood relics and of course, her press clippings. There's the framed series of stills from her brief run in *Les Mis* before it closed—and there's the empty spot beside them where a portrait of her and Jason used to hang.

There are her plants, her books, her CDs. The Waterford vase her father and stepmother gave her last Christmas—why a *vase*?—and this morning's empty coffee mug and yesterday's *Daily News* and the telephone.

On the shelf above the mantel is her eclectic collection of angel figurines—all of them with dark hair. When she was a little girl, she once asked her grandfather why angels always seemed to have golden hair, and none brunette, like Clara. Naturally, her grandfather began a mission from that day forward to find and buy for his only granddaughter every dark-haired angel in the metropolitan area.

Good old Grandpa.

On the end table is a framed black-and-white photograph that catches Clara's eye tonight. Her grandmother, Irene, looking like a forties' pinup girl—busty, wearing dark lipstick, hair in sleek waves—smiles out at her. She must have been in her early twenties when the picture was taken, blissfully unaware of what her future would hold.

Clara pulls her eyes away from the photo. She can't look at it—not tonight.

Beside the window, a foil-wrapped red poinsettia droops thirstily, a smattering of curled leaves littering the sill. She bought it at the supermarket on a whim a few weeks ago.

I should water it.
No, the plant can wait.
I should call someone.

She reaches for the cordless receiver, wondering whom to call.

Not her mother.

Nor her father, who lives across the river in Jersey

with his third wife and their two young sons. Clara just saw them all on Thanksgiving. Dad mentioned something about an upcoming business trip that would take him out of town for most of Hanukkah week. He also said he would be spending Christmas in the Midwest this year, with his in-laws.

You don't mind, do you, Clara? he asked anxiously, and she wondered what he'd do if she said yes, she did mind. That he's supposed to be here, with her, sleeping on the couch, waiting to see what Santa brought.

But she didn't say that. He hasn't done that in years, and anyway, she gave up on believing in Santa—and her father—ages ago.

Somewhere around the time he scheduled one of his honeymoons to coincide with one of her Broadway openings. He told her his tickets were nonrefundable.

So when he said he was going to Indianapolis for Christmas, Clara told him that it was fine, that she would be spending the holidays with her mother and Stan in West Palm Beach anyway.

He looked miffed.

She felt guilty.

Once a child of divorce, always a child of divorce . . . even when you're twenty-nine.

So, no, she won't call her father. She'd only get Sharon, and her stepmother is hardly Clara's trusted confidant. Not due to any particular animosity, but rather because of a general indifference, on both their parts.

Who, then, if not her parents, can Clara lean on?

Her longtime therapist, Karen Vinton, of course.

But of course there's only so much she can do. There are lines a therapist can't cross.

Who, then, Clara wonders, feeling more needy and

alone with every passing second, *is my most trusted unpaid, unprofessional confidant?*

It *was* Jason. For so long that she's almost tempted to dial his number. But that wouldn't be fair. She shouldn't turn to him now, when he still isn't over their breakup. He might think there's hope for them, when all she wants to hear from him right now—from *anyone*—is that there's hope for *her*.

She runs through a mental list of assorted longtime female friends—her cousins Rebecca and Rachel, her gay sidekicks from her stage and soap days—considering and quickly dismissing each of them. Everyone is terrific when it comes to dishing over margaritas and wedding showers for mutual pals. She wholly appreciates the impeccable fashion advice and metaphoric applause when her actress ego needs it most.

But when it comes to a life-and-death situation like this, she isn't compelled to reach out to any of them.

When you get right down to it, she's much closer to some of the people she's recently met on the movie set. Accelerated friendships are as common a commodity in the entertainment industry as they were back in Clara's summer camp days. Sharing a rustic cabin or a makeup trailer for a mere couple of months, one can forge unwavering bonds that might take half a lifetime to establish back in the "real world."

Clara's co-star, Michael, knows more about what's going on in her life than her parents do, while she's privy to more of Michael's secrets than his soon-to-be-ex-boyfriend is. They spend a lot of time together on set and off—particularly now that both their publicists are currently encouraging tabloid rumors of romance. After all, Michael's secret lifestyle requires the occasional smoke screen, and being linked with an A-list star certainly won't hurt Clara's new film career.

So yes, Michael is a trusted confidant; she can lean on him if she needs to.

Then there's Albany Jackson, who plays Sue, Violet's scripted best friend; Tessa Milks, the stand-in who's teaching Clara how to knit; and Jesus deJesus, the acerbic makeup artist who keeps her in stitches and in false eyelashes . . .

She'll tell all of them soon enough. Tomorrow morning, bright and early, at the location shoot up in Westchester, in the real Glenhaven Park.

But not now.

She slowly returns the receiver to its cradle, missing Jason for the first time since he left.

Or maybe . . .

No, it isn't Jason she misses. It's the relationship itself. The intimacy of a real relationship. She misses coming home to somebody; misses knowing that she is the most important person in somebody's world; misses crawling into bed beside a warm body every night.

But not Jason's.

No, their romance had long since run its course when she finally found the guts to call it quits. In theory, he should have been Mr. Right: the perfect complement to her theatrical lifestyle. He was the product of a solid small-town family, had a stable corporate job, believed in marriage, and children . . . in that order.

On paper, he was everything she had ever wanted. She knew, because in the midst of her soul-searching about him last spring, she made a list of pros and cons.

The only con was one that, in the end, she couldn't live with. Or rather, it was something she couldn't live without.

Passion.

The initial sparks that brought them together lasted only a few months.

Yet somehow, waning chemistry didn't stop Clara from moving in with him or accepting his proposal and a hefty diamond last Christmas.

She craved stability; Jason provided it.

Which is why, she tells herself sternly, *you're thinking of him now.*

Now, when she's feeling like a kite caught up in a tornado, with a tether that's frayed to a thread and about to snap, Jason would be able to bring her back down to earth. Levelheaded, logical Jason would hold her steady through the long night ahead. Through the many long nights that surely lie ahead.

But cancer isn't a good reason to get back together, Clara tells herself sternly. *It's probably the worst, most desperate reason there is.*

Stoically, she reminds herself that she chose to be alone when she set him free.

Alone is what she is, and alone is where she'll stay. At least, for the time being.

Alone sucks, she thinks glumly.

Maybe if it weren't the holiday season . . .

Yes, and maybe if I weren't scared to death, despite what Dr. Svensen says, that this might be the last Christmas I'll ever have . . .

Well, maybe she'd feel stronger than she does now. Stronger, and less needy.

When the going gets tough, though, the tough don't curl up and cry.

They steel themselves for whatever lies ahead, and they fight.

I'll fight tomorrow, Clara decides, as the tears begin to fall at last. *Tonight, I'll curl up and cry.*

Chapter 2

Two days later, it's official: Clara will be spending Christmas alone in New York.

She called Florida yesterday when she knew her mother would be at her weekly holistic cooking class and broke the news to her stepfather that she wouldn't be able to get away for Christmas.

Stan was disappointed, but said he understood how important this movie was to her.

"We'll miss you, but we know you'll be spending the holiday doing something that makes you so happy, even if it is work," he said, and it was all Clara could do not to burst into tears.

Since then, she's screened two calls from her mother, who sounds teary and wants to talk. She hasn't returned them yet. She can't. She doesn't trust herself not to break down and tell her mother the real reason she can't come.

She's tentatively scheduled the lumpectomy for the week before Christmas, with endless rounds of tests between now and then. She has also met with the breast surgeon, the oncologist, the radiologist.

Later tonight, back in Manhattan, she's going to her standing weekly appointment with her regular therapist. She's been seeing Karen for years, ever since her parents decided she needed help dealing with the divorce.

Karen became her trusted confidant. And yes, there are times when Clara's relationship with her feels more personal than professional.

But of course, they never cross that invisible doctor-patient line.

Nobody knows Clara like Karen does. She helped her process not just her parents' divorce, but, through the years, her grandfather's death, her breakup with Jason, and of course, her ongoing issues with her mother.

It isn't that Clara doesn't get along with her mom, because for the most part, she does.

The problem is that Jeanette has never been a rock for her daughter the way mothers are supposed to be—not even when Clara was still a child and desperately needed one. There were countless times, especially right after the divorce, when it was Jeanette who crumbled and Clara who took on the maternal role. It was emotionally exhausting—and sometimes, still is.

Of course, things have been better since Clara's stepfather, Stan, came along. Not perfect, but better.

Finding out about Clara's cancer would do her mother in, no doubt about that.

Which is why she's not going to tell her. In fact, she's not in the mood to discuss it with anyone, really.

"Maybe I'll skip my appointment with Karen," she muses aloud to Jesus.

"You can't do that. I'm sure she's worried about you."

"She doesn't know anything about this. I never even bothered to tell her about the lump," she tells Jesus, watching in the mirror of her location trailer as he coats her lids with smoky shadow that matches her green eyes. "That's how unconcerned I was about it."

"Well, hopefully she'll be able to help you work through your anxiety. I know my shrink has done wonders with my ostraconophobia."

That, of course, would be his irrational fear of shellfish, which he is slowly overcoming with cognitive therapy.

"Okay, darling . . . blink."

Clara blinks.

"Again."

She blinks again.

Jesus studies her face with critical dark eyes, stroking his clean-shaven chin—which matches his clean-shaven head. And his clean-shaven chest, as well as anatomical hinterlands he mentioned in one of their too-much-information conversations, the kind that tend to unfold amidst hours of mind-numbing between-take on-set boredom.

There isn't a whole lot she doesn't know about Jesus deJesus, including his oft-mentioned conviction that he is the reincarnation of Coco Chanel. This he discovered during a past-life hypnotic regression conducted by one of his many therapists or gurus or whatever he calls that particular member of his new agey posse of advisors.

Jesus frequently expounds on the concept that everyone's spirit, after physical death in this world, is reborn in a new body. The concept has its roots in various religions in which Jesus has dabbled, from Hinduism and Buddhism to Hollywood-chic Scientology and Kabbalah.

Clara actually read a couple of the books he forced on her, and was unexpectedly absorbed. Of course, she would never admit to anyone—least of all Jesus deJesus—that his far-fetched reincarnation theory makes sense. Nor is she convinced that the legendary

Coco Chanel has returned to earth as a hairless, chubby man who runs away shrieking at the mere sight of shrimp.

Jesus dabs a bit more shadow on Clara's lids, and reaches for the liquid liner with a flourish. "So how are you feeling overall?"

"You mean, mentally? Or physically?"

"Both."

"You know. I'm hanging in there."

"Hold still. You're hanging in there mentally, or physically?"

"Both." She sighs, holds still, gazes at her face in the mirror.

At least she looks like her usual self: wide-set eyes, high cheekbones, pert nose, heart-shaped mouth. Jesus expertly masked the shadows under her eyes with plenty of pancake foundation; you'd never know she hasn't slept more than restless half-hour spurts since the diagnosis.

How reassuring to see her familiar reflection, considering that she's been feeling as though she's temporarily inhabiting a stranger's body.

Every time she looks down at that small, gauze-covered scar, she glimpses the most innocuous-looking enemy portal imaginable. And she can't help but wonder whether Dr. Svensen was wrong, whether perhaps her records got mixed up with somebody else's at the lab.

How can she, Clara, possibly be ridden with deadly, toxic cancer cells when she feels absolutely fine?

"Listen, I'm here if you need a friend instead of a shrink," Jesus is telling her. "And you should make an appointment with Jezibel, my life coach."

"I don't think I—"

"She's amazing. I'll give you her number."

"No, that's okay, Jesus, I doubt I'll—"

"I need something to write on."

Because it's easier than arguing, she opens a drawer, rummages around, and plucks one of her photo business cards from a rubber-banded stack. On the front is her head shot, on the back, her contact info.

"Just put it on here," she tells Jesus.

"Don't you have any scrap paper?"

"Does this look like an office?"

"Got a pen? Or do you want me to use eyeliner?"

She sighs and relinquishes a Sharpie she keeps handy for signing autographs. Which doesn't happen as often these days as it did when she was on *One Life to Live*. Soap fans are a dedicated breed.

Jesus scribbles something, then hands the card back to her. "Promise me you'll call Jezibel."

She sticks it into the shallow lone pocket in her vintage forties skirt. "Thanks, but I really don't think—"

"Um, hello, you need to close your mouth so I can do your lips now."

"Okay, but just so you know, I don't need—"

"Ah-ah-ah," he cautions.

Forced to close her mouth so that he can apply the vintage deep red lipstick, she contemplates the day that lies ahead.

She still hasn't found the nerve to break the news of her illness to the powers-that-be, particularly Denton Wilkens, the director. She will, before the day is out, but she isn't looking forward to it.

What's the worst that can happen?

It's not as though he can recast the Violet role at this stage in filming . . . can he?

No, but he's going to have to scramble the production schedule to accommodate her surgical recovery and treatment. As the world's most notoriously anal-retentive director, he'll hardly welcome the disruption—particularly on a film this close to his heart, and one he's wanted to make for years.

Glenhaven Park is Denton's hometown; he was born there on December 7, 1941.

"The world I came into that day," he dramatically told the cast at the first read-through, "was a far different world than it had been the day before. I was born the day America's innocence died."

Denton can be a little over the top . . . but not necessarily more so than any other director Clara has ever known.

"Just think," Jesus muses, expertly giving her the lips of a forties film siren, "you'll be able to channel all this personal angst into your role as Violet. Maybe you'll win the Oscar."

"Yeah, posthumously," she says darkly.

Jesus curses. "You just smudged. Stop talking."

"Sorry," she mumbles through a clenched mouth.

"You're no ventriloquist, honey. But move your lips one more time"—he brandishes the crimson lipstick tube—"and you might just be a clown."

Sitting mute and motionless, Clara wonders when would be a good time to talk to the director about her illness. Definitely not until she's finished filming her scene today—the one in which city girl Violet steps off a train in Glenhaven Park, slips on the icy platform, and literally bumps into her future husband for the first time.

It'll be difficult enough to muster believable passionate attraction for a man who, she happens to know, has been battling a nasty stomach bug the last few days, *and* is having a torrid and clandestine affair with the best boy. She might be a pro, but given her current emotional state, it will be more challenging than usual to separate the closeted actor Michael Marshall from fabled all-American hero Jed Landry.

"All right, you're all set, Violet," Jesus proclaims, taking a step back to admire her face. "Off to the hairstylist you go."

"Thanks, Jesus." She removes the black vinyl drape and peers out the window of the trailer at the frosty gray dawn, pulling her terry cloth robe more tightly around her. "You know, it actually looks like it's going to snow. Wouldn't that be great?"

"Snow? Great? I'd rather be on a tropical island, shellfish and all, in a thong with a piña colada."

"A thong?" She raises an eyebrow and attempts to block out the mental image of Jesus deJesus in a thong.

"A sarong?"

She makes a face. "I'll take the snow. And a parka."

"Oh, come on." Jesus shudders, looking at the overcast sky. "You wouldn't kill to be lying on a beach right now?"

"Not in December," she says, remembering that today is the first of the month. "In December, I want snow. It puts me into the Christmas spirit. Only twenty-four shopping days left."

"Fa la la la freaking la," Jesus replies in a monotone.

She sticks out her tongue at him.

Then, as Jesus warns, "Don't you go messing up those perfect lips with that slimy tongue!" she realizes that she forgot, for a merry moment, about her plight.

"And anyway," Jesus adds, "it's not supposed to snow. It's supposed to warm up to fifty and rain."

Fifty degrees and rain?

So much for being in the Christmas spirit, Clara thinks glumly, and steps out into the gray December morning.

In the heart of formerly-countryside, now-suburban Glenhaven Park is a town green that looks like something out of *It's a Wonderful Life.* Especially today, thanks to the Oscar-winning art director's holiday magic.

Store windows are artificially frosted and some, like the five-and-dime, display packets of holiday cards, compartmentalized boxes of metallic ornaments, and bags filled with fancy ribbon candy. Every lamppost is wrapped in shiny silver garland. Nostalgic strings of wide-spaced, bright-colored bulbs line the gingerbread eaves above most front porches; flocked trees decked with bubble lights and tinsel stand in picture windows; door wreaths abound.

As long as you don't look at the vast condo community sprawled on a hillside above the Congregational church, overlooking the town, you might actually believe you've stepped back in time.

A wide, grassy strip runs the length of the town, encompassing three blocks. A brick path meanders among trees and shrubs, wrought-iron benches and tall posts that appear to hold gaslights.

On either side of the green, Victorian-era homes and businesses that line the sidewalks have been stripped of anything post-WWII. Flags with fifty stars have been replaced with flags bearing forty-eight. In place of SUVs and foreign sports cars are vintage roadsters parked in driveways and diagonally along the curbs. The Internet cafe has been transformed into a telegraph office; the trendy clothing boutique now advertises STYLISH WOMEN'S HATS and MODERN SLACKS.

A half mile up the commuter railroad tracks, an

authentic diesel locomotive—painted a cheery red—has been positioned. It's ready to steam into town towing old-fashioned domed, corrugated railroad cars, and dispatch Clara and several extras on the platform to block the first scene.

Clad in platform shoes with high wedge heels, a trim-fitting gray wool skirt suit, black wool coat, and brimmed black velvet hat, Clara boards the train with a crowd of period-costumed extras.

She's struck, as she was during rehearsals, by the dated rotating mohair seats and ornate lighting fixtures. What a far cry from the modern commuter railroad she takes out to her father's place in Jersey.

"It smells like smoke in here," one of the extras comments, fanning the stale air.

It *does* smell like smoke.

Repulsed, Clara clasps her wrist against her nostrils to inhale instead the potent fragrance of the essential oil she dabbed all over herself this morning. A blend of lavender and geranium, the concoction is, quite suitably, called Calming.

God knows Clara can use as much of that as she can get these days.

The scent was wholeheartedly recommended yesterday by Luna, the aromatherapist at her mother's favorite health store. Clara stopped in on a whim to load up on organic produce, herbal supplements, books on holistic medicine . . . as much supposedly healing merchandise as she could carry.

"Do you think this was once a smoking car?" one of the extras asks.

"They were all once smoking cars, dude," somebody replies.

Cigarettes. Why did you have to smoke all those cigarettes when you were younger?

Cancer. You have cancer.

Her thoughts catapulted back to her diagnosis, Clara can't help but wonder if things might be different now if she hadn't.

You can't second-guess everything you ever did, she reminds herself. *What good is that now?*

What is, is.

Nothing to do but accept this. Accept it, and fight it.

"Clara?" someone prods impatiently, and she realizes that nearly everyone is in their places now.

Everyone but the bit actor playing the conductor, and the leading lady.

Fighting the overwhelming urge to scratch the itchy spot where the rough woolen collar brushes her bare neck, Clara takes her designated spot standing beside the door. She's supposed to be the first passenger off the train.

Her character, a disillusioned office worker, is eager to reach her small-town destination and begin her new elementary school teaching position at the redbrick schoolhouse.

Little does Violet know that she's about to be swept off her feet by the so-called swooniest fella in town.

"Here you go, Clara." With a grunt, Lisa, the prop mistress, sets an authentic 1941 Samsonite Streamlite suitcase on the floor at her feet.

"It looks heavy. It *is* heavy," Clara exclaims, lifting it slightly to test the weight. "What's in this thing? Sandbags?"

"I stuck a bunch of outfits from wardrobe inside. Stuff we decided not to use. You can go through it after the shoot and keep what you want."

"Are you kidding? I can't wait to get back into real clothes when this shoot is over. I don't know how women back then dealt with being this dressed up every day—and can I ask why this suit doesn't have more than one pocket?"

"For what? Your iPod?"

"Nope, it won't fit. I keep that right here." She grins and lifts her jacket, showing Lisa the slim device tucked into her waistband. The skirt fits loosely, and she can't seem to get used to the fact that it's a size twelve—which, as the wardrobe mistress has repeatedly reminded her, is the equivalent to a modern four, her usual size.

"Hey!" Lisa protests. "You can't carry one of those in the scene. This is supposed to be 1941, remember?"

"Shh! Nobody knows it's here. And I'll take it out when we shoot later. It comes in handy in this endless blocking."

"What if it falls out of your skirt?"

"It won't."

"It might. Hand it over."

"Oh, relax, I'll just pop it in here." Clara opens her large black leather clutch purse and drops it in. "There. Nobody will ever know it's there."

"*You* will. It might interfere with your authenticity."

"Nah, I'm a pro, and anyway, we're not shooting yet." Clara sighs and scratches the back of her neck again. "God, I would kill to be wearing a sweatshirt and jeans."

"And here I thought you were a glamour queen actress," Lisa says dryly. "So much for the Hollywood illusion."

"Yeah, but I look like one today, right?" Clara asks with a grin, reaching up to pat her head beneath the trim hat. The hairstylist tamed her brunette mane into a controlled pompadour high above her forehead, with sleek waves falling to her shoulders.

Her smile fades as she remembers that it won't be long before her hair is falling to the ground in clumps.

"Places, everyone!"

At last the train is ready to steam toward Glenhaven Park for the first run-through.

Clara clutches her purse in one hand and grabs a pole with the other in anticipation of the train's movement. Time to conjure an expectant, exhilarated feeling.

You're going off to start a new life . . .

The train starts chugging. It quickly picks up speed.

"How can you ride facing backward?" asks an extra seated nearby. "Doesn't it make you feel sick?"

Clara merely shakes her head, trying to focus on her character's motivation.

It's 1941 . . . you're Violet . . . off to start a new life . . .

"Hey, did you drop this?" somebody asks, and hands her something from the floor.

She looks down to see the photo business card she had tucked into her shallow pocket earlier. Jesus had used it to scribble his life coach's phone number . . . which she has every intention of throwing away.

But there's no place to toss it now, so she opens the purse and tucks it in.

Nearly losing her balance as the train rounds a bend, she holds the pole more tightly, wondering if they should be going this fast. Positioning her too-tight vintage platform shoes farther apart to keep her balance, she glances at the landscape flying past the window.

Get into character. Come on. You're an actress.

Yes, an actress with a hell of a lot more on her mind this morning than work. But there will be plenty of time to brood later.

The train hurtles forward toward Glenhaven Park; she stares at the back wall of the car, convincing herself that she's Violet. Violet, living her uncomplicated 1941 life, embarking on a new adventure in a brand-new place.

Any second now, you're going to meet the man of your dreams . . .

Yes, and he's going to go off to war and die.

But Violet doesn't know that now.

Violet is all hope and anticipation.

Lucky, lucky Violet. Healthy. Happy. About to make a fresh start.

What I wouldn't give to be in her shoes for real, Clara thinks wistfully. *Not forever.*

Just for now.

Just for the happy stuff . . . like not having cancer and falling in love with Jed Landry.

"I don't know . . . maybe I like the blue one better after all. What do you think, Jed?"

Mustering every shred of his threadbare patience, he pretends to study the woolen muffler Mrs. Robertson is ostensibly about to purchase for her son—after a good twenty minutes' deliberation, with Jed as a reluctant participant and model.

"The red looks more Christmasy." He points at the muffler in her hand. "Definitely the red."

There's a moment of silence as she contemplates that. A train whistle sounds in the distance. Jed can hear the 9:33 chugging away from the station across the green, and fervently wishes he were on it.

"But Theodore will be wearing the scarf for the rest of the winter," Mrs. Robertson protests, thrusting the scarf away. "He won't even open it until Christmas morning. Maybe I should—"

"The red will be keen in February, too," Jed cuts in hastily, flicking his gaze to the clock hanging just beyond the stovepipe on the far wall. "You know, with Saint Valentine's Day, and George Washington's birthday and all."

"George Washington's birthday?" Mrs. Robertson's eyebrows rise toward the tilted brim of the black felt hat she bought here at Landry's Five-and-Dime last winter—a purchase that enveloped well over an hour of Jed's time and a month's worth of patience.

This morning, she was waiting by the door when he arrived to open the store at nine, barely giving him time to shovel the new-fallen snow from the sidewalk before starting in with questions.

He isn't in the mood. Especially not today.

Not when Alice, the increasingly inept young woman he hired as Christmas help, has yet to show up.

Not when it's the first of December, and his thoughts are consumed by his father. It's been two years. Two years since—

"I beg your pardon, Jed, but what on earth does George Washington's birthday have to do with a red muf—"

"George Washington cut down a cherry tree. Cherries are red."

At that, Mrs. Robertson's eyebrows disappear altogether.

Jed waits for her to inform him that it's the most ridiculous thing she's ever heard.

Certainly, it's the most ridiculous thing he's ever uttered behind the counter at this store.

Or anywhere.

"Why, you're right!" Mrs. Robertson exclaims. "It's settled. I'll take the red." She hands it over with a smile and opens her handbag.

Relieved, Jed yanks a length of brown paper from the roll bolted to the counter, hoping she won't suddenly change her mind again—or, worse yet, remember one more thing on her Christmas list.

As soon as the thought crosses his mind, he chides himself. The holiday shopping season is barely underway and the store is particularly quiet for a Monday morning, thanks to the bitter cold in the wake of last night's storm.

Shouldn't he be trying to encourage browsing, rather than hustling one of his well-heeled customers out of the store?

Probably. But he's had about all of Mrs. Robertson that he can take for one morning.

Anyway, he's not a natural salesman, like Pop. Or Gilbert. Jed wasn't cut out to run the store; he's only here by default.

He probably wasn't cut out to be a lawyer, either. If fate hadn't intervened, he might have eventually realized that and left Boston—and Carol—after all.

So what were you meant to be, Jed Landry? A lifelong bachelor? A soldier? A vagabond?

Who knows? I'm just anxious to find out.

"Oh! I almost forgot!" Mrs. Robertson interrupts his restless thoughts. "Do you have any Mickey Mouse watches? My Patty has her heart set on one for Christmas."

"I'm sorry, we're all out," Jed lies.

That's just swell. Lying to a customer on the anniversary of Pop's death.

As he briskly wraps the red scarf in brown paper and ties it with string, he vows that he'll make up for it with his next customer.

That isn't good enough, an inner voice scolds.

"Mrs. Robertson, maybe Patty would like something else instead . . . like a musical snow globe?" he suggests as a nearby display catches his eye.

"A snow globe?" Mrs. Robertson echoes dubiously. "I don't know if Patty would—"

"All the little girls love them," Jed cuts in, walking over to the display. "These just arrived this week and they're selling out fast."

He picks up the nearest glass globe, one that has a dark-haired ceramic angel inside. "This model is very popular."

"But the others have more than one angel inside. And they're all golden-haired, like my beautiful Patty."

"Yes, but this one is musical . . . and it's the last one I have in stock."

He feels around on the felt base for the key, then winds it quickly.

A tinkling melody promptly spills forth.

"What song is that?" Mrs. Robertson asks with interest.

" 'Hark the Herald Angels Sing.' " Jed sets the globe carefully on the table again.

Mrs. Robertson waits until the melody begins to slow as the mechanism winds down. Then with a shrug, she says, "You say all the little girls want musical snow globes?"

"All of them," he confirms with only a slight pang of guilt. "Should I wrap that up for you, then?"

"I don't know . . . where was it made? I hope not in Germany."

"I believe Switzerland."

"Are you sure?"

"Positive," he says, but she's already picking it up to see for herself. She turns it over to look at the bottom, accidentally tapping it, hard, against the edge of the display table.

"Switzerland," she confirms, and flips it right side up again. Then she peers at it. "The glass is cracked and the angel's wing is broken off. Look."

She thrusts the globe into his hands.

He frowns. She's right. The tip of one of the angel's gossamer wings has cracked right off. The shard is lying amidst the reflective white flakes at the bottom of the snow globe.

And you're the one who did it when you bumped it against the table, Jed silently scolds Mrs. Robertson.

"Now, Jed, you know that I can't buy broken merchandise as a gift," she says chidingly, and briskly deposits the snow globe back on the table with a thump.

"How about a different one?"

"The others aren't musical. What good is that? I'll just take what I already have, thank you."

"Merry Christmas, Mrs. Robertson," he calls as she sails toward the door with her parcel tucked under her arm. *And good riddance.*

"Oh, I'm sure I'll see you before Christmas," she promises.

"I certainly hope so," he lies with a fake smile so clenched his jaw hurts.

A tinkling of bells and a whoosh of cold air as the door opens, then closes, and he finds himself alone in the store.

With a heavy sigh, he picks up the damaged snow globe and shakes it. The angel is obliterated by a flurry of white flakes, the tip of her broken wing quickly sinking amidst the temporary storm. Examining the glass, he sees that it's a surface crack; nothing is leaking from it. He winds the key and is relieved to hear "Hark the Herald Angels Sing" spill forth.

Still, nobody is going to pay full price for a wounded angel.

He finds a piece of cardboard and makes a sign that reads HALF-PRICE, AS IS. Then he clears a spot on the sale merchandise table for the snow globe and props the sign against it just as the song winds down.

That done, he consults his watch again.

Where on earth is Alice? This is the third time she's been late in the two weeks since he hired her. On both occasions, she claimed to have overslept. The first time, he readily forgave her. The second, he warned her that if it happened again, he'd have to fire her.

Reluctant to make good on that promise, he decides to give Alice another twenty minutes. If she isn't here by ten o'clock, he'll call Mrs. Bleaston, the woman who runs the rooming house where she lives, to see whether she's on her way.

If she isn't, he'll have to ask to speak to her and tell her not to bother coming in—today, or ever again. He doesn't relish that prospect. She's a newlywed, and her husband is in the army, stationed somewhere in the South Pacific.

All right, then. If she does show up, he'll give her another chance. Just one more, and only because he feels sorry for her. Besides, it isn't easy to find Christmas help once the season is underway.

Anyway, he doesn't want to fire anyone if he can help it. He isn't any better at handling employees than he is customers, when you get right down to it.

Jed steps out from behind the counter to straighten a towering display of boxed lead tinsel. Spotting a gap on a nearby shelf above the bin filled with packets of gift wrap, he makes a mental note to order more scotch cellulose tape dispensers.

In fact, next year, he really should have more on hand before Thanksgiving to ensure that he won't run out so early in—

Wait a minute.

Next year, you won't be here, remember?

By then, he'll have enlisted. He'll be . . .

Well, anywhere but here.

The thought is as comforting as a steaming cup of cocoa would be, right about now.

The century-old building is drafty this morning, and he wishes he had layered long underwear beneath the plaid wool shirt and high-waisted trousers he's wearing under his canvas apron.

Crossing over to the plate glass display window, he notes that the curved marquee beneath the vertical Majestic sign across the street has been changed. *Tarzan's Secret Treasure* has replaced *They Died with Their Boots On.*

Doris thinks Johnny Weissmuller is the cat's meow. Maybe he'll surprise her and take her to see the new movie tonight after she finishes her homework.

Or maybe not, he decides as he replenishes a display of ribbon candy.

She'll expect popcorn and a Coke, Necco Wafers and Licorice Snaps, and she'll insist on sitting in the very front row and chattering nonstop as the film unfolds, asking a zillion questions about what's happening on screen, and things that have nothing whatsoever to do with the movie.

Jed sighs. It sure would be nice if he could see a movie with a female who doesn't share his last name . . . or isn't scheming to.

Take Betty Godfrey. She's real whistlebait and a terrific gal, when she isn't implying that she'd love to get engaged. If she'd just stop dropping hints and take one for a change, he might ask her out again . . .

Or not. Betty Godfrey is hardly his dream woman. He's better off keeping his options open, just in case his dream woman walks through the door tomorrow . . .

Which is about as likely as a man on the moon.

Wishful thinking is of no use to anyone, Mother always liked to say . . . back when Pop was still alive.

Now, Jed suspects, wishful thinking is the only kind Mother ever does.

If only he could snap his fingers and make Pop walk through that door again.

Pop . . . and the girl of his dreams.

A miracle, Jed decides. *That's what we need around here. A miracle . . .*

The whistle blows.

Shouldn't the train be slowing down by now? Clara wonders, suddenly on edge. She doesn't know why, but her body feels almost as though it's been zapped with a surge of electricity, every nerve ending tingling with . . .

Apprehension?

A bit of fear?

They're going so fast . . . they might overshoot the station if they don't slow down.

Clara bends her head to peek out the window and gauge how close they are to town. She catches a fleeting glimpse of the low stone wall. Then she sees the back of the wooden WELCOME TO GLENHAVEN PARK signpost.

The train slows abruptly with a deafening, high-pitched squeal of brakes as it rounds a curve.

Clara is thrown off her feet, toward the back of the car, slamming her head against the hard edge of the nearest seat.

"Ow!"

Her hand flies up to rub her temple. The pain is so

stunning that for a moment she sees nothing but a blinding glare.

Then it subsides just a bit and she's left with a dull ache.

Terrific.

Just what she needs in the midst of filming.

A lovely bump above her eye.

A bump to match my lump, she thinks grimly.

Cancer. I have cancer.

She shakes her head.

I'm Violet. Violet doesn't have cancer.

Violet is happy, giddy, naive—about to fall in love.

At last, the train is slowing down. Turning to face forward, she looks out the window and sees a vintage Packard tooling along the road beside the tracks. In the front seat is a young extra dressed in a military uniform.

And . . . that's funny. The ground is dusted with snow.

She doesn't remember seeing snow when she left her trailer a little while ago.

But you did tell Jesus the sky looked like it, she reminds herself, rubbing her sore forehead.

Yes, and Jesus said it was supposed to warm up and rain.

Some snowflakes must have fallen while they were setting up the scene back there. A lot of snowflakes. Enough to cover the ground and rooftops.

How the heck did I miss it? she wonders, and decides it must be fake snow, part of the set decoration.

Then she catches a whiff of cigarette smoke.

Glancing around, she sees that two of the female extras have swiveled their seats to face each other and are puffing away.

She wrinkles her nose in disgust. Period authenticity is one thing; a public health hazard is another.

She opens her mouth to object when the conductor appears in the aisle. "Station stop is Glenhaven Park. Glenhaven Park. Next stop, Brewster. Please exit to the rear of the car."

Clara gapes at him, wondering why he seems different. For some reason, she thought the conductor was a much older, rotund character actor type.

He isn't. He's a skinny beanpole of a guy, with pockmarked cheeks and an overbite. She can't help but feel as though she's never before laid eyes on him in her life.

Good Lord, am I becoming so much of a diva that I'm no longer noticing the little people?

Pushing aside the troubling question, she bends to lift the suitcase Lisa stuffed with clothes.

I'm Violet. Expectant. Exhilarated. New life.

The train chugs to a halt.

She gazes out at the platform, wondering why the crew isn't in place.

The door opens and she steps out into the brisk December chill, purse tucked under her arm, suitcase in hand. *Brrr.* Is it her imagination, or has the temperature dropped a good thirty degrees in the last ten minutes?

She descends from the train, trying not to wobble in her narrow 1940s' heels. The wooden platform is caked with snow and ice—which *must* be real, because it's pretty darned frigid out here.

Hmm, she could have sworn the platform was made of concrete . . . and shouldn't the crew have salted it?

Oh, wait. They probably left it genuinely slippery for authenticity.

You take three steps, and then you slip, she reminds herself, moving forward, lugging the suitcase with her.

Yes, she slips, and Michael catches her.

So where is he?

And where are the other actors who are supposed to follow her off the train, chatting?

She doesn't want to blatantly turn her head to look, but she seems to be the only one who got off the train, and Michael doesn't seem to be on his mark. *Oh, well.* He must be there. And the cameras and lighting, too. They're just more unobtrusive than she would expect.

Start walking.

One step . . .

Two . . .

Three.

"Oh!" Clara cries out, slipping on cue . . .

And falling to the hard planks with an excruciating thud as the train chugs off into the distance.

Dazed, she looks around the empty platform.

Empty?

Wait a minute.

Where are the other extras who were supposed to disembark with her?

Where's Michael?

Where's Denton?

And where are the damned cameras, and the lighting crew, and . . . ?

Clara frowns.

What the . . . ?

I'm alone out here.

She slowly gets to her feet and brushes the powdery snow off her skirt. Her breath puffs white in the wintry air.

Shivering in the wind, she looks around, bewildered.

Glenhaven Park looks just as it should: flags flying, vintage automobiles parked along the green—now blanketed in white.

She can see costumed extras bustling along the sidewalks. Swing music even plays faintly from a distant radio.

The crew has thought of everything.

Everything but me, Clara thinks ruefully, uncertain what to do next.

Maybe Denton called a meeting in one of the trailers. Maybe he's going to adjust the blocking schedule because of the snow.

It doesn't make sense—none of this makes sense—but it's the only explanation Clara can come up with.

She looks in the direction where the location trailers were parked in an A&P supermarket lot down the street.

That spot is occupied by a large Victorian mansion with a mansard roof.

Huh?

Where's the supermarket?

She squints, blinks.

No trailers.

No parking lot.

No A&P.

Maybe she's mistaken.

Maybe the trailers were on the opposite end of town.

She turns her head—still throbbing from the bump on the train—to look the other way.

No trailers.

No parking lot.

No supermarket.

All she can see, beyond the white steeple of the Congregational church, is the tree-lined hillside overlooking the town.

Her heart pounds so violently, her knees weaken so abruptly, that it's all she can do to remain on her feet.

Just the hillside.

Nothing *on* the hillside but trees.

Nothing.

Somehow, an entire condominium complex has vanished into thin air, along with the rest of Clara's world.

Chapter 3

At the sound of a car horn honking in the street, Jed looks up to see wiry, bespectacled Arnold Wilkens, a childhood friend, passing by the five-and-dime in a new blue Packard. Arnold waves at him, and Jed waves back, wondering whether his wife Maisie has had their first baby yet. She must be due any minute now, judging by her enormous belly when she stopped in the store to pick up some pink knitting yarn a few weeks ago.

"Why not blue?" Jed asked.

"I'm betting it's a girl," Maisie said with the same self-confidence she'd displayed since their kindergarten days. "And we're going to name her Daisy."

Of course they are. Because it rhymes with Maisie. Poor kid.

"Well," he said, "Arnold thinks it's a boy."

"Arnold took the Dodgers in the World Series," Maisie retorted with a what-does-he-know? shrug.

"A lot of people did." Jed excluded, of course. Being a Yankees fan, he was thrilled when the Bronx Bombers pulled off an unlikely victory against their crosstown rivals.

"How about a nice pale yellow yarn?" he offered Maisie.

"No, thank you. If Arnold is right by some chance,

and this baby is a boy, he'll just have to wear pink booties and sleep in a pink nursery, because we're painting this weekend.''

Jed has no doubt the baby will be a girl.

Maisie has a way of knowing things she can't possibly know. Women's intuition, she likes to call it.

Arnold calls it phonus bolonus.

Which makes a fella wonder why he married a gal like Maisie in the first place. Then again, with his wiry build and thick glasses, Arnold, who is now an accountant, has never exactly been known as what Jed's sisters might call a Hunk of Heartbreak.

About to return his attention to the store, Jed notices big fat flakes in the air—drifting lazily, almost horizontally in the air as opposed to falling furiously as they did early this morning.

He turns away from the window—then back, realizing that he just glimpsed a familiar figure coming down the block.

It isn't roly-poly Alice.

As he trains his eyes on this woman, he's so caught up in admiring her shapely legs—even as he notes that she appears to be wearing stockings, and wonders where she managed to find them—that he momentarily forgets to look up to see who she is.

When he manages to tear himself away from those glorious gams, he realizes that he doesn't know her after all.

Or does he?

He takes in the well-made hat and coat, the waves of chestnut hair curled fashionably above her shoulders . . .

Even from here, he can see that she's a real dish.

He can also see that she's hauling a large suitcase. Is she coming or going?

Coming. Definitely. Because she seems lost. He can tell by the way she's looking around, as though she's searching for something.

She must have just stepped off the train from Manhattan. In fact, everything about her says Glamour Puss.

Still, there's something familiar about her . . .

Jed is almost one hundred percent positive that he's seen her someplace before.

So certain is he that he raps on the plate glass window to catch her attention.

She looks up, startled.

Her smile is at once tentative, relieved, and laced with recognition.

So I must know her, Jed realizes, watching her approach the store. *And obviously, she knows me.*

It's about time, Clara thinks, waving at the guy in the window of the old-fashioned five-and-dime. At last, a temporary haven from the icy wind, and a familiar face.

Not nearly as familiar—or as welcome—as, say, Michael's would be. Or Denton's.

But this costumed bit player—whom she must have met in passing on the set at some point—is better than a total stranger.

She just can't help wondering why she didn't recognize any of the other vintage-fashion-clad extras she glimpsed hurrying along the sidewalks as she walked over from the train station. Maybe she was just too busy trying to figure out what on earth was going on with the set . . . and the scene she's supposed to be blocking.

She supposes something could have come up and caused the camera crew, Denton, and Michael to beat a hasty retreat.

Maybe Michael's contagious stomach bug has infected the whole production.

Or maybe there was a problem with the filming permit. The town's administration is a stickler for rules.

It just would have been nice if somebody had mentioned the abrupt change in the schedule to the cast and crew on board the train.

Yet a communication breakdown doesn't explain the vanishing condo complex on the hill. A cluster of buildings can't just walk away.

Then again, Hollywood magic can make anything possible. Clara has seen, at the hands of capable set designers, the southwestern desert become a tropical island beach, a wall of white Styrofoam blocks transformed into an ancient Roman villa.

All right. Maybe they've created some kind of optical illusion to camouflage the condos.

It would have been nice if somebody had mentioned that, too.

And what about the enormous bronze statue on the green—the one that depicts the eleven lost soldiers of Glenhaven Park? Obviously, it's been removed for the duration of filming. Yet she could have sworn the set designer tried—and failed—to have the statue relocated. The town refused to allow it to budge an inch. Yes, and Denton had to alter a number of long, establishing shots as a result.

Clara glances again at the spot where the statue should be. Nothing there now but a towering maple tree. The kind of tree that can't be plunked down by a set designer to hide an unsightly bare spot. The kind of tree that takes centuries to grow . . . and wasn't there last week. Or yesterday.

But that's crazy. You must be imagining things.

And no wonder. It's so cold, and her head hurts,

and this suitcase weighs a ton. Is it so surprising that she can't think straight at the moment?

Noticing that the actor in the store is now out beneath the striped awning, holding the door open for her, Clara covers the last stretch of icy sidewalk quickly, and gratefully.

"Come on in . . . chilly out today, isn't it?" he asks pleasantly as she steps over the threshold and deposits her suitcase on the worn wooden floor with a thud.

"That's the understatement of the year." Her teeth are chattering as he closes the door behind her.

"Have we met?" he asks, and she turns to find him looking curiously at her.

"I don't know . . . I'm Clara," she says politely.

"I'm—" Instead of introducing himself, he frowns, peering into her face. "I thought you looked familiar, but I didn't realize . . ."

You were the star.

How often has she heard that? People are always saying she comes across as a regular gal because she doesn't put on airs like some actresses.

". . . I was wrong," he concludes the sentence unexpectedly.

He was wrong?

She looks into his eyes and sees that he doesn't seem to have a clue who she is. Either that, or he's a terrific actor.

He smiles pleasantly, revealing teeth so white she wants to ask who did them and how much he paid. She's had her own professionally whitened twice in the last year by two different oral health care experts, with less than perfect results.

She wonders why this guy's dentist didn't repair the slight gap between his front two teeth while he was at it. Then again, if it weren't for that barely visible flaw, he would be almost too handsome.

He's clean-shaven with angular features, a full mouth, and a deep cleft in his chin. His hair, so dark it's almost black, is neatly trimmed over his ears without a trace of sideburn. It's so short it spikes up on top with the help of some gel, as though he combed it straight up from his forehead with his fingers. His eyes, wide set beneath straight, sooty slashes of brow, are the striking blue of the sky on a clear winter day.

Clara is so busy noticing his good looks that it takes her a moment to confirm that the lack of recognition is mutual. She's never seen this guy before. He must be a local. She thought he looked familiar when she spotted him from afar. But up close and personal like this, he's as much a stranger as anyone else in this town.

Disconcerted by his expectant blue gaze, she looks away and is startled to find that the dime store's interior now matches the forties' facade. It isn't just the pressed tin ceiling, exposed pipes, soda fountain, or antique register . . .

The set dresser went to a lot of trouble to track down authentic-looking merchandise, too. Everything on the shelves and in the bins—from Christmas decorations to clothing to penny candy—is either an incredibly realistic reproduction, or in terrific condition for being at least sixty-five years old.

Just last week, this was an Internet cafe. She checked her e-mail on a computer right over in that corner, now occupied by a display table holding a pile of bright blue boxes and a sign that reads PARAMOUNT STAR-LITES.

"Are we shooting interior scenes here?" she asks,

wondering why anyone would bother to go to these lengths if they're not—and she could have sworn they aren't.

About to lift her suitcase and move it away from the door, he looks up and frowns as though he doesn't comprehend.

He must not speak English, she realizes in the split second before she recalls that he did, indeed, speak English when he greeted her.

"Shooting?" he asks blankly without a trace of an accent.

"I thought this place was just for exterior shots," she clarifies, and is met with an even more puzzled expression.

Oh. Maybe he's a little slow, like Eddie, the bag boy at Gristede's near her apartment. That would explain, too, why he was knocking on the window and waving at her as though she's a long-lost friend. He probably knocks and waves at everybody.

"Never mind," she says sympathetically. Marlene, the casting assistant, must have hired him for his looks. He can't possibly have a speaking part.

"Say, what's in this thing?" he asks, grunting as he moves her suitcase. "Rocks?"

"I thought sandbags," she tells him, surprised that he manages to sound so . . . well, fluent. "But Lisa said it's just vintage clothes."

"Vintage?"

"You know Lisa. She lives her art, and she wants the cast to live it, too." She glances out the window as a huge black vintage automobile rumbles by, a horizontal evergreen tied to the roof. Very charming, very realistic. "I've got to keep an eye out for the crew and find out what happened to my scene."

He seems as though he's about to ask a question,

but thinks better of it. Instead, he asks, "Can I help you find something?"

"Definitely. Denton would be a great place to start."

"Denton?" he echoes, then nods as though a light bulb went on. "Oh! Right this way."

He ushers her past a display of ladies' hats and retro cosmetics to a row of shelves. Gesturing at a small stack of pastel clothing of some sort, he asks, "What size?"

"Excuse me?"

"Sizes three and up come with a roll collar now. See?" He lifts a folded garment and unfurls it to reveal a child's one-piece footed pajamas with a trap door in back.

Clara just stares.

"Too big?" he asks. "Or too small?"

"What are you doing?"

He looks taken aback. "Showing you the Dr. Denton's. You asked for them, didn't you?"

She can't help but laugh. Uneasily. And notice that he speaks with the distinct vintage speech pattern she's been working to learn. He must have a speaking part; maybe they even share the same voice coach. But this bit actor manages to make the dialect sound far more natural than she's been able to manage so far.

"No, I meant . . . I was looking for *Denton.*"

"What's that?"

What's that, he asks. Not *Who's* that.

Not that *who's that* would be any more acceptable a question, under the circumstances. He should know. Unless . . .

Unless she's mistaken about this guy being part of the cast.

Because anybody remotely involved with the movie would know who Denton is. In fact, anybody with the slightest knowledge of pop culture for the past three decades would know who Denton is. When it comes to Hollywood directors, he's like Woody, or Spike, or Ang. No last name needed.

Right. So maybe this guy is just some freak who wandered onto the set.

Or maybe . . .

"Am I being punked?" she asks, looking around for a camera crew and a bunch of practical joker colleagues.

"Pardon?" Again, he looks utterly clueless.

Okay, so he's just some random freak. Hopefully not a dangerous one. Clara checks to see how many steps it would take her to get to the door and away from him.

"Are you all right?" the freak asks politely.

"I'm fine."

"You're shivering."

No, I'm shuddering. Big difference.

"Why don't you sit down? Can I get you a cup of hot coffee?" He nods at the glass percolator, then at the row of stools along the soda fountain.

She hesitates. She'd be tempted to sit and feed her caffeine addiction even without too-tight dress shoes and an unshakable chill from the sub-zero temperatures.

But shouldn't she be . . .

Where?

Shooting a scene?

She can't exactly do that single-handedly, so . . .

"I'd love a cup of coffee," she informs the dimwit heartthrob, setting her purse on the counter. "I don't suppose you have any fat-free hazelnut creamer in here, do you? That would be heaven."

He hesitates. "I'm afraid not."

Figures. So much for her vow to avoid artificial sweeteners from now on—not that the fat-free creamer would have been much healthier.

But she'll have to worry about chemicals and cancer later. Right now, she just needs coffee and a reality check.

"What about Splenda?"

"Splendid?" he echoes—sort of. "What is?"

"What?"

"You said something is splendid?"

"No . . . never mind," Clara says with a sigh, settling on a stool beside a *Life* magazine display featuring a cover close-up of a Boeing B-17 above the ten-cent price tag.

"I'll just take black coffee," she decides. "And your cell phone, if I can borrow it." Too bad she didn't stick hers into the antique purse. A lot of good the iPod does her now.

"My what?"

"Your . . . cell . . . phone," she articulates, and wonders why she's bothering. Obviously, this guy is clueless. About everything.

"Phone?" He gestures at an old-fashioned black one at the far end of the counter. "Go ahead."

"That works?"

"Why wouldn't it?"

"I thought it might be just for show." She shrugs, lifts the heavy receiver, and waits for a dial tone.

Instead, she hears a woman's voice.

"Somebody's on the line," she informs the guy behind the counter, who's watching her with an expression of . . . concern.

Almost as though *she's* the crazy one. *Yeah, right.*

"It's the switchboard operator," he says with a slow, troubled nod.

"The operator? But . . ."

She trails off, her head swimming in confusion, and hangs up the receiver.

"What about your phone call?"

"It can wait," she says, sinking onto a vinyl-topped stool. "I just need that coffee. Please," she remembers to add, realizing that her tone is bordering on hysteria.

"Coming right up, Clara."

"Thank you . . ." She interlaces her icy, trembling fingers on the marble counter. "What did you say your name was?"

"I didn't," he says with a smile, extending his hand to shake hers. "But it's Jed. Jed Landry."

Jed Landry.

The name slams into her like a two-by-four, taking her breath away.

That's when she realizes why he looks so familiar—and that he isn't crazy after all.

She is.

She must be, because she recognizes not just his name—Jed Landry is the character Michael is playing in the film—but also his face.

She saw it just a few weeks ago in a black-and-white photo in the Glenhaven Park archives—the hero soldier who's been dead for over six decades.

Chapter 4

The poor thing seems to have wilted before Jed's very eyes.

He watches her grasp the edge of the counter with violently trembling hands, and takes a moment to note that she isn't wearing a wedding ring before he goes on to wonder what's wrong with her.

Is she ill? Feeling faint? It doesn't seem that way. Her body has gone limp, but her face is alive with . . .

Shock? Fear?

Why on earth is she staring at Jed as though she's seeing a ghost?

"You . . ." She falters, tries again. "Your . . . name . . ."

"Jed Landry," he repeats, perplexed by her reaction. She looks as though she's about to keel over. "Jeepers creepers, are you all right?"

She just shakes her head weakly.

He comes out from behind the counter to stand beside her, fighting the sudden, inexplicable urge to touch her. In a gentlemanly way, of course. Just to keep her from slumping off the stool, as she seems in danger of doing any moment now.

"You're Jed . . . Landry?" she croaks at last.

"That's right." He hesitates, then asks, "Have we, ah . . . met?"

She doesn't reply.

No matter. He knows the answer to his own question. He might have thought she looked familiar out there, from a distance, but he's never crossed paths with her before in his life. He would remember a woman this beautiful. And, well, this . . . batty.

When she finally manages to speak again, her voice is so raspy it's all but inaudible.

Either she's coming down with something, or . . .

Or she's terrified.

He draws the latter conclusion judging by the look in her wide-set green eyes. He has no idea what's frightened her, but clearly, she's on the verge of panic.

"Look, miss . . . I don't know what's eating you, but you seem—"

"What's today?" she asks hoarsely, urgently, clutching his sleeve. "Tell me! What day is it?"

"It's Monday."

"No, it's . . . it's Friday." She's almost desperate. "Friday the first. Right?"

"No. It's the first, but it's Monday," he says, feeling vaguely foolish to be arguing with her—with anyone— over the day of the week.

"It's Monday?" she echoes slowly. "You're sure?"

"I'm positive. See?" He grabs this morning's newspaper from the stack at the end of the counter and holds it up, pointing to the date above the screaming black headline ALLIED SUCCESSES CAUSE JAPS TO ASSUME MILDER ATTITUDE.

She frowns, peering at the *Glenhaven Gazette* with the intense scrutiny of a kindergartner trying to master the alphabet chart. "Monday . . . the first . . ."

"That's right."

"But . . . that's a prop."

"How's that?"

"The newspaper . . . it's not real?"

Is she asking him, or telling him?

"If it's not real," he says slowly, deciding she's delusional in either case, "then what do you think I'm holding in my hands?"

"No, I mean . . . the paper's a set prop, and the date . . . the *real* date . . . it's two thousand and—" Her voice seems to give way; she breaks off, lifts a trembling hand to her face, her fingertips furiously probing her forehead.

"Two thousand . . . what are you talking about?"

"The year! For God's sake, what year is this?"

"What *year* is this?" He gapes at her. She's truly deranged—though not dangerously so. At least, he hopes not.

"What year do you *think* it is?" he asks cautiously, careful not to make any sudden moves as he takes a step away from her.

"Just tell me." She squeezes her eyes closed, looking for all the world like a child in dread of an imminent vaccination. "Please . . . just say it."

He shrugs. "It's 1941."

"No!" Her eyes fly open.

"No?"

"It can't be." She is incredulous.

"It can't be?" he echoes, equally incredulous. "It can't be 1941? What *can* it be?"

Clara winces and removes her hand abruptly from her head. That's when he spots it.

No wonder she's dazed, he thinks, gazing at the slight hint of purple swelling above one pencil-shaded, perfectly arched eyebrow.

He is swept by a prompt rush of relief that at least she's not deranged. Not permanently, anyway.

"What happened here?" he asks, stepping closer to her again, and reaching out to boldly tilt her chin up so that he can inspect her forehead. "Did you bump your head?"

"Oh . . . yes. On the train. But . . . "

"I'll get you some ice." He moves briskly around the counter and in a matter of seconds has created a makeshift ice pack from a towel. He holds it out to her. "Here . . . this will help."

She takes it and presses it to her head, murmuring, "Thank you."

"You're welcome. Is there somebody you want me to contact for you? A friend, or . . . your husband?"

He waits for her to tell him that she isn't married, even as he chides himself for the shameless ploy. But he can't help it. What red-blooded fella can overlook the opportunity to ascertain the availability of a beautiful doll like her?

Unfortunately, a simple "No, thank you," is her only reply.

"You say you bumped your head on the train?" he asks. At her nod, he asks, "Did you come up from the city just a little while ago? On the 9:33?"

Her head bobs again, most of her face shrouded by the towel so that he can no longer see her expression.

Encouraged by the fact that she hasn't snapped at him again, he continues the line of questioning. "What are you doing up here in Westchester? Visiting somebody?"

She hesitates for so long he suspects she doesn't remember. He read somewhere that head injuries can cause amnesia.

Then she says, from behind the ice pack, "No, I'm here for . . . a job."

"You're looking for a job? Well, it's your lucky day"—*and mine*—"because I happen to be in desperate need of a salesgal."

You are, are you? a disbelieving voice asks in his head. *What about Alice?*

Well, what about her? She's not here. And Miss Whistlebait here just said herself that she's in town looking for work . . . didn't she?

"Oh, I'm not . . . I don't need a job," she says, lowering the towel and looking him in the eye at last. "I've got to get back to—the city," she finishes awkwardly, as though she were about to say something else.

Disappointment takes hold somewhere in the vicinity of his heart . . . which had no business beating a little faster just because of her, in the first place.

He turns away, gladly, to pour her coffee.

The bell on the door jangles abruptly as somebody steps in from the street.

"The next train doesn't come through until ten twenty-one," he informs Clara, setting the cup in front of her before turning toward the front of the store. "So it looks like you're going to be here a little while longer."

Old Minnie Bouvier is gingerly wiping her black galoshes on the mat. "Good morning, Jed," she calls as he strides toward her. "My, but it's brisk out there this morning."

"That it is, Mrs. Bouvier." From the corner of his eye, he sees Clara abruptly turn her head toward the newcomer. "How can I help you today?"

"I'll take two dozen pint-sized canning jars. They've got Florida oranges at twenty-five cents a dozen over at the grocery. I'm putting up the last of my marmalade this week, before I start in on the holiday baking."

"Well, I can hardly wait for that. I count on you to

bring me one of those delicious fruitcakes of yours every year."

"Oh, I'll be bringing you a few, don't you worry. That reminds me—I need heavy brown paper to line the pans . . ."

Jed points her in the right direction, then keeps one eye on Clara as he counts the jars into a sturdy carton.

She's still sitting there on the stool with the coffee untouched in front of her, and she's fretting. Even from several yards away he can see her wringing her hands and biting her lower lip.

Maybe he should lock up the store after Mrs. Bouvier leaves, and take Clara over to see Doc Wilson. She might have a concussion. She sure as heck is confused, and she probably shouldn't be boarding a train back to the city by herself.

For a split second, he fancies himself going with her—and all but snorts out loud when he realizes how outlandish an idea *that* is.

For one thing, she's a complete stranger who for all he knows is married or engaged, ring or no ring.

For another, he has a business to run. He can't go chasing after every Able Grable who happens to cross his path.

The trouble is, it isn't every day that an Able Grable crosses his path here in Glenhaven Park, unless you count the gals he's known all his life. And he doesn't.

"I can deliver these later this afternoon, Mrs. Bouvier," he informs his customer, having finished counting and packing. "Or maybe sooner . . ."

If Alice ever shows up.

"Oh, there's no rush." She deposits her purchases— a roll of brown paper, a metal cookie cutter shaped like a bell, and a popgun, a gift for her great-nephew—on the counter. "I'll take these with me now. How is your mother, Jed?"

"She's doing just fine," he lies as he totals her purchase.

There's no reason to tell Mrs. Bouvier that his mother has fallen into a state of depression these last few weeks.

It's because of Christmas, of course.

Another Christmas without Pop, who joyfully embodied the holiday spirit.

That first holiday after he died, with the harsh loss raw as a coastal nor'easter, was a blur of shock and overwhelming grief.

The one that followed brought the first anniversary—and, in the wake of initial disbelief, a somber permanence that settled over the Landry household like a burial shroud.

It's been two years now. Two years, today.

Two years already, Jed thought when he stepped into the dim, chilly kitchen early this morning to see the still-empty spot at the head of the big table in the breakfast alcove. Sometimes it seems like just yesterday that Pop was sitting there enjoying his morning paper, a cup of coffee, one last Lucky Strike before heading out to open the store.

Only two years, Jed thought later this morning when Mrs. Robertson, oblivious to the shortages created by the war in Europe, demanded to know why there are *still* no silk stockings for sale, and why he can't tell her when there will be. Sometimes it seems like a lifetime since he was striding jauntily and carefree along a Cambridge street, a stack of books under one arm, Carol under the other.

Two years.

Shouldn't it be getting a little easier? Shouldn't

there be some mornings when Lois Landry doesn't emerge from her lonely bedroom with heavy footsteps and telltale red, swollen eyes?

Jed honestly expected his mother's grief to diminish as yet another year drew to a close, but time seems to have had the opposite effect on her.

And it isn't just Mother. Facing yet another holiday season without Pop is hard on all of them. Grandma sighs a lot, and not just over the news from overseas. Granddad shuffles around the house halfheartedly, glancing often at the chessboard sitting untouched on the shelf. His son-in-law was the only one in the house who knew how to play.

Gilbert sent a letter claiming that he couldn't be home until Christmas Eve, and had to be back on campus before New Year's. Penny and Mary Ann have been bickering even more than usual.

Meanwhile, Doris pesters Jed every chance she gets about when they're going to take the cartons of decorations from the attic, and put up the outdoor lights, and cut down a tree . . .

Those were tasks Pop always tended to—only he didn't consider them tasks.

The first year without him, of course, the Landry home was newly in mourning; there were no decorations, no lights, no tree. Last year, it was Jed who took over the seasonal rituals, halfheartedly, because Doris insisted and Pop would have wanted him to.

But he only agreed to indoor decorations: a small Christmas tree and the stockings. Outdoor lights for all the world to see would have seemed garish on the first anniversary of Pop's death.

This year, he supposes, the decisions—and the decorating itself—will fall to him again.

And what about next Christmas? Will he be on

some frigid European battlefield or in an island jungle in the South Pacific, longing for home? Will Gilbert know how to string the lights along the porch eaves and remind Doris to hang the shiny lead tinsel on the tree strand by strand, rather than in clumps?

"Oh, look, it's snowing again," Mrs. Bouvier announces as she accepts her package from him.

Jed follows her glance out the plate glass window and a wistful feeling falls over him.

You don't have to go, you know, he reminds himself. *You can always stay right here in Glenhaven Park. Forever.*

Unless, of course, he's drafted.

Which he will be, sooner or later—he knows it in his gut, the way he knew that his father's health was failing long before Doc Wilson delivered the dreadful verdict back in the spring of '39.

Anyway, he doesn't want to stay here and bide his time waiting for war to hit home and the government to decide his fate. He'll enlist in May, right after Gilbert gets home, just as he planned.

"I'll be seeing you later, then, Jed," Mrs. Bouvier says, and departs into the swirl of white flakes.

Jed returns his attention to his visitor, who can't really be called a customer because she isn't shopping. She's just sitting, and staring. Not at him, but into space, which gives him another opportunity to surreptitiously look her over from head to toe, with renewed appreciation.

She sure is classy.

Much too classy for a small-town fella like me, Jed can't help thinking. *Still . . .*

She looks up, suddenly, and catches him staring at her.

He is alarmed to see that the bump above her eyebrow is so much more pronounced, in size and color, that he can easily see it from where he stands several yards way.

"You really do need to keep ice on that," he advises, quickly covering the ground between them.

"I know . . . but it's cold."

"It's supposed to be cold. It's ice." He picks up the towel, now sopping wet, and secures it better around the clump of melting ice. He offers it to her. When she doesn't take it, he gently presses it against the bump himself.

She flinches when it makes contact with her skin, but to his surprise, she lets him hold it there. It's an oddly intimate situation, to be standing so close to her that he can, if he lowers his eyes to her legs, easily see that she *is* wearing the real thing. Silk stockings. If Mrs. Robertson were here she might offer to buy them from her on the spot.

Standing this near to Clara, Jed can smell the delicate scent that wafts deliciously in the air between them. He wants to ask her what fragrance it is, so much lighter than the heavy floral aroma of that Evening in Paris perfume he's been selling like hotcakes.

Betty Godfrey bathes herself in it, as far as he can tell. It's all he can do not to sneeze whenever she's cozying up to him.

He inhales again and is seized by a momentary—and wholly inappropriate—fantasy that involves burying his face in Clara's fragrant neck.

He can't do that.

But he can ask her what scent she's wearing.

No, he can't, either.

That would be much too forward of him . . . wouldn't it?

Of course it would, Jed! You barely know her. Wait, you don't know her at all.

"You're shivering," he notes. "I'm sorry . . . I know it's cold, and this isn't comfortable for you, but if you don't ice that bump—"

"It's okay. It's not just that I'm cold, I'm . . . " She trails off, but he has the strangest sensation that he can read her mind . . . and that she was about to say *scared.*

He provides the word for her, but as a question, and isn't surprised when she nods.

"What are you scared of?" he asks.

She hesitates. "A lot of things. But . . . I don't want to talk about them."

Jed frowns, running his thoughts over a list of possibilities. He settles on the most likely and most frightening scenario he can conjure. "Is somebody after you? Did somebody hit you? Is that why you have that bruise?"

"No!" she says quickly . . . so quickly that he's certain she must be lying.

Jed is instantly infused with the same brand of anger he experienced as an overprotective older brother called in to disperse Waldie Smith and his cronies with a few well-thrown punches.

If some goon did this to an innocent woman . . . well, Jed would love to get his hands on him and give him a taste of his own medicine.

I guess I am capable of violence after all, he finds himself thinking as he says aloud, "Clara, you can stay here with me for as long as you need to. I won't let anything happen to you."

"I can't . . . I have to get back home. And that's . . . that's part of the reason I'm afraid."

"Because he's there?"

"Who?"

"The fella who—did this." He removes the ice pack

to inspect the injury again, gingerly grazing it with the very tips of his fingers.

"Nobody did this. There's no . . . *fella.*" The word seems so awkward on her tongue that he decides she must be lying. But she persists, "I told you before, I hit my head when I was on the train."

"Then why are you afraid to go home?"

"I'm not afraid to go home. I'm afraid I won't be able to *get* there," she says cryptically. "And when I do manage to get back, *if* I do . . . I've got a lot of stuff going on that I have to deal with. That's all."

"Like what? What do you have to deal with?" When she remains silent, he tries another tactic. "Do you live with your parents? Your husband?"

"I'm not married," she says—*at last, at last.*
She isn't married!

Absorbing that delightful news, he asks, "You live with your parents, then?"

"No— But this has nothing to do with where I live, and you wouldn't understand, so . . . " She starts to stand. "You've been very nice to me, but I have to—"

"Careful," he advises, seeing her start to sway.

She quickly sinks to the stool again as he guides her, gently holding one slender upper arm. There's nothing to her; beneath the sleeve of the velvet jacket he can tell that she's scrawnier than his kid sister.

"Are you hungry?" he asks, concerned.

She shakes her head.

"You're not drinking your coffee. Too hot?"

After a slight pause she nods, but she looks uncertain enough to make him wonder if she even took a sip.

"How about a milk shake, then? It'll make you feel better." And put some meat on your bones, as his grandmother would say.

"No, thank you," she says politely.

"Let me make you a chocolate milk shake," he insists. "You can just sip it."

"I can't!" she protests, as though he suggested that she drink the blood of a freshly slaughtered boar.

"Why can't you?"

She responds in a tone that suggests she doesn't appreciate having to spell out things that are pure common sense. "Because . . . I have to watch my weight."

He blinks. "How's that again?"

She studies him for a moment, as though trying to assess his reaction, then admits, this time with considerable reluctance, "I'm watching my weight."

"Watching your weight do what? Plummet until there's nothing left of you?"

For the first time since he offered her Dr. Denton's, he sees a glint of amusement in her eyes.

So that's it. She was kidding, obviously. She sure has a quirky sense of humor.

"Never mind." She glances at the newspapers on the counter. "Things are so different . . . here."

He can't help but feel a little defensive at what sounds like a vague insult, coming from a cosmopolitan gal like her. "We're only about forty miles from the city, you know."

"That isn't what I meant."

"No? What did you mean?"

"You couldn't possibly understand." Again, her gaze flicks to the bold black headlines about the war.

"Try me." It's a challenge . . . one she seems to accept with a sparkle in her eye despite her pain, her confusion, her inexplicable fear.

"Where I come from—"

"New York? That's where you're from?"

She seems to hesitate for a split second before answering, "Yes."

"Lived there all your life?"

She nods, then tells Jed somewhat guardedly, "In my world, people tend to worry about a lot of things that, I have to admit, all of a sudden seem pretty . . . frivolous."

"Such as . . . *milk shakes*." He shoots an exaggerated comical expression at her.

For the first time since she walked into the store, a pleasant, tinkling sound spills from her lips. But the laugh quickly ripples back into silence like a music box that needs to be rewound.

"What are you scared of, Clara?" he asks softly, watching her face transform once again into a mask of trepidation.

"I just . . . I really need to get back home. What time did you say the next train leaves for the city?"

"Ten twenty-one. I'll walk you over to the depot when it's time."

"That's all right, I can find it. I just came from there."

"You shouldn't be walking around by yourself."

"Where I come from, grown women come and go as they please."

"They do that where I come from, too," he says, frowning, "when they're in familiar territory and don't have tremendous lumps on their foreheads."

"Oh . . . " A shadow crosses her face. "Trust me . . . this particular lump is absolutely the least of my worries right now."

Jed nods thoughtfully, wondering again what it is that's got her so spooked.

But he's pretty darned sure she isn't about to tell him.

Chapter 5

First cancer, now this . . . this . . . this bizarre hallucination she can't seem to escape.

This is about as cataclysmic as things can possibly get, Clara has concluded, marveling that she's still able to function on any level.

Yet here she sits, somehow having a coherent conversation with dead Jed Landry . . . *in 1941,* no less.

It's almost as if focusing on the superficial details keeps her from facing the mind-bending situation itself.

"How about a Coca-Cola?" Jed is asking. "If you won't drink a milk shake, will you drink a Coke?"

Just the details, Clara. Stick to the conversation. All you have to think about is answering the question.

Will you drink a Coke?

No, she won't. Not unless it's Diet—which she highly doubts is available here in the, um . . . past.

And anyway, that's an indulgence she can no longer enjoy . . .

Talk about superficial. Here she is, trapped in some alternate universe, and she's lamenting her self-imposed diet soda ban?

Well, it's certainly preferable to lamenting the loss of everything even remotely familiar to her.

Plus, it's much easier to be self-disciplined about arti-

ficial sweeteners when they've ceased to exist even in your fantasies, she realizes with the tiniest hint of irony.

As if there's anything even remotely amusing about any of this.

"I'd rather have water, thanks," she tells the still-hovering Jed, realizing he's not going to leave her alone until she allows him to hand her a beverage of some sort.

"Just *water*?"

"Just water," she assures him.

She watches him go around to the other side of the counter, where he picks up a glass.

A *glass* glass. Not a paper cup.

Paper cups must not have been invented yet, either.

Good Lord, is this 1941? she thinks as renewed panic begins to well up again. *Am I really in 1941?*

How on earth could this have happened?

Breathe, Clara. Don't panic. And don't hyperventilate, for God's sake.

Air in, hold it . . . air out.

Air in, hold it . . . air out.

Jed turns around. "Do you want a straw?"

A straw. Does she want a straw . . .

Air in, hold it . . . air out.

Jed is waiting.

A straw? Does she want a straw?

She manages to shake her head and smile.

He smiles and turns his back again, running water at the sink.

Okay. If you must think about what's going on here, then do it rationally.

And there's only one possible *rational* explanation.

This *hasn't* happened. Not really.

I'm just dreaming.

Of course she is.

Like Clara in *The Nutcracker* ballet . . .

Or like Dorothy. Glenhaven Park is her own personal version of Oz. She even bumped her head right before she started dreaming, just like Dorothy did in that Kansas twister.

But . . .

It's just . . .

Well, shouldn't she have woken up by now?

Because whenever she's dreaming, and in the dream she suddenly comprehends that it is, indeed, a dream . . . she wakes up. Always. Instantly.

She has never before, after being struck by the realization that she's in the middle of a dream, managed to continue it. Especially against her will. *Especially* when the dream happens to be a nightmare.

The good thing about nightmares—if there is anything *good* about nightmares—is that sooner or later, you always wake up.

Not that this particular nightmare has been *entirely* nightmarish.

But only because of Jed Landry.

She's just barely managed to hold it together—in part because deep down in some innately flirtatious and decidedly unreasonable part of her psyche, she doesn't want Jed to decide she's a looney tune.

No, God help her, she wants Jed to think she's desirable . . . and if he does think that, then it's certainly mutual.

He happens to be much better looking than any Hollywood heartthrob she's ever known—including Michael Marshall, last year's cover boy for *People* magazine's annual Sexiest Man Alive issue.

How could Clara never have noticed until just today that most actors' looks are just so . . . premeditated?

The big-screen heroes whose handsome faces cover the tabloids—men most women would kill to meet in person, as she has—spend way too much time in the gym, and painstakingly applying hair product, and shopping.

Conversely, Jed Landry's sex appeal seems utterly incidental.

Who knew a barbershop haircut and a canvas apron could make a man look so good?

He doesn't just look good, he also smells good. She's pretty sure it isn't expensive cologne. It's . . . well, she could swear it's just plain old soap. Maybe a hint of pipe tobacco. And plain old masculine skin. *His* skin.

She got a good whiff of him when he was leaning over her, holding the ice pack against her forehead. It was all she could do to remain in control of her emotions.

She *was* shivering, but not because she was cold.

And not merely because she was afraid, either.

"Here you go." Jed slides a glass of tap water across the counter. "Are you sure that's all you really want?"

Tap water. Hmm.

"This is perfect," she tells him with forced enthusiasm, reminding herself that no five-and-dime circa 1941 is going to be serving Evian or even Poland Spring.

She sips, watching him watching her over the rim of the glass.

He's such a sweet guy—or fella, as he might say— with his tender concern about her head, and his old-fashioned manners . . .

Old-fashioned?

Does anything about Jed Landry technically qualify as old-fashioned when this is his era? And when this moment has already unfolded, or is currently unfolding, almost three quarters of a century ago?

Does any of that even make sense?

Clara tries to wrap her mind around the thought, to rephrase it, but only winds up more confused.

How can *now* be in the past? How can *she* be in the past?

She can't be. Therefore, she must be dreaming.

It's that simple.

Okay, you can wake up now, she tells herself for the umpteenth time since she figured out what's going on here.

Or rather, what her subconscious *thinks* is going on here.

But she doesn't wake up.

So how can she help but wonder if this *isn't* a dream?

Well, if it's not a dream, then what the heck is it, Clara?

How the heck should I know? she shoots right back at the inner voice, as irritated by the ridiculous questions riddling her stream of consciousness as she is by the fact that she can't seem to stop talking to herself.

But there's nobody else to talk to. Not about her predicament, anyway.

Certainly, she can't ask Jed Landry—regardless of whether he really exists—if he thinks she could possibly have fallen through some kind of cosmic time warp.

Could such a thing possibly happen?

I wouldn't know that, either . . . I always did suck at science, she recalls grimly. Then she reminds herself that it's unlikely that her all-time favorite teacher, Mr. Kershaw—who ironically taught her all-time least favorite subject—covered cosmic time warps back in high school physics. If he had, she'd have been paying attention, because time warps are infinitely more interesting than studying tedious formulas all day.

When it comes to time warps, Clara's only frame of reference is Hollywood.

God knows there have been countless time travel movies—including the *Back to the Future* remake she auditioned for just last year. She didn't get the part. Last she heard, the movie itself had been scrapped, anyway. Presumably, some studio honcho figured out that not every halfway decent box office hit is begging to be remade. Certainly not a mere twenty years after the first version.

"Feeling any better?" Jed asks.

No. She won't feel better until she's awake—or returned to her own century, as the case may be.

Unfortunately, she can't climb into her DeLorean and accelerate herself Back to the Future, as Marty McFly did in the old movie.

However . . .

Doesn't it make sense to assume that since it was the train that delivered her to 1941, the train might just be her means of escape?

That, or waking up, dammit.

This is ludicrous.

Wake up! Wake up, Clara!

She squeezes her eyes shut, certain that when she opens them, she'll see Michael and Denton and Jesus deJesus hovering above her like a trio of Kansas farmhands, telling her that she hit her head and dreamed the whole thing.

All right, then. She just needs to concentrate. Really concentrate.

There's no place like home. There's no place like home. There's no place like—

"Clara?"

She opens her eyes and there's Jed Landry again, back on this side of the soda fountain, blue eyes laced with concern.

"I'm sorry . . . " She swallows a lump in her throat. "I just want to go home."

"Maybe I can drive you, if I can borrow a car and—"

"You can't," she says desolately. "I have to take the train."

"Well, if you'll wait until I can drive—"

"I can't wait and I can't drive home . . . I have to take the train."

"I don't think you should. Not alone. Not when you're so . . ."

He trails off, too polite to say *mentally unbalanced* or whatever it is that he's thinking about her.

"What about your folks, then? Can't they come up from the city and get you?"

"No."

"I'm sure if they knew—"

"They're not even in the city. My father lives in New Jersey and he's probably away on a business trip anyway, and my mother lives in Florida."

"They don't live together?" he asks in obvious dismay.

"No, they're divorced."

"That's a shame. I'm so sorry."

Judging by his sympathetic tone and expression, divorced parents are uncommon in 1941. She hesitates, wondering if she should assure Jed that it's really okay.

But she opts not to . . .

Because she realizes that it *isn't* okay.

Divorce might be the norm, but it's never okay.

Coming from a broken home is painful no matter what decade you live in—no matter how old you are.

"What about your mom and dad?" she asks Jed, supposing they're madly in love. As far as she's been able to tell, Glenhaven Park in 1941 is small-town Americana at its vintage best: an insular, idyllic place despite the horrific events unfolding in the rest of the world.

But Jed winces as soon as the question has left her lips, and she realizes that his parents' marriage might be as painful a subject for him as her parents' marriage is for her.

"We, ah, lost my father. Two years ago today, actually."

I'm sorry seems such a trite response, but what else is there?

So she says it softly, inadequately.

Then, needing to comfort him further, she allows herself to lay a hand on his sleeve. Her fingertips encounter woolen fabric as rough as her own suit, and she fantasizes, just for a moment, about the warm skin and defined biceps that lie beneath.

Jed looks down at her hand, then up at her, clearly startled.

Maybe women didn't touch strange men back in his time. But she doesn't move her hand away. She can't. Not having seen the tears that rim his blue eyes.

He clears his throat a few times.

Then he says, "I should be over it by now."

"Over it? I don't think you ever get over it, really, Jed." Funny how strange his name sounds. It isn't the first occasion it's crossed her lips, by far.

Running lines with Michael, she's said it many times. Said it in anger, in passion, in delight—whatever emotion the script demands.

But she's never said it to *him*. The real Jed Landry. *Who is either a figment of your imagination or a ghost.*

Looking very much alive, he says, "I guess I never really expected him to die. Not even while he was doing it, and I was watching. I figured he'd pull through somehow. He always managed to. That was how he was."

"What do you mean?"

"My dad's nickname was Lucky when he was a kid. Which I think he might have come up with himself, since he really, really hated his real name."

"What was it?"

"Abner. But Lucky Landry suited him better—back then, anyway. He was known around town for surviving a lot of close calls. He had smallpox when he was a baby. Then, when he was about seven, he was hit by a milk wagon and broke both his legs and a couple of ribs. And when he became a doughboy, my grandmother was convinced he'd never come home alive."

Clara finds herself picturing the fat white Pillsbury Doughboy from the commercials, and hides a quick smile.

Somehow, she's pretty sure that's not what he means.

"Your father worked in a bakery?" she asks, pleased at having quickly made the danger connection. Maybe Jed's grandmother feared her son would get burned in a raging brick oven inferno.

"A bakery?" Jed is looking blank.

"You said he was a doughboy . . . "

"In the Great War."

"He was a baker in the Great War?" she asks, vaguely embarrassed but not quite sure why.

"He was a *soldier* in the Great War."

"Oh." She nods as though she understands what baking has to do with fighting in the Great War.

At least she's aware that he's talking about World War I, which was called the Great War back before there was a World War II.

Suddenly, she is struck by just how much Jed Landry doesn't know.

America isn't even officially in the war yet. Pearl Harbor hasn't been attacked, but it will be . . . less than a week from today, she realizes, after a quick calculation.

Denton's dramatic proclamation comes back to her. *The world I came into that day was a far different world than it had been the day before. I was born the day America's innocence died.*

Maybe she should warn someone. Jed, or better yet, warn the president. Maybe she can somehow get to FDR and—

What? Heroically change history? Save the world? Preserve America's innocence?

You're dreaming all this anyway, Clara, remember?

"So my father made it through the war, and that horrible flu that killed all those people," Jed is saying, "and he survived the Depression. Then he was hit with the one thing he couldn't survive."

"What was it?"

"Lung cancer."

There it is again, rearing its ugly head to invade her dream like the murderous Mouse King did Clara's in Tchaikovsky's ballet.

Cancer.

The one word that never really leaves her consciousness . . . not even when she's asleep.

"They couldn't treat it?" she manages to ask Jed, who shakes his head bleakly.

"It was cancer," he repeats, as if that explains everything.

And it does.

In this day and age, a diagnosis like yours isn't the automatic death sentence it used to be.

Haunted anew by Dr. Svensen's words, Clara comprehends that for Jed's father, just as for her own grandmother, there were no effective treatments. They were trapped in a world without options . . .

And now . . . am I trapped there, too?

Alarmed as the chilling notion hits her, Clara withdraws her hand from Jed's sleeve. Age-old instinct sends her restless fingers straight to her head, where she encounters her hair confined by the velvet hat and stiff spray.

It seems like a lifetime ago that she donned her retro costume and boarded the train to shoot her scene . . .

Dear God, if I'm not dreaming this, then it really was a different lifetime.

If I'm not dreaming this, and I'm really stuck in 1941, then . . .

I'm going to die.

Just like Grandma, and Jed Landry's father.

And Jed.

Jed is going to die.

Unlike his father, he won't come home from the foreign battlefield. He'll be killed on a beach in France on a June day.

A wave of emotion rises within her to collide with one of sheer panic.

Overcome, she bolts from the stool.

"What happened?" Jed asks, startled.

She doesn't reply, just takes off running, running as

fast as she can despite liquid knees and ridiculous high-heeled platform dress shoes.

"Clara! Where are you going?" Jed calls, scrambling after her.

"Home," she hurls over her shoulder, then jerks the door open with a jangle of bells and bursts out into the street.

A wall of cold air and swirling snow hits her head-on.

She flinches momentarily but resumes the race.

There are more people out on the street now, despite the blustery weather. She weaves her way among the scattered pedestrians, vaguely aware that they're turning toward her in bewilderment as she flies by.

Midway down the next block, her path is blocked by a slow-moving quartet of chatting young women pulling young children along on wooden sleds with runners.

Clara darts between two oversized automobiles parked at the curb and steps into the street. Her foot promptly sinks into gray slush so deep that it rises above the thick soles of her shoes to soak her stockings.

Ignoring the icy chill that shoots up her leg, she waits for an antiquated pickup truck to pass, then scurries across the wide avenue and on toward the train station.

Her head hurts and her cold, wet feet are killing her. The air is bitter, snow falling on a diagonal wind from the gray sky.

Several times she nearly loses her balance on the slick sidewalk, yet she rushes on, determined to catch the southbound train.

Finally, she trips on an uneven slab of concrete and goes down hard for the second time this morning.

Assorted male pedestrians, all in overcoats and fedoras, most of them smoking cigarettes, rush over to help her up.

"Are you okay, doll?" one of them asks.

Another gallantly brushes a few snowflakes from her sleeves, politely ignoring her more provocative body parts that are now presumably covered in white.

Clara wriggles away from them, murmuring that she's fine.

"Wait, honey, is something wrong? Why are you running?"

In the distance, she hears a train whistle from the north.

"I—I have to catch the train," she blurts, and takes off toward the depot again.

Behind her, she can hear the men calling out to be careful.

Then she hears something else.

Someone is shouting her name.

For a moment, she wonders if it's Michael or Denton—if somehow, she's awakened from the nightmare at last.

She turns her head.

No, she's still dreaming . . . or still in 1941 . . .

Because the voice belongs to Jed. He's striding down the street on the opposite side, toting a large piece of luggage and her purse.

She forgot all about them.

But it doesn't matter. She can't go back now. If she misses the train—

Helplessly, she ignores Jed and hurries on. She'll have to leave everything behind.

The suitcase, the clothes it contains, her iPod—and Jed Landry.

She couldn't care less about the bag—it's a meaningless prop.

Yet, desperate as she is to get back to New York, the present, familiar territory . . .

She can't help feeling . . .

Wistful.

It's ridiculous.

Absolutely ridiculous, because even if he really does—did?—exist . . .

There's no place for Jed Landry in Clara's world.

And she has no intention of staying in his if she can help it.

"Wait, Clara!" he calls again breathlessly.

She glances over her shoulder to see him stepping recklessly into the road to get to her.

"Jed, no!"

A car swerves to miss him. Its horn emits an old-fashioned *ah-ooga* in unison with another high-pitched whistle from the train, sounding much closer this time.

Oh, Jed, be careful.

She turns away, knowing there's nothing she can do . . . knowing, too, that his life isn't in danger.

He'll be okay . . .

Today.

Swept by helplessness, she forces herself to cover the last stretch of sidewalk to the depot.

The whistle sounds again, loudly, drowning out Jed's urgent shouts.

She mounts the steps to the platform two at a time as the big antique locomotive pulls into the station. She's vaguely aware of curious stares from the cluster of people waiting there: a few businessmen dressed in overcoats and hats, and several uniformed soldiers who shoot curious—and appreciative—stares in her direction.

She can again hear Jed calling her name.

Don't look back. Whatever you do, Clara, don't look back. Just get on the train.

It slows to a stop.

"Clara, just wait one second!"

His voice is so plaintive. She starts to look over her shoulder for him. Maybe, if he's close enough, she can grab the suitcase and tell him goodbye . . .

"Need a hand?" One of the soldiers, a red-headed guy with a freckled face and a friendly grin, materializes at her elbow, obstructing her view of Jed.

"I'm fine," she protests, but he ushers her onto the high step.

There's nothing to do but move from there into the smoky, crowded car with the other boarding passengers.

The train begins to move again, and she leans toward the nearest window, hoping for a last glimpse of Jed.

Why, she has no idea. She just wants to see him one more time before he disappears forever.

For a moment, the deserted platform is all that's visible in the sliver of glass between the large hats of two women seated by the window.

Then, through a thickening curtain of falling snow, she spots him.

He's poised on the depot steps, still holding her bag, searching the train windows as though he's looking for her.

She waves, a futile gesture, and feels ridiculous when she catches the red-headed soldier looking at her.

"Goodbyes are tough, aren't they," he comments.

She merely nods, closes her eyes and inhales the smoky air deeply, trying to steady her nerves as the train chugs away from Glenhaven Park . . .

And Jed Landry.

And, please God, 1941 . . .

If she opens her eyes, will she wake up at last, back in her own century?

"Miss?" Somebody touches her arm. "Take my seat."

I'm definitely still dreaming.

She knows it even before she opens her eyes to see a young uniformed soldier standing and gesturing at the mohair cushion he just vacated.

On a modern-day commuter train, the seats are cushioned in stiff vinyl, and nobody offers one to a woman unless she's enormously pregnant, or elderly.

She slides into it gratefully, thanking him. He tips his cap and steps away, down the aisle, past the red-haired soldier who helped her up the steps.

In the process of lighting a cigarette, he catches her eye and offers the pack.

She shakes her head.

He comes over anyway. "Are you Jed Landry's girl? I saw him chasing after you back there at the station."

Jed Landry's girl.

Why does the quaint phrase immediately send a ripple of pleasure through her? And why can't she quite bring herself to tell him that no, she isn't Jed Landry's girl?

She hears herself asking instead, "You know Jed?"

"Sure. I went to grammar school with his brother Gilbert. Jed was a coupl'a years ahead of us. He's a good egg."

She smiles faintly at the quaint phrasing. "He is a good egg."

The soldier sticks out his gloved hand. "I'm Walter O'Mara."

"Clara McCallum." She shakes his hand politely, wondering why his name sounds so familiar.

Walter O'Mara . . .

"You can't be from Glenhaven Park," he said, "or I'd know you. It's too small a town."

"No, I'm from the city."

"Going back home?"

God, I hope so. She merely nods.

"I wish I were." He exhales a stream of smoke.

"Where are you going?"

"Fort Eastkill. My National Guard company was mobilized into the army."

Fort Eastkill.

He's one of them, Clara realizes, staring into the friendly, freckled face of a soldier who is little more than a boy.

He's one of the eleven Glenhaven Park servicemen who was killed—who *will* be killed—in the Normandy invasion.

She swallows hard over the knot that constricts her throat and squeezes her eyes closed to block out Walter O'Mara's unwitting innocence.

"Those fellas are part of my company, too," he informs her, and she opens her eyes to see him gesturing at the other soldiers who boarded with them at Glenhaven Park.

She nods and turns away, staring blindly out the window. She can't bear to look at him, at any of them, knowing what's going to happen to them all . . .

And to Jed.

Oh, Jed.

I wish . . .

No, that's silly.

He was just part of my dream. And now that part is

over, and any second now the whole dream will be over, and I'll be home.

Except . . .

He was so real.

Jed. She touched him, smelled him, can even now see his face in her mind's eye as the train sways rhythmically, its forward motion lulling her frenzied torrent of thoughts.

She leans her head back against the seat, exhaling heavily, trying not to remember . . .

And then, inexplicably, trying not to forget.

The whistle blows.

She can see every contour of Jed Landry's face so clearly, etched against the darkened screen of her closed eyelids.

She finds herself wondering what it would have been like to kiss him.

Just once.

Her breath catches in her throat as she imagines him taking her into his arms and hungrily lowering his mouth over hers the way Michael does in their big love scene.

Except that kissing Michael is nothing like kissing the real Jed Landry. She knows that, just as she knew that beneath his stiff woolen shirt was a magnificently sculpted masculine chest, taut abs, well-defined biceps . . .

Terrific. Now you're fantasizing about seeing a man who doesn't exist—not in your world, anyway—shirtless.

Clara yawns, suddenly weary.

Much too weary to prop open her eyes again, much less fight the searing images of her fantasy love scene with Jed Landry.

So she lets them come, borne on a welcome haze

of romantic illusion as the southbound train chugs on toward the city.

Jed didn't even lock the store when he raced out into the snow, coatless, chasing after Clara.

What would Pop say about that?

That I'm an irresponsible goof, and anyone could have walked in and robbed the place blind, Jed thinks grimly as he steps back inside. To his relief, he sees that the store is empty—and, at a glance, the merchandise and cash register seem intact.

He drops Clara's heavy suitcase with a thud and eyes it—as well as the pocketbook in his hand—dubiously.

Now what? What is he supposed to do with this?

What *can* he do? He'll have to stash her things in the storeroom and hope she'll come back to claim them.

What if she doesn't?

You can always track her down in the city, he tells himself.

But how? He doesn't even know her last name.

A quick inspection of her suitcase reveals no identification tag. Not on the outside, anyway.

He glances at the handbag, turning it over.

Maybe he should—

No. Absolutely not. He can't open a lady's pocketbook. That's just too . . . personal.

So is the suitcase. He can't possibly go rifling through her belongings . . . though his pulse does quicken shamefully at the very notion of the dainty unmentionables that are undoubtedly stashed inside.

Jed moodily abandons the suitcase and returns to the soda fountain, stashing the pocketbook behind the counter. Picking up the barely touched glass of water, he sees that the rim is stained with her red lipstick.

I can't wait and I can't drive home . . . I have to take the train.

What did she mean by that?

She's an enigma, through and through. Nothing about her adds up, now that he has a chance to go over everything she said and did.

Why, if she arrived in town with luggage—meaning she had every intention of staying for awhile—would she promptly turn around and flee like the demons of hell were chasing her?

She sure wasn't all that upset when she first set foot in the door. Her agitation seemed to grow with every minute she spent in the store . . .

More specifically, in Jed's company.

In fact, now that he thinks about what transpired, it wasn't until he actually introduced himself that Clara's demeanor changed from vaguely confused to downright panicky.

Her behavior makes no sense. No sense whatsoever.

Then again . . . she *did* bump her head.

Hard enough to leave a bruise . . . and perhaps, hard enough to leave her so dazed she didn't know whether she was coming or going.

I shouldn't have let her get on that train alone, Jed thinks helplessly.

To be fair, he did try to stop her. But maybe he didn't try hard enough. He could have run a lot faster if he'd left the bags—at least the suitcase—behind . . .

But the bags were the reason he was chasing her in the first place—or so he had tried to rationalize to himself as he seized the pocketbook from the counter and the bag from the floor, then impulsively ran after her.

What was he thinking? He wasn't thinking. If he had been, he would have remembered to act like a sensible grown man, not a dizzy schoolboy with a crush.

Still . . .

If anything happens to her, it will be my fault.

And there's a good chance that he'll never even know what becomes of her.

A good chance?

If she doesn't take it upon herself to come back to Glenhaven Park for her bags, he'll never see her again.

Unless . . .

Again, he picks up her handbag, speculating. There must be some kind of identification inside.

But he shouldn't check.

Really, he shouldn't . . .

Should he?

"Good morning, Jed!" Alice explodes through the door as he wavers, her hat askew and pudgy cheeks ruddy from the cold. "I'm sorry I'm so late . . . I know you're probably sore at me but I can explain . . ."

Jed stashes the bag back under the counter and turns away. "It's all right, Alice," he says absently, his mind on the enigmatic woman who dashed out of his life as unexpectedly as she came into it.

"It . . . it is? It's okay?"

Jed blinks, sees Alice gaping at him. "It's fine," he says with a shrug, not in the mood for her explanation—or his own required recourse. "Just go hang up your coat and get your apron on."

She nods and scurries away.

After a moment, Jed lifts Clara's suitcase and carries it toward the back room. If Clara comes back for it, he'll have it for her.

And if she doesn't come back . . . well, he might just decide to go looking for her.

Chapter 6

"Last stop, Grand Central. Please take a moment to gather your belongings before you exit the train. Last stop, Grand Central Station."

Clara opens her eyes with a start, looking around in confusion.

She's on the train . . . ?

The train!

It all comes back to her—*Glenhaven Park, 1941, Jed Landry.*

A dream.

That's what it was. Just a dream.

It must have been, because she's definitely in familiar territory now: on a modern commuter train car with rows of regular—i.e., uncomfortable—benches.

And the cancer! Was it part of the dream?

Please, God . . .

After glancing around quickly to make sure she's not being observed, she pulls the neckline of her jacket back slightly. Is it her imagination, or is there a strong hint of cigarette smoke clinging to her clothing?

She lowers her eyes to peer down inside her blouse.

A black chill seeps over her at the sight of the gauze bandage covering the biopsy site.

That part was real.

But the rest . . .

Jabbed by a pinprick of doubt, she realizes she'd better double-check, just to be sure she really is safely back in the present.

"Excuse me . . ."

She looks up to see her seatmate—a bearded guy with a ponytail and a nose ring.

"Can I get out?"

"Out! Yes! I'm sorry!" Fighting the urge to hug him in all his scruffy twenty-first century glory, she stands quickly.

Instinctively, she checks for a bag and realizes in dismay that she doesn't have one.

But I did . . .

In my dream.

Feeling numb, she slips into the aisle with the other passengers filing slowly toward the open doors at the far end of the car.

And in my dream, Jed was chasing after me with that huge suitcase and my prop purse . . .

She shakes her head to clear it, but she can only remember how Jed looked, and the sound of his voice, and the masculine smell of him . . .

It seemed so real.

But it wasn't.

She's not in Glenhaven Park, and she's not in 1941. She's wide awake, in the city, in her own decade . . . isn't she?

Sneaking surreptitious glances at her fellow riders, she's reassured to see iPods, Snapple bottles, nylon backpacks, cell phones . . .

She's definitely in her own decade.

As she steps with the crowd onto the cavernous station platform, she notices some of the other passengers shooting inquisitive glances in her direction.

Not glances of recognition: *Wasn't she with Michael Marshall in that magazine picture I saw . . . ?*

No, these are looks of blatant curiosity, as in: *What is* up *with that freak?*

It takes her a moment to figure out why.

Oh. She's still dressed in her forties costume, black velvet hat and all.

So startled that she stops walking altogether, she wonders how it's possible.

"Excuse me," a man says brusquely, jostling her from behind.

"Sorry," she murmurs and resumes shuffling with the crowd toward the steps leading up to the main terminal.

If she's still dressed for her scene . . . then where is she coming from?

Straight from the set, obviously.

But she takes a car service, not a commuter train, back and forth from the city to the location shoot in Westchester County every day.

What was she doing on a Metro-North train?

Another man bumps into her, not even bothering to excuse himself.

For a split second, she wistfully recalls the gentlemanly behavior of all those gallant strangers back in 1941 . . .

Then she reminds herself that she wasn't really *there*; it was just a dream. A dream from which she has finally awakened . . .

And you most definitely don't want to go back, she informs herself firmly.

Emerging into the vast main concourse, she takes in the marble floors, stone walls, enormous arched windows, and vaulted turquoise sky sprinkled with golden constellations. For a moment, she wonders whether she's back in the past.

No, the terminal may have been restored to its prewar appearance, but the people bustling through it are decidedly contemporary. She's still in the present.

You never left in the first place. You just imagined that you did.

Clara glances toward the famous four-face brass clock above the information booth, sees that it's 11:20.

Specifically, 11:20 A.M., judging by the light filtering through the doors leading out onto Forty-second Street.

The thing is . . .

This whole dream scenario would make far more sense if she were waking up safe and sound in her own bed first thing in the morning, just as Tchaikovsky's Clara did under the Christmas tree.

That would mean her subconscious had conjured the entire day, including the time in the trailer with Jesus, and setting up the scene on the train.

Instead, it's almost as if she began the day wide awake in the present . . .

then took an imaginary detour to the parallel date and time in the past . . .

then picked up the day almost where she left off, yet somehow regaining consciousness on the train she boarded in 1941 . . .

about an hour—and sixty-five years—later.

No, not the same train, she reminds herself.

But a train, and one that traveled the same route as the one she boarded in her dream.

How did she get here?

There's just one way to find out.

She reaches automatically for her pocket, and her cell phone—then remembers she doesn't have that, either.

Only after making her way through the crowded

terminal to a bank of pay telephones does she realize that she also lacks money. She has no purse, no wallet . . .

What now?

You can always call collect . . . can't you?

It's been years since she's done that. Does it still work the same way?

Lifting the receiver, she dials zero, then, after a moment's thought, Michael's cell phone number.

She informs the operator who comes on the line that she's making a collect call, then waits nervously as it rings once . . . twice . . .

Michael usually doesn't answer unless he recognizes the number on his caller ID. In fact, even then, he rarely picks up his phone.

This time, for whatever reason, he does, on the fourth ring. *Hallelujah.*

"I have a collect call from Clara . . . will you accept the charges?"

"Clara? God, yes . . . I was hoping this was . . . Clara, are you there?"

"Hi, Michael," she says tentatively as the operator clicks off. "Where are you?"

"Where am I? In my trailer, eating saltines and drinking ginger ale."

Oh, right. The stomach bug.

"Where the hell are *you*?"

Feeling as foolish as she is frightened, she admits, "I'm in, um, Grand Central Station."

"What are you doing there?"

I have no idea.

Before she has a chance to come up with a plausible explanation, Michael goes on, "Listen, everybody's going crazy looking for you."

"Who is everybody?"

"Everybody on the set. Somebody said you were in the middle of blocking your train scene, and you just took off."

"What do they mean by that?"

"I don't know, that's just what I heard. One minute you were there, on the train, and the next, you were gone. When the train pulled up to the platform for our scene, you weren't on it."

"No, I was on it," she protests defensively, without thinking. "You were the one who wasn't on the platform!"

There's a moment of silence.

Then Michael says slowly, "I was there, Clara. And so was Denton. And the rest of the crew, and the camera equipment . . . Everything was set. But you weren't there."

"I . . . I'm sorry," she murmurs, thoughts spinning. It doesn't make sense. Nothing makes sense.

"Look, I figured you must have just freaked out or something—you know, with everything you've got going on."

The cancer. He knows; she told him about it yesterday.

"I didn't want to say anything to anyone," Michael goes on, lowering his voice, "but you'd better explain it to Denton. And fast. Right now, according to Bobby"— Bobby would be the unit production manager—"Denton thinks you're on drugs or something."

"Drugs?" she echoes incredulously.

"Yeah, I guess this is what used to happen on the set of his last film when he was directing that strung-out crackhead who ended up winning the Golden Globe. Anyway, I tried to convince Bobby you aren't on drugs, but I don't know if he believed me."

"I'll call Bobby as soon as I get home."

"Home? You're not coming back?"

"I can't." Not without a cent in her pocket—or a clue how she got here.

Michael pauses, then asks, "Do you need anything, Clara?"

Just a reality check, she thinks grimly. Aloud, she assures him that she's fine—or rather, that she will be. "I just have to pull myself together. It's been a rough couple of days."

"I know it has. But you're going to get through this. You're a tough cookie."

"Well, today, I think the cookie is crumbling."

After hanging up, she steps out onto the street into a steady drizzle falling from a gray sky.

She'll have to walk all the way home to Eleventh Street. That's over thirty blocks . . . in shoes that feel like torture devices.

She'll just have to take it slowly. At least the fresh air will give her a chance to clear her head.

Forty-second Street is teeming with midday traffic and pedestrians. She makes her way to the opposite side and rounds the corner onto Park Avenue, heading downtown toward her apartment.

Wishing she had an umbrella, she notes that it's an unseasonably warm day for December.

How strange that it was just snowing . . .

In my dream.

That's all it was. She hit her head on the train before blocking her scene, then blanked out everything that happened after that—like finding her way out of the vintage train car and onto a southbound train—all the while dreaming that she had gone back in time.

It just seemed so real . . .

All of it.

Especially Jed Landry.

Why was he a part of it?

Then again, why wouldn't he be?

She supposes it only makes sense that she would dream about him . . . she was, after all, preparing herself to fall in love with him.

Just . . . not with the *real* Jed.

With Michael playing Jed.

If she was going to fantasize about Jed Landry in her dreams, wouldn't she see him as Michael? Why would she see him as . . . himself?

It isn't as though she's even given much thought to that black-and-white photograph she glimpsed weeks ago in the Glenhaven Park library, in the local history room. She's given it no thought at all, really.

Yet she must have filed Jed Landry's image away in her subconscious.

Right, and it was jarred loose when I smacked my head, she thinks wryly.

And now that he's in her brain, floating around—well, she can't seem to shake him. She can still see him as clearly as she did when he was standing right in front of her . . .

In the dream.

Just as long as she keeps reminding herself that none of it is real—that Jed Landry isn't alive at this very moment in some alternative universe—she'll be fine.

Because if he were . . .

Well, she might just have a bittersweet afterthought about leaving him behind.

At last, Clara limps the final few steps along West Eleventh Street toward her building. She averts her eyes as she passes a trenchcoat-clad man from a neighboring building. She can feel him watching her from under his black umbrella as he clings to his dog's leash, waiting for it to do its business along the curb.

She can just imagine what she looks like at this point: still wearing the vintage costume, soaked to the bone, her hair bedraggled and makeup undoubtedly smeared all over her face. If she had collected a dollar for every curious stare she attracted in the course of her journey down from Grand Central Station, she could have bought a car in no time and driven herself the rest of the way.

Grimacing, she forces her swollen feet up the steps to the door and buzzes the building super's apartment on the ground floor.

If he isn't here, she's going to have to get to a phone and call Jason. He still has his set of keys . . . if he didn't toss them into the East River.

Please be home, Mr. Kobayashi. Please let one thing go right for me today. Pleasepleasepleasepleaseplease . . .

"Yes?"

"Mr. Kobayashi, it's Clara McCallum. I'm locked out. Would you mind . . . ?"

The door buzzes promptly, unlocking with a click.

She opens it and steps in out of the rain at long last. Relieved to be home, she closes the door behind her and leans against it with a sigh.

What a nightmare.

Beyond the inner vestibule door, she can see Isamu Kobayashi, an elderly man with surprisingly jet-black hair. He ascends from his apartment and shuffles toward the door, wearing a robe and slippers, as usual. She undoubtedly caught him in the midst of what seems to be his favorite pastime: watching one of the old cop shows to which he's addicted.

He was doing that the very first time she met him, when she first came to see the apartment. She could hear the distinct *Dragnet* theme blasting from his television.

She remembers the details of that sweltering July day very well, with good reason, because something strange happened. Something she hasn't been able to explain to this day.

The moment Mr. Kobayashi first saw her standing there in the hallway with Kim, the Realtor, his jaw dropped.

At the time, that didn't strike her as unusual; he was probably a fan of her soap. Or so she assumed.

"Wait here a minute," he said, and she assumed he was going to get the keys to the vacant apartment or something.

That wasn't it.

He handed her a package wrapped in brown paper and marked with her handwritten name, all but faded. It was wrapped with string and sealed with a yellowed, brittle strip of tape.

"This is for you," he said.

"Oh, how sweet. Thank you. What is it?"

"I don't know." At her questioning look, he elaborated, "A man dropped it off and said to give it to you whenever you came."

Puzzled, Clara smiled politely, tucked the package into her bag, and exchanged a knowing glance with Kim, assuming the old man must be slightly senile or something.

She fell in love with the apartment at first sight, and agreed to rent it on the spot.

It wasn't until she got home later that night that she remembered the package.

She opened it somewhat gingerly, uncertain of what she was going to find.

Certainly not the fuzzy red mittens with the white

snowflake pattern her grandmother knit for her mother when she was a little girl. Along with a matching red hat, they were part of a set Jeanette had given to Clara years ago, but she rarely wore them. Mittens just weren't in style; she preferred sleek leather gloves.

She always assumed the hat and mittens were tucked away in a dresser drawer, but when she opened it to check, only the hat was there. Puzzled, she put the mittens in with it, and the set was whole again.

Obviously, she unwittingly lost the mittens somehow, at some point.

But how on earth had they come into Mr. Kobayashi's possession?

Even he seemed clueless. When she asked him, he just repeated that a man had given him the package and told him to hold it for her.

"When was this?" she asked.

His answer told her that he really was senile. "Oh, years ago. When I was a little boy."

Not wanting to embarrass him, Clara dropped the subject. To this day, she's stumped about how her mittens landed in her super's hands, but at least she hadn't lost them forever. She wore them all last winter, and plans to this year as well.

But at this moment, she isn't dwelling on the mittens as she comes face-to-face with Mr. Kobayashi.

"Oh! What happened to you?" he asks in his Asian-accented English. "You look like a drowned rat."

"I know . . . I'm sorry to bother you, but I don't have my keys."

"You got mugged? Did they steal your purse?"

Clara hesitates, then nods. It's easier than attempting to explain what really happened. She simply doesn't have the energy to provide even an abridged version.

Unfortunately, in addition to watching old cop

shows, Mr. Kobayashi's other favorite pastime is conversation. He's the chattiest man Clara has ever known—and oddly, he has rarely come across as senile since that first day she met him. Maybe that was just a momentary memory lapse.

For the most part, she usually doesn't mind chatting with him. But today, right now, she just wants to get into her apartment and out of these clothes.

"You poor thing! They attacked you! You're all bruised!" Mr. Kobayashi has spotted her forehead. "Let me call the fuzz for you."

The fuzz?

Okay, he's definitely seen a few too many outdated cop shows. She wants to smile, but manages not to. He's so earnest, so concerned.

"I'll call the doctor, too," he offers.

"No, I don't need a doctor or—or the *fuzz*, Mr. Kobayashi, but thank you. I'm sure I'll be okay."

"But you're hurt! You need ice on that."

That's it. His kindness, combined with the reminder of Jed Landry gently applying an ice pack to her head, suddenly has Clara feeling like she's going to cry.

She opens her mouth to explain that she's really fine, but she can't seem to push the words past the lump of emotion in her throat.

"Did you get a good look at the perp so you can ID him in a lineup?" Mr. Kobayashi asks then, sounding like Starsky, Hutch, and Baretta all rolled into one.

Okay, now she feels like she's going to laugh *and* cry all at once.

She manages to tell him, straight-faced, that the perp got away.

"That's a shame. But maybe he dumped your purse somewhere. Usually these swine just want the bread and toss the rest."

"The bread?" she echoes in bewilderment, before realizing that he's talking about the money.

The bread.

Bread . . .

Bakery . . .

Doughboy . . .

Her momentary amusement with Mr. Kobayashi's outdated cop jargon segues right back to Jed Landry with disarming ease.

Jed, and his comment about his father having been a doughboy.

The thing is, if that was all a dream . . . then how could it contain information she's never heard of?

For a moment, she's stricken anew by the possibility that she might really have traveled back to 1941 this morning.

Then she comes to her senses.

Who says any of those details in the dream were authentic? You probably just made up the stuff you never heard of before.

Like doughboy.

"Mr. Kobayashi," she says, dragging her errant thoughts back to the matter at hand, "if you could just let me into my apartment, I would really appreciate it. I know I'll be fine. I just need to rest."

"First, you need to get ice," he says, pulling out his key ring and leading the way to the stairs. "Then call the fuzz. Then rest. Okay?"

"Okay." *Except for the part about the fuzz and the ice.*

Shaking his head as he climbs the steps above her, the diminutive man says, "Such a shame this happen to nice dame like you."

This time, she does smile. He can't see her.

"I've lived in this city all my years—seventy years, you know that? Seventy years right in this house."

She does know that. He likes to tell anyone who will listen about what the neighborhood was like in the old days. The neighborhood, his life, the house . . .

She knows that his parents were household help for the Sloans, the last people to live here when it was a one-family home. After Mr. Sloan passed away years ago, his heirs sold it for a small fortune and it was turned into apartments like most of the other townhouses on the block. Apparently, Mr. Kobayashi came with the building.

"All these years, the city has gone downhill. Now, nobody is safe around here. You can't be too careful."

"No, I guess you can't."

"You poor thing. You're a nice person. Why did this have to happen to you?"

"It's just been a really bad day," she admits, her smile vanishing.

"You should watch TV when you rest," he suggests. "*Dragnet* is good. It's coming on soon. That will take your mind off troubles, cheer you up."

Dragnet. Right, very cheerful.

They've reached her door. He unlocks it and she steps over the threshold. "Thank you so much, Mr. Kobayashi."

"You so welcome. Oh! I almost forgot!" He slaps himself on his hair, still jet-black despite his advanced age.

"What?"

"Somebody was here looking for you today."

"Looking for me? Who was it?"

"She didn't say her name. Just rang the bell and asked if you live here. I told her no, in case she was a nutcase, but she pointed to your last name on the buzzer panel," he says apologetically.

"That's okay," Clara says with a sigh. "What did she look like?"

"Old lady. White hair. Glasses." He shrugs.

It was probably another die-hard *One Life To Live* fan. They pop up from time to time, seeking autographs and complaining about Arabella Saffron's untimely demise.

"I'll check on you later," Mr. Kobayashi says, turning to leave.

"Oh, that's not necessary. I really am fine."

"I'll check on you," he says, and departs with a wave, shuffling back down the stairs in his robe and slippers.

Safe and warm in her apartment, Clara unwedges her feet from the hideous shoes and kicks them into the corner. In the bathroom, she slips off the wet clothes and throws them into the claw-foot tub. Oddly, the stench of stale cigarette smoke again reaches her nostrils. She picks up the jacket she was wearing and sniffs it.

It definitely smells like smoke.

Which proves . . .

Absolutely nothing.

Sitting on the closed toilet seat, she unpeels the seamed silk stockings, which are hopelessly snagged, and deposits them into the trash.

Looking down again at her breast, she gingerly touches the gauze bandage. The site beneath it is still sore. But in a few days . . .

The lump will be cut out, leaving her permanently disfigured.

Oh, my God.

Without warning, a wail escapes her throat. Even

as she tells herself that she should just be damned grateful for the surgery and her prognosis for survival—and grateful that she isn't losing her entire breast—she can't help but mourn the imminent loss.

She buries her face and sobs, long and hard and loud. If the flood of bitter tears alone could wash away the heartache, she would be healed.

Instead, she merely feels ravaged in their wake, more depleted than ever before.

She rises to her feet shakily, takes her robe from the hook on the back of the door and puts it on, needing to hide the bandage and all it signifies.

As she ties the sash around her waist she catches sight of her reflection in the medicine-chest mirror.

Good God. I look like hell.

Her forties hat is waterlogged; beneath it, her hairdo is lacquered to her head. Her eyes are raw and red, her expression ravaged, her makeup is down around her chin, and the crimson lipstick is hopelessly smudged.

How ironic that Clara, who wouldn't deny that her success in the entertainment industry is based as much on her beauty as on her talent, has transformed into this . . . this visual monstrosity. She can't bear to look at herself.

Is this what it's going to be like from now on . . . after the surgery? Will she dread seeing herself naked afterward? Will she be able to ever again share her body with anyone else?

One thing at a time. For now, I just need cold cream, she tells herself. *Cold cream, then a hot shower for about an hour, and about a week of sleep . . .*

Except that she can't sleep. She has to see Karen.

Maybe she'll help me . . .

Oh, who am I kidding?

No one, she thinks bleakly, *can possibly help me at this point. Not in the way I need.*

What she needs is a magic genie who could miraculously sweep away her cancer as if it never existed.

Sure. That'll happen.

With a weary sigh, she begins pulling out the pins that secure her sodden hat to her matted hair. Each tug makes her wince in pain.

She isn't looking forward to donning this getup all over again tomorrow . . .

Nor is she looking forward to calling the unit production manager to explain her vanishing act.

And no, she's not looking forward to the appointment later with Karen, either.

So what are *you looking forward to?*

Not much of anything, she realizes. Except, perhaps, sleep.

Maybe I'll dream about Jed Landry again.

That possibility sparks a glimmer of interest. Now that could possibly be something to look forward to. Especially since this time, she'll know it's just a dream.

Not that *he* can possibly help her . . .

No, she has already determined that no one can do that. No human, anyway.

But then, Jed wasn't human—he was a part of her dream. And there was something about dream Jed . . . strong, solid, capable dream Jed . . . that made her feel . . .

Safe.

Gazing into the mirror, she watches her brow furrow and her teeth come down on her bottom lip.

It was definitely just a dream.

Right.

Right?

Clara turns thoughtfully away from the mirror, the hairpin removal task momentarily abandoned.

Padding barefoot to the living room, she goes straight to the bookcase and peruses the row of titles.

It's on the top shelf: the big leather-bound dictionary her grandfather presented to her at her elementary school graduation, along with a dark-haired porcelain angel, of course. The dictionary's first page is inscribed in spidery handwriting: *For Clara-belle, with love from Grandpa on your special day.*

She flips the pages to the Ds and scans the entries. There it is.

As she reads the definition, her heart starts pounding all over again.

Doughboy (dō′boi) n. An American infantryman in World War I

She never knew that.

Are you sure? Maybe you read it somewhere.

No, she would have remembered. She would have remembered because the word *doughboy* would have brought to mind her father, and the way she used to poke him in the stomach to make him giggle like the fat white Pillsbury Doughboy on TV.

But if she never knew that a doughboy was a World War I soldier, then how could she have conjured it in her dream?

If the Jed Landry she encountered was a figment of her imagination, then he could know only what *she* knows . . . isn't that correct?

Suddenly, she's utterly depleted. Her head is spinning and once again, nothing makes sense.

She closes the dictionary and shoves it back on the shelf.

Later, she thinks wearily, trudging to the bathroom again. *I'll worry about all of this later.*

Chapter 7

"Jed? Have you been away?" Sarah Wenick calls through the dusk as he passes by her two-story Dutch Colonial that evening on his way home.

He shakes his head, marveling that the neighborhood gossip happens to be outside on a gusty December evening like this. Chestnut Street is all but deserted, families tucked cozily inside houses gaily illuminated with strings of colored lights.

Yet there's Sarah on her top step, plainly visible in the pool of light from an overhead fixture. She's bundled into a woolen coat and a headwrap, fiddling with the string of darkened lights tacked around her front door. One of the bulbs must have burned out.

"Hello, Sarah, no, I haven't been away," he calls back to her. "I'm just coming from the store."

"Oh . . . I saw the suitcase and I thought . . ." She trails off, waiting for him to elaborate.

He merely nods and tips his hat with a gloved hand.

If he were a gentleman, he'd offer to help her replace the bulb, knowing her husband Clark is working the night shift down at the plant.

Well, he *is* a gentleman . . . under most circumstances.

He just isn't in the mood to explain the suitcase to his perennially nosy next-door neighbor . . . or, in turn, to his mother, who will surely hear about it from Sarah promptly.

"Good night, Sarah."

"Good night, Jed. Give Lois my best."

His galoshes make a squeaking sound in the snow as he trudges up the Landrys' driveway next door, covered in several inches of fresh white powder since he shoveled it early this morning.

Pop's snow-blanketed DeSoto is parked in front of the detached garage, right where Jed left it when he drove it home a few weeks ago with a flat tire. He hasn't got around to fixing it yet. Good thing nobody drives the car but him—though Gilbert will want to when he gets back, and Penny keeps begging him to teach her now that she's almost seventeen.

He figures he'd better oblige her one of these days. Mother doesn't have a license, and Gilbert would never have the patience to teach Penny.

But he'll have to become more patient if he's going to take over where I leave off next spring, Jed tells himself—not for the first time.

He can't help but worry about how Gilbert is going to manage the household in his absence. He'll have to grow up quickly . . .

Just like I did.

Jed pauses beside the car, remembering how proud Pop was when he scraped together enough to buy it— how lovingly he cared for it, polishing it every week until the chrome shone like mirrors.

I really should fix that tire, Jed thinks guiltily.

It just hasn't been a priority. Not with everything he needs within a few blocks' walking distance of the house.

Well . . .

Not everything.

Clara lives in New York.

But that's all he knows about her . . .

So far.

He hasn't opened her pocketbook or her suitcase—not yet. It seemed far too brazen a thing to do in the store, especially with Alice underfoot.

But when it came time to close up the five-and-dime for the evening, there was no question about his leaving Clara's belongings there. He opted to bring them home with him for safekeeping—and, all right, possibly for further investigation.

If she hadn't left her bags behind, it would have been much easier to forget her.

Who are you kidding, fella?

All right, Jed probably wouldn't find it easy to forget her under any circumstances. It isn't every day a beautiful doll like her walks into his life . . .

then out again, without any plausible explanation.

If she hadn't left behind the suitcase and pocketbook, he'd be helpless when it comes to finding her again.

If that's what he decides to do.

Forget about her. That's what you should decide to do.

Even if . . .

Say he finds her, in New York. What then? Does he just hand over her bags and wish her well?

Somehow he knows that seeing her again, one last time, won't be enough.

But what else is there?

Falling in love, getting married, settling down . . .

That wasn't part of his future plan. Not for a coupl'a years, anyway. After he's enlisted, and done his part for his country, and seen something of the world beyond Glenhaven Park.

Then again . . . he's seen it. Some of it. He's seen New York and Boston, and the Catskill Mountains where they spent a week every summer before the Depression, and once, right after he got the DeSoto, Pop drove the whole family to the Jersey shore for the day.

Maybe that's all the world travel Jed really needs.

Maybe if he found the right girl tomorrow—

Or, more specifically, *today*—

Maybe he'd be content to just stay put here in Glenhaven Park forever.

Maybe.

Jed can see his mother's silhouette against the filmy white curtains in the window as he passes the back corner of the house. He pictures her there in the kitchen, bustling from stove to sink to icebox, preparing supper with help—and a lot of bickering—from his sisters.

They eat later than usual on Monday nights, because it's laundry day and Mother doesn't finish until after five o'clock.

It must be nearly six now.

Mother will be sending Doris out to summon him for supper any minute.

First, however, he wants to examine Clara's bags. His curiosity has been building all day, as has his anticipation of actually finding her address.

He steps into the garage, which was formerly a carriage house, and is far too small to house the monstrous DeSoto. Anyway, it's filled to its shadowy, cobwebby depths with unused remnants from his grandparents' household, plus the Landrys' yard equipment, outgrown bicycles, and lawn furniture nobody's bothered to bring out for two summers now.

Jed hauls the suitcase up the steep, rickety flight of

stairs leading to what was once a loft overhead. Now it's a one-room apartment with indoor plumbing Pop installed back in '38. He'd planned to use the space as a workshop; he always did like to tinker with things.

But those days were over for him soon after he finished whitewashing the walls and sanding the wide-planked floors.

Pop's tool bench still sits in one corner of the large room. Jed likes to look at it, remembering how he was once Pop's proud helper. Hunched over some splintered furniture or broken appliance, cigarette burning between his lips, Pop would tell him what he needed; Jed loved to reach in, rummage around until he found the right tool, and bask in Pop's approval.

Jed hasn't opened the tool chest since his father passed away. When something needs fixing around the house, it's Granddad who usually does the repairs, using his own set of tools, before Jed can get to it.

He should probably move Pop's tool chest back down to the garage; the apartment is cramped enough as it is. But he doesn't have the heart to do that just yet.

The remainder of his meager floor space is occupied by furniture odds and ends, including the twin bed, bureau, and desk Jed moved up here from the house. His grandparents brought their own bedroom suite when they took over his old room. The heavy mahogany four-poster and massive wardrobe still seem out of place up in Jed's dormered boyhood room, against a backdrop of decades-old pastel wallpaper picturing baby farm animals: lambs and chicks and calves.

No less out of its element is the wobbly wooden dinette table that once stood in the Landrys' breakfast nook and is now tucked into a dormered nook of Jed's garage loft. He has countless memories of hearty meals eaten at that table with his parents and Gilbert when they were a well-fed family of four, back before the Depression—and the girls—came along.

Now the nicked wooden surface, its faded yellow paint worn away completely in some spots, is covered with household bills, books, magazines, and a basket of folded clothing Mother must have brought up earlier.

Jed drops the suitcase by the table and pushes the tabletop clutter aside to make room for the pocket-book.

He stares at it as he removes his coat, hat, and gloves, tossing them all on one of the rickety, painted chairs.

Then he lowers himself into the sturdiest of the four, the only one he uses for sitting, and takes a deep breath.

Does he dare?

If you don't open that pocketbook, you'll never see her again.

But he can't know that for certain.

He can't know that she won't show up tomorrow to reclaim her things . . . and his heart.

Face it. That's not going to happen, Jed.

And you can either forget her . . . or try and find her.

He hesitates.

Then, with a trembling hand, he unfastens the clasp on Clara's pocketbook.

Karen Vinton, a beautiful African American woman dressed in a gauzy purple print skirt and a brown shawl she crocheted herself, looks up from the phone in her hand when Clara steps into her reception area.

"There you are! I was just about to call you. You're fifteen minutes late."

"Sorry. Subway trouble." Living in Manhattan, you can blame anything on that.

In reality, the subway got her here in a flash, and Clara spent the next half hour wandering aimlessly around the neighborhood, trying to work up the courage to break bad news to someone who cares about her.

She reluctantly follows Karen into the adjacent office, a rectangular space as nondescript as the waiting room: a tidy desk in one corner, a cluster of blond wood chairs covered in nubby gold fabric, a nondescript framed still life on the wall, and a tall window covered in metal blinds.

"So how was your week?" Karen Vinton's stack of silver bracelets jangle as she closes the door and turns to face Clara with a smile.

"It was . . . okay."

Jed Landry flits into her mind, then stubbornly refuses to budge.

That's been happening all day. The dream hasn't faded in the hours since she awakened, as dreams usually have a way of doing.

She can still recall every unsettling detail.

She finds herself wishing she could tell Karen about it, but how would she even bring it up?

"What's on your mind, Clara?"

"Do you mean . . . right this second?"

Karen nods.

"Can I tell you about a dream I had?" she hears herself blurting, much to her own surprise—and dismay.

"Sure."

Clara hesitates. Why did she have to go and say something about the dream?

Because you don't know what to make of it . . . and

you're starting to think you might be losing your mind. Who better to decide whether that's the case than a shrink who knows you inside and out?

She takes a deep breath, and finds herself spilling the whole story—prefacing today's events with the cancer diagnosis.

Karen takes that in stride—unsurprising, really, considering that it's her job to remain calm and listen.

She starts asking questions about treatment, but Clara holds her off with a terse, "I just want to tell you about the dream, okay?"

"Okay."

Clara reveals the entire dream, and how she met Jed—even that she was attracted to him. And how she awakened on the Metro-North train with no memory of how she might have gotten there—not in real life, anyway.

She winds down by admitting that her feet were raw and bleeding by the time she made it downtown, and how Mr. Kobayashi had to let her into her apartment.

She also mentions that when she called Bobby, the unit production manager, he was remarkably understanding about the whole thing and promised to pass along the information to Denton. The director promptly sent an enormous bouquet of flowers, closely followed by a messenger service delivering her call sheet for tomorrow as well as her bag containing keys, wallet and cell phone, which she'd left in her trailer up in Westchester.

"And that's it," she says, looking at Karen at last. "What do you think?"

"About . . . ?"

"All of it. The whole dream. It was a dream . . . wasn't it?"

"Do you think it was?"

"Of course!" She stares at Karen, who is watching her intently. "I mean, what else could it have been?"

Karen remains silent. Waiting, apparently. She's good at that.

Clara knows from experience that she'll just sit there for as long as it takes for Clara to answer her own question.

"What I don't get," she admits, shifting her weight uncomfortably, "is how I *lost* a few hours of my morning. I mean, I didn't feel like I was losing it when I was dreaming . . . but I figured I'd wake up and find myself in the same place where I was when I started dreaming. Instead, I guess I blanked out . . . and I woke up in the same place where I was in the dream when it ended . . . on the train to the city. How could that happen?"

"Temporary dissociative amnesia can be triggered by both psychological and physical trauma."

"Is that what I have?"

"I'm not saying that, but given your cancer diagnosis—and the head injury—your experience isn't all that unprecedented . . . except . . ."

Utterly unnerved by the final word and the way Karen trails off wearing an intent frown, Clara prods her. "Except . . . what?"

"If we assume that your experience this morning should be attributed to the bump on your head, we would have to rule out retrograde amnesia, because you seem to clearly remember the details leading up to the accident . . . correct?"

"Right. I remember specifically how the train slowed down all of a sudden, and I flew backward through the air, and hit my—"

"Backward?" Karen cuts in. "Don't you mean forward?"

"No, backward," Clara repeats slowly, though how that might have happened is momentarily puzzling to her. Usually, a lurch on a moving train would cause you to fall forward . . . wouldn't it?

Again, she regrets not paying better attention in high school physics class.

Karen is silent for a few seconds, as if trying to ascertain whether what Clara described is physically possible.

Then she continues with a shrug. "You say you didn't immediately lose consciousness after you hit your head."

"I don't think I—wait a minute, of course I didn't. If I had, everyone there would have seen me. They'd have known what happened. But according to them, I just . . . vanished."

"You wandered out of the car you were in, and then off the train."

"I guess so. Nobody saw me go, and I don't remember it. Except that I *do* very clearly remember the train pulling into the Glenhaven Park station, and finding the empty platform, and everything that happened after that."

Karen hesitates.

Then she asks, "Have you ever heard of dissociative fugue?"

"No. What's that?"

"It's a psychological disorder—"

"Oh, God, here we go." Clara rakes a hand through her hair. *I'm losing it. I knew it.*

"Why do you say that?"

Ignoring the question, Clara asks impatiently, "What kind of disorder?"

"Do you want the textbook definition, or layman's terms?"

"Textbook." She's familiar with layman's terms: *crazy*.

"It's a disorder in which the patient experiences a spontaneous episode of sudden travel away from home, marked by amnesia about some or all of his or her past life. And she may, during this episode, experience the reemergence of some event or person representing an earlier trauma."

Clara is shaking her head before Karen is finished speaking.

"That's not what happened," she says resolutely. "I never for a moment forgot my past life. I knew exactly who I was the whole time."

"But you did experience what you say were memory blanks?"

"Only about what happened to me, physically, while I was dreaming or hallucinating or whatever I was doing. I don't remember getting on the train back to the city," she says impatiently, sick of going over this aloud after having dwelled on it ever since it happened. "I mean, not in the present day. I remember getting on the train in 1941, in the dream. But it was a different train."

"How?"

"You know . . . old-fashioned. Like a train would be in 1941."

Karen is silent, mulling that over.

"What are you thinking?" Clara asks at last.

"That I'm not entirely sure what's going on with you, but that it's acceptable to have escapist fantasies when you've just been diagnosed with a life-threatening illness."

"So that's what you think happened to me this morning?" Clara asks doubtfully. "Just a fantasy?"

"I don't know, Clara. We have a lot more work to do before I can make any kind of diagnosis . . ."

"But what are you thinking this might mean?" she presses, unable to let it go. "Why did this happen to me?"

"You mean this particular episode? I would say the fact that it involved traveling back to the past might indicate that the forties represent nostalgia for simpler times, and that this man—"

"Jed Landry?" Clara asks, her heart beating a little faster.

"Right, that he might represent your repressed longing for a man who knows nothing about your life or your illness, a man who has no preconceived notions about you. A hero to come along and save you from all this."

Clara rolls her eyes, ignoring the little voice that tells her there might be a hint of truth to it. "I don't want to be rescued," she says firmly. "You and I both know that I can take care of myself—and of my mother, for that matter."

"Have you told her yet?"

"No. And I'm not going to."

"Don't rule it out. You might need her. Or someone."

"I don't."

"Are you sure? A cancer diagnosis is traumatic under any circumstances, and you wouldn't be human if you weren't just a little bit insecure about your ability to face the challenges ahead."

A lump rises in her throat, making it impossible to speak.

"Then there's that bump." Karen leans forward and peers at Clara's forehead. "You need to have that looked at. You might have a concussion."

"Do you think it might have caused the whole . . . amnesia thing?"

"I'm concerned about it. Do you have a headache? Blurred vision? Are you nauseous? Sleepy?"

"Not really . . . not any more than I normally would be after getting up in the dark to go to work."

"Does your head hurt?"

"Just if I touch the bump itself, but it's just sore. I'm sure I'm okay."

"If I were you, I'd go to the doctor just to be sure."

"I will . . . tomorrow." Glancing at her watch, she sees that their forty-five minute session—which today was reduced to a half hour—is almost up.

"I don't want you to go home alone tonight. Is there anyone who can come by for awhile tonight, just in case your head starts bothering you? I'd do it myself, except I've got tickets to a concert."

"I'm fine, Karen. It's no big deal."

"But I don't like it that you live alone. You must have a neighbor you can count on . . . someone who would be willing to check in and make sure you're all right."

A neighbor you can count on.

Drew Becker pops into her head.

Why, she doesn't know, because he's a total stranger. Not someone she can count on.

She imagines herself knocking on his door and asking him to keep an eye on her in case she develops brain damage.

Sure. As if.

"I'll be fine," she assures Karen. "And I have an early location call tomorrow morning, so . . ."

"So I'm calling you on your cell first thing, to make sure you're all right."

Clara sighs. "Must you?"

"I must." Karen flashes a brief smile. "And listen, let's make another appointment, sooner than next weekend." She briskly takes out a desk calendar and flips the page. "How's Monday?"

"Monday? Karen, I'm way too busy to squeeze in—"

"I'd like to see you again on Monday," Karen says firmly, pencil poised over the page. "Six o'clock."

"I'm shooting that day. I can't possibly get here by then."

"So name the time. When can you make it?" When Clara doesn't reply immediately, Karen says decisively, "I'm putting you down for eight thirty Monday night. Okay?"

"Okay, I guess."

She thinks I'm going crazy, Clara decides, watching Karen write her name in the book. *And I'm not so sure she's wrong.*

A tube of lipstick in a deep red shade . . .

A powder compact . . .

A comb . . .

A lace-edged handkerchief . . .

That's it. That's all Jed finds in Clara's pocketbook. No wallet, no identification, no . . .

His probing fingers encounter one more object in the folds of the taffeta lining.

He draws it out.

What on earth?

Jed finds himself holding a peculiar flat, rectangular metallic . . . er, *device* of some sort.

It fits in the palm of his hand, about two inches wide by four long, and it weighs only a few ounces, if that. The back—or is it the front?—is smooth, and in the center is etched the outline of an apple with a bite taken from it. Beneath that are the letters I-P-O-D, followed by a series of apparently coded numbers and letters.

The other side has a rectangular indentation on one end, and a circle below it. At the top of the circle, where the twelve would be on a clock face, is the word MENU. There are sequences of triangles and slashes at three, six, and nine. A thin, pliable, coated white wire comes out of the narrow edge of the contraption; it splits into two cords with cushioned circular objects attached to the ends.

What on earth is this thing?

It almost looks like . . . some kind of transmitter.

A sick feeling twists Jed's gut.

Is Clara a modern-day Mata Hari?

That would explain why she was so skittish; why she didn't reveal her last name; why she wasn't carrying any identification—

Something suddenly creaks in the garage below.

Jed goes still, listening.

Not a sound, but he can feel somebody there. It must be Doris. Lately, she's been eavesdropping and sneaking around. She claims it's because she thinks the family is talking about her behind her back, but Jed is convinced she's just plain nosy.

He tosses the odd device back into the pocketbook, along with the cosmetics and other items, and quickly shoves the whole thing into the laundry basket with his stack of clean shirts and underwear.

"Doris," he calls, "I know you're there."

"How did you know?" a disappointed voice asks from the stairs outside his door.

"Because I know everything."

"You do not." His sister pokes her freckled face through the doorway. "What are you doing?"

"Nothing."

Nothing other than entertaining the chilling possibility that the woman he found so enchanting might actually be a spy.

"Why are you just sitting there?" Doris asks.

"I'm not."

"It looks like you are to me."

Gee whiz, sometimes Doris really gripes his middle kidney.

"Never mind what I'm doing. What do you want?"

"Mother says it's time to eat."

"Go tell her I'll be right there, will you?"

She stares at him for another long moment, then changes her mode. "After supper, can we string some lights outside? Please, Jed? We're the only house on the block without them."

He can't argue with that.

"Come on," his sister cajoles. "Pop wouldn't like it if we were the only house around without Christmas lights for three years in a row."

Jed can't argue with that, either.

"All right," he tells his sister absently, his thoughts on the mysterious woman who crossed his path today.

It's his patriotic duty to turn everything over to the government . . .

Isn't it?

Absolutely.

Just . . .

What if he's mistaken?

As a teenager, he saw the movie about Mata Hari's life, starring Greta Garbo. In the final scene, she was led away to be executed by a firing squad.

He cringes.

Loyal American citizen or no, he can't bear the thought of any harm falling to Clara . . . if that's even her real name.

"Jed, are you sure you're okay?" Doris asks, still watching him from the doorway.

"No," he snaps, "I'm not okay."

She flinches. "What's wrong?"

He hesitates.

He can't possibly confide in his kid sister. He doesn't dare confide in anyone. Not until he figures out what's going on.

"Never mind," Doris says softly. "I know what it is."

"You do?"

She nods. "It's December first. Nobody's having a good day. Mother cried all afternoon into the clean laundry, and . . . well, that's why I thought we should put up some Christmas lights. To cheer everybody up."

"I think that's a great idea, Doris." Jed smiles despite his own heartache, and decides his patriotic duty can wait until tomorrow.

This time, at least, I have an umbrella, Clara thinks as she climbs out of the subway at West Eighteenth Street and heads toward Sixth Avenue. An umbrella, and comfortable New Balance sneakers.

But her feet still ache from this morning's hike downtown, and she can't imagine how she's going to squeeze them into those uncomfortable shoes again tomorrow morning.

She reaches Sixth Avenue and the brightly lit brick and terra-cotta facade of what was once Siegel Cooper, the city's largest department store. Now, continuing with the last decade's suburbia-invades-Manhattan trend, it's a Bed Bath and Beyond.

She and Jason had an ongoing argument about whether to register here when they got engaged.

He wanted to stick with Fortunoff, even after she pointed out that some of her entertainment industry friends weren't as well-off as his Wall Street cronies and couldn't afford to spend more on a place setting than a typical month's rent.

When she called him stuffy and conventional, Jason at last grudgingly agreed to compromise: they would register at Fortunoff *and* Bed Bath and Beyond. For Clara, the victory was hollow. Jason grumbled the entire time they were browsing in Bed Bath and Beyond and refused to consider the fun green margarita glasses, the square striped throw pillows, the woven place mats, or the flannel duvet.

He wanted traditional.

Of course he did.

After they broke up, it only seemed fair that he take responsibility for returning the *traditional* engagement gifts that had come from his family and friends, and she the ones from hers. She hoped to find satisfaction when Jason had to haul all that fine china and crystal around town, while she dealt with the everyday linens, an electric coffee grinder, and a couple of muffin tins.

But there was no perverse satisfaction. Just . . . sadness. Sadness that he couldn't be who she needed him to be. Nor could she, for him.

There was relief, too, when the last relics of their engagement had been safely returned to the stores.

She never wanted the muffin tins or grinder in the first place, but Jason insisted. "Wouldn't it be great to wake up to freshly ground coffee and hot blueberry muffins on a cold winter morning?"

It didn't occur to her until later that his role in that oh-so-traditional male fantasy was relegated to waking up; she was supposed to brave the cold winter morning for fresh blueberries and the imported Colombian coffee beans he loved, then do the baking and the grinding.

As if.

Clara turns south toward her apartment and waits for the light to change, glad to put Bed Bath and Beyond—and the accompanying memories of her former fiancé—behind her.

The sidewalks of Greenwich Village are teeming with activity despite the cool, misty weather. It's a Friday night; the bars and restaurants and stores are jammed with people.

Normally, Clara would be energized by the neighborhood scene. She might even stop into her favorite cafe for an espresso and eclair. But tonight, nothing could energize her, not even caffeine and chocolate. She's emotionally and physically drained.

Seeing Karen was more cathartic, even, than she anticipated. At least she was able to spill her strange tale to a professional . . .

Yeah, one who thinks I'm certifiably nuts, she thinks wryly.

Dissociative fugue?

She knows Karen told her what that meant, but it's a blur now. She'll have to look it up online later, when she'll be able to retain information.

For now, it's just good to know that there might be a reasonable explanation for what happened this morning.

Reasonable. But frightening, nonetheless. The prospect of having suffered some kind of psychiatric . . . *episode* . . . is about as comforting as having breast cancer.

Rounding the corner onto West Eleventh Street, Clara quickens her pace despite her sore feet, glad this grueling day is about to come to an end at last.

All she wants to do is fall into bed and sleep.

Maybe I'll dream about Jed again.

That would be good.

It would prove that she was also dreaming this morning—not having some kind of frightening fugue.

It would give her a chance to see Jed Landry again, too. Dream Jed.

Just as closure, of course. Because she didn't really get to say goodbye, and she feels like she should have.

Even if it was just a dream.

"Ms. McCallum?"

About to climb the steps of her townhouse, she turns to see who called to her. Her eyes search the sidewalk, but there's no pedestrian in the vicinity.

Puzzled, she turns back to her building, pulling her spare set of keys from her pocket.

"Ms. McCallum!"

Swiveling her head again, she realizes that the female voice came from a large black car parked at the curb. The driver's side window is rolled down, and a white head is poking out into the rain.

"Would you mind . . . can I please talk to you for a moment?"

It's the woman who was here earlier, Clara realizes. *The one Mr. Kobayashi told me about. It has to be.*

"How can I help you?" she asks, keeping a safe distance.

Instinctively, she arranges her keys in her hand like a weapon, the way she was taught in an urban self-defense course she once took. The key ring is clenched in her palm; a jagged-edged key protrudes from the space between each of her fingers. If need be, she can rake her fist like a claw across the face of an assailant.

"I just need to talk to you, dear," the would-be assailant warbles. "If you'll just come over here, please . . . I can't get out . . . it takes me so long to move around and it's so raw out there I don't want to catch my death."

Clara contemplates the situation.

The woman might just be a harmless elderly *One Life To Live* fan seeking a brush with celebrity and an autograph.

Yes, or she might be a lunatic stalker with a gun.

Like Mr. Kobayashi said earlier, you can't be too careful these days in New York.

"Please, Ms. McCallum. I've been waiting such a long time . . . and I've been trying all day to catch you."

Catch me?

All right, Clara definitely doesn't like the sound of that.

She turns away abruptly and mounts the stairs two at a time.

Moments later, she's safely inside her building, feeling partly foolish for her frantic escape from a little old lady, and partly as though she's had a close call.

But after all she's been through today, she's not about to dwell on this. Every actress has her share of odd fans.

Clara climbs the second long flight of stairs to her apartment, yawning. As she covers the last few steps to her door, she spots something propped on the knob.

It's . . . a CD?

A Christmas CD.

Bing Crosby smiles up at her, wearing a Santa hat.

There's a note, too, written in red Sharpie on a plain white sheet of paper: *I thought this might cheer you up! Love, Santa*

She smiles.

Mr. Kobayashi. Trying to help her get over her terrible day. He did say he would check on her later.

How sweet of him. She'll be sure to thank him tomorrow.

Tomorrow.

Yes, and she'll return to the set and put all of this behind her.

Tomorrow will be a better day, definitely.

Yawning again, she dials into her voice mail.

You have three . . . new . . . messages, an automated voice informs her.

"Hi, Clara, just wanted to let you know I'm thinking about you . . . " It's Jason. And he sounds uncharacteristically nervous. "I wanted to talk to you about something and it's pretty important, so I was thinking it would be nice to get together for coffee or dinner. Oh, and I saw an article about the movie in *Entertainment Weekly* and I've been wondering how it's going. So give me a call and we'll hook up, okay? I really need to talk to you," he repeated in conclusion before hanging up with a quick "Bye."

Entertainment Weekly? Jason has never read that magazine. *Forbes* and *Business Week,* yes. But until this moment, she'd have doubted he'd pick up an issue of *EW* even if she was smiling out from the cover.

I wish, she thinks, and presses DELETE.

She'll decide later what to do about Jason. She hasn't the energy to even think about him tonight, let alone make plans to see him.

Next message . . .

"Clara! It's me, Rachel!" her cousin announces in her thick Lawn Guyland accent. "Rebecca and I were wondering if you have Bubbe's brisket recipe somewhere. She wrote it out for us the other day but it has grape jelly in it. I think she's losing her marbles. Give me a call even if you don't have it. Maybe we can do lunch. If not we'll see you at Hanukkah in two weeks, right? I can't wait to hear all about the movie. I told everyone at work that you get to kiss Michael Marshall. Okay, bye."

Clara smiles and shakes her head, realizing she really misses her cousins—lovable self-proclaimed Jewish-American Princesses. She'll have to call Rachel back and tell her that she clearly remembers Bubbe preparing her famous brisket . . . and spreading a mixture of grape jelly and ketchup over the meat. She can just imagine Rachel's reaction . . .

But once she gets over the grape jelly, she'll want to do lunch. And she'll want to know how Clara has been . . .

And I can't tell her, Clara thinks, her hand drifting up to gingerly touch her sweater above the biopsy site. *So I'd better not call her back. Not yet, anyway. Not until I know I can talk to her without breaking down and telling her what's going on.*

Nor does she dare, yet, to speak to her mother—and of course, the next message is from her.

"Clara, it's me, Mom." She always starts out that way. As if Clara doesn't know her voice by now. "I'm just calling to talk to you about Christmas, honey. I know your shooting schedule—is that what you call it?—is crazy, but Stan and I were thinking maybe you could just fly down for Christmas Day. You know—catch a flight in the morning and be back by that night. They can't be filming on that day, can they? We would pay for your ticket as part of your present, and . . . well, I just want to see you. I miss you. Give me a call back, okay? I know you're busy but . . . just call me. I love you. Bye."

Clara sits holding the phone, guilt trickling in. She can't just avoid her mother forever. *Maybe I should tell her,* she thinks. *Maybe it would be good to share this burden with somebody . . .*

Somebody who loves her, that is.

She can't help but long to be nurtured. To cry in somebody's arms. To be held and comforted and promised everything is going to be all right . . .

But Mom isn't that person, she reminds herself. She can just imagine the look on her mother's face. It wouldn't be filled with hope.

And right now, what I need is hope.

Hope, and strength, and courage.

She just wishes she knew exactly how to find—and cling to—those precious commodities.

Chapter 8

Today is going to be a better day all around.

Clara has been telling herself that ever since her feet hit the floor after the alarm went off in the wee hours this Saturday morning.

Determined to keep grim thoughts about the breast cancer and the looming surgery at bay today, she intends to prove that she's the most responsible actress since the venerable Meryl Streep.

She's off to a good start, on the set before sunup, a full fifteen minutes before her call time.

As usual, she has begun the day in worn jeans, a warm parka, and sneakers that are a blessing on her wounded, blistered feet. She also wears a ski cap pulled low over her forehead to obscure the lovely purplish black bruise that lingers above her brow; she's counting on Jesus to work his cosmetic magic to conceal it.

In the shopping bag she's toting are the suit and shoes she wore yesterday. Everything could stand a good cleaning; the stockings, of course, are in the garbage can back home.

Lisa isn't going to be happy with her. Oh, well.

You can't please all of the people all of the time, Clara thinks philosophically.

Ironic, then, that it is distinctly possible to please

none of the people none of the time . . . and yesterday, she managed to do just that.

But this is a fresh start, she thinks as she dutifully heads over to check in with K.T., the second assistant director.

Tall and broad-shouldered, with sun-streaked shaggy brown hair and a perpetual tan—a real one— he looks like he should be in front of the camera, rather than behind it.

He smiles when he sees her, which is a good sign.

With any luck, Michael was exaggerating the on-set reaction to her disappearance yesterday. He does have a tendency to be quite the drama queen.

"How are you feeling today?" K.T. asks, looking her over as he signs her in. "Everything okay?"

"Everything's great."

"You sure?"

Maybe Michael wasn't exaggerating.

Clara can't help but discern that K.T. seems a tad . . . overconcerned.

"I'm positive," she assures him, hoping he can't hear the waver of doubt in her voice.

She gives him her breakfast order: coffee, tomato juice, fruit, and oatmeal. Healthy, healthy, healthy.

"No Diet Coke today?"

"No Diet Coke today," she replies, surprised K.T. would even have taken note of her usual morning quirk—or its absence.

"Okay, well, here are your sides." He hands her the thin sheaf of script pages that cover the material they'll be shooting today. "Take care."

Leaving him to radio the first assistant director that she's on the set, she heads to her trailer, wondering what he meant by *Take care.* Does he think she's in some kind of trouble? What did he hear about her?

You need to relax, she scolds herself. *You're just paranoid. Everything is fine. Everyone has probably forgotten all about your taking off yesterday.*

Denton's assistant, Andre, is waiting outside her trailer, wearing his trademark impractical shiny black shoes and, beneath his wool coat, a bright pink shirt—Denton's trademark wardrobe color.

My father always said it takes a real man to wear pink, he likes to say.

Maybe Denton can get away with it based on star stature alone, but Andre certainly isn't a real man, Clara can't help but think.

His weasly little body is wrapped in a black cashmere scarf that's longer than he is, and he's smoking a clove cigarette with gloved fingers. An arrogant, terminally pretentious recent film school grad who's here by virtue of being related to someone who knows someone who slept with someone, Andre is by far one of Clara's least favorite people on the crew.

"Denton wants to see you right away," he says importantly.

Uh-oh. "Do you know what about?"

"No. He's in his trailer."

As Clara makes her way through the early morning chill, she wonders if Denton is going to fire her. She wouldn't be surprised. Her upcoming treatment is going to mean reshuffling the January shooting schedule to accommodate her.

She climbs the three metal steps and knocks tentatively, mentally rehearsing what she's going to say.

No time for that: the door is thrown open almost instantly by Jack, the director of photography. He nods a greeting and gives her a long, curious once-over before telling Denton he'll see him in a little bit.

The crew is definitely gossiping about me, Clara realizes, slipping past him into the trailer. She wonders if they know about her breast cancer diagnosis, or if other rumors are spreading.

"Come on in." Clad in jeans and a rose-colored designer sweater that looks luxuriously soft—and ridiculously expensive—Denton is seated at the table.

He's a small man, wiry, and usually wears a pair of thick wire-rimmed glasses. He doesn't have them on now, which makes his face look oddly naked. He blinks several times as he looks up from the lined script spread before him, each page marked with different colored ink that indicates which material has been shot.

"You're looking well this morning, Clara," he greets her. "At least, from here . . . without my glasses. Meaning I probably can't see much beyond a foot from my head, so you might very well look like hell," he adds with classic Denton quirkiness.

"I probably do," she informs him, knowing there are dark circles under her eyes, thanks to a restless—and dreamless—sleep. At least she's still wearing the hat, meaning he has no hope of spotting the bruise on her forehead.

"I'm sure I'll look better after makeup," she tells him.

"Right, and I'm sure Jesus is anxious to get started on you. Just have a seat for a few seconds, will you?" He pulls out a chair adjacent to his, blinks, and takes a sip from a white porcelain mug.

"Vanilla soy latte." He raises the mug in her direction. She nods, knowing Denton's quirks well enough to realize that he's merely informing, not offering.

Stifling a yawn, she tells herself she'll swing by the

catering tent and grab a cup of real coffee on her way back to her trailer, lest she fall asleep in the makeup chair. Breakfast won't come until later.

Denton sets his mug down and steeples his fingers beneath his chin. "So Bobby told me what's going on."

She nods, uncertain what to say to that.

When Denton doesn't make it easier for her by continuing, she says, "I'm going to be fine, it's just . . . the next few months will be a challenge. Personally, I mean . . . not professionally. I'm a hundred percent on board here, Denton. Just so you know that."

"Good. And we're a hundred percent behind you, just so you know that. Look, what happened yesterday is . . ."

She holds her breath, wondering what he's going to say. *Unconscionable? Deplorable? Grounds for dismissal?*

"Forgiven," he concludes, and she exhales in relief.

"Thank you. It won't happen a—"

"I know you're under a lot of pressure, and I understand that you may have needed to get away," he continues, talking over her. "I just wish you had asked for a break, instead of just taking off in the middle of blocking. That cost this production—"

"I know, I'm so sorry. It won't happen again." *Whatever it even was,* she thinks uneasily. "I promise I've got my act together, and I'm ready to get back to work."

Denton sips his vanilla soy latte thoughtfully. "What about your treatment? What's going on with that?"

"I'll know more next week, after I've consulted with the doctors again." She doesn't want to tell him too much. Not yet.

"Surgery? Radiation? Chemotherapy?"

All of the above, she thinks grimly. Aloud, she says only, "I'll let you know as soon as I know."

"Do that." He raises two fingers to his temple, then thrusts them away in a mock salute, clearly dismissing her as he turns back to the script.

She pushes back her chair.

"Thanks for coming by, Clara."

"Thanks for understanding."

He nods, not looking up from his notes. "Good luck."

She exits the trailer, wishing she had a pair of dark sunglasses to hide the tears welling in her eyes.

This is so damned hard. All of it.

A cancer diagnosis is traumatic under any circumstances . . . you wouldn't be human if you weren't just a little bit insecure about your ability to face the challenges ahead.

Okay, so maybe Karen was right. Maybe she's feeling more insecure, deep down, than she realized.

And maybe she does have a subconscious longing to be rescued from the nightmare her waking hours have become.

Not, of course, by her mother.

But it's going to take more than an imaginary hero to do the job, she tells herself. *Jed Landry isn't going to pop up and rescue you no matter how nice that would be.*

She might as well stop feeling sorry for herself and get it together. She's got a job to do, and she's going to prove to Denton Wilkens that when it comes to her work, she's a pro, just like she said.

Sniffling, Clara bows her head against the brisk air and the curious stares of the crew as she hurries off to makeup and wardrobe.

*   *   *

Jed runs his fingers over the lacy slip, reminding himself that he has every right to be going through the contents of the suitcase for the third time since he first opened it late last night.

Yes, but his patriotic duty shouldn't involve imagining what Clara might look like in this lingerie—or any of the other items he's stacked neatly on his newly made bed. On the nearby table lie the contents of her pocketbook, including the strange device he found.

But other than that, to his relief, he's uncovered no further evidence that she's a spy.

Nor, to his dismay, has he found any evidence of her last name or address.

That's not all that's eating him.

There's something strange about the collection of clothing in the suitcase. The garments are all in different sizes, which doesn't make sense if they belong to one woman. Which, ostensibly, they do.

But why would one woman have a dress in size ten, another in size fourteen, and another in a twenty?

Having three sisters as well as running a store, Jed is perhaps more familiar with ladies' clothing than your average fella, and he'd swear that slender Clara is no bigger than a size twelve . . . if that.

Even more intriguing—or perhaps, incriminating— the clothes she packed aren't all suitable for the same season. Several blouses and playsuits are unmistakably meant for warm weather, and there's even a bathing suit.

A bathing suit?

In Glenhaven Park, in *December*?

It's almost as if . . .

Well, if he had to come up with a plausible explanation for the eclectic assortment of clothing, Jed would guess that she might have packed in a hurry, throwing everything in—inadvertently including her much larger roommates' or sisters' clothing—and paying no heed to the weather where she was going.

Or . . .

The luggage could be a dupe, its contents mere filler, and its carrier masquerading as an guileless young woman on an innocuous journey.

Jed greatly prefers the prior scenario . . . though why she might be forced to pack in a haphazard rush is beyond him.

Was she running away from something?

Someone?

Again, he remembers the bruise over her eye.

She said nobody hit her; she claimed to have bumped her head. Was she lying?

Is she the victim of some vicious aggressor? An abusive husband?

Or is she some kind of undercover informant committing an act of treason?

Slowly, he repacks her suitcase, trying to come up with sound arguments for Clara's innocence. It would be a heck of a lot easier if her bags had yielded more answers than they did questions.

So. He can either go right to the police . . .

Or he can keep her things here for her for another twenty-four hours, in case she comes back.

You're a fool, do you know that? Here you are, mooning over a woman who's most likely up to no good. A woman who might even be an international spy.

Yes, but the idea seems preposterous, despite the so-called evidence before him.

Clara seemed as American as he is—though there was something unusual about the way she spoke that set her apart from anyone he's ever known.

It wasn't an accent—rather, the slightest hint of an unfamiliar dialect. She sure didn't sound like any of the city girls he's ever met, and she claimed to have been born and raised there. He wants to believe her.

Why? Why do you care? She's a complete stranger, for crying out loud.

But he can't help himself. He needs to give her the benefit of the doubt. When—*if*—she does return in the next twenty-four hours, he'll demand an explanation. If it's satisfactory . . .

What will you do?

Ask her to go dancing?

Maybe, he thinks stubbornly, and all but quivers at the mere thought of whirling around a swanky nightclub with Clara in his arms.

And if her explanation isn't satisfactory . . . ?

Then I'll have to report her.

What matters, above all, is that this time, he won't let her slip away.

But she has to come back to him, first. Back to Glenhaven Park.

He returns to the table, picks up the pocketbook and opens it, about to replace its contents.

In the depths of the lining, something catches his eye. Something that blends right into the satiny gray taffeta.

He reaches in. His fingers encounter a rectangular piece of cardboard, one edge wedged into a frayed seam. He has to tug on it a bit before it comes free. No wonder it didn't fall out when he dumped the bag upside down.

What is it?

"Jeepers creepers," he breathes, realizing he's holding a small black-and-white photograph. A woman gazes up at him: a woman with long, loose wavy hair, very little makeup, and a natural-looking smile.

It takes him a moment to realize that it's Clara, looking drastically different than she does in person. Her hair . . . her face . . . her expression . . .

She's so casual. Utterly relaxed. Not a trace of tension or fear in her clear, wide-set eyes.

Scribbled across the photo is the name *Jezibel*, followed by a series of numbers separated by hyphens.

Jezibel? Is that her name?

Jezibel.

It doesn't seem to fit. But . . .

Turning the card over with a trembling hand, Jed sees that something is printed on the back.

Clara McCallum.

That must be her name—her full name.

Beneath it is an address on West Eleventh Street in New York, followed by a series of number clusters separated by dashes.

Jed stares at the card, turning it over and over, realizing what this means.

New York—and Clara McCallum—here I come.

"Leavin' . . . *on that midnight train to Georgia,"* Gladys Knight sings in the background, accompanied by the Pips and Jesus deJesus.

"Uh-oh, are you still on your seventies' music kick?" Clara asks with a groan as she settles into the makeup chair.

His only response is a falsetto train-whistlelike *"Whoo-hoo"* in unison with the song lyrics.

"God, I miss my iPod," she mutters.

"What happened to your iPod?" Jesus interrupts his singing to ask.

"Oh, I, uh . . . lost it."

"That's a shame." He tosses a tube of foundation in the air, catches it, and sings into it, *"Goin' back to find . . . a simpler place and time . . ."*

Unexpectedly struck by that line, Clara closes her eyes to shut out a vision of Jed Landry's face.

It's still there.

"I'd rather live in his world . . . than live without him . . . in mine."

"God, do you really have to sing that song?" she snaps at Jesus, opening her eyes to glare at him.

Taken aback by her outburst, he reaches over and turns off the CD player. "What's wrong with you?"

"Nothing. I just don't like that song."

"Well, I don't like 'It's the Most Wonderful Time of the Year,' but I didn't complain when you insisted on playing it over and over the other day."

"Yes, you did. Repeatedly. And you threatened me with that ugly orange-apricot lipstick until I promised never to play it again with you in earshot."

"Oh. Right. Whatever." Jesus shrugs. "Listen, you should probably know that the entire world is talking about you."

"So I've heard." Clara reaches for her coffee, placed in arm's reach. She takes a sip, then says, "So tell me what the entire *world* is saying."

"Let's see . . . that you're on crack—"

"Crack?"

"Or heroin. I've heard both versions." Jesus drapes her in a black vinyl cape.

"Good Lord. What else have you heard?"

"That you're having an affair with K.T., that you're bulimic, that you're pregnant . . ."

"With K.T.'s baby?" she asks, amusement mingling with dismay.

"You tell me, honey." Jesus—and just about everyone else on the set, gay and straight alike—has a crush on the good-looking second assistant director.

"It's not true. Not one bit of it. Did you tell them?"

"I told them it wasn't true. But"—Jesus dabs thick foundation along the trenches beneath her eyes—"I wasn't about to tell anyone what's really going on. That's your business. And you're obviously losing sleep over it, Raccoon Girl."

"I know. It's been brutal."

"You're going to be just fine after all this, you'll see."

"And if I'm not, I can be reborn as somebody fabulous, like Coco Chanel."

"Don't even joke about that!"

"I know, I know . . . you take your past lives very seriously."

"That's not what I meant and you know it. You're going to survive. You'll get it all behind you, the tests, the surgery, the treatment . . . it seems like it's going to last forever, but it isn't. You'll have a normal life again."

"I know I will . . . but . . ." *It isn't just the cancer.*

She wants more than anything to confide in him about what happened to her yesterday. The problem is, she doesn't know what happened to her yesterday.

Better to shrug it off and vaguely attribute her absence from the set to her illness.

But what if it happens again?

What if, when she boards the train again this morning to shoot her scene, she finds herself in a repeat performance: blanking out and imagining that she's back in the past?

She simply can't let that happen.

No way.

But if she had any idea how it happened in the first place, she'd have a better chance of preventing it from happening again.

There's a knock on the trailer door.

"Who is it?" she calls.

"Albany." Her friend appears in the doorway behind her, reflected in the mirror before the makeup chair. She's costumed as Violet's friend Sue, in full makeup with her golden hair swept up in a wavy pompadour. "I heard what happened to you."

"That I'm an addict?"

Albany's pencil-darkened brows shoot toward the swoop of hair above her forehead.

"Pregnant with a crack baby?"

Albany shakes her head, laughing. "No."

"Then what did you hear?"

"That you freaked out and ran away in the middle of a scene because K.T. was flirting with Lisa."

"Good Lord. I swear that's total bull, Albany."

She grins. "I thought so. But I was worried about you anyway."

"Have you got a minute? Or ten? I'll tell you what's really going on—"

"Not now. I've got to go back to wardrobe and change into my dress for the wedding scene, and you're supposed to meet me over there."

"Wedding scene? I thought we were doing the depot scene."

"We were . . . until the sky opened up and it started pouring. It wasn't supposed to rain until this afternoon. Denton's putting the scene on hold."

"Until when?"

"Who knows? It's probably going to rain all day."

Thank God, Clara thinks, turning her head to look at the ominous sky beyond the rain-spattered windowpane. At least she won't have to worry about a repeat performance of her notorious vanishing act.

Not today, anyway.

Maybe, by the time Denton's ready to get back to that scene, she'll know what happened to her yesterday—and how to keep it from happening again.

Every time the door jangles to signal a new arrival in the five-and-dime, Jed hopefully jerks his head in that direction.

But it's never Clara.

Nor is it Alice, who has once again failed to show up for work.

No, just a constant parade of local shoppers, too many of them with impossible requests . . . and he's just about got whiplash from all this wishful head swiveling.

All he wants is to get down to Manhattan to find Clara.

Instead here he is, swearing to Mrs. Robertson, yet again, that he really *doesn't* have silk stockings in stock.

"I don't think you're being honest with me, Jed. I heard that you had a stash."

"Where did you hear that?"

"I don't remember. But I'm sure somebody mentioned it."

"Mrs. Robertson, if I had silk stockings in the store, I'd be happy to sell them to you, believe me."

Anything to get you off my back, you old biddy.

"I just don't understand why you can't get them."

Gritting his teeth, he reminds her—again—that most silk is imported from Japan, and the government cut off trade with Japan several months ago. He offers her an alternative but Mrs. Robertson, who perceives the war as a major personal inconvenience, refuses to consider the "newfangled" nylon stockings.

"You're charging too much for them," she accuses. "No one in her right mind would pay that for a pair of stockings."

He watches her browse for a good fifteen minutes, asking countless questions about the merchandise. As he answers them, his thoughts are on Manhattan, and Clara. He still hasn't fixed the DeSoto's flat, but he's pretty sure he'll be able to borrow a car from one of his buddies. That's the best thing about living in a small town—somebody is always there when you need a favor.

"Oh, look, there's the dear little musical snow globe you tried to sell me," Mrs. Robertson comments, spotting the damaged music box on the sale table. "I can't imagine who would want an angel with a broken wing, even at half price."

Jed merely shrugs.

"I'll give you ten cents for it," Mrs. Robertson announces, pulling out her change purse as though it's a done deal.

Jed shakes his head. "I'm afraid I have to stick with the marked price."

"You aren't willing to bargain?"

"I'm sorry," he says, as if he really is. Meanwhile, he promises himself that at this point, he wouldn't sell her the sweet, wounded little angel if she offered him twice the original cost.

No sooner does Mrs. Robertson grumble her way out the door with just the morning paper than Betty Godfrey sashays in.

She's wearing fashionably thick-soled shoes and a sweeping fur coat. Beneath a tall, tilted hat, her strawberry blond hair is carefully parted on the side and draped over one eye in an exaggerated imitation of Veronica Lake's peekaboo style.

"Jed Landry! Where have you been?"

"I've been right here," he says mildly as she marches right up to the counter, enveloping him in a cloud of Evening in Paris perfume. "Where else would I be?"

"You said you would call on me over the weekend, you naughty thing, and you never showed up."

"I did?" He frowns, trying to remember when he might have made such an unlikely commitment.

"Yes, don't you remember?"

"Refresh my memory, why don't you."

"I stopped in here on Friday afternoon to buy some navy thread for the divine dress I'm making, and I told you I had to hurry home because I had an apple pie in the oven, and you said that you like apple pie, and I said, why, then, come on by and have a piece."

Hmm. Jed *does* like apple pie.

But the rest of it . . . well, he's fairly certain he would not have made any brash promises to the likes of Betty Godfrey. Knowing her—and he does, all too well—she'd expect a ring and a vow in return for the pie.

"But you never showed up, Jed," Betty concludes unnecessarily, obviously waiting for an explanation.

"Sorry you were disappointed, Betty. I guess it must have slipped my mind. What can I help you with today? More thread? Different color?"

"Oh, I think I'll just browse." She makes no move to do so.

He nods, and begins to unpack a carton of music boxes that arrived this morning.

"You know, Jed . . ." Betty leans toward him, elbows propped on the counter, her pretty face cupped in both hands, her one visible eye gleaming with what appears to be accusation. "I heard a rumor about you."

"About me?" *Oh, for crying out loud.* "What's that, Betty? I suppose you heard that I've got a stash of silk stockings. Well, let me tell you, it isn't—"

"No, I heard that you were chasing a dame through the streets yesterday morning, hollering at her."

"Well, you don't say." He shrugs, thinking that this is the worst thing about small towns. A fella can't get away with anything.

Betty just nods.

Jed can't help but notice that she seems to spend an awful lot of time waiting for him to say something. And that he seems to spend an awful lot of time trying to think of something to say.

This, then, is clearly not a relationship made in heaven—not that it's news to him.

"Well, where'd you hear about this rumor?" Jed mildly asks Betty at last, shifting his weight, filled with renewed longing to flee Glenhaven Park.

"First from Gladys Van Tassel, and she heard it from Floyd Mead. I don't know where he heard it."

I do, Jed thinks, remembering that Floyd's twin brother George was one of the eager fellas who helped Clara up when she tripped and fell.

"I told Gladys, 'Jed would never make such a public scene.' But now that I've heard it from a couple of people, well . . . I told them all that I was sure she was a customer."

"She was."

"And I said that she must have shoplifted something from you, and that's why you were chasing her. Was it?"

"No." He looks around the empty store, wishing for

a distraction—like Mrs. Robertson coming back to go at it another round about the silk stockings, or break more fragile merchandise.

"Then why?"

"She left something behind. I just wanted to give it to her."

"What was it?"

"A couple of bags, Betty, that's all." He wishes he didn't feel so gosh-darned defensive about it.

"Did you catch her?"

"No, I didn't." *But I will.*

"Well, some people are saying you were chasing her like a love-crazed fool."

"Oh, they are, are they?" he mutters.

"Are you in love with her, Jed?"

"I don't even know her, Betty."

She smiles coyly and winks at him. Or maybe it's just a blink. He can't tell, what with that hairdo of hers.

Veronica Lake might look sexy with one eye, but Jed swiftly concludes that on everybody else—including Betty—the style is somewhat ridiculous.

You don't see Clara going around half-blind.

No sir, when she was here, both of her big green eyes were clearly visible—and frightened.

If she were a spy, Jed muses, you wouldn't expect her to be frightened. As the legend goes, Mata Hari was calm and collected right until her last moment, blowing kisses to the firing squad before they executed her.

There was nothing calm about Clara.

Again, Jed longs to drop everything and rush to the city to find her—not just to put his curiosity to rest or do his patriotic duty.

She needs me, he finds himself thinking irrationally.

"Say, there's still half a pie left over at my house, Jed," Betty is cooing. "Why don't you come by after you close the store later? My mother is out at her bridge game and she won't be home until late."

"I can't. I have to be . . . someplace else."

"Tomorrow, then?"

"I'm afraid that's no good, either."

"Then Thursday?"

"I would think that pie of yours might be moldy by then, Betty," he can't help saying.

She shoots him a one-eyed scowl and straightens up, adjusting her hat. "What a thing to say!"

"I'm sorry. It's swell of you to invite me, but I'm afraid I'm just too shorthanded and busy here at the store to squeeze in much of anything else at this time of year."

"That's just your loss, then, Jed Landry." Betty flounces out of the store without a backward glance.

He watches her go, thinking his life would be much simpler if he could will himself to fall in love with Betty.

But he can't do that any more than he can stop obsessing over the troubled mystery woman.

He looks impatiently at his watch.

At least six hours to go before he can depart on his mission to find Clara.

Find her . . . and then what?

Chapter 9

A steady rain is falling as the black town car eases down Fifth Avenue.

The driver has the radio tuned to AM, 1010 WINS, with its endless news, traffic, and weather.

And thanks to Jesus deJesus, Clara's head is tuned, as it has been since this morning, to an endless replay of "Midnight Train to Georgia."

Which wouldn't be so bad if it didn't remind her of Jed Landry.

But then, today, what hasn't?

Determined to keep those disturbing thoughts at bay, she sits huddled in the backseat, gazing out at the surprisingly heavy Saturday night traffic.

Or perhaps not so surprising. *After all,* Clara remembers, *it's December now. Manhattan is always extra crowded at this time of year.*

Mesmerized by the red brake lights reflected on the shiny pavement, she can't help but remember happier holiday seasons.

From the time she was a little girl, her grandfather always took her to see *The Nutcracker* on the first Saturday night in December, just as he always did her mother. In fact, Clara was named for the little girl in the ballet, who was given the unexpected Christmas gift of a nutcracker—then saw it come magically to life in her Christmas Eve dream.

Maybe she and I have more in common than just a name, Clara finds herself thinking—and immediately drags herself away from that topic.

She'd rather dwell on pleasant, uncomplicated thoughts tonight. Like her annual *Nutcracker* outing with Grandpa.

He always called it "a date with my best gal"—and she thought the words always sounded a little hollow. When she got older, Clara came to understand that his real "best gal" had been his beloved Irene. Grandpa liked to talk about how he didn't mind getting older, because it meant that he was getting closer to seeing his Irene again.

Though sometimes, when he looked at Clara, he would smile and say it was almost the same thing. *Almost.*

Clara-belle, you look more and more like your grandmother, he used to tell her.

He was the only one who ever called her Clara-belle.

God, I miss him, she thinks, turning her head against the seat back and blinking away unexpected tears.

So much for pleasant, uncomplicated thoughts.

It's been awhile since she cried over her grandfather, who lived to the ripe old age of eighty-three.

"In your sleep—that's the way to go," he liked to say, as the years piled on. "None of this wasting away slowly. One day you just don't wake up, and boom! It's over."

Which was exactly what happened a few years ago. He had a sudden heart attack in his sleep. *Boom! It was over.*

For Clara, the only comfort in the wake of his death

was that he did it his way—and that he was at last with his true best gal again.

She knows that; she can feel it . . . and sometimes, when she's alone, she can almost convince herself that she just glimpsed the two of them out of the corner of her eye.

Yes, and she once made the mistake of saying that to Jason.

"You believe in ghosts, Clara? Are you kidding me?"

"I believe that my grandparents are together somewhere. And that sometimes, they're with me."

"But . . . they're dead." As if she didn't know. "Where is it that you think they are? In heaven?"

"Maybe. Or maybe back here on earth."

"You mean reincarnated?"

"Maybe. Who knows? Maybe they were both reborn as babies right now, and they're going to grow up and find each other and fall in love all over again."

"Sometimes I really worry about you, Clara. Some things you get into your head are just . . . out there."

And everything in *his* head was just . . . completely pragmatic. He's never believed in anything. An afterlife, or reincarnation, or miracles, or Santa Claus, or God, or creative thinking, or . . .

Or Clara herself.

Not even when her yearly income surpassed his.

"Mine is a salary," he would say. "It's not going to go away tomorrow."

Implying that her income—and her career—could evaporate in a puff of smoke any minute.

And, okay, it very well could.

But Clara is accustomed to the unpredictability of her life. She thrives on the whimsical nature of her business, on being paid for creativity.

Jason, who possesses not an ounce of whimsy, just didn't get it.

She can just imagine what he would say if she tried to explain what happened to her yesterday.

Covering a tremendous yawn, she's grateful that she isn't due back on the set until Monday morning, when they'll shoot the train scene.

What a relief it will be tomorrow to catch up on her sleep, maybe go to the gym, or catch a movie.

Or she could—

No. Absolutely not. That's a bad idea.

One she's been toying with all day, but a bad idea nonetheless.

Spotting the familiar green awning of the landmark prewar apartment building on the corner of Fifth and West Eleventh—Mr. Kobayashi said Marlon Brando lived there back in the forties—she straightens in her seat.

Almost home. She zips her parka to her chin as the town car turns onto West Eleventh Street, past the looming Gothic facade of the First Presbyterian Church on the corner.

Gazing down the block, she can see Christmas lights twinkling from several buildings, isolated to the windows of apartments occupied by particularly festive tenants. Swept by a wave of nostalgia, she wonders what it was like when all of these nineteenth century townhouses were single-family homes.

The car glides across Sixth Avenue, where the elevated trains once ran. Mr. Kobayashi once said that one of his earliest childhood memories was watching the overhead trestles being demolished when the avenue was widened. He also wistfully told her about the beautiful architectural complex that used to stand on the corner. Rhinelander Gardens, it was called, and it looked like something out of New Orleans' French Quarter. Mr. Kobayashi said the structures were razed back in the fifties to make way for P.S. 41.

Trying to block out the school, along with Ray's Pizza on the opposite corner, Clara pictures the neighborhood back in Jed Landry's time—then finds herself feeling both wistful and vaguely uneasy.

"Here we are, Ms. McCallum." Don, the driver, double-parks in front of her building and gets out to open her door. "Careful not to get wet. You don't want to get sick."

If you only knew, she thinks grimly.

Holding an umbrella above her head, Don escorts her up the steps to her door. He tips his cap and is gone.

I should thank Mr. Kobayashi for the sweet note and Bing Crosby CD, Clara reminds herself as she steps into the warm, dry, well-lit vestibule.

She descends to his apartment on the basement level and knocks.

No reply other than the squealing tires and wailing sirens of a police car chase, clearly audible from the television inside.

She knocks again, harder.

This time, the volume is promptly lowered and she hears footsteps, chains rattling, bolts sliding.

"Ms. McCallum!" The super peers out at her in surprise. "What happened? Did you get mugged again?"

"No, I'm all set tonight, see?" She holds up her purse and her keys.

"You got your stuff back!"

"Er—yes."

"Where did the perp leave it? Dumpster? Trash can? Mailbox? I saw that one once, on *Columbo*."

Ignoring the query, she quickly changes the subject. "I just wanted to thank you again for letting me into the building yesterday, and for that sweet little gift you left at my door. That really cheered me up."

"Sweet gift?" Mr. Kobayashi frowns. "What sweet gift?"

"You know . . . " Clara smiles. "The CD."

He just looks at her blankly.

So he's going to play dumb.

"Thank you so much, Mr. Kobayashi."

"I don't know what you mean."

All right, maybe she should just let him be a secret Santa if that's how he wants it. And that definitely seems to be how he wants it.

"I didn't leave you a sweet CD gift," Mr. Kobayashi says nervously, with a glance over his shoulder.

"You didn't?" she asks, playing along.

"No! I'm a married man!"

Hearing a pot lid rattle in the kitchen, Clara realizes that the semireclusive Mrs. Kobayashi must be eavesdropping. *Oops.*

"I'm sorry, I guess it was somebody else," she says hastily.

"I guess so. It wasn't me."

Hmm. His tone is so forceful and his expression so stern that she's almost inclined to believe him.

But if he didn't leave the CD at her door, then who did? It's not as though somebody could just walk into the building off the street and up the stairs to her door. Nobody roams the halls unless they live here.

Although . . .

She has a sudden, disconcerting memory of the mystery lady lurking in the shadows of her building last night, wanting to talk to her.

Well, no worries about being stalked by a fiend if it came from her. There's nothing sinister about a Bing Crosby CD, that's for sure.

When she reaches the second floor, Clara finds herself thoughtfully glancing at Drew Becker's closed door. She can hear music playing on the other side.

Christmas music, she realizes with a smile, recognizing Perry Como's croon . . . and going absolutely still.

Drew Becker?

Maybe.

Well, who else could it have been?

Jason?

He did pop up on her voice mail, saying he had to talk to her about something important.

He still has the keys. He could theoretically have done it . . .

But he wouldn't. It would be too sweet a gesture, too . . . whimsical. As she was just reminding herself earlier, Jason doesn't have a whimsical bone in his body.

So . . . what, you think Drew Becker does?

Chewing her lower lip, she ponders the likelihood that her new neighbor left the CD and the note. After all, they were just talking about Christmas, and how she would be spending the holiday alone this year . . .

And she did seem to have some kind of split-second connection with him when they first met in November, and again on the stoop the other day.

Split-second being the key. And it wouldn't be the first time she's experienced a passing attraction to someone since Jason. Or before Jason, for that matter.

Still . . .

You've got more baggage than a cross-country flight. And Drew isn't your type.

So what's up, then?

You just want to focus your romantic attention on somebody other than the mythical Jed Landry, right?

Wrong.

Romantic? This isn't about romance. This is about being neighborly. And gracious. And getting into the holiday spirit.

That's *all* this is about.

In Drew's apartment, Perry Como sings about a man who lives in Tennessee heading for Pennsylvania and some homemade pumpkin pie.

Clara can't help echoing along under her breath, "*. . . some pumpkin pie.*"

That was always one of her favorite Christmas songs.

Smiling, Clara walks slowly over to the door and raises her hand to knock.

Then, mingling with the lyrics "*. . . From Atlantic to Pacific,*" Clara distinctly hears a laugh on the other side of the door.

A female laugh.

". . . *Betty . . .*" rumbles a male voice.

She immediately lowers her hand and turns away.

So Mr. New-In-Town already has a girlfriend. Betty. That sure didn't take long.

Oh, come on, Clara. Why do you even care?

Why? Because this is obviously Lust After Totally Inappropriate Men Week.

First Jed Landry, now Drew Becker . . .

Not that she's lusting after Drew Becker.

Still . . .

Next thing you know, I'll be calling Jason back, she thinks as she hurries up the last flight of stairs to her apartment, shaking her head in dismay.

No way. She's as finished with her ex as she is with . . .

Well, with daydreaming—or any other dreaming—about Jed Landry.

As for Drew Becker . . .

Maybe he left the CD.

And maybe he didn't.

Maybe it was the old lady.

And maybe it wasn't.

She can only hope that somehow, everything will be much clearer after she's had a good night's sleep.

Standing on the street in front of the Wilkens bungalow, Jed is reassured by the lamplight spilling from the windows.

Somebody's still awake at almost ten o'clock on a Tuesday evening. With luck, it will be Arnold and not Maisie.

Of course, the mere possibility that it might be Maisie who answers the door is almost enough to send Jed scurrying in the opposite direction.

But if he does that, there will be no chance of getting to the city tonight. He can't patch the tire on his father's DeSoto—he tried and quickly figured out that it needs to be replaced. Unfortunately, the dealer is closed for the night.

He then ran down a list of pals in an unsuccessful attempt to borrow a car or convince somebody to give him a lift to Manhattan. Nobody was ready, willing, or able.

He saved Arnold for last, due to the Maisie factor.

But it's worth a shot. With any luck, she's sound asleep and will never even realize the Packard is gone. He'll promise Arnold that he'll have it back in a couple of hours: just long enough to drive down to West Eleventh Street, find Clara, and . . .

And then what?

That's the part he hasn't worked out yet.

But he will, while he's driving.

And if it gets any later, he'll have to rule out the plan in its entirety. At least for tonight.

His mind made up, jaw set in determination, he walks up the shoveled path to the front door. After only a moment's hesitation, he raises the brass knocker and lowers it. Gently. Just two times. So as not to wake the formidable lady of the house.

Too late, he realizes when the door is thrown open by none other than Maisie herself.

It's all Jed can do not to recoil in horror.

Standing on the doorstep, Arnold's wife seems to tower over him like some kind of creature from a Bela Lugosi or Boris Karloff film. Her face is covered in some kind of white goo, her belly protrudes at a frighteningly distorted angle from her sweeping robe, and her hair is covered by a kerchief tied high atop her skull.

"Say, Maisie, is Arnold around?" Jed attempts to ask casually, hating the slight squeak in his voice. It's the first day of kindergarten all over again, and he's just been informed by Maisie that he spelled his own name wrong.

He dared to argue with her, only to be told, *All right, then, your name must be Jug! Jug Lundy! Miss Corcoran, Jed thinks his name is Jug Lundy! Everyone, this is Jug Lundy!*

Luckily, that nickname lasted only about ten minutes.

But Tattletale Maisie followed her all the way to the altar.

"Do you have any idea what time it is? Arnold is asleep!"

"Actually, I figured he might be awake and you might be asleep since you're . . . sleeping . . . for . . .

two . . ." He trails off with a halfhearted smile that isn't returned.

"Do you honestly think I can get a moment's sleep with this?" Maisie gestures at her belly. Without waiting to hear what he thinks—as if she ever has cared—she continues, "I'm telling you, Jed, I'm uncomfortable sitting, lying, standing, walking . . ."

Yelling, Jed thinks. *Nagging, harping, complaining . . .*

"This is just the hardest thing I've ever done," she goes on. "Which is why men don't have to do it."

Right, and women don't have to go to war, Jed wants to point out.

"Gee whiz, Maisie, that's too bad," he murmurs instead, thinking this was a mistake. Big, big mistake.

"Jed, seriously . . . what are you doing here?"

"I was going to ask Arnold for a favor, but—"

"What kind of favor?"

"Oh, never mind."

"Maybe I can help."

Seriously doubting it, yet willing to grab on to a shred of hope for seeing Clara tonight, Jed explains that he wanted to borrow their Packard for a few hours.

"Why?"

"I have to go down to Manhattan to . . . pick up some merchandise," he lies, feeling guilty. But no way is he about to tell Maisie about his real mission.

"Well, I'm sorry, Jed, but we can't help you. We need our car here because I could go into labor at any second."

Maisie in labor. Now there's a scary notion.

Poor Arnold.

"Thanks anyway, Maisie," Jed says, turning away. "Good luck with everything."

"You, too."

Yeah. Luck. That's what it's going to take at this point. Luck, or the milk train, which doesn't come through for another couple of hours. He can hardly show up at Clara's door in the wee hours.

Jed shuffles the five blocks back to Chestnut Street, his breath puffing white in the chilly night air.

He might as well forget about finding Clara tonight. But he isn't giving up.

No, sir.

Nights are the worst.

Lying alone in the dark, Clara can no longer keep the reality of her illness at bay. No matter how exhausted she is—especially tonight—she finds herself restlessly immersed in dire deliberation about what her future might hold.

That, and the increasingly haunting lyrics of "Midnight Train to Georgia."

I'd rather live in his world . . . than live without him . . . in mine . . .

Finally, realizing that sleep will indefinitely elude her if she stays in bed, she gets up and goes to the living room, turning on every light along the way to dispense the wee-hour December gloom.

Knowing there will be nothing worth watching on television at 2:40 on a Sunday morning, she doesn't bother to pick up the remote. She sits on the couch and flips through Thursday's unopened mail, remembering that she didn't even bother to remove it from the box the past two days.

No, she's had other things on her mind.

Like time warps, and dead soldiers, and getting fired, and old lady stalkers . . .

No, don't you dare even start with any of that, she

warns herself, having managed so far to ward off disturbing thoughts about everything but the cancer.

She goes to the kitchen and puts a cup of water into the microwave. Chamomile tea will help her to relax.

Waiting for the water to heat, she realizes that it's too quiet. Almost eerily so, despite the hum of the microwave and a distant siren floating up to the closed window.

You can't help but become immersed in your own disturbing thoughts when it's this quiet. Thoughts, and old song lyrics that persist in running through your head.

Goin' back to find . . . a simpler place and time . . .

Returning abruptly to the living room, she puts on the new Bing Crosby CD.

Instantly soothed as the opening strains fill the room, she smiles at the irony: Bing's "Silent Night" has dispelled her own uncomfortably silent night.

She retraces her steps to the kitchen and returns moments later, steaming mug of tea in hand.

Now what?

"Slee-eep in heavenly peace," Bing croons from the stereo.

"Yeah, don't I wish," Clara murmurs.

She can't seem to relax. Not with her thoughts repeatedly turning to the looming lumpectomy and the treatment to follow.

What if none of it is successful?

What if the doctors missed something?

What if the cancer has already spread, is spreading now . . .

No! Stop that, Clara.

She needs a distraction. Something other than tea and tunes.

Maybe if she reads . . .

Looking around for a magazine, she finds herself zeroing in on her desk in the far corner. More specifically, on the case containing her laptop.

She hasn't checked her e-mail in a couple of days.

It takes a few moments for the laptop to power up and go through its various scans against viruses and the like, thanks to all the protective software Jason installed for her.

She can't help but note the irony: her computer is shielded against toxic invaders, but her body is not.

You'd think with all the marvels of modern technology that somebody would come up with some sort of . . . cancer-proofing device. Yes, a wristband or medallion, or a microchip that could be implanted to ward off carcinogens and instantly kill malignant cells.

Maybe someday . . .

After all, look how far we've come since the forties, Clara can't help thinking, remembering Jed's father, and her grandmother.

You've got mail, a disembodied voice informs her.

Clara ignores it, thinking about Jed's father.

Lucky Landry.

Lucky Landry?

Could she possibly have made that up?

Maybe she read it somewhere when she was doing her research up in Glenhaven Park . . . though she doesn't recall coming across any information about Jed's father.

What was his real name?

Arthur?

No, Abner.

She contemplates that. Did Abner, aka Lucky Landry, even exist? If so, did he really die of cancer?

Clara opens a search engine, then sits, fingers poised over the keyboard, wondering what to type.

She settles on *Jed Landry*.

Her fingers are shaking so badly as she types that it takes several tries to hit the right letters. She hits ENTER and waits, holding her breath, her e-mail and her mug of tea entirely forgotten now.

The long rectangle on the lower left corner of the screen begins to shade in as the page opens. Clara watches it, wondering what she'll find.

All at once, she finds herself facing a lengthy list of *Jed Landry* hits.

She opens the first link—and is frustrated to find the official Michael Marshall Web site, with home page news about his latest role. With a sigh, she goes back to the search page results and begins to open and close links with growing frustration. The first dozen or so are related to Denton's movie: cast lists, articles, Michael's fan pages. Then she hits the jackpot with an excerpt from an archived article from the *Glenhaven Gazette*.

It's dated July 15, 1944.

ANOTHER LOCAL MAN CONFIRMED LOST IN EUROPE

A telegram from the War Department last night officially brought to ten the number of local casualties in the first wave of the Allied invasion at Normandy on June 6. Previously reported missing in action, Sergeant Jed Landry of 21 Chestnut Street, son of Mrs. Lois Landry and the late . . .

Heart pounding, she clicks on the link to the full article . . .

And discovers that she has to register on the paper's online site and pay to access the archives.

Cursing under her breath, she does her best to hurry

through the painstaking process: choosing a user name and password, and digging out her credit card, entering personal and payment information . . .

Then, all at once, there it is.

The complete article, accompanied by a photo of Jed in uniform. It's the same photo she saw in the library's historical exhibit, yet suddenly, the man in it is a stranger.

He looks so different from the Jed Landry she met in the five-and-dime . . .

In my dream, she reminds herself.

There is no twinkle in this Jed's eyes, which are framed by a faint but distinctly visible network of fine lines. They're focused on some far-off point, slightly narrowed, as though he doesn't like what he sees. His jaw is set in resignation. The stubbly, unruly dark hair is now military-short.

It's almost as though he knows, Clara thinks, staring into his face. *As if he knows, but somehow, he isn't afraid.*

Tearing herself away from the picture, she scans the article's lead again, picking up where she left off.

With the name *Abner.*

Jed's father.

Could I possibly have known that, and forgotten? Clara wonders anxiously. *And my subconscious conveniently plugged it into my dream?*

What about his death? How did Abner Landry die? If she just had a date, then she could check . . .

Wait a minute.

Didn't Jed say something about its being the anniversary? Yes! What was it, exactly, that he said?

Two years ago today, actually.

Heart pounding, Clara scrolls through the *Gazette* archives until she finds the first of December, 1939.

Page by page, she clicks through the paper, searching for a death notice. But there's none for Abner Landry, just for a Minerva Medford who died at the ripe old age of ninety on November 28 . . .

Wait a minute.

Realizing that it takes a few days after a death before an obituary appears in the paper, Clara impulsively switches to the December 3, 1939 edition.

A few clicks . . . and there it is.

On page four, beneath the headline COMMUNITY PILLAR SUCCUMBS TO LUNG CANCER . . .

Lung cancer.

Just like Jed said in her dream.

Scanning the article, she gasps, spotting a familiar phrase: *Commonly known by his childhood nickname, Lucky* . . .

There is no way. Absolutely no way that any of this is pure coincidence, or that Clara somehow noted, then forgot about, all of the information and it made its way from her subconscious to her dream . . .

And yet, it couldn't be anything but a dream, Clara tells herself firmly, her hand poised, trembling, on the mouse pad.

A dream, an episode, a hallucination, a fugue . . .

Abruptly bringing up the search engine over the open newspaper archive, she enters the words *dissociative fugue.*

Choosing the first of thousands of hits that pop up, she is linked to a clinical information site. She scans the criteria: spontaneous travel from familiar surroundings . . . most commonly follow disasters, wars, or situations of extreme personal distress . . . the afflicted person forgets his or her true identity . . . when the person "wakes up," he or she has little or no recollection of what transpired during fugue state . . .

Clara quickly closes out of that screen.

But I never once forgot who I really am while I was going through it, she thinks, *and when it was over, I didn't forget what happened in my state of . . .*

Well, whatever it was.

So it doesn't fit.

Nothing fits.

She closes her eyes, trying to remember every detail of that short, fateful train trip. She remembers talking to Lisa and the extras, and facing the back of the train as it sped along, and how she bumped her head when she was thrown toward the back of the train as it slowed abruptly . . .

Wait a minute.

Karen brought this up during Clara's account at the therapy session last night, too.

If the train suddenly braked, wouldn't she have been thrown *forward*?

Of course she would have. If you're riding in a car and somebody slams on the brakes, you fly forward, toward the windshield, not back against the seat. That's why you wear a seat belt.

Why, then, on the train, did Clara have the sensation of being thrown backward?

She has no idea.

No, she's quite clueless about the laws of physics.

Shaking her head, she returns her attention to the computer and the open *Glenhaven Gazette* site. Reluctant to see Jed's unfamiliar photo again, and to read about the circumstances of his—or his father's—death, she hesitates.

Then, impulsively, she pulls up the newspaper for December 1, 1941.

ALLIED SUCCESSES CAUSE JAPS TO ASSUME MILDER ATTITUDE

The headline leaps out at her, as hauntingly familiar as if . . .

Well, as if she saw it just yesterday.

Again, she finds herself wondering how she could have known. She never searched old newspapers when she was in Glenhaven Park.

Could this one have been on display in the library's historical exhibit?

No. It couldn't have been.

There was plenty about December 7, the day that would live in infamy . . .

Plenty, predictably, about D-Day, and V-E Day, and other relevant dates during the war years.

But nothing about December 1. That would have stood out for its sheer incongruity. She would have remembered.

She scrolls forward again, until she finds the *Glenhaven Gazette* dated December 7.

Nothing.

Oh, right. She remembers that she needs to look at the following day's paper.

Sure enough, the December 8 headline screams US DECLARES WAR.

The pages are filled with details about Pearl Harbor, the stateside reaction, the government. Clara reads about the attack and its aftermath with more fascination than ever before, feeling as though it's no longer just something that happened in a history book.

It was real, she was there . . .

No, she just feels as though she was. It seemed so real, all of it . . .

Particularly when she begins to notice that the paper contains ads for familiar businesses she's seen on the Main Street of modern-day Glenhaven Park . . . or did she see them in the past, in her dream?

And it isn't just the ads . . .

A name jumps out at her from a small article of local news, buried in the middle of the newspaper.

Bouvier.

Accompanying the article is a photo of an old woman she instantly recognizes: it's the customer who stopped in Jed's store for canning jars while Clara was there.

Clara clearly remembers being struck by the woman's last name at the time; it was the maiden name of the former—but in 1941, it would have been future—first lady. When she heard Jed mention it, she almost expected to look up and see a young Jacqueline Bouvier standing there.

Naturally, she didn't recognize the old woman who promised to bring Jed a couple of Christmas fruitcakes. But she remembers how affectionately he spoke to her, and how it seemed as though she had been shopping in his store for years.

According to this article, Mrs. Minnie Bouvier, eighty-six, of 59 Oak Street, was struck by a car as it rounded the corner of Main and Oak at dusk on Saturday. She died the next day at Glenhaven Park hospital. Her next-door neighbor mentioned that Minnie had asked to borrow a spice she needed for a recipe, but the neighbor was out of it as well.

"She said she'd just walk over to the store," a Mrs. Lorraine Barker was quoted as saying.

"I warned her not to go, as it was getting dark and starting to snow. But she really wanted to finish mixing her fruitcakes. She said she'd been trying to get to them for days."

Fruitcakes.

A chill slips down Clara's spine.

Yet another detail.

And one too many for comfort.

She tries to turn her attention back to the article.

    No charges were pressed against the distraught driver of the blue Packard that fatally struck Mrs. Bouvier. En route to the hospital with his laboring wife, Mr. Arnold—

Clara reaches out and snaps the laptop closed, unable to continue.

It's just too much. Too much to absorb in one evening . . .

Though she wonders, if she tries for the rest of her life, whether she'll ever manage to wrap her mind around any of this.

It's almost as if . . .

"I was really there."

There.

She said it aloud.

And somehow, it didn't sound half as outlandish as she expected.

Pushing back her chair, she heads for her bedroom, determined to get some sleep.

And tomorrow, she won't rest, or go to the gym, or see a movie.

No. Tomorrow, she'll pay a visit to an old friend.

One she hasn't seen in over a decade.

The only person in the world who might be able to explain why the impossible suddenly seems distinctly possible.

Chapter 10

The first southbound commuter train stops in Glenhaven Park at precisely 5:40 A.M. on weekday mornings.

Today, Jed plans to be on it. Wearing a brown fedora and his only decent suit, baggy with wide lapels and high-waisted trousers, he waits on the platform. He's joined there by a smattering of businessmen he's known most of his life, encompassing the generation between his and his father's.

In his hand is Clara's heavy suitcase. He stashed her pocketbook inside, not wanting to be seen carrying it.

"Jed Landry, what are you doing headed for the city at this time of day?" Harold Pogue, a Park Avenue lawyer, asks, curiously eyeing the suitcase. "Starting a vacation?"

Lifting the bag as though it's weightless—and thus, empty—he tells Harold, "No, I need to pick up some merchandise downtown. I'll use this to get it home." Frightening how comfortable Jed is with the lie he's been rehearsing all night.

He didn't sleep when he climbed into his bed after setting the alarm.

Nor does he sleep now, as he leans back in a cushioned seat after boarding the train.

Anticipation dogs his every breath, along with a hint

of dread at what he might find—or not find—when at last he reaches West Eleventh Street.

It would probably have been easier to wait until he can fix his father's car and drive down, but he simply couldn't hold out another day.

The train is the way to go. With any luck, he'll be back in Glenhaven Park by nine o'clock to open the store.

Darn that Alice, anyway. If she were someone he could count on, he'd simply have asked her to cover for him until he could get there. But she didn't show up at all yesterday, nor did she ever call with an explanation. Jed figures she's as good as fired; he'll just have to wait until she turns up to drop the axe.

He isn't going to waste any time worrying about it now, when Clara McCallum is almost within his grasp.

As the train rattles toward the city, he removes her photo card from his wallet and stares at it.

Who are you, really? he asks her smiling, carefree image.

More than an hour seems to pass before the train pulls into Grand Central Station, but checking his watch, Jed sees that it's right on time.

He exits with the other passengers, whose population has grown steadily at every stop and is now a bona fide horde.

It's been years since Jed took the subway in Manhattan. So long, in fact, that he has to consult a map on the mosaic tiled wall of the station below the terminal.

Hmm . . . Which line will get him closest to West Eleventh Street: IRT, IND, or BMT? It takes just a few seconds to conclude that the IRT Lexington Avenue express to Fourteenth Street looks like the best route. He fishes a nickel from his pocket and feeds it into the wooden turnstile.

The train arrives within minutes. Every rattan seat is occupied; he stands holding on to a porcelain strap as the train hurtles through a black tunnel to the next stop.

Less than five minutes after boarding, he's outside at last, heading down Broadway, the suitcase weighing heavily on his arm.

For the first time since the commuter train entered the tunnel a few miles north of Grand Central, he's able to glimpse the sky. It's gone from black to milky charcoal, rimmed by the slightest hint of golden light that seems to promise a nice day.

This is almost too easy, he thinks as he turns west onto Eleventh Street. *It can't possibly be this easy.*

He walks down the block, noting the descending order of the addresses as he nears Fifth Avenue: 25, 21, 15, 11 . . .

Having reached the sprawling Beaux Arts apartment building on the corner, he crosses lower Fifth Avenue. He can see Washington Square Park a few blocks to the south, with its famed marble arch.

Does Clara stroll in the park on nice afternoons? he finds himself wondering, and pictures her there, in dappled shade on a glorious summer afternoon.

He realizes that he's seeing the black-and-white Clara in the photo, though—not the Clara he met in person. A stroll in the park seems far too idyllic a pastime for the skittish woman with the bruise on her head and fear in her eyes.

He pauses to set the suitcase down on the sidewalk and pull the card from his pocket again.

What happened to you? he asks the serene woman in the photo.

Again, he wonders about the name *Jezibel*, scribbled across the card. Is that her real name? Her alias?

He flips the card to check her address against the buildings to his left. Still a ways to go. Eleventh Street's designation transformed from East to West when he crossed Fifth Avenue and the numbers are ascending from the beginning again. She lives in the hundreds; he's just passed number 16, 18 . . .

He lifts the suitcase with a grunt and resumes his pace. The street noise seems to have gone down a decibel, and there are more trees. More pigeons and squirrels, too. It's as though he's in a whole new realm of the city now. The hubbub of Union Square seems a thousand miles away, rather than a mere few blocks.

Here, traffic and pedestrians are sporadic. Bare limbs spread overhead against the gray morning sky. Century-old brick homes with wooden trim and double-hung paned windows are set back from the sidewalk. Many are fronted by short, wide flights of stairs that lead to graceful entries. Beneath, basement windows rise to eye level. The tiny concrete patches of sidewalk footage are protected by low black wrought-iron fences.

Jed reaches the intersection with Sixth Avenue and is startled to find it oddly open and bright. It takes a moment for him to realize why: he hasn't been down here since before the elevated train trestle was razed two years ago.

Now there's a clear view up the avenue, formerly the city's famous Ladies' Mile. From this angle he can't see much detail on the sprawling Beaux Arts buildings that once housed the glorious department stores of the Gilded Age. Many lingered well into this century before closing or moving to more desirable uptown locations.

Jed is familiar with the area's history because his mother once worked down here, as a shopgirl at Siegel Cooper a few blocks north. When Pop was courting her, they used to meet by the famous lobby fountain with its shooting jets and colored lights.

Jed remembers taking the train down here with his parents once in a while on Sunday afternoons when he was little, before the Depression hit. He was struck by the way Mother and Pop would hold hands as they strolled, laughing and reminiscing about what used to be.

What used to be . . .

Jed can't help but notice that, freshly sprung from the shadows of the el, the once-elegant buildings now seem as faded and run-down as the widowed Lois Landry does.

Melancholy seeps in, and he quickly turns away from the memories, focusing his thoughts again on Clara.

So this is her block. On the left is Rhinelander Gardens, a series of three-story apartment buildings set back from the street beyond well-landscaped front yards. Unbroken balconies run along the buildings' facades, marked by lacy ornate ironwork.

Though momentarily intrigued by the unusual century-old architecture, Jed doesn't linger; Clara's address is farther up the block.

Has she ever eaten at that quaint little Italian restaurant, or noticed the high broken limb creaking in the wind on that elm tree just ahead? Are any of the briskly striding pedestrians her neighbors?

He looks more closely at them as they pass, and can't help but note the stark difference between these folks and the uptown commuters.

Here, there are scattered well-heeled types to be sure, but there are also dungarees on men and women

alike. Rather than briefcases, some people carry port-
folios and instrument cases, or nothing at all. A few
seem aimless, others shifty; many are obviously less
than well-off. Though it has its share of elegant old
homes, this doesn't strike Jed as a particularly safe or
desirable neighborhood.

Why does she live here, then?

Who or what is she, really?

Greenwich Village, he knows, has been inundated
with artists, writers, and theater people over the past
few decades. Clara doesn't seem to be any of the
above—though he should probably know better than
to think he can begin to guess anything about her
based on one short, edgy encounter.

You just never know. She could be a burlesque
dancer, or a poet, or, yes . . . a spy.

That she lives here among the Bohemians and architectural remnants of forgotten New York neither adds
to nor detracts from his espionage speculation. He just
can't help but wonder why someone like Clara would
make this neighborhood her home . . . unless she had
no choice. Perhaps she can't afford to live uptown,
though this suitcase certainly contains a lot of nice
clothes for someone on the fringes.

Nice clothes in all different sizes.

Realizing he might be close to solving the enigma
one way or another, he checks the nearest address.
Hers is only a few numbers away.

He walks on, and his heart seems to be beating in
his ears.

Here. This is it.

He stops and surveys the tall townhouse.

It's slightly shabbier than the one on the left and
much nicer than the one on the right, proving the
neighborhood clearly is in flux.

Once, this was a grand townhouse. Now the paint is peeling from the trim around the door and windows. English ivy creeps halfheartedly up the front of the building, obstructing most of a ground floor window, and there is a Christmas wreath on the front door. Those splotches of green are the building's only bright spots in the midst of the bleak December landscape.

Jed checks his watch. It's just past seven o'clock.

He wonders whether he should knock now or wait until a slightly more respectable hour. He can't afford to let too much time pass if he expects to get back home and open the store . . .

Then he hears the voice.

"Hey, mister . . . what you doing?"

Sunday morning, Clara is awakened from a sound sleep—a sleep that had refused to descend until the sun came up—to a distant tapping sound.

It takes her a moment to realize that it's coming from her door.

She jumps out of bed and hurries, barefoot, to the next room, rubbing her bleary eyes, wondering who it can be.

In fact . . .

She slows her pace as she approaches the door, remembering that people can't just pop in. Not people without keys to the building, anyway.

Or crazed killers who slip in when nobody's looking.

Frowning, she peers through the peephole . . . and smiles.

The building super is standing there, holding a tremendous pinkish white poinsettia plant.

Wishing she were presentable, she unlocks the door and peeks out. "Hello, Mr. Kobayashi," she croaks in her morning voice. "What have you got there?"

"This is for you." He thrusts the foil-wrapped pot at her.

"Thank you! It's so sweet of you to—"

"No!" He looks downright alarmed. "Not sweet of me! This isn't a sweet gift from me! I'm a married man!"

"I know, I know . . . don't worry." Confused, she wonders if Mr. Kobayashi has a crush on her, and what she's supposed to do about it—and the sweet gifts he won't own up to even when he hands them directly to her.

"I found this here," he says then, and gestures at the black rubber doormat.

"You . . . found it?"

"On the mat. Someone left a sweet gift. Not me."

"No, not you. Of course not." And she believes him.

"I just found it when I was coming to give you soup."

"Soup?"

For the first time, she realizes that he is also holding a plastic container.

"My wife made it. When I told her last night you got mugged by street scum and beat up to a pulp, she said, 'Isamu, my soup will help that poor girl.' She says her soup will help everything. Here. For you. Homemade *nabeyaki udon*."

"Thank you so much." Clara accepts the soup, balancing it on her arm, touched. Touched, and wondering who could have left the gorgeous poinsettia on her mat. "Please thank Mrs. Kobayashi for me, too."

He nods and pads away in his slippers, down the stairs.

There's a note, Clara realizes, spotting a corner of white peeking out from amid the leaves.

She locks the door again, shoves the soup in the nearly empty fridge, and hurriedly opens the small florist's card.

In red Sharpie, someone has scrawled, *May your day be merry and bright! Love, Santa.*

You again, Clara thinks, bemused. *But who are you?*

The small, accented voice seems to have come out of thin air.

Frowning, Jed looks around.

There is nobody in sight.

He hears a giggle.

Only then does he catch sight of the little boy squatting in the subterranean shadows of the brownstone's front steps.

He's about five, with a cap of shiny black hair and mischievous black Asian eyes. Clad only in a short-sleeved shirt and dungarees, he's shivering.

"Shouldn't you be wearing a coat?" Jed asks, and the child shakes his head. "Well, what are you doing out here?"

"Hiding," is the reply.

"From whom?"

"Mama. She want to give me grilled fish for breakfast." The boy makes a face.

"I take it you don't like grilled fish?"

"Not for breakfast. I sick of fish! Every day, every day, fish."

"You don't say."

The child nods vigorously.

"I see where that would be a problem," Jed says thoughtfully, setting the heavy suitcase on the sidewalk. "Say, where do you live?"

The child points up at the townhouse.

"Really? In there? What's your name?"

"Isamu."

"Hello, Isamu. Nice to meet you."

"What's your name?" the boy asks haltingly and somewhat self-consciously, using the same inflections as Jed in a clear attempt to perfect his American accent.

"I'm Jed."

"Nice to meet you."

"Say, Isamu . . . if you live here, you must know Clara."

The boy is expressionless.

"Clara McCallum," Jed elaborates, and, for good measure, adds, "Miss McCallum. She lives here, too."

The child shakes his head.

"What do you mean?"

"Just Mama . . . Papa . . . Mr. Sloan . . . Mrs. Sloan," Isamu informs him. "Oh. And me."

"That's everyone who lives in your apartment?"

"In whole house." The little boy waves a hand at the townhouse.

"What about Jezibel? Do you know her?"

"No."

Jed reaches into his pocket and crouches down beside the low wrought-iron fence, on the same level with the child on the other side of the rails. "Come over here, Isamu. Let me show you something."

The child obediently approaches the fence.

Jed pokes Clara's card through a space between the black bars, picture side up. "Does she live here?"

"No."

"Have you ever seen her before?"

Isamu shakes his head solemnly.

Suddenly, the door opens and a woman's voice calls out from the doorway overhead.

Jed straightens to see a worried-looking middle-aged Japanese woman on the stoop shouting, "Isamu! Isamu!"

"He's right here, ma'am." Jed tips his fedora at her. "You must be his mother."

Obviously relieved to see her son, the woman just gapes. Then she says something in Japanese to Isamu, whose long-winded reply is of course inscrutable to Jed. He's pretty sure it involves him, though, because both mother and son are now eyeing him inquisitively.

"What did she say?" Jed asks Isamu.

"She want to know why you here, what you want, who you are."

"What did you tell her?"

"I say I don't know. Maybe you detective like Dick Tracy, protector of law and order." This time, Isamu perfectly nails the booming inflection of the announcer on the popular radio show.

"No, I'm not a detective, Isamu . . . I'm looking for my . . . friend. Clara. I thought she lived here. See? This address is on the back here."

"I show Mama," the boy tells Jed, and plucks the card from his fingers.

Jed watches him dart up the steps to his mother, who turns the card over and over, scrutinizing it, as her son speaks to her in their native tongue.

Jed's heart sinks as she looks down at him and shakes her head, shrugging to indicate that she doesn't recognize Clara, either.

"She never know this girl," Isamu informs him, descending the steps and returning the card to Jed's grasp. "Mr. Sloan own house. He live here with Mrs. Sloan. We live in basement. Take care of things."

Jed shoots a probing gaze up at Isamu's mother, waiting on the stoop, her arms folded against the chill. Is she telling the truth?

Even if *she* weren't, he'd probably be able to tell if the little boy were lying. And he doesn't seem to be.

There wasn't a hint of recognition in Isamu's face when he spoke Clara's name, much less when Jed showed him her photo.

"Isamu!" the mother calls sharply, beckoning.

"See you, mister," the little boy says before scurrying up the steps, where he is promptly herded into the house.

The door closes sharply behind them.

Jed looks again at the address printed on the card, then checks it against the number above the townhouse's door.

They match.

Wait a minute . . . maybe he's on the wrong street!

Maybe he wasn't paying enough attention on his way over, and he's actually on West Tenth Street . . . or West Twelfth . . .

He picks up the suitcase, turns, and retraces his steps to the corner, striding quickly despite the weighty bag in his hand.

The white lettering on the arched blue sign is clearly visible before he even reaches the corner.

West Eleventh Street.

He had the street right.

Again, he checks the lettering on the card. Just one more time, to be absolutely certain . . .

No, he had the address right, too. And it matches the address range listed in the arched panel above the street name on the sign.

Obviously, the card—like the clothing in the suitcase, and everything else about Clara McCallum—is just part of an elaborate charade.

It's all he can do not to pitch the card into the nearest trash can, and deposit her luggage along with it.

But he can't do that.

It's important evidence.

The authorities are going to need it.

Feeling as though he's been sucker punched in the stomach, Jed slowly makes his way back to the subway.

That Jonathan Kershaw—the *right* Jonathan Kershaw—is listed in the Manhattan white pages is perhaps the first thing that's gone smoothly for Clara in the past forty-eight hours.

It would be too much to hope for that her former high school physics teacher might not only be home when she called, but remember her.

Yet he was, and he did.

"Clara! You're a big movie star now. Do you have any idea how proud I am of you? To hear Sandra Nelson tell it, she's single-handedly responsible for your success."

Sandra Nelson was, of course, her high school drama teacher. The one who, when casting the sophomore musical, assigned the plum parts of Dolly Levi and Irene Molloy to two other girls, leaving Clara to giggle her way through a supporting role as frivolous Minnie Fay.

She's come a long way since *Hello, Dolly!*, thank goodness.

And a long, long way since she last spoke to Mr. Kershaw.

He seemed surprised to hear from her, and even more surprised when she asked to see him—in person. Today.

But he readily agreed, and now here she is, climbing out of the subway on the southern fringes of the Upper West Side neighborhood where the retired, divorced Mr. Kershaw has been living for decades.

Somehow, since having made the initial contact with

him this morning, she's managed to temporarily clear her head of the unsettling thoughts that have haunted her these past few days. Just knowing she's going to see him has brought a temporary reprieve—though for all Mr. Kershaw knows, the purpose of her visit is a nostalgic trip down a figurative memory lane, not a scientific inquiry into whether a literal one is remotely possible. And for all she knows, he's going to confirm that she's lost her mind.

But right now, she isn't thinking ahead. Nor is she looking back. She's just walking up Amsterdam Avenue, content for a change to be in the moment.

She's taken great pleasure in avoiding makeup on her day off and her face feels wonderfully unadulterated, as does her hair, falling loose and squeaky-clean from beneath a cozy red knit hat that covers her bruise.

She's cozy and comfortable in jeans, sneakers, and a sweatshirt, a red down jacket, and of course the treasured—and mysteriously returned to her—pair of warm red mittens with a white snowflake pattern that exactly match the hat on her head.

"Why do you go around wearing mittens?" Jason frequently asked last winter.

"Because when I wear them, my fingers can keep each other warm."

That didn't fly with Jason. Of course he believes that mittens—sentimental value notwithstanding—are impractical, mostly because you can't wear them while dialing a cell phone or pressing the numbers on the ATM keypad.

"So what? You can't stash things in your gloves, but you can in your mittens," Clara would point out to her ex-fiancé. "Like money, your license, credit cards, your keys . . ."

"Or you can wear gloves and keep those things in your pockets, where they belong," said Jason the killjoy.

"I don't always have pockets."

"Then carry a purse."

Today, gloriously unencumbered—by purse, or gloves, or Jason—she carries only some cash in her right mitten, her keys in her left. She even left her cell phone at home, not wanting to hear from anybody for awhile. Not on her day off.

The air is crisp, the sky a brilliant winter blue. Church bells are ringing and for the time being, all is right with the world.

She smiles to herself as she passes an open doorway and hears Bruce Springsteen's exuberant "Santa Claus Is Comin' to Town" playing somewhere above.

It's a heck of a lot more welcome than "Midnight Train to Georgia."

As she waits for the light to change, she catches a whiff of Sunday brunch—or perhaps a dozen different Sunday brunches from a dozen different restaurants—wafting on the cold breeze. She finds herself swallowing a sudden flood of saliva and remembers that she hasn't eaten anything yet, and it's past one o'clock. She put Mrs. Kobayashi's soup in the refrigerator and forgot all about it.

Come to think of it, she didn't eat much yesterday, either. Or the day before.

Guess you've learned the ultimate magic bullet for an actress's appetite control, she thinks wryly. *Cancer diagnosis with a time travel chaser. Next thing you know, your Levi's are bagging around your hips.*

Nearing Mr. Kershaw's cross street, she slows her pace a bit. It isn't that she's changed her mind about seeing him . . . she just wants to put it off until the last possible moment because she has no idea how he's going to react to her question.

She allows herself to gaze into a few boutiques as she passes, admiring the glitzy holiday merchandise; the tinsel, garland, and lights.

Then she allows herself to think about the pink and white poinsettia from her mystery Santa. But only for a moment: then she dismisses the thought and any speculation about the Santa's identity. It's just too much right now.

Still . . . it would be so nice if I could just get into the spirit.

Wistful again, she can't help but pine for a simple, joyous Christmas shopping mission. How carefree her life used to be when there was nothing heavier weighing on her mind than whether to get her stepmother a gift card or attempt to buy her something to wear.

This year, everybody's getting gift cards, Clara tells herself briskly, *and that's that.* She doesn't have the time, the energy, or the inclination to shop. *And if that's not sad, I don't know what is.*

Too soon, it seems, she finds herself walking down a tree-lined quiet side street that reminds her of her own block in the Village. Nestled among the brownstones is Mr. Kershaw's boxy yellow brick prewar apartment building.

Here goes, Clara thinks as she heads toward the entrance. Several elderly men, bundled in bulky coats and caps, are sitting and talking in plastic chairs in a small patch of winter sun.

As Clara passes, she notices that one of them is wearing a black baseball cap with WWII printed in gold above the visor. It's all she can do not to stop and stare, suddenly struck by the realization that this with-

ered old man was a young and heroic soldier, like Jed.
And that Jed, had he lived, would now be a withered
old man.

Well, of course he would. Why is that so
surprising—and disappointing?

*Because he's lost to you either way, whether he lived
or died,* comes the startling reply from a wayward
inner voice. *That's why.*

He's not lost to me. *He's nothing to* me, protests her
voice of reason. *Just a vision in a dream . . .*

*Right. So that's why you're here to see Mr. Kershaw?
Because you're still convinced it was a dream? A dream
about a man named Jed who had a father named
Abner, also known as Lucky Landry, who died of lung
cancer on December 1, 1939, all of which you couldn't
possibly have known unless . . .*

Okay.

Okay.

Clara swallows hard, attempting to steel herself for
whatever lies ahead.

On the long panel of buzzers beside the entry, she
finds the name Kershaw beside 14E. *Here goes,* she
thinks again as she removes her red mitten, careful not
to drop her keys, and presses the cold metal button.

The door clicks promptly. He's waiting for her.

She steps into the Pine-Sol scented lobby. In a by-
gone era, it might have been elegant, with glass chandeliers, marble floors, and ornate moldings. Today, it
seems a little forlorn: the chandeliers are strung with
cobwebs, the floors are worn, and the moldings could
use a fresh coat of paint.

With this prime location, though, it won't be long
before the place goes co-op. Then it will be completely
overhauled and populated by moneyed Wall Street
types like Jason.

Clara takes the elevator to the fourteenth floor, noticing that there's no thirteen, in keeping with many of the city's older high-rises including the Chrysler Building and Rockefeller Center.

Which means that this is *the thirteenth floor,* she thinks as she steps out into the corridor. She's never been particularly superstitious—unlike a surprising number of Manhattan builders—but she hopes that this isn't a bad omen.

Mr. Kershaw opens the door before she even reaches it. At least, she assumes he's Mr. Kershaw. The balding, rotund man in bifocals looks nothing like the dashing teacher she remembers. All that's familiar about him is his attire: even in retirement, he's wearing tan corduroy trousers and an olive green cardigan sweater over a wrinkled white dress shirt and bow tie.

Then he smiles, and she realizes with relief that he's entirely familiar, after all—and she's missed him.

This is the man who gave her a hall pass, no questions asked, the day she cut study hall to kiss Adam Dumont behind the bleachers. The man who regaled the class with heart-wrenching stories about Bianca, his beloved only child, overcoming impossible odds to survive a brain tumor. The man who was clapping in the front row at Clara's first off-off-Broadway performance at sixteen, and admitted afterward that he didn't "get" the play.

I guess I'm just too scientific to be very creative, he said with a rueful laugh.

To which Clara responded, *I guess I'm just too creative to be very scientific.*

Which is exactly the reason I'm here today, she thinks, as she walks toward him.

"Clara McCallum! Look at you! You even walk like a movie star!"

Somehow she doubts that, especially in blistered feet and sneakers—but it's a nice thing to say.

When she reaches him there is an awkward moment of not knowing whether to greet him with a hug or handshake. She opts to let him take the lead, but he seems to be doing the same, so they share an uncoordinated hug-shake.

"Come on in, Clara," he says with a laugh.

The place is huge. Rent-stabilized, without a doubt. A retired educator could never afford it otherwise.

Gazing around, Clara sees just the architectural touches one would expect to find in a vintage building like this: crown molding, built-in bookshelves, parquet floors, tall, deep-silled windows.

But the sparsely furnished apartment, like its resident himself and the lobby thirteen floors below, has seen better days. There are bubbles and creases in the wall opposite the door, painted a manila-paper beige that might very well once have been white. In the living room, a jagged crack runs through one windowpane and ominous water stains spread across the ceiling above the nubby sand-colored couch.

"Have a seat," Mr. Kershaw offers, gesturing at the couch after taking her coat. She removes her hat reluctantly, wishing she had thought to cover her bruise with makeup. And it would be nice if she were wearing something a little more presentable than this old navy blue hooded sweatshirt, a relic from the 2004 American League playoff game she attended with Jason.

"My goodness, what happened to your forehead?"

"I walked into a door," Clara says seamlessly. "You know me . . . always a klutz."

"It was always the opposite, as I recall," he replies

with a furrowed brow and another dubious glance at her head.

"Oh, well, I guess the clumsiness came later. I swear, there are some days that I can't believe I was ever a dancer."

You're chattering because you're nervous. Cut it out.

She falls silent, twisting her hat in jittery fingers, wishing she could put it back on . . . pull it low over her face, and slink right out the door.

This was definitely a bad idea.

"In that case, please have a seat before you hurt yourself," Mr. Kershaw says with a grin, and she can't help but laugh.

"Can I get you something?" he asks graciously. "Seltzer? A cup of hot tea?"

A double cheeseburger would be great, Clara thinks, and her stomach promptly growls at the savory image that pops into her head.

"No, thank you," she tells him, sitting on the couch. On the metal TV tray that serves as an end table beside it is a framed snapshot of a young family: mother, father, blue-swaddled baby.

Seeing Clara glance at it, Mr. Kershaw proudly announces, "I'm a grandpa. My daughter had a baby last spring. That's Bianca's little Tyler, and her husband Jack."

Bianca. The little girl who wasn't supposed to live past her sixth birthday. Moved, Clara offers a heartfelt, "Congratulations . . . that's wonderful."

"It sure is. They live on the West Coast, but they're coming for Christmas. I've been busy redoing Bianca's old room as a nursery, and turning the spare bedroom into a guest room."

"Wow . . . how many rooms do you have?" she exclaims.

"Eight, including the maid's bedroom. Not that I

have a maid. My ex-wife got everything else in the divorce—the furniture, the money, half my pension. I got to stay here."

"It's rent-stabilized," she guesses.

"Rent-controlled," he clarifies, almost gloating.

Ah, New York, Clara thinks, in complete understanding. A city where rent control is the equivalent of a middle-class teacher's lottery win, and multimillionaires line up to claim apartments vacated when their half-century tenants die off.

A fat cat with dense ebony fur appears out of nowhere to jump onto the cushion beside her, purring . . . or is he growling?

Terrific. First the thirteenth floor, now a black cat.

"Hawking, get down right now!" Mr. Kershaw scolds. Ignoring him, the feline begins to lick its paw. "You're not allergic, are you, Clara?"

"No, it's okay. I like cats," she lies. Jason had two. She prefers dogs.

Good thing I'm not superstitious.

"I'm afraid Hawking thinks he owns the place." Mr. Kershaw lowers himself into a well-worn armchair opposite the couch. "Well. To what do I owe the pleasure of your company this fine afternoon?"

She decides to cut right to the chase. "I need to ask you a question."

He nods, focused on her face with the same intensity with which he used to focus on the formulas and theories he tried so hard to convey to her.

She finds herself feeling guilty now that she didn't work harder, do better. At the time, she told herself that physics—like algebra, and chemistry—was not something that would come in handy in the real world. Not her world, anyway.

Hah.

"Do you think time travel is possible?"

He doesn't even bat an eye. Good old Mr. Kershaw.

"I do, yes."

He does. Yes.

Her breath catches in her throat.

The only response she can muster is one word: a strangled-sounding, "Why?"

"My ideas are based on the work of several renowned physicists, Einstein among them. Do you remember his special theory of relativity?"

She squirms uncomfortably.

Even if her thoughts weren't racing in the wake of his unexpected answer, she highly doubts she could recite Einstein's theory if her life depended on it.

He grins. "No, hmm?"

"It's not really fresh in my mind."

Hawking, seemingly disgusted with her, leaps off the couch and pads away in search of more scintillating company.

"Well, I could offer a refresher," Mr. Kershaw says, "but I'm sure that can wait for another time, so I'll simply say that the theory would seem to permit time travel to the future based on the fact that our perception of time is relative to our motion—it can speed up or slow down depending on how fast one thing is moving in relation to something else. Have I lost you?"

"Yes," she admits.

"Let me give you an example. Over thirty years ago, a physicist named Carrol Alley synchronized two atomic clocks, put one on a plane and flew it for several hours, then compared it to the one that stayed earthbound. He found that the one on the plane was behind the one on the ground. Meaning time had slowed down for the clock on the plane. It had thus traveled into the future."

Clara can't seem to find her breath, her voice.

It's real, then. It's possible.

Rubbing his chin the way he often did as a teacher, only this time *sans* chalk dust on his fingers, Mr. Kershaw goes on. "You've probably heard, if you're well-versed in current events, that there has been considerable discussion about astronauts being able to travel great distances over many years without aging as they do on Earth?"

She shakes her head, ashamed to discover that she must be woefully ill-versed in current events.

Undeterred, Mr. Kershaw explains, "This would mean that when the astronauts finally arrive at a distant planet they would be much younger than if they had stayed on Earth."

"But . . ." She clears her throat, trying to collect her thoughts. While encouraging, all this talk about outer space seems somewhat off the mark. "What about time travel into the past? Is that possible, too?"

"Ah, the next big question. Based on Einstein's theory of gravitation . . ." He pauses. "Any chance you remember that one?"

She shakes her head, feeling more unintelligent with every passing moment.

"I can't help but feel that I've failed you, my dear."

It takes her a second to see the twinkle in his eye and realize that he's joking. Thank goodness.

"In any case," he goes on, "based on that theory, we could assume that anything containing energy could warp space-time."

Clara nods as though that makes perfect sense.

"Take light, for example. A physicist named Ronald Mallett believes that two intense beams of light circling in opposite directions could distort time into a linear dimension similar to space . . . am I making any sense to you whatsoever?"

"Yes," she lies breathlessly, "keep going."

"In a nutshell, Clara, Mallett's plan could theoretically work if we had all the technology necessary to implement it. The same goes for wormholes, the old sci-fi standby."

"I don't read much . . . um, science fiction."

"No? Well, briefly, wormholes are a hypothetical space-time gateway, also based on the theory of gravitation that could allow time travel using relativistic time dilation if sufficient energy were provided."

After deciphering his words, she clarifies, "So what you're saying is that time travel to the past could happen?"

"With sufficient energy, theoretically, yes. But our current technology is simply incapable of harnessing or producing that level of energy—many times the magnitude of the sun's cumulative energy."

"So it *can't* happen?"

"I repeat . . . *current* technology is incapable, Clara."

"So . . . what are you saying, exactly?" she asks slowly. "That it might *become* possible?"

He nods emphatically. "Think of this: around the turn of the last century, a world-renowned mathematical physicist named Lord Kelvin declared that 'heavier than air flying machines are impossible.' Just a hundred years ago, a respected astronomer named Simon Newcomb announced, and I quote, 'No possible combination of known substances, known forms of machinery, and known forms of force could be united in a practicable machine by which men shall fly for long distances through the air.' "

"You memorized that word for word?"

He nods modestly. "I find it absolutely fascinating. Do you think, back then, that anyone in their wildest dreams ever imagined that in their lifetime, a man could fly across the country in a plane, much less walk on the moon?"

Flabbergasted, she simply shakes her head.

"Just a few years after Kelvin and Newcomb made their statements, the Wright brothers came along and figured out how to harness energy and make the seemingly impossible, possible. An everyday miracle, if you will."

"So you're saying that scientifically, time travel isn't impossible, either."

"Theoretically, it isn't impossible. Scientifically, it may not be possible *yet*."

May not be, Clara notes. *Not* isn't.

"All we would need to do then," she says slowly, "is figure out how to harness the energy. Like the Wright brothers did. Is that right?"

"I wouldn't say *all*, but . . . " He shrugs. "Look, Clara, I taught physics all my adult life. I consider myself a scientist, and scientists never claim absolute knowledge. The most fundamental scientific theory can be disproved if new evidence is presented. That's what makes it such a fascinating field."

"I never thought of it that way," she murmurs.

"As fascinating?"

"Exactly. I thought it was pretty much the opposite."

"You mean boring."

She smiles faintly. "Sorry."

"It's okay. You're not the first."

"I can't believe what you're telling me. It seems so . . . simple."

"Occam's razor." He tilts his palms as though that explains everything.

"Naturally, I have no idea what you're talking about . . . but I'll assume you covered it in class."

He nods. *"Pluralitas non est ponenda sine necessitate."*

She blinks. "Pardon?"

"It's Latin."

"No fair! I never even *took* Latin."

With a grin, he translates, "Entities should not be multiplied unnecessarily. Or, to restate the rule by complying to its own form: kiss!"

"Kiss?"

"K-I-S-S. Keep it simple, stupid!"

She can't help but laugh. "I figured sooner or later you'd come right out and call me stupid."

He laughs, too. "Hardly. In fact, you were one of my brightest students—you just chose to apply yourself in areas other than physics. And look at you now."

"Still clueless about physics," she says wryly. "So where, exactly, does Occam's razor come in?"

"For your frame of reference, in science, we apply it to uncertainty in metaphysical concepts. Basically it says that when you have competing theories, the least complicated is the most likely to be correct."

"Time travel isn't all that uncomplicated . . . is it?"

He shrugs. "Could be. It all depends on the evidence."

"You make it sound like anything, even what a person would logically believe is impossible, might be possible."

"Could be," he says again. "The thing is, Clara, I'm not just a scientist. I'm a parent. And thirty years ago, I was told that my daughter's chances of survival, based on scientific evidence, were basically nonexistent. But I prayed for a miracle." He leans over to pick up the framed photo and waves it in the air. "This is my miracle."

"Your daughter."

"Maybe Bianca just somehow managed to beat the incredible odds. The nonexistent odds. Or maybe something we can't understand or comprehend in this lifetime—some kind of energy—intervened to make this happen. Another everyday miracle. Who's to say? I just know that nothing is impossible. *Nothing.*" His voice is hoarse.

Clara nods slowly, her eyes swimming in tears, moved not just because of his daughter's inspiring story, but because she can't help thinking of Jed Landry. Jed, and all the other Glenhaven Park men who had no idea they were marching off to their deaths in the war.

"So it is possible," she tells Mr. Kershaw, "to go back in time and, maybe, change something that was supposed to happen? You know . . . save somebody's life?"

"Ah, the classic paradox." He's already shaking his head, setting the picture of his family on the tray again and leaning back in his chair, arms folded. "That scenario would seemingly violate the law of quantum mechanics that says that what you do in the present is an inevitable product of the past."

Her heart sinks. "So you can't change the past."

"There are different theories—some involving alternate universes—but my personal conclusion based on the hypothetical research that's been done at this time is that no, you can't."

"But you said yourself that nothing is impossible because science isn't absolute."

"I did. And you were paying attention. Very good."

"I don't know if it's very good, considering that I'm completely confused."

"There is very little about the possibility of time travel that isn't completely confusing, even for somebody like me."

"Which means there's absolutely no hope for somebody like me."

And no hope of going back in time to save Jed Landry.

"I wouldn't say that. You're here, aren't you? Which leads me to ask . . . *why* are you here? Why are you asking me about time travel? Researching a new movie role?"

She doesn't hesitate before responding with a concise, "Yes."

Better to lie than attempt the truth. Even now. Even with him.

"Mr. Kershaw," she says, remembering one last thing. "I have another question you can probably answer. If a person is in a moving vehicle that suddenly brakes, are they always thrown forward?"

"Of course. You're referring to the inertia of direction, which goes back to Newton's laws of motion."

At this point, she notices, he doesn't bother to ask her if she remembers Newton's laws of motion.

"So there is no way a person can be thrown backward."

"You would be thrown backward if a car suddenly accelerated."

She closes her eyes, trying to recall if there was any possible way she misinterpreted what happened on the train.

No. She distinctly recalls the screeching of the brakes as it slowed before the curve.

"Would you like me to show you a textbook that illustrates Newton's laws?" Mr. Kershaw offers.

She thanks him, but tells him that she has to get going. Her brain is too overwhelmed at this point to absorb much of anything.

"Well, anytime you need an expert on the set, you know where to find me," he says with a wink as he leads her to the door. "Except, of course, over the holidays, because I'm planning on spending every second with my daughter and her family while they're here. If I've learned anything in my life, it's that nothing is more precious than spending time with people you love. And if you've learned nothing else from me, I hope you'll learn that."

"Thank you, Mr. Kershaw." Clara stands and hugs him, this time without a hint of awkwardness. "That's one lesson that I swear I won't forget."

Chapter 11

Now what? Clara wonders, rising from the park bench, tossing the wrapper from her second hot dog into a trash can, and brushing the crumbs off her jeans.

Now she should probably go home before it starts to rain, that's what.

Above the tree line and skyscrapers at the southern edge of Central Park, she can see that the blue sky has given way to an ominous bank of clouds.

She entered the park from the West Side on a whim, needing to walk and process everything Mr. Kershaw told her. She meandered quite a considerable distance before she came across the hot dog vendor and realized she was still famished. She decided to take a break to eat and watch the skaters on Wollman Rink.

Now she heads slowly down the path leading to the southeast, leaving behind the white rink crowded with skaters.

It was a welcome diversion, and as much fun to see the professionals executing perfect twirls and jumps as it was to watch the beginners: stiff-legged preteen girls in cute outfits, wobbly husbands clinging sheepishly to their wives' hands.

Then there was the little girl who teetered over to the edge of the ice, entranced by the skilled skaters gliding by. Clara could see the longing in her eyes even from where she sat, yards away, on the bench.

"Wait, Brittany! Wait for me!" her mother shouted as she hurried to lace her own skates, but the little girl diligently ignored her.

Brittany had obviously never been on skates before, but she stepped out gamely and pushed right off, gliding across the ice, arms outstretched in elated imitation of the magnificent solo skaters . . .

Until she fell.

And put her hand to her injured mouth, took one look at the crimson smear that covered her fingers, and started screaming.

Clara watched her mother comfort her, dry her tears, blot her bloody lip.

She found herself filled with renewed longing for that kind of maternal nurturing . . . and reminded herself, again, that her mother probably can't provide it. Not in the way Clara needs, anyway—without looking at Clara with that same desolate expression she always gets whenever anybody even just mentions the word *cancer*.

Clara couldn't help but wish her mother were more like Brittany's, who coaxed the shell-shocked child right back onto the ice again with a firm but patient smile. She encouraged her daughter to start slowly this time, to stick to the edge of the rink until she found her footing, to keep her balance.

For Clara, spying on Brittany and her mother was more than a melancholy reminder of her relationship with her own mother. It was also a welcome deviation from . . .

Well, from pure panic.

Which has subsided at last, a good hour after having left Mr. Kershaw's apartment.

If everything he said is true, then she's convinced

that what happened to her on Friday morning was
no dream.

She really was back in 1941.

She knows that now, not just intellectually, but spiri-
tually. She slipped through some kind of warp or
wormhole or whatever a physicist or science fiction
writer would choose to call it, and she was instantane-
ously thrown sixty-five years into the past.

Meaning the Jed Landry she encountered was the
war hero himself, not a figment of her vibrant
imagination.

And Glenhaven Park seemed authentically vintage
not because of a set designer's magic . . . but because
it was the real deal.

Real magic.

Or, to quote Mr. Kershaw . . .

An everyday miracle.

I believe in miracles, she thinks, taking her red knit
mittens from her pocket and tucking her icy hands
into them again. *I believe in miracles.*

That's her new mantra.

Funny how all it takes is something so simple—
validation from a trusted friend, and a willingness to
suspend disbelief—to make everything fall into place.

Not everything.

She still has cancer. She's still facing it alone, along
with a dismal holiday season.

But at least I know now that I'm not crazy.

At least there's a reasonable explanation for what
happened.

Reasonable from a physicist's point of view—and
from the viewpoint of someone who chooses to believe in everyday miracles.

*Now I know that it really did happen, but I still don't
know why.*

If she wasn't meant to go back in time to make a difference—to save Jed, and Walter, and the others . . .

Well, then, why was she there at all?

Maybe she was never meant to understand that.

Or maybe, she was meant to understand, and she left before she could.

Maybe she could still find a way to understand it . . . if she just had another chance.

If I could just go back.

To 1941.

Just one more time . . . one last time.

But why? Why would she even consider doing that? It was scary enough the first time—

Only because you didn't know for sure that you could come back home.

If she were able to somehow get back to 1941 again, she would still be powerless to change anything.

Yet . . .

Mr. Kershaw himself said that science isn't absolute.

He could be wrong about the ability to change things.

What if I could save Jed Landry? What if that's the reason I was there in the first place—to warn him?

What if I had my chance to do that . . .

And I ran away.

She shivers, arms folded, head bent as she walks, huddled as much against the chill from within as from the wind that rustles the dry leaves clinging to a low branch.

Yes, she ran away. She ran because she was frightened. Scared out of her mind.

And who wouldn't be? She stepped off the train into 1941, for God's sake. That's enough of a shock to freak out anyone.

But the shock of it wasn't the only reason she bolted.

It was because I was afraid for my life.

I was stuck in the past with no treatment for my disease, and staying there would have meant dying.

I was worried I'd never get back . . .

But you did.

Yes. She did. All she had to do was get on the train, and she was somehow able to travel right back through that inexplicable portal to the present.

Her conversation with Mr. Kershaw echoes in her mind:

The Wright brothers came along and figured out how to harness energy . . .

So you're saying that scientifically, time travel isn't impossible . . .

Theoretically, it isn't impossible. Scientifically, it may not be possible yet.

All we need to do is harness energy.

She said it . . . and he didn't argue. It was all about physics and energy.

Okay, not *all*. He did dispute that.

Yet maybe it isn't all that complicated. Not when you add to the equation some greater energy, some greater power, than she—than anyone—can possibly comprehend.

It happened. To her.

Meaning it's potentially there. The energy.

She knows it exists—that it provided the final component needed to propel her to the past . . . and then back again.

And now that you know that you can come home . . .

What's stopping you from going back?

*   *   *

Jed has just dispatched the last of the lunchtime rush customers when he spots a familiar blue Packard pulling into a diagonal parking space beyond the plate glass storefront.

Arnold Wilkens climbs out and heads across the sidewalk toward the five-and-dime, wearing a heavy overcoat and a cap with fur earflaps.

Maisie isn't with him, to Jed's relief. He isn't in the mood for her. His temper has been short as it is today, ever since he arrived back from the city to open the store forty-five minutes late and found Alice waiting out front.

She had the nerve to complain about the cold and his absence.

In response, Jed fired her on the spot without the slightest qualm.

Watching her storm off down the street, he expected to feel a hint of remorse, but he felt only relief.

Even now, hours later, his only regret is that he's had to man the store single-handedly once again. He's been inundated with Christmas shoppers, which is a good thing, businesswise. But today, Jed would much prefer to be left alone to figure out what he's going to do about Clara. Instead, he's spent the day forcing small talk and smiles, filling requests and ringing up purchases.

Then again, he knows *what* to do about Clara.

He just doesn't know *when* he can possibly bring himself to do it.

He can't help but feel a perhaps ill-advised urge to hold out just a little longer before going to the police.

Perhaps *ill-advised*?

What is going on with you, Jed?

Arnold asks precisely the same question the moment he enters the store.

"What do you mean?" Jed asks, striding toward the soda fountain.

Arnold is right on his heels. "Maisie said you showed up at our door in the middle of the night all wild-eyed and crazy. She said you wanted our car."

"I wanted to borrow your car . . . and it wasn't the middle of the night. It was ten o'clock, and I figured you'd be up and she'd be in bed."

"She never sleeps," Arnold informs him gloomily. "She just walks the house, hour after hour, like some kind of . . ."

"Hideous spook?" Jed supplies, recalling Maisie's appearance when she answered the door.

Arnold blinks agreeably behind his thick lenses. "I was going to say night watchman, but . . . yes, hideous spook will suffice. And it's impossible for me to get any sleep—she keeps poking me to tell me that she's uncomfortable, or that she thinks this is it, she's in labor . . . and she never is."

"Well, sooner or later she will be," Jed promises, as though he knows the slightest thing about such matters. "Any day now, the baby will be here, and things will be back to normal, and you'll be able to get plenty of sleep."

"I guess you're right. As I always say . . ."

Chiming in with Arnold, Jed choruses, "Sometimes the longest way round is the nearest way home."

Then he pops the caps off two bottles of Coca-Cola and hands one to Arnold.

"Thanks." Arnold gulps some Coke and suppresses a burp.

"Is Maisie still sure the baby's going to be a girl?"

"So sure she told me I can name it if it happens to be a boy."

Jed nods knowingly. "She's sure all right."

"So . . . why did you need to borrow my car last night?"

"Because the DeSoto has a flat, and I had an errand to run in the city."

"What kind of errand?"

"You know. Just . . . business." Jed takes a deep swig of his own Coke, wishing he had never gone to the Wilkens house last night.

"What kind of business?"

"Cripes, Arnold, who are you, Dick Tracy?"

Dick Tracy . . .

He finds himself thinking again of the little Japanese boy at Clara's supposed address. Isamu.

"Come on, Jed," Arnold says wearily, "give a fella a break. My whole life is columns of numbers and a wife who looks like she stepped out of . . ."

"A horror film?"

"I was going to say a magazine ad for maternity clothing, but horror film will suffice. Cigarette?" he asks, taking a pack from his pocket and offering it to Jed.

"No, thanks."

He watches Arnold light up, then tuck the pack and matches away again.

Around the cigarette clutched between his teeth, Arnold says, "Come on, humor me, won't you, Jed?"

"I really don't want a cigarette, Arnold." He's never been much of a smoker. Not cigarettes, anyway.

He prefers a pipe. He has a couple of nice ones that used to belong to his father. Whenever he lights one, the pungent sweetness of the tobacco seems to carry him back to happier times.

"I didn't mean humor me by having a cigarette." Arnold exhales a stream of smoke from his nostrils. "I mean tell me about your mysterious mission. Did it have anything to do with that city gal you were chasing down Main Street the other day?"

Here we go again, Jed thinks. "Where'd you hear that?"

"Maisie told me—and she heard it from Betty Godfrey the first time, but it's all over town now. Who is she?"

"I don't know," Jed admits, and sets his half-empty bottle on the counter. "Say, Arnold, can I show you something?"

As the Lexington Avenue express pulls into Grand Central Station on its southbound journey toward Greenwich Village, Clara has every intention of staying on the subway.

Fourteenth Street—her home station—is the very next stop. The train isn't all that crowded; she even managed to get a seat.

Why, then, as the doors rattle open, does she find herself standing? Striding purposefully toward the exit?

What is she doing stepping out onto the platform with all the hell-bent bravado of feisty little Brittany back at the rink?

Yeah, and look what happened to her.

She got hurt . . .

But then she gave it another shot, Clara remembers. She dried her tears and she set out on the ice again, knowing she might take another nasty spill. She allowed her mother to coax her out because she so obviously wanted to glide across the rink with the wind in her face, and she realized that it was possible.

It's almost as though Clara's legs have taken on a life of their own, propelling her to the top of the stairs, then on up the ramp marked TO METRO-NORTH TRAINS.

She comes across a monitor listing northbound trains on the Harlem line and stops to check it. Just because . . .

Well, she doesn't really know why.

She just knows that she has to.

Wow. What a coincidence.

The next departure for Glenhaven Park is in less than five minutes from a distant track on the upper level.

If it weren't leaving for, say, another hour, she wouldn't hang around Grand Central waiting. She would talk herself out of this ridiculous impulse—at least for today.

Or, if it was leaving in the next sixty seconds, she'd realize she couldn't possibly make it, and, again, forget the whole thing. At least for today.

But it's leaving in five minutes, and . . . well, why not today?

Five minutes.

The upper level.

It's now or never.

She'll have to run if she wants to make it . . .

I do, she realizes all at once. *I want to make it.*

I have to make it.

Her legs are already back in action, her whole body oddly tingling again as she hurtles herself up the stairs, across the main terminal toward the track . . . and Glenhaven Park . . .

And, with any luck at all . . .

Pleasepleasepleasepleaseplease . . .

1941 and Jed Landry.

Jed has second thoughts about showing Arnold Clara's belongings as he leads the way to the back storage room, but it's too late now.

His friend's curiosity has been whetted. And anyway, it will be prudent to get a second opinion . . . won't it?

Maybe. Or it might be better to just keep this whole thing to yourself.

Without voicing his suspicions about Clara, he shows Arnold the handbag and its contents, the suitcase and its contents. Not trusting Doris not to snoop, he brought it to the store.

Arnold does a lot of low whistling and saying, "Jeepers creepers!"

He is, of course, particularly interested in the tiny transmitter. At least, in what Jed assumes is a transmitter. Because . . .

Well, what else can it possibly be?

He watches his friend turn it over and over in one hand, inspecting it, as he puffs away on the cigarette he holds in the other.

"What do you think?" Jed asks at last, and holds his breath for the reply.

"Golly, Jed . . . I think she's a Nazi spy, that's what I think. And her code name is Agent Jezibel."

"I just don't buy it," Jed hears himself saying. "She can't be a Nazi."

"Well"—Arnold gestures at the photo card—"she sure doesn't look like a Jap."

"No, but—" Jed breaks off, not wanting to go there.

"But what?"

Jed is reluctant to tell him about the Japanese mother and son who live at Clara's supposed address.

Yet, the more he thinks about it, the more he wonders if they were covering for her, all of them working for the Japanese government.

"Jed?" Arnold prods.

"You're right. She might be a spy."

"Might be? If she isn't, then what is this?" Arnold waves the silver device at him. Then, lowering his voice to a whisper, he adds, "For all we know, the Nazis could be listening to us right this second."

"Why would they want to listen to *us*?"

"Maybe they think we know government secrets."

Jed shakes his head. "I doubt that, Arnold."

Still . . .

What if that thing is some kind of transmitter and . . .

And Clara herself is listening?

He never thought of that.

"You've got to take this stuff right to the police," Arnold is saying in a stage whisper as he stubs out his cigarette in an ashtray Jed hands him. "Or—wait. The FBI. That's who you should go to. They handle Nazi spies."

"You're right. I'll do that," he promises distractedly, wishing Arnold would leave.

He has an idea.

An outlandish idea, to be sure.

But now that it's stuck in his head . . .

Beyond the rain-spattered window of the Metro-North railroad car, the urban landscapes of Harlem and the Bronx have long since given way to the low skyline and bare treetops of suburbia.

"Station stop . . . Bedford Hills," proclaims a disembodied electronic voice as the doors glide open.

Just a few more minutes to go. Clara shifts nervously in her double seat, relieved that the chatty female passenger who was sitting beside her got off the train in Chappaqua a few stops earlier. Clara wanted only to stare out the window and prepare herself for whatever may—or may not—happen.

She might arrive in Glenhaven Park to see a condo complex, an A&P supermarket . . . and, in the center of the green, the bronze statue commemorating the eleven local sons killed on D-Day.

Or she might find woods where the condos should be, a Victorian mansion on the supermarket site, a tremendous maple tree growing in the statue's future spot . . .

And Landry's Five-and-Dime across the way . . .

And Jed, alive and well, in 1941.

One thing is certain: she's in for an emotional upheaval in either case.

Too restless to sit, she stands and moves to the wide aisle between the two sets of exit doors on either side of the car.

Please let it happen, she pleads silently, clinging tightly to a metal pole.

Returning to the storage room after Arnold has gone, Jed picks up the transmitter again.

For a dubious moment, he just looks at it.

Then he lifts it to his lips.

"Clara . . . Clara, can you hear me?" he asks, feeling slightly foolish, yet at the same time slightly exhilarated by the mere notion that she might be out there somewhere . . . *listening.*

"Clara, hello—Clara?"

"Station stop . . . Katonah."

Nearing the end of the line, only a smattering of seats are filled. No one is paying the least bit of attention to Clara, other than the flirtatious young conductor.

"Getting off at this stop?" he asks as the doors open.

"The next one."

"Tired of sitting, huh?"

She nods distractedly.

She can't sit down. Nor can she face forward.

Everything has to be just as it was the first time it happened.

Though of course, certain key elements are missing.

This is a sleek, modern commuter train as opposed to the vintage car in which Clara was riding that day.

And she herself is still wearing jeans, sneakers, and a down jacket: distinctly twenty-first century clothing.

But maybe none of that is relevant.

Maybe, if she keeps trying to put herself in a 1940s frame of mind, just as she was doing on Friday morning, the contemporary trappings won't matter.

This time, however, she isn't concentrating on becoming the fictional Violet.

This time, she's just Clara . . . willing herself back to 1941, and Jed Landry.

Please, take me back.

Beyond the window, she notices, the familiar low stone wall has materialized, running alongside the track bed.

Please take me back.

They're passing the wooden signpost now.

WELCOME TO GLENHAVEN PARK.

Please take me back . . .

"If you can hear me . . . you have to come back. I need to talk to you. Please, Clara. Please come back."

Jed pauses, listening, half-expecting a reply.

Not a sound: the room is hushed.

He closes his eyes, willing the impossible.

"Please come back, Clara. If you can hear me . . . Please come back."

*   *   *

Please take me back . . .

The track is starting to curve; the train slows ever so slightly.

Please take me back.

Clara closes her eyes to block out the rows of blue vinyl upholstered seats, the glare of the overhead lights, the wide, modern windows.

Please take me back.

She focuses every bit of her concentration on 1941.

Please take me back.

Her body is beginning to tingle as if from an electric current.

Please take me back.

And . . . there seems to be a far-off humming in her ears.

Please take me back . . .

"Please come back, Clara . . . "

She can't hear you. This is crazy.

Yet he can't seem to make himself stop.

"Please come back . . ."

Jed pauses to listen.

Do you honestly think she's going to answer you?

No, he honestly doesn't.

So there is no surprise when he can hear only the beating of his own heart . . . then, at a great distance, the far-off whistle of a train making its approach to the depot.

No other sound. Not even a crackle of interference from the transmitter—if that's what it is.

Put it away and get back to work now.

You know you're not going to hear her voice.

"Please come back, Clara," he persists ludicrously,

ears trained on the stillness, until he realizes that it is gradually broken by a distant rumbling.

"Please come back, Clara . . ."

The train. He looks at his watch. It comes through every day at this time. Nothing unusual about the train . . .

Unless . . .

Unless Clara is on it.

Chapter 12

"Station stop . . . Glenhaven Park. Glenhaven Park.
Please watch your step as you leave," the conductor
calls.

Clara's eyes snap open.

Conductor?

Yes. The station announcement was just made by a
living human, as opposed to a robotic recording.

Through a haze of cigarette smoke—*cigarette
smoke!* she marvels with the wonder of George Bailey
discovering Zuzu's petals—she spots a uniformed conductor coming down the aisle.

"Glenhaven Park! Next stop!"

He isn't the same conductor who just asked her if
she was getting off the train.

No, and Clara sees that on either side of the aisle,
the seats are occupied by women in sleek hats and
red lipstick and shoulder pads, men in baggy suits and
fedoras, or military uniforms . . .

Literally in the blink of an eye, the seats have become mohair and the lighting fixtures are bare bulbs
and the people are smoking and . . .

And the train is stopping and the door is opening
and . . .

And . . .

How did this happen?

Clara stands frozen for just another moment, pondering the miracle.

Then she hurtles herself forward, toward the door, down the steps, onto the platform . . .

A *wooden* platform.

A wooden platform and a wooden depot house and on the nearest wall, someone has drawn a line with an odd little caricature of a man's eyes peering above it, and the words KILROY WAS HERE.

And it isn't raining; the sky is a study in whitish-purplish-gray above a snowy landscape. It's cold, much colder than it was in the city, where she stashed her red hat and mittens in the zippered pockets of her down jacket.

It feels different, here. It feels . . .

Like 1941.

Still, she isn't sure . . .

Not even when she looks toward the hills for the condominium complex and finds only woods—nor when she looks for the supermarket and finds a Victorian mansion . . .

Maybe I'm hallucinating, or dreaming, or having an episode, or . . .

She walks slowly across the empty platform and down the steps, her rubber-soled sneakers making a thumping, hollow sound on the snow-coated boards.

The familiar stretch of village green and Main Street await.

Even from here, she can see the old-fashioned houses and people and cars . . .

But this might not be real.

It might just be in my head.

It might just be that I want it so badly that—

"Clara!"

She whirls around in the direction of the voice . . .

And there he is.

Jed Landry, running coatless toward the depot, calling her name.

That's when she knows . . .

It's real.

Clara is running—but this time, she isn't fleeing from Jed.

She's running toward him.

That, to him, is easily as astounding as having seen her materialize on the platform just now, almost as if he willed her here.

That isn't the case, of course. He knows that she came to town in the regular way; he witnessed her stepping off the train from down the block just as he was racing toward the station on a ridiculous, glorious whim.

I must look like a crazy fool.

He can feel people turning to watch him as he sprints past and knows that he's creating another spectacle for the whole town to gossip about, but he doesn't care. He doesn't care if he winds up in Hedda Hopper's column tomorrow.

All he cares about is Clara.

He wonders, as he covers the last twenty yards between them, what he should do when he gets to her.

It would seem rather silly to stop short, walk up, and shake hands.

Yet it wouldn't be right, either, to seize her and kiss her as though she's his long lost-love . . .

Would it?

Who knows?

Who cares?

Whatever happens, happens, he tells himself, racing toward the finish line with a final, elated burst of energy.

In every wishful Clara scenario he's created these last two days, never did he imagine that she would launch herself fervently into his arms.

Yet that's exactly what happens when they reach each other.

"Jed, I can't believe it." She encircles his neck in an embrace and he can feel her breath warm against his skin.

"What are you doing here?" he asks in wonder, holding her close, not caring who or what she really is. "Did you hear me calling you?"

"Calling me?" she echoes.

"Never mind," he says quickly, realizing that she either doesn't know what he's talking about—or isn't ready to admit anything about the transmitter. "I just can't believe you're really here."

Her face is buried against his neck just above the collar of his dress shirt, her skin tantalizingly warm against his. "I had to come back."

"For your bags," he remembers, pulling up to look at her.

"My bags . . . ?"

"Your suitcase, your pocketbook . . ."

Your spy transmitter . . .

Though now that she's here, the word *spy* is utterly incongruous.

Clara McCallum, if that's her real name, may be an enigma, but whatever she's hiding can't possibly mean him—or anyone—any harm.

"Oh, my bags . . . I almost forgot." She smiles.

That's when he notices . . . she looks so different.

Everything about her . . . her face . . . her hair . . . her clothes . . .

Her lashes, her lips, her skin are startlingly free of cosmetics. She radiates a simple, wholesome beauty, her face framed by a tumble of unfettered waves that beg his fingers.

Gone are the trim, prim suit, the silk stockings, the fashionably high platform sandals. Her figure is obliterated by some kind of quilted, satiny red parka. With it, she wears long, sadly worn, uncuffed dungarees, and thick-soled, chunky white shoes that appear to be made of rubber and leather.

"I know what you're thinking," she says softly, and he looks up to see her watching his face. "No, wait . . . I really don't know what you're thinking. But I can imagine."

He smiles faintly, trying not to look down at her curious clothing again. "I was just . . ." He trails off, not wanting to insult her.

"Wondering what I'm wearing?" She smiles back, but only with her mouth.

He tries to decipher her strange expression before a gust of wind blows her hair across her face, obliterating it.

"It doesn't matter what you're wearing," he tells her truthfully, watching her duck her head, then toss it.

She's trying to get the hair out of her eyes, he realizes, *and she doesn't want to let go of me to do it.*

He doesn't want to let go of her, either. He wants to hold her closer—wants more than that.

"It *does* matter what I'm wearing," she's protesting. "I look ridiculous."

"No. You look beautiful." Giving in to temptation,

he reaches down and brushes the stubborn strands away from her face. Her hair is spun sugar in his fingers.

"But . . . I can't go around looking like this."

"Yes, you can. All that matters is that you're here."

"You know what? That's all that matters to me right now, too."

She looks into his eyes, and he gets the sense that she wants to tell him something else.

But instead of saying another word, she stands up on her tiptoes and, incredibly, brushes his lips with her own.

The contact is feathery-swift: angel's wings. A kiss as gossamer as the soft strands of hair still draped in Jed's fingers.

"I'm sorry, I didn't mean to—"

"No." Before she can pull away, Jed's mouth instinctively claims hers with a hunger he hadn't known he possessed, a hunger that can't possibly be sated with one brazen kiss.

Miraculously, Clara doesn't stop him. Her mouth opens against his and he deepens the kiss, daring to allow his tongue to caress hers for a few tantalizing seconds until he remembers where they are: in the middle of Main Street, in broad daylight . . .

Undoubtedly with an audience.

Summoning a supreme tide of willpower, Jed manages to break the kiss. For her sake. He can just imagine what people will say about her.

He opens his eyes reluctantly, uncertain what he'll find.

One glance at Clara's face, flushed with the heat of requited passion, and . . .

To hell with what people think or say.

Nearly consumed by the powerful, primal urge to

kiss her again, it's all he can do to find his voice. He wants to ask her if he's dreaming. But if this were a dream, they would be alone together, away from prying eyes.

He reluctantly allows the downy strands of her hair to fall away from his grasp at last, fighting the urge to entwine his entire hand in that lustrous mane and kiss her again.

"I can't believe you're really here, Clara."

"I can't, either." Again, the flicker of an inscrutable expression in her gaze.

"I honestly didn't think I'd ever see you again."

"I didn't, either. And it wasn't easy for me to get back here, but . . . I had to find a way."

"What do you mean? Why was it so hard for you to get here?"

She hesitates. Shrugs.

Then she breaks eye contact, lowering her gaze.

In that moment, for Jed, the real world begins to intrude.

He hears a car door slam in the distance, tires crunching along the snowy pavement, faint swing music on a far-off radio, the gleeful shouts of children sledding on the hill behind the redbrick elementary school down the block.

Though he doesn't dare to turn his head, he can feel the stares of curious bystanders scorching him like hot rays on a July beach.

He and Clara can't just stand indefinitely on the street, talking . . . kissing.

"Can you come back to the store with me?" he asks, belatedly remembering that he dashed out the door without a moment's hesitation, thus recklessly abandoning his business for the second time this week.

He braces himself for her to say no.

Or that she'll come just to pick up her things before catching the next train back to the city.

But when she looks up at him again, she's smiling.

In a voice that rings almost serene to his ears, she replies, "Of course."

Jed is silent as they walk toward the five-and-dime.

Clara is grateful for the chance to collect her thoughts.

She's actually done it!

She's successfully transported herself back to 1941, propelled by a force more powerful than many times the magnitude of the sun's cumulative energy . . .

An energy that could only have come from within.

And in the end, is that really so surprising? Can science ever possibly begin to interpret the potency of pure human emotion?

Occam's razor. The simplest explanation.

I needed to be here, for him, she thinks, glancing over at Jed Landry. *And so I am.*

This time, knowing that she's really traveled back in time, she pays more attention to the details. This is what the world was really like sixty-five years ago.

No, this *is* the world, sixty-five years ago.

Eyes wide with exhilarated wonder, she takes in the oversized cars tooling along the avenue, the quaint stores with their deco-lettered signage, the passersby who look as though they just stepped out of a Frank Capra movie . . .

And who, she can't help but acknowledge, are looking at her as though she just stepped out of a spaceship.

They can't possibly suspect anything, she assures herself.

After all, even Jed doesn't seem suspicious.

Yet she keeps catching people staring at her, far more politely and surreptitiously than they do in Clara's century—but still staring.

I have to do something about these clothes.

And she will. First chance she gets. Jed said he has her bag; there must be something in it that she can wear.

They've reached the five-and-dime.

Jed closes the door firmly behind them, shutting out the outside world at last.

If he took her in his arms again right here and now, Clara wouldn't stop him.

But he just clears his throat and says, "Here we are."

Yes, here they are. Clara looks around at the tin ceiling, the worn wooden floor, the vintage merchandise, drinking it all in like a welcoming cup of steaming cocoa.

On a nearby table, she spots a snow globe with a smiling, dark-haired angel inside. Picking it up, she shakes it and a blizzard erupts beyond the glass, momentarily obscuring the angel.

"Why is this marked *as is*?" she asks Jed, wishing she could add it to her own collection of brunette angels.

"Because her wing is broken and the glass is cracked. See?"

She peers at the globe and spots the angel's wounded wing tip. "Yes, but you can barely see it. I would buy this in a heartbeat."

Yes, because she's scarred, just like me. And . . .

"She's all alone in there," Clara notices. "All the other snow globes have more than one angel." And, of course, they all have golden hair.

"That's because she's special. And this globe is

musical . . . see?" Jed takes it from her and winds a key in the bottom.

Clara smiles, recognizing the delicate melody: "Hark the Herald Angels Sing."

Too bad she doesn't have 1940s currency in her pocket. If she did, she'd buy the snow globe to display with her angels on the mantel back home.

Carefully setting it back on the table, Jed returns his attention to Clara, eyeing her ski parka with renewed ambivalence.

"Can I take your . . . uh, coat?" Clearly, he uses the term loosely.

Hmm. What is she wearing underneath it?

It takes her a moment to remember: it's her old hooded Yankees sweatshirt—emblazoned with the Red Sox and Yankees insignias and the words AMERICAN LEAGUE CHAMPIONSHIP SERIES 2004. She clears her throat. "I'll keep my coat on for now, thanks."

He looks surprised. "Are you sure?"

Oh, trust me, I'm positive.

She simply nods, wondering how long she can get away with this.

Not just keeping her coat on.

This whole . . . charade. How long before he figures out that she's not just a regular 1940s gal dropping by for a visit?

Should she break the truth to him?

How would she even begin?

If she's going to save him—and she still has no clue whether that is even possible—she may at some point need to tell him, in a calm, straightforward way, what she knows and how she knows it.

Right. And then he will very calmly place a straightforward call to the local psychiatric hospital.

But right now, he isn't looking at her as though he

thinks she's crazy. He's taken a step closer, looking at her as though he's thinking pretty much the same thing she was a moment ago: that he wouldn't be opposed to taking her into his arms again and—

"Hello, Jed," trills a voice.

A woman's head, wearing a brimmed hat, pops out from behind a shelf at the back of the store.

"Oh, hello, Mrs. Shelton. I didn't realize anyone was in here."

"I came in a few minutes ago. I thought you must be back in the stockroom," the customer informs him, flicking a curious gaze over Clara. Her eyebrows rise visibly as she takes in the outfit and hairstyle—*or rather,* Clara realizes, *the lack of both.*

"Can I help you find something?" Jed asks politely.

"I was just looking for a chenille bed jacket for my sister Gertrude as a Christmas gift." Her eyes remain fastened disapprovingly on Clara. "But I don't see any here."

"We have quite a few bed jackets in stock." Jed crosses the floor to help her, shooting an apologetic glance over his shoulder.

Clara shrugs to show him that it's all right.

Of course, it isn't. Why did that woman have to pop up just as Jed was going to kiss her again?

Why? Because this is a dime store, not a bedroom. And you're not here to lust after Jed Landry, you're here to figure out if you can save his life, remember?

Mr. Kershaw might not believe that's possible, but there are plenty of physicists who probably wouldn't believe any of this is possible.

But what if . . .

No. It's real. You know it's real.

Still, as soon as Jed disappears behind a clothing rack with Mrs. Shelton, Clara strides over to the display of newspapers on the counter. She wants to check the date, just to be absolutely sure.

And . . .

There it is.

Wednesday, December 3, 1941.

A little thrill shoots through her at this latest validation that she really is here . . . *not,* she reminds herself again, *that there was any lingering doubt.*

1941 is real, and Jed is real, and, for that matter, so is the attraction she thought she sensed from the moment they first met.

But what good is that going to do either of us?

On that dark thought, a group of chattering schoolboys enter the store from the street, obviously fresh from the last bell. They're wearing caps and wool coats, carrying lunch pails and their books bound by straps slung over their shoulders.

"Say, ma'am, do you have any pop gums?" the tallest and boldest of the boys asks, and to Clara's relief, he appears completely oblivious to her attire.

Okay, then, what's a pop gum? Some kind of candy? Bubble gum?

She quickly surveys the row of labeled glass canisters on the counter. Peppermint sticks, lollipops, bubble gum, licorice . . .

Clara glances over her shoulder.

"What are you doing?" the ringleader kid asks in a tone that makes Clara fairly certain that she shouldn't be looking for pop gums amidst the penny candy jars.

"What was it that you asked for again?"

"Popguns."

"Pop *guns*?" she echoes, just to be sure.

Nodding, the boys exchange glances.

Then she catches one of them looking down at her

right sneaker as though he's never seen such a thing
before . . . and is about to ask what it is.

"Hang on a second, um . . . fellas," she inserts stra-
tegically, lest anyone dare suspect that she's not completely at home here in 1941, where children are
apparently free to roam the streets in search of weap-
ons. "I'll go check."

Clara slips to the back of the store, where she finds
Jed holding up a pale pink chenille bed jacket for Mrs.
Shelton's perusal.

"Excuse me . . . sorry to interrupt, but there's a
group of boys up there who want to buy popguns."

"Can you do me a favor and show them where they
are?" Jed asks.

"I can . . . if you tell *me* where they are." Not to
mention *what* they are.

"Oh—past the dolls, in the bin next to the spinning
tops, on the shelf below the board games on the
side wall."

Clara nods. All right, so they're talking *toy* guns,
here. You learn something new every . . . *second*.

"Does she work here?" Mrs. Shelton asks in
surprise.

Without missing a beat, Jed says firmly, "Of course
she works here. What did you think?"

Mrs. Shelton sputters some kind of reply meant to
indicate that she knew all along that Clara was an
employee . . .

When in reality, Clara thinks, amused, *she took one
look at me and figured I was either a charity case or a
refugee from the house of ill repute.*

"Would you like me to finish straightening the
Christmas card display after I help the boys, Mr.
Landry?" she asks Jed for good measure.

After all, she's a trained actress. She can certainly play this store clerk role without much effort.

"That would be swell, thanks, Miss McCallum."

As she turns on her heel, Jed sneaks a wink at her.

Her stomach does a series of Olympic-caliber acrobatics at the unexpected intimacy of it.

What a shame that nobody winks anymore, she finds herself lamenting as she returns to the front of the store.

Then again, it might not be quite so sexy back where she comes from. She tries to envision a modern guy—a city guy—say, Jason—winking at her. She promptly concludes that the gesture would have a considerable cheese factor.

But here in the small-town past, winking is sexy.

Especially when Jed Landry's doing it.

Yes, his wink is sexy . . . and his kiss was even sexier.

She still can't quite believe he actually kissed her. Then again . . .

You're the one who started it, she reminds herself. *You kissed him first. What did you expect?*

She didn't expect anything because she didn't exactly plan it. It just happened.

Besides, that was a happy-to-see-you-again peck. Never in her wildest dreams did she expect to find herself in Jed's arms, being passionately devoured.

All right . . . maybe in her *wildest* dreams.

But for all she knew when she first heard him calling her name, Jed was running toward her to chew her out for abandoning him at the depot with her luggage the other day. Yes, he could very well have been angry—or at the very least, seriously annoyed.

So what did she do? She threw herself at him and kissed him.

She couldn't help herself. It felt right.

At the time, anyway.

What about now? What about him?

Does he think it was presumptuous of her?

Probably. It's unlikely that women go around passionately throwing themselves at men they barely know here in 1941.

She was just so overwhelmed by joyous relief to see him again, after all that's gone on since she left here.

ANOTHER LOCAL MAN CONFIRMED LOST IN EUROPE

She pushes the horrifying newspaper headline out of her mind, replacing it with another memory of kissing Jed.

Not the chaste kiss she gave him—no, the one that came after.

That's the one that counts, because it confirms that the emotion she felt when she first saw him again was—*is*—mutual.

Nobody has ever kissed her that way—not even in her soap opera era, when unbridled passion was the order of many days on the set.

But then, her leading men were just acting.

Jed wasn't. Somehow, she's sure of that.

What if nobody ever kisses her that way again?

After all, she'll be mutilated after her surgery . . .

Oh, come on, Clara, how can you be so superficial? Do you really believe no worthwhile man will ever want you again just because of an imperfect breast?

Not intellectually.

Yet when she looks into her future, she can't fathom intimacy: baring herself, ravaged body and shaken soul, to anyone.

Somehow she knows that it's going to take her a long, long time to find her way back into a relationship . . . if she ever does.

So it was worth coming all the way back just for one amazing kiss from Jed Landry—*not that it's the main reason you're here,* Clara reminds herself as she returns to the schoolboy posse.

"All right, follow me, fellas."

She leads the way over to the toy section, where she checks out the stack of board games on the nearby shelf while the boys rummage through the bin.

In addition to chess and checkers sets, she's surprised to see some of the same games that are popular today: Monopoly, Sorry, Parcheesi.

There are also quite a few that apparently never caught on, including one particularly lame one called Bunny Rabbit, in a pastel box. Kids in 1941 were more easily entertained, by the looks of it.

Clara pictures the big Toys "R" Us store in Union Square, with its aisles of games stacked floor to ceiling. And what about electronic games: Game Boy and PlayStation and Xbox?

Watching these unspoiled 1940s kids laboring over which no-frills wooden popgun to choose, Clara can't help but feel a twinge of longing for simpler times.

Maybe I shouldn't go back home again, she thinks.

Maybe I should just forget about my real life and hang out here and kiss Jed Landry, she thinks. *Forever.*

That tantalizing prospect lasts all of an instant.

I'd rather live in his world . . . than live without him . . . in mine.

No.

She has to go back.

She has to have surgery, and chemo . . .

And Jed won't be here for very much longer, anyway, she reminds herself . . . only to be swept by a surge of sorrow.

You have to save him.

Even if you can't stay here with him, you have to save his life.

She can't bear the thought of anything happening to him. Now that he's kissed her, now that she could be falling in—

No. No way.

I am not in love with him. I barely know him. He doesn't even exist where I come from.

So loving him is absolutely out of the question.

I just can't let him die.

There must be a way to save him.

And she can't go home until she figures out what it is.

Chapter 13

"Miss?" one of the boys asks, and Clara sees that he's holding out a quarter.

The others are digging through their pockets for the coins to pay for their popguns.

"It'll be just a minute before Mr. Landry can ring you up."

That announcement is met with a deafening series of protests.

"It's all right," Jed calls. "Take the money, Clara, and make change at the register. I've got my hands full here."

Clara can't help but feel like a bona fide sales clerk as she handles the flurry of purchases, marveling that a few cents can actually buy something and a quarter can get change. For that matter, a dime can get change.

In this world, pennies count. In Clara's world, people—like Jason—vacuum them up and never think twice about it.

The boys head for the exit, popguns in hand, obviously on their way to do battle with a rival posse.

A police officer on his way into the store holds the door open for them, greeting most of them by name before sauntering in.

He's probably about thirty, but he looks, Clara notices in amusement, like a little boy in costume. He's scrawny, and can't be more than five-foot four, with a freckled complexion, sandy brows and lashes, and a blond brush cut barely visible beneath his cap.

His eyes narrow the instant he spots Clara standing behind the register, and miraculously, he transforms into a formidable authority figure.

I have to find a way to change out of these clothes, she tells herself. She's attracting far too much attention this way.

"Good afternoon, miss," the officer says politely, though his gaze is anything but friendly. "Is Jed around?"

"He's helping a customer."

"He is, is he?" He sounds skeptical.

She notices then that the man's hand strays to his belt . . . and that he's got his fingers resting on his gun.

Does he think I'm robbing the place or something?

Before she can assure him that she's no criminal, Jed materializes at her side.

"Hello there, Pete," he says with the easy smile of a longtime acquaintance. "How's that new puppy of yours?"

"He's doing just fine, Jed." The officer's fingers are still on his gun, his wary gaze fastened on Clara despite the fact that Jed obviously doesn't think she's a robber.

Why?

The cop doesn't appear to be questioning her sense of fashion. Nor is he looking at her out of idle curiosity. And he certainly doesn't recognize her from *One Life to Live.*

So what is it?

Is it a power thing? Does he try to overcompensate for his diminutive build by playing tough cop? Or is this something more . . . personal? Something that involves Clara?

"What can we do for you today, Pete?" Jed is the picture of casual as he leans against the counter, positioning himself between Clara and the police officer. She can't help but sense that it's a deliberate move. Deliberate . . . and protective?

What is going on here?

"I just got a call from Maisie Wilkens, Jed."

Maisie Wilkens? Clara wonders if she could be any relation to Denton Wilkens. Come to think of it, Denton is due to make his entrance into the local world in just a few days.

She can't help but marvel at the irony that she could ostensibly stick around here long enough to change his diapers.

"Maisie Wilkens is completely off her nut," Jed announces with conviction and a tight-sounding laugh. "Arnold said she keeps imagining that she's going into labor . . . imagining all sorts of ridiculous things, really."

Going into labor?

Whoa. Maisie Wilkens could very well be Denton's mother.

In fact, she must be. This is a small town; how many women named Wilkens could possibly be on the verge of giving birth around here?

"It's gotten so bad," Jed goes on, his voice an unnatural register higher, "that Arnold has been calling her Crazy Maisie. That's how wild her imagination is these days."

Clara's momentary amusement—and revulsion—at the idea of Crazy Maisie and newborn Denton in diapers evaporate when she sees that Pete is still fixated on her.

To Jed, he says brusquely, "I wondered if I could

talk to you about something for a few minutes, Jed. In private, since I see you've got . . . company," he adds, acknowledging Clara again with a nod and a look that's anything but cordial.

"Oh, this isn't company," Jed corrects him, a slight waver in his voice. "This is Clara McCallum, my new clerk. Clara, this is Pete Kavinski, an old school pal of mine."

"It's nice to meet you . . . officer." She extends her hand.

Pretending not to see it, Pete tells Jed, "I didn't know you hired a new clerk."

Is it strictly her imagination, or is there some dark undercurrent passing between the two men?

"Well, I usually don't run these things by you, Pete," Jed replies with a grin. But Clara can see that it's forced; the strain in his jaw muscles is plainly visible.

"What happened to the gal you had working here the other day? The one who helped me pick out a leash for Sparky?"

"Alice? I had to let her go."

"Why is that? She was helpful. Friendly, too."

"She was . . . when she bothered to show up."

"I see. And you just happened to come along and take her place?" The question is directed at Clara, with undue emphasis on the word *you*. Clearly, this is an official interrogation.

Okay. Whatever.

You're an actress. Play your role, and don't let his attitude throw you.

"I saw the *Help Wanted* sign in the window," she explains, "so I came in to fill out an application."

"That's funny. I didn't see a *Help Wanted* sign in the window."

"Well, I took it down," Jed says logically.

But he's growing more nervous by the second. She can hear it in his voice, see it in his clenched hands.

Why? What's going on here?

Clara is half-convinced that this pint-sized cop likes to throw his weight around, creating drama in a small town where there can't be any crime to speak of.

Yet she can't help but wonder if there might not be something else . . .

Probably something that has nothing to do with me, she assures herself, *even though it sure feels like it does.*

"Jed, I really need to have a word with you," Pete persists, just as Mrs. Shelton calls out from down the aisle.

"Mr. Landry? Do you have this bed jacket in yellow?"

"That *is* yellow, Mrs. Shelton," Jed replies after glancing distractedly at the garment in her hands.

"But this is just so . . . bright. Like margarine. I would prefer a pale yellow for my sister. More like butter."

"Would you like me to go help her?" Clara offers, seizing the opportunity to escape the police officer's inexplicable scrutiny—and to prove that she really does work here.

Which you don't, she reminds herself.

But that's Jed's story, and she's sticking to it.

"That would be swell, thank you, Clara," Jed says. "I'm pretty sure we have some pale yellow bed jackets out in the back room."

Grateful for the chance to flee, Clara hurries to the back of the store.

* * *

"What's going on, Pete?" Jed hisses the moment he's sure that Clara is safely out of earshot.

"Maisie Wilkens told me you're harboring a lady Nazi spy here, that's what."

"Maisie said *that*?" Jed feels sick to his stomach. "She doesn't know what she's talking about."

"What she said"—Pete keeps a watchful eye on the back room, and one hand still poised on his gun— "was that this woman had been here and left evidence behind, and that I needed to pick it up and get it to the FBI. But she told me that Arnold told her that you claimed you never saw her again," Pete adds.

The word *claimed* obviously implies that Jed must have been lying.

"Like I said, Maisie doesn't know what she's talking about," he repeats in a terse whisper. "It's like I just told you, she's so berserk over this pregnancy that Arnold's calling her Crazy Maisie."

He silently begs forgiveness for the white lie, not daring to cross his fingers inside his apron pocket. Not with old Eagle Eye Kavinski acting like J. Edgar Hoover himself.

"So you're saying this woman is . . ." Pete shrugs. "Who is she? I need you to level with me here, Jed."

"She's my new clerk, like I told you."

"How much do you know about her?"

"I know that she's not a Nazi spy, and I'm sure as heck not *harboring her,* whatever that's supposed to mean."

All at once, a light seems to dawn on Pete.

He leans closer and murmurs under his breath, barely moving his lips, "Is she holding you hostage? Forcing you to defend her? Because I'm armed, Jed, and I can—"

"No!" Jed protests sharply, with a sickening lurch of his gut.

There is a prompt clacking of high heels from the back of the store, and Mrs. Shelton peers around a rack. "Is everything all right up there, Mr. Landry?"

"Everything is fine, Mrs. Shelton."

"Do you think I should come back another day?" she asks, looking uneasily from Jed to the police officer.

"I think that might be a good idea," Jed tells her, his gaze locked on Pete Kavinski's. "There's still plenty of time for Christmas shopping."

Mrs. Shelton scurries past them, perhaps anxious to escape the tension—or, just as likely, eager to get out on the street and spread the word that Jed Landry and Officer Pete Kavinski are at odds over the beautiful stranger in their midst.

"Look," Jed tells Pete in a low voice the moment she's gone, "you and I both know that I'm as patriotic as they come. Do you honestly think I'm involved in some kind of espionage?"

"You? No. *Her?*" Tilting his head to indicate Clara in the back room, Pete throws up his hands.

At least he's released his grip on the gun.

"Take my word for it, Pete . . . she's no Nazi spy."

Jed pushes aside a pesky image of the little Japanese kid living at her address. The one who said he didn't recognize her picture.

He still doesn't know why Clara lied about where she lives, or why her wardrobe encompassed a hodgepodge of sizes, or why she was carrying that transmitter . . . heck, if it even *was* a transmitter . . .

But sometimes, a fella has to go with his gut.

His gut and his heart.

All he knows, at this point, is that he trusts her.

And for no good reason . . .
Other than that kiss.
It was just a kiss.
One heck of a kiss . . .
But still, just a kiss.
And for now, it will have to be reason enough.

He looks at Pete, the runt of three local brothers. The oldest is now a rugged marine serving overseas, the middle son, a swaggering New York City cop. Jed remembers Pete—who back then was known to one and all as PeeWee—forever tagging along after them, trying to catch up. He never did.

The perennial kid brother has something to prove. Snagging a Nazi spy right here in Glenhaven Park would do it.

Darn that Maisie, anyway. Doesn't she have enough to worry about between nagging her husband and knitting baby booties? Must she also dabble in international espionage?

If Jed doesn't figure out a way to diffuse this situation, Clara's going to be hauled away in handcuffs.

"Pete, you and I have both known Maisie since she ratted you out for dipping Karla Kent's braid in the inkwell back in kindergarten," he points out on a whim. "Which you only did to get Karla back for pouring that cup of water on your lap and telling everyone that you wet your pants."

Recognition flits into Pete's gray blue eyes. "Hey, I had forgotten all about that. Was I ever sore at her!"

"Maisie?"

"Her, too. And that Karla used to gripe my soul just as bad. Thanks to those two brownnoses, Miss Corcoran chewed me out good, and she put a black ink dot on the tip of my nose and made me keep it there all day."

"Right, and Maisie made sure nobody in the school missed seeing it at recess, remember?"

"Yeah, I remember." Pete scowls.

"Old Tattletale Maisie. Remember?"

"Sure do. That's what we all used to call her. Even Arnold. Say, do you remember that time back in high school when he gave that blond bombshell Babs Woodfield a lift home after chess club, and Maisie found out about it? Remember how she went and spread rumors all over town that Babs was necking with that drip Orson Babcock in the balcony of the Odeon?"

"How can I forget? Poor Babs really got into a lather about it."

"Well, she should've. It was a lie. Ask me how I know that." Pete elbows him in the ribs. "Go on, ask me."

"How do you know that?"

"Because I'm the one who was with Babs Woodfield in the balcony of the Odeon." Pete chuckles. "That Babs was some solid sender."

"She sure was. No matter what Maisie said about her," Jed adds purposefully. "There's nothing meaner than a jealous girlfriend. Or wife."

"You can say that again."

Jed drives in the final run. "Especially when it's old Tattletale Maisie—and she's nine months pregnant and bigger than a house."

Pete absorbs that for a second.

"You know, Crazy Maisie has a nice ring to it, too." Pete's grin is wicked. "You say Arnold made up that one?"

Cringing inwardly, Jed says, "He sure did."

There will be hell to pay if any of this gets back to the Wilkenses. Which, of course, it will.

Then again, they deserve it. Both of them.

And you should have known better than to let Arnold in on anything and think he wouldn't go running back to tell his wife.

All right, so maybe Jed can't really blame Arnold.

How can he, when he himself was all set to go to the FBI with the contents of Clara's suitcase and purse?

But not anymore. Now all he wants is to be alone with Clara—no matter who or what she really is.

"Listen." Jed claps his old friend on the shoulder, "I don't want to waste any more of your time on this hooey, so . . ."

"Giving me the bum's rush, are you, Jed?" Pete asks almost good-naturedly. "Can't say I blame you. She's a hot little number."

"Who?" Jed asks, all innocence.

"Who? Maisie's so-called lady spy, that's who. You might want to go help her out in the back room, if you know what I mean."

"Oh, I know what you mean," he says with a hubba-hubba bob of his eyebrows for added effect. "And listen, Pete, if I do run across any Nazi spies around here, I'll be sure to send them your way."

"Well, all reet." With a jovial wave, Pete is out the door.

Jed exhales gratefully through puffed cheeks.

Close call.

It took Clara all of sixty seconds to ascertain that there are no butter yellow chenille bed jackets in the store's back room.

Obviously, Jed was as eager to get rid of her as she was to flee . . . but in a purely supportive way, of course. She gets the comforting impression that he's irrevocably on her side—and that the law officer, for whatever reason, is not.

If only she had some idea why the lines are drawn in the first place . . .

Unless it was her imagination?

Nah. That cop was looking daggers at her from the moment he spotted her, even after Jed vouched for her.

But right now, Clara has other things to worry about.

Like how she's going to save Jed's life.

She paces the stockroom, past shelves of assorted merchandise: housewares, clothes, toys, stationery supplies.

What if she simply tells him the truth?

The truth being that she's been miraculously—or perhaps magically—transported here from the twenty-first century.

Yeah, that'll go over really well. The proverbial men in white coats will be here to cart her away before you can say *asylum.*

Unless . . .

What if he believes her?

There's always a chance—slim, but a chance—that he might.

He stuck up for her out there, didn't he? With the cop? There he was, heroically coming to the rescue and giving her a perfect alibi for being here when she didn't even anticipate she might need one . . . let alone understand why.

Then again, Jed's willingness to tell a white lie about her working in the five-and-dime as a clerk doesn't mean he's likely to buy a bizarre time travel tale.

Why *would* he believe her? Even *she* thought she was crazy until Mr. Kershaw provided the scientific evidence.

Evidence . . .

Hmm.

Well, there's always her sweatshirt. She can take off her coat and show him. AMERICAN LEAGUE CHAMPION-SHIP SERIES 2004.

But what will that prove?

It will prove that someone—say, a deluded Red Sox fan—can get a sweatshirt imprinted anywhere, with anything they want it to say . . .

Although maybe you can't do that here in 1941.

Still, the shirt alone isn't necessarily sufficient evidence. Not the same as it would be, say, if she were able to tell Jed the Yankees were going to play—and lose to—the Red Sox in the future playoffs before the fact . . . and then he were able to see it unfold, just as she predicted.

Too bad that's not going to happen for another sixty-three years.

And anyway, Clara is baseball fan enough to know that these playoff series didn't even exist back in 1941. Only the World Series.

Historic details aside, the shirt is out as proof. What else can she use, then?

She does have some cash and her Metro North ticket receipt tucked into her mitten. The bills would be imprinted with future years, and the receipt would be dated December 3, 2006. But she supposes that those things could easily be faked, as well—if there were any possible reason to pull such a hoax.

Jed doesn't know her well enough to believe that she wouldn't.

For now, there's nothing to do but try to fit in, once again, here in the past.

In the far corner of the storeroom, she spots the prop suitcase she abandoned here the other day. The one Lisa said was filled with vintage clothing.

If nothing else, Clara thinks, hurriedly unzipping her parka, *you can get out of this sweatshirt before somebody spots it.*

Somebody like Pete the Unfriendly Cop.

Jed opens the door to the stockroom with nothing on his mind but having a serious talk with Clara.

One look inside, however, and conversation—serious or otherwise—is the last thing on his mind.

Even in the dimly lit room, he can clearly see that Clara is nearly naked.

She's turned at an angle but most of her left side is visible; she's wearing some kind of flimsy black brassiere and skimpy black lace panties like nothing Jed has ever seen before.

Not that he's seen much intriguing lingerie outside the collection of girlie magazines he confiscated from Gilbert's clubhouse years ago. Not unless you count his ex-girlfriend Carol's thick white torpedo brassieres, rigid, durable nylon girdles, and billowing underpants and slips.

Which he doesn't.

Though if he ever did, he wouldn't after *this*.

Clara's undergarments amount to little more than three V-shaped transparent lace triangles held together by narrow wisps of ribbon.

Jed finds it hard to believe that he actually ever considered her scrawny. Her figure is all taut skin and gentle curves, from the swell of her breasts to her flat tummy, rounded hips and lithe thighs and the shapeliest legs he's seen this side of the silver screen. Heck, no. Even Betty Grable's famous gams don't hold a candle to these.

He watches Clara bend to remove something from

the open suitcase on the floor at her feet—and swallows hard, realizing that it's a garter belt.

This is wrong. You need to stop watching her. Now!

But somehow, Jed can't force himself to turn away. He's as helplessly captivated by the exquisite woman before him as he is disturbed by his own voyeurism.

Not a breath escapes his lungs in the interlude as she slips the first seamed stocking over her toes and rolls it ever so carefully up her leg. He exhales only when she grapples awkwardly with the clip.

It takes her so many tries to get it fastened that he has to wonder if she was wearing dungarees earlier because she simply hasn't the patience to don stockings every day.

Then he's back to holding his breath in rapt regard as she unfurls the second swathe of sheer silk, inch by painstaking inch, up the magnificent length of her other leg.

Alas, this one is no easier to attach to the garter belt.

Watching her fumble and hearing her curse softly under her breath, Jed briefly wonders whether all women have this much trouble with their stockings every day. It goes a long way toward explaining why, with his mother, his grandmother, and three sisters in the house, he often finds himself waiting impatiently for them to get ready to go anywhere.

Clara bends over the suitcase again, and his attention is diverted back to the matter at hand. He watches her rummage through the clothes, shaking her head as though she doesn't like the looks of anything there.

Which is odd, since she supposedly packed it all.

Finally, she pulls something out, briefly inspects it, and approves it with some obvious reluctance.

She lifts it over her head to pull it on. Jed duly admires her toned arms and the curve of her throat and the way her long hair swishes lazily across her bare shoulders before the fabric swoops down to obliterate the glorious view.

The dress is short-sleeved.

Huh.

Short-sleeved. In December.

Jed watches Clara smooth the snug-fitting skirt over her narrow hips, as if trying to make it drape properly. But it doesn't. Even he can see that it's cut for a woman more petite in stature. The hem falls just above her knee, revealing slightly more of her leg than is fashionable—not that he's complaining.

Nor is he dissatisfied when the crepe fabric strains slightly across her full bosom as she lifts her arms to adjust the square neckline.

He can't help but wonder why the ill-fitting dress was in what she claimed was her own suitcase.

She buttons on the matching belt, which accentuates her waist.

Then she looks down to inspect herself and shakes her head, less than pleased with the finished effect. She sighs a disappointed sigh and it's all he can do not to speak up.

No, you're beautiful, he wants to assure her. Yet concealed in the shadows just beyond the doorway, he doesn't dare give himself away now. She would have every right to slap him across the face and storm out of here forever.

". . . shoes," he hears her mutter as she digs through her suitcase with little concern for the clothing, which has gone from neat stacks to a rumpled heap.

You'd think a woman would be more careful with her wardrobe . . . unless it isn't her wardrobe. He can't think of a single unincriminating reason why it wouldn't be. But there are plenty of incriminating possibilities.

She stole it . . .

She's on the lam and grabbed the wrong bag . . .

It's part of the charade and she really is a spy . . .

Okay, Jed, that's enough speculation about spying.

Which, ironically, he is doing *while* spying. On her. A pastime that has admittedly lost some of its allure now that she's fully clothed, aside from the shoes.

Shoes she can't seem to find . . . which, now that he thinks back on his own investigation into her belongings, might be due to the fact that she didn't pack any.

Which she would know . . . if she were the one who packed the suitcase.

All right, that does it. It's time to get to the bottom of this.

Jed backs up a few inches, clears his throat loudly, knocks on the door frame, and sticks his head into the storeroom as though he's just showing up.

"Oh . . . you changed," he comments, as though he's surprised.

"I did. I felt . . . I mean, those clothes were . . . I just wasn't . . ."

"Comfortable?" He didn't mean to help her out of her verbal trap—far better to hear what she has to say for herself—but he doesn't regret it when he sees the spark of gratitude in her eyes.

"Exactly. I wasn't comfortable in those jeans and sneakers. This, um, *dress* feels much better."

He nods as if that's a perfectly logical thing to say, even as he watches her once again attempt to adjust the neckline, the drape of the skirt.

Meanwhile, he's thinking, *Sneakers?* Those big

white shoes of hers look nothing like any sneaker he's ever seen. Sneakers are dark-colored, like regular shoes—or bright-colored cotton with open toes like the new Kedettes he had in stock this summer.

Clara gives up trying to conform her too-small dress to her luscious figure and looks at him again.

He wishes he could read her mind . . .

And he sure hopes she can't read his.

Because if she can, she knows that he's not seeing the dress at all.

No, he's seeing what's underneath the dress. He can't seem to help himself. Now that he knows, in graphic detail . . .

Well, he can't seem to banish the provocative image of her, all but naked and breathtakingly beautiful.

"Oh, by the way," she says, "I couldn't find it."

He blinks. "Hmm?"

"The pale yellow chenille bed jacket for that lady. Are you sure it's back here?"

"I'm sure it's not," he admits. "And Mrs. Shelton is long gone. I was just trying to save you from Pete."

"Thanks. I don't think he liked me."

If she only knew.

Aloud, Jed says, "Well, he can be a little bit of a . . ."

"Pain in the—er, neck?"

"Exactly."

"So it had nothing to do with me?"

He shakes his head.

She obviously doesn't believe him.

"I don't believe you," she says, in case he missed the skyward roll of her pupils.

"I know you don't." He shrugs helplessly. "And you know what? I'm having a hard time figuring out what to believe myself."

"What do you mean?"

Here goes nothing, he thinks, taking a deep breath.

Whatever Clara is expecting Jed to say, it isn't "I checked out your address this morning. On West Eleventh Street in Manhattan."

Her stomach churns.

Her address? How could he possibly know her address?

"Somebody else was living there," he goes on. "And they never heard of you."

She searches her mind wildly, miraculously managing to pluck pertinent information from a maelstrom of panicky thoughts.

"Mr. and Mrs. Sloan," she blurts, grateful that she never entirely tuned out her chatterbox building super—and hoping she got the year right. She's pretty sure Mr. Kobayashi said the Sloans were there at least until after the war.

If Jed's raised eyebrows are any indication, she's correct about that.

"Yes," he says, with a slow nod. "The Sloans. That's the name."

"You talked to them?"

"No, not to them. To a little boy . . . and his mother. But she didn't speak any English."

A little boy . . .

Comprehension swoops over Clara like a bracing sea breeze on an August afternoon.

"They were Japanese!" she shouts like an exuberant game show contestant determined to ace the final round. "Right?"

Jed nods, but he still looks unsettled. "Right."

"What was the little boy's name? Wait, I'll tell you. It was Isamu. Right?"

"Right," Jed says again, and she realizes that she probably shouldn't be quite so jubilant about discussing her supposed neighbors. "He spoke English. And he liked to talk."

If you only knew, she thinks, trying to picture Mr. Kobayashi as a child . . .

And as a child, of course, he would never have heard of Clara McCallum.

"How is it that you found my address in the first place?" she asks Jed.

Wordlessly, he reaches into his pocket, pulls something out, and hands it to her.

Oh. Her card. With the name and telephone number of Jesus's life coach written on the front.

She should have remembered it was in her purse.

What now?

"Oh, that Isamu," she says with a grin and a wave of her hand. "He's such a mischievous little imp. He's always pretending he doesn't know me."

All right, that was lame.

Clearly, Jed is in agreement. "Why would he do that?"

"He thinks it's funny," she says with a kids!-what-are-you-going-to-do? shrug.

"His mother didn't know you, either."

"I thought . . . she didn't speak English."

"I showed her your picture. Isamu translated for me that she didn't recognize it, either . . . or so she claimed."

Oh, that Mrs. Kobayashi . . . she's such a mischievous little imp isn't going to cut it this time.

Clara just looks at Jed, wondering what she can possibly say that will make any sense.

But before she can speak, Jed does.

"Clara," he says with a forthright lift of his chin, "are you working for the Japs?"

In that first moment of confusion, all she can think of is her cousins Rebecca and Rachel.

Then she realizes he doesn't mean JAPs; he means Japs—as in *Japanese*.

Her jaw drops.

Working for the Japs? In wartime?

No wonder the police were here.

She shakes her head, dumbfounded at the paranoid conclusion Jed seems to have drawn based on . . .

What? The fact that she has Asian neighbors?

How can he be so small-minded? So prejudiced? So . . .

Politically incorrect?

This *is* a different era. In Germany, at this very moment, her grandmother's uncles and aunts are imprisoned in Auschwitz, never to be seen again.

In this century, African Americans are relegated to the back of the bus. Martin Luther King Jr.'s fiery "I have a dream" speech is still decades away.

So much for the Good Old Days, Clara thinks grimly.

It's understandable that to Jed, the so-called Japs are the enemy. In fact . . .

December 7 is mere days away.

The Japanese are plotting their sneak attack on Pearl Harbor at this very moment.

What if I'm supposed to stop it?

What if she's here in December 1941 not to save one man's life, but hundreds of lives? What if she's destined to change the course of history?

"You haven't answered my question." Jed pins her with a level look. "Are you working for the Japs?"

"You really think I'm some kind of . . . traitor?" she asks, incredulous despite her newfound grasp of where he's coming from. "Just because my neighbors are Japanese?"

"And because of the . . . the . . ." He takes a deep breath. "I have to admit something, Clara. I'm not the least bit proud of it, but I did it because I was trying to find your identification so that I could return your belongings, and . . ."

"What? What did you do?"

"I looked inside your pocketbook. And I found . . . this." He reaches into his pocket and pulls some-thing out.

She looks into his outstretched palm—and laughs out loud.

She can't help herself. It's amusing to see him hold-ing out her iPod as though it's some sort of . . .

Oh.

He has no idea what it is, but she can just imagine what he's thinking.

As the ludicrous picture falls into place, complete with the nosy cop, Clara recognizes the seriousness of the allegation. Her laugh fades, along with the slight-est hint of humor in the situation.

She's going to owe him an explanation . . . and she'd better come up with a plausible one, fast.

"What is this, Clara?"

Stall him.

"What do you think it is?"

"Some kind of . . . device."

She nods. So far so good.

"It looks like a transmitter," Jed goes on. "And I thought . . . I mean, I couldn't help it. I figured . . ."

He figured that she was—she *is*—a wartime spy transmitting secret messages to the Japanese.

"This isn't a transmitter, Jed," she says quickly. "At least, not in the way you're thinking."

"So you didn't hear me calling you?"

She shakes her head, even as she remembers his odd comment a little while ago, on the street. He said he was calling her to come back.

He wanted me here.

The realization strikes a spark of euphoria. For a giddy instant, she's fifteen again, just finding out that her crush on the cute soccer goalie is mutual.

Then she glimpses the lingering misgiving in Jed's eyes and the spark is gone. Reality crashes over her: she's all grown up, and he isn't Adam Dumont, and they don't have a chance in hell of any kind of relationship.

"Let me show you what this is, Jed."

Abruptly, she takes the iPod from his hand, earbuds dangling, and presses the center button to turn it on, illuminating the screen.

Scrolling down the inventory of downloaded playlists, she almost wishes she had downloaded Jesus's *Super Seventies* CD. Gladys Knight and the Pips would be a good alternative to Green Day and the Black Eyed Peas.

She needs something more classic, something that was around back in the forties. Too bad she's never been much of a fan of swing music, or vintage crooners, or . . .

Wait a minute. There.

Perfect.

"Here . . . put these on." She hands him the cord.

He stares at the earphones as if he has no clue what—

Oh. Right. He probably doesn't know what they are. Of course he doesn't.

"Here, I'll help you." She steps closer, stands on

her tiptoes, and rests one hand on his shoulder poised to insert the first tiny speaker into his ear.

Enveloped all at once in that familiar soap-tobacco-skin scent, she experiences another giddy fifteen-year-old moment. Caught up in a seductive fantasy, she can't seem to move on, entranced by the sensual images infiltrating her head.

She can see the muscles in Jed's neck working as he swallows audibly, and she wonders if he's feeling the same provocative tension.

All he would have to do is turn his head and they would be face-to-face . . .

And I could kiss him again.

"What is that sound?" he asks, and for a second she's convinced he must hear her heart pounding.

Then she realizes he's talking about the faint buzz of music coming from the iPod, the song she selected from her Christmas playlist.

Swiftly getting hold of her recalcitrant emotions, she gently puts the earphone into his right ear.

He jumps. "What the—?"

"Shh, hang on . . ." She places its twin into his left ear, then takes a step back and watches his face.

His blue eyes are wide with shock.

"Is this music coming from that little thing?" he shouts at the top of his lungs.

She grins. "Yup."

"Well, I'll be . . ."

She watches him listen, as mesmerized by his rapt expression of wonder as he is by the music.

"What song is this?" he bellows at her.

Amused by his deafening decibel, she motions for him to remove the earphones.

He obliges with obvious reluctance. "This is incredible. What is it?"

"The song? That's 'I'll Be Home for Christmas' . . . you've heard it before, right?"

"Never."

Uh-oh. She could have sworn it was a huge hit in the forties.

The question is . . . *when* in the forties?

"Who is it?" Jed asks.

"Frank Sinatra." Surely he's heard of . . .

"Who?"

"Frank Sinatra. The singer."

"You mean the kid from Jersey who sings with Tommy Dorsey?"

Well, do you?

"Uh . . . yes?"

"I didn't even know he had a record. Is it new?"

Is it?

Or is it a year or more into the future?

She nods; what else can she do?

"It's going to be huge, I'll tell you that," Jed says enthusiastically. "I should have this one in stock. What did you say it was called?"

" 'I'll Be Home for Christmas,' but I . . . I don't think it's out on record yet," Clara says feebly.

"How can it not be on a record?" He peers at the iPod. "What *is* this thing, anyway? And if there's no record where is it getting the music?"

"It's . . . kind of complicated. You know—new technology. I don't really understand it myself."

At least *that's* not a total lie. She comprehends as much about consumer electronics as she does physics.

"So all along, this was just some kind of radio? A one-way radio that plays music?" Jed asks.

"As opposed to a two-way radio a spy might use?" She raises an eyebrow at him. "That's right."

He seems to be digesting this information.

Then, with a lingering trace of suspicion, he asks, "What about your neighbors? Why didn't they know who you were?"

Yes, why is that, Clara? Are you going to explain that it's because you aren't born yet, and won't be for another four decades?

"The thing is, Jed . . . I've had some trouble with a stalker lately."

Again, not a total lie, she thinks, remembering the elderly autograph seeker who assailed her the other night in front of her building.

And what about the secret Santa? Not that unexpected holiday gifts qualify as harassment, exactly . . . but it's still unnerving.

"You've had trouble with a *what*?"

Can it be that stalkers, like iPods and Frank Sinatra, are a wave of the future?

"Somebody has been harassing me, and . . . Isamu and his mother were trying to protect me. They didn't know who you were so they didn't want to give out personal information to a total stranger on the street."

A very logical explanation if she does say so herself. Although . . . maybe she should have toned it down a little, because Jed now seems dangerously provoked.

"Is this fella who's harassing you the one who gave you that bruise?" he asks, his blue eyes dark with ire.

"Oh, this?" She touches her head gingerly.

"Yes, this."

In an instant, he goes from wrathful to tender, as he gently brushes her hair back from the sore spot.

"I got this when I walked into a door."

"You said you got hurt on the train."

Oops.

"I did," she says quickly. "I walked into a door on the train."

There's a long pause.

Then he says, "I think you're making that up to protect whoever did this."

Well, you're half-right.

"Clara . . . I have to ask you . . . is he your husband?"

"Is who my husband?"

"The brute who—"

"I'm not married, Jed . . . and really, there is no brute. I'm just clumsy."

He studies her doubtfully. "You don't have to be afraid, you know. I'd protect you. If he followed you here and dared to even look at you cross-eyed, I'd—I swear he'd be eating a knuckle sandwich."

She smiles, warmed by the notion of big, strong Jed protecting her—even if it is from a nonexistent adversary.

If only he could protect me from the real threat . . .

Her smile fades as she remembers her illness.

"You're safe here with me, Clara. I want you to know that."

She nods, wishing it were true . . .

Wishing she could, in turn, keep him safe.

Maybe I can, though. Maybe there's a way.

"Where are you staying while you're in Glenhaven Park?"

Startled by the question, she stammers, "I—I'm not sure."

"You don't have anyplace to go?"

"No, I guess I . . . didn't think that far ahead."

"Then you're coming home with me. Nothing improper, I swear," he adds hastily, even as she is engulfed by an image of Jed's bed . . .

More specifically, of being in Jed's bed with Jed.

In Jed's arms.

"No, nothing improper," she agrees, ducking her

head to hide the heated flush she can feel creeping over her cheeks.

After all, men were gentlemen back in 1941.

At least, Jed is.

Although maybe it's just an act, pipes a lascivious little voice in her head. *Maybe once you're alone with him, in private, you can break him out of that—*

"I'll have to let my mother know to set the table for one more for dinner," he tells her, and her wanton vision evaporates.

"You live with your mother?" She hopes the question reflects casual interest as opposed to blatant disappointment.

"Not under the same roof . . . she and my sisters and my grandparents live in the main house. I've got a separate apartment over the garage. You can stay there."

"With you," she says with a nod, even as she reminds herself that she can't possibly spend the night. She has an early location call tomorrow.

Then again, maybe she can catch the first southbound train in the morning.

It would be worth it, for the prospect of one precious night with Jed.

"Oh, I'd stay in the house," he assures her. "On the couch."

"I can't put you out of your bed!" she protests.

No, I want to be in it with you. Naked with you, to be specific. One last time for me—for us.

"Oh, I don't mind at all. In fact, I won't take no for an answer. You can stay as long as you like."

Yeah? How about the next sixty-five years?

She musters a smile and a polite, "Thank you. That's really nice of you."

"In the meantime . . . I really can use some help around here. How about it?"

"You want me to work here in the store? For real?"
He nods.

Tell him you're not sticking around.

Not longer than one night, anyway . . .

She can only hope that will be enough time for her to figure out what she needs to do to keep him from going off to war and getting killed. And maybe even prevent the sneak attack on Pearl Harbor.

Somehow, after the complicated iPod incident, she senses that a straightforward warning to Jed—or, for that matter, FDR himself—isn't going to cut it.

"I didn't come here to work, Jed." *I came to save you. And the world.*

"I know, but I had to fire my clerk this morning, like I said. And with Christmas and all . . . well, I can't swing it by myself."

"Of course I'll help you," Clara hears herself saying.

"That would be swell. Let's go up front and I'll find an apron for you."

"Some shoes would be good, too," she says ruefully, glancing down at her stocking feet. "I seem to have forgotten to pack mine, and I can't wear those with a dress."

"No, you can't," he says in a tone that tells her exactly what he thinks of her sneakers. "I've got a shoe rack over by the ladies' coats. You can pick out any pair you like—my gift."

"Thank you." She starts back out into the store.

"Oh, wait, Clara? One thing . . ."

Uh-oh. "What is it?"

"Mind if I hear the rest of the song?" he asks, already inserting the iPod earphones with the agile expertise of a twenty-first century tween. "This Frankie kid isn't half-bad."

Chapter 14

"This is it," Jed informs Clara, leading the way up the snow-packed sidewalk to his childhood home nestled in a row of two-story wood frame houses.

He's glad Doris talked him into putting up the Christmas lights the other night.

After a two-year dearth, the Landrys' house blends in with the gleaming festivity up and down the snow-blanketed block, just as it always did when Pop was alive. Strings of fat oval multicolored bulbs underscore the eaves, and the spotlit front door is festooned with a wreath and shiny gold tinsel garland. Pop would be pleased.

Jed watches Clara giving the house a thorough once-over, as charmed by her childlike red mittens— her late grandmother made them, she explained—as he is by her rapt expression.

He's noticed, as they worked together in the store all afternoon, that she has a quirky way of intently absorbing even the most ordinary details. She acts as though she's seeing the most mundane everyday thing—whether it be a candy bar, or a pair of shoes, or even just a coin—for the very first time.

"This is a beautiful house," she pronounces. "Have you lived here all your life?"

"Well, until I moved to the garage apartment out back," he reminds her. "That's where you'll be staying. But my mother probably has dinner waiting, so I'll take you out there after we eat."

"That would be good," she murmurs, teetering a bit in her high-heeled shoes on the uneven surface as she resumes heading up the walk.

"Are you all right?" He shifts her suitcase to his other hand and takes her arm to steady her.

"It's just hard to walk in these shoes in the snow."

"I should have given you a pair of galoshes before we left."

At least he did think to loan her a warm wool coat to wear in place of her strange, slippery parka, along with a stylish brimmed hat. She once again looks the part of the elegant beauty, even without lipstick or her hair done up.

He catches her sneaking a curious peek at the lamp-lit windows as they climb the shoveled front steps. Beyond the drawn shades, he knows, Mother and the girls are bustling to prepare a dinner fit for unexpected company.

"Who is this gal, Jed?" Mother asked when he called home to say he was bringing an impromptu houseguest.

"An old friend—from college," he improvised.

He was worried that Clara wouldn't want to go along with that, but she took it in stride when he mentioned it just now as they walked the few blocks to Chestnut Street from the store.

Perhaps it should bother him that she seems willing to be anyone he wants her to be—newly hired store clerk, old college friend . . .

But it doesn't.

Just as long as she isn't the person he *doesn't* want her to be: a spy.

He still presumes that she's lying about the bruise on her head, and perhaps even about being married.

But that hasn't stopped him from repeatedly reliving the intense kiss they shared out on the street today . . . and longing for another one. In private.

That will have to wait awhile, though.

Opening the door, he calls, "Mother? I'm home."

Swing music, crackling with slight static, greets Clara as she crosses the threshold, along with a wave of savory-scented warmth.

Looking around the entry hall as she stomps the snow from her shoes on the mat, she takes in the living room to the left, the dining room to the right, and the garland-draped stairway straight ahead, bordered by ascending picture frames on the wall. Beneath it is a low telephone table with a built-in bench. The black rotary dial phone rests on the table beside a thin bound booklet labeled *Glenhaven Park Telephone Directory.*

Clara discerns at a glance that this house is a home in the truest sense of the word. The rooms glow with cozy lamplight and flickering firelight, burnished woodwork, amber-toned vintage wallpaper, and floor-length gold draperies. The hardwood floors and area rugs are comfortably worn with use, as is the chintz furniture in the living room. The dining room is formal, with built-in cabinets displaying rows of fine china. Bric-a-brac seems to cover every available surface, including the tall wooden radio cabinet.

Clara makes sure that her money and keys are securely tucked into the bottom of her red mittens before slipping them into the pocket of her coat. Jed helps her take it off and hangs it, along with his overcoat, in a crowded closet beneath the stairs.

"Mother?" he calls again.

A pot lid clatters somewhere in the back of the

house, and heels clack their way toward the front hall.

A woman appears. She has sad blue eyes and salt-and-pepper hair pulled severely back from a haggard face that, judging by her delicate bone structure, must once have been beautiful. From the neck down, she might have stepped out of a fashion magazine ad as opposed to a suburban kitchen. That's because she's wearing a dress and pearls and stockings and heels—a far cry from the terry cloth tracksuit and slippers that make up Clara's own mother's household uniform.

Even more disconcerting, Mrs. Landry is smoking.

Well, of course. Back in 1941, nobody knew that cigarettes are carcinogenic.

"Mother, this is my friend Clara, visiting from Cambridge."

"It's wonderful to meet you." The woman politely extends her right hand.

Clara shakes it, noting the ironic juxtaposition of the gold wedding band she still wears on the same hand that holds the cigarette aloft.

"It's nice to meet you, too, Mrs. Landry," she says politely, trying to block out the memory of the ar-chived newspaper headline.

COMMUNITY PILLAR SUCCUMBS TO LUNG CANCER

"Hi, I'm Doris."

Startled by the nearby voice, Clara turns to find a freckle-faced girl with red pigtails standing right at her elbow. She looks to be about twelve and is wearing jeans and an oversized blue sweater that must once have belonged to Jed or his father. Her eyes are the same deep shade of blue as her big brother's.

"Where did you come from?" Clara asks with a laugh as she shakes Doris's extended hand.

"Oh, Doris is always sneaking up on people," Jed says, ruffling his kid sister's hair affectionately. "Aren't you, toots?"

"Yes, she is, and it really gripes my middle kidney," another voice announces from overhead.

"Oh, ish kabibble," Doris retorts, looking up at the stairs.

Clara follows her gaze to see a pretty, slender teenager starting down the flight. Directly on her heels is a look-alike, a few inches shorter.

Both girls have shiny auburn hair curled in pompadours above their foreheads and falling past their shoulders in careful waves. They're wearing similar knee-length wool skirts, white blouses with rounded collars, cardigans, dark-colored cuffed socks, and oxfords.

"That's Penny, and that's Mary Ann," Jed tells Clara. "Did I mention I've got three sisters? How lucky am I?"

"Really lucky, actually. I don't have any sisters. Brothers, either."

"Well, I've got one, and you can have him, too."

"Jed, you know that isn't kind."

"I'm just teasing, Mother. You know that I love Gilbert. It's Mary Ann that I'd give away to the first taker."

Arriving at the base of the stairs, his middle sister swats his arm and sticks out her tongue. He grabs her hand and holds it behind her back as she squirms, giggling, refusing to say *Uncle* on her big brother's command.

"Why don't you have any brothers and sisters, Clara?" Doris asks.

"Doris, don't be nosy," Penny scolds.

"I'm not being nosy. I'm being friendly."

"All right, that's enough," Mrs. Landry declares, as Clara wistfully contrasts Jed's household to her own quiet, unorthodox urban upbringing. As much as she has always lamented her parents' divorce, as much as she has always craved domestic stability, never until this moment did she entirely grasp all that was missing from her life as an only child in a small city apartment.

"Supper is ready," Jed's mother declares. "Come on. Grandma and Granddad are already sitting down."

"In the kitchen?" Doris is blatantly disappointed. "But we have company, Mother!"

"I'd have set up in the dining room," Jed's mother tells Clara somewhat apologetically, "but I need Jed's help getting the extra leaf into the table. And anyway, we have an extra seat with Gilbert away."

"Where is your brother?" Clara asks Jed as they all head down a dimly lit hall toward the kitchen.

"College. Penn State. He graduates this spring, then he'll be home to take over here with the store and the family."

He says it in a low voice, almost as though he doesn't want his mother and sisters to overhear.

"What about you?" she asks, wishing she didn't already know. A sick feeling twists in her gut.

"Well, I was thinking I'd join the army once Gilbert's back home, but . . ." He shrugs, shooting her a meaningful glance, slowing his pace as the others disappear around the corner into the bright kitchen.

"But . . . what?"

"That was my plan when I didn't think I had anything to stick around here for."

Clara's heart skips a beat. Is he hinting that he might change his plans . . . because of her?

She knows, based on the movie's true-to-life script, that Jed wasn't drafted; he enlisted. It was his own choice.

What if she can influence that?

"What about now?" she dares to ask him, and holds her breath for the answer. "Do you think there might be some reason to stick around?"

"Now . . . who knows?"

"Jed? Can you help me to lift this roaster out of the oven?" his mother calls.

"Coming, Mother." Jed looks at Clara. "We'll talk later."

Not certain whether to be relieved or dismayed at the interruption, Clara follows him.

The kitchen is large by Manhattan standards, but smaller, she supposes, than a modern suburban kitchen would be. The floor is speckled aqua linoleum. The cabinets are white metal with long silver handles. The white enamel stove is enormous, particularly in contrast to the icebox across from it. The low double sink stands alone, rather than set into a countertop the way sinks are today.

As she looks around, taking it all in, Clara's thoughts are whirling with possibilities.

Maybe she's here in the past so that Jed will fall in love with her and stay in Glenhaven Park instead of going off to the war in Europe. She can't help but feel exhilarated by the mere thought of settling down here with him . . .

Even though it's flat-out impossible.

If she stays here in 1941, she'll eventually die of the cancer that's growing within her. She can't survive without treatment.

So what does this all mean?

Is she supposed to sacrifice her own life to save Jed's? Is that how it works?

How can you even imagine such a thing? He's a stranger, really . . .

And yet, he's not a stranger at all. Right now, there

is no one else in this world—or in her own world—who matters to her as much as this man does. Only with Jed does she feel safe, and happy, and—ironically—irrevocably alive.

"Mom and Dad, this is Clara, an old friend of Jed's from Cambridge," Mrs. Landry announces to an elderly, white-haired couple seated in a breakfast nook at a large chrome table with an aqua Formica top. "Clara, this is my mother, Etta, and my father, Ralph."

"It's so nice to meet you both," she manages to say cordially, even as she is struck by the perception of having crossed a vast bridge through time. Jed's grandparents might very well have been born before the Civil War even ended.

And they're long dead now, in my time, she reminds herself.

Jed's mother probably is, too. And Jed himself—not something she wants to dwell on right now.

"Where did you say you're from, dear?" asks Jed's grandmother, her gaze solemn behind thick glasses.

"I'm from New York, but I met Jed in college," she remembers to say, feeling a little guilty.

"Did you go to Harvard Law, too?" Doris asks in surprise.

Before Clara can acknowledge that she did, Penny disdainfully informs her sister, "Women aren't allowed to go to Harvard Law, Dumdora."

As unnerved by that unexpected discrimination as she is by the close call, Clara reminds herself that in some ways, the good old days are anything but.

Doris pulls her pigtails horizontally from her head, crosses her eyes at her sister, and retorts, "Aw, go chase yourself, Henny Penny."

"You're not allowed to call me that anymore! Jed said, remember?"

"Well, you're not allowed to call me Dumdora, either!"

"Jed never said that."

"I'm saying it now," Jed announces from the stove, where he's looking into the oven.

Doris sticks her thumbs in her ears, wiggles her fingers at Penny, and lets loose a loud, wet raspberry.

"Doris! That's enough."

Under her mother's warning glare, Doris turns to Clara and in an exaggeratedly sweet tone, offers, "You can sit here, in Gilbert's chair."

"Thank you," Clara murmurs, sliding into it, acutely aware that even Jed's puerile kid sister is an old woman now . . . if she's still alive at all.

A lump rises in her throat as she watches Jed carry a steaming roaster pan to the table, laughing with Mary Ann about something.

"What have we got here tonight, Lois?" Jed's grandfather asks, looking with interest at the heaping platters she's set before them.

"Roast chicken and potatoes, bread and margarine, Brussels sprouts, and corn. Oh, and I've got canned peaches for dessert," Mrs. Landry adds, as though that's a rare treat.

It must be, because Doris squeals and claps her hands in delight.

"What was in that basket Minnie Bouvier dropped off this afternoon?" Jed's grandfather asks.

Startled, Clara recognizes the name.

Minnie Bouvier.

What was it she read in the *Glenhaven Gazette* about her?

"She brought some marmalade," Jed's mother is saying. "We'll have it in the morning with toast."

"Oh, I was hoping it was some of her famous fruitcake."

Fruitcake . . .

It comes back to Clara as Jed speaks up. "Don't worry, Granddad—Minnie was in the store on Monday and she promised she'll be bringing her fruitcake along soon."

No, she won't. Clara remembers with a nauseating lurch of her stomach that the elderly Mrs. Bouvier will be struck by a car . . . where was it?

On the corner of Oak and Main, at dusk . . .

When?

On Saturday, she remembers. She was going out to the grocery to get ingredients for her fruitcakes, and she was killed.

But what if . . . ?

Maybe I can save her, Clara tells herself. *If I stay here, I can save her.*

And if I can, that will mean I can save Jed, too.

"Mother, remember when you used to make fruitcake?" Doris asks.

"Yes—in fact, I always used Minnie's recipe. I like that one because it calls for currants and dates."

"Do you still have it?"

"The recipe? It's in my file over there." Taking a long drag on her Pall Mall, Mrs. Landry gestures at a small wooden box on the counter.

"Why don't you make some fruitcake this year, then?"

"I don't think so, Doris." Clara catches her flicking a gaze at the empty chair at the head of the table—the only one that doesn't have a place setting.

That, she realizes, must have been Abner Landry's seat.

"But Mother," Doris protests, "it would be such fun to—"

"Come on, toots, sit down," Jed cuts in pointedly as he takes his own seat beside Clara, just to the right of his father's chair.

It won't be long before Jed's place, too, is forever vacated, Clara thinks with an ache in her throat.

"Well, we're still getting our tree on Sunday morning, right, Jed?"

"Right."

"Oh, goody!" Doris launches into a loud, off-key rendition of "Oh, Christmas Tree."

"Will you please stop singing that?" Mary Ann bellows, hands over her ears. "Or at least, learn a new verse?"

"Mary Ann!"

"Mother, I can't take it anymore. She's been singing the same thing over and over for days. It gripes my middle kidney."

"And you've been saying that, over and over, for days," Jed says, amused.

"I could sing 'Oh, Tannenbaum,' but then it would be a Nazi song," Doris declares with a gleam in her eye.

"Doris, will you please say grace tonight?" Mrs. Landry asks with a sigh, having stubbed out her cigarette and taken her place opposite Jed.

Jed reaches across his father's vacant spot to take his mother's hand. With the other, he clasps Clara's, his grasp reassuringly warm as he gives her fingers a squeeze. On her other side, Doris reaches for her fingers.

"Dear Lord, we ask you to bless this food," Jed's little sister begins, her red head bowed like the others.

As Doris recites a prayer of thanks, asking God to

bless "dear Pop in heaven, Gilbert at school, and all the poor soldiers all over the world," Clara lifts her face to dab her eyes against her shoulders before somebody spots her tears.

Her vision cleared, she is struck by the bittersweet sight of the Landry family, linked hand-in-hand around the table, their chain unbroken . . .

For now.

"Watch your step," Jed warns Clara, opening the door to the garage. "It's kind of hard to see in here, and the place is filled with years' worth of junk. Here, let me help you."

He reaches out to grab her hand, and can feel that there's something stashed inside the mitten she's wearing. Earlier he might have wondered what it is, might even have been suspicious that she's hiding something incriminating.

Not anymore. Throughout dinner and dessert, as he watched her charismatically interacting with his family, he realized that he instinctively trusts her.

And he doesn't just *trust* her . . .

He's falling for her, hard and fast.

And now, at last, he'll be alone with her . . . if only for a little while. He told his mother he was going to get Clara settled in his apartment before returning to the house to spend the night on the sofa.

"How long will you be staying with us, Clara?" his mother asked.

"At least a few nights—I had to let Alice go, so she's helping me out in the store for awhile." Jed spoke up before Clara could say a word. He could tell by the hesitant look on her face that she wanted to correct him, but she didn't.

Nor did she amend Doris's delighted observation

that Clara will be here, then, this Sunday when they go up to the woods to chop down a Christmas tree. She even chimed in when Doris sang a loud, off-key stanza of her new anthem, "Oh, Christmas Tree," giggling with his little sister as though she's part of the family.

But she isn't. And she'll have to leave Glenhaven Park and return to her life—whatever that may be—sooner or later, Jed knows. Unless . . .

No, it's too soon to even think about anything like that.

For now, he decides, he'll simply live in the moment.

Lugging her heavy suitcase, he leads the way across the crowded concrete floor and up the creaky stairs.

"Sorry it's so crummy in here," he feels obligated to say as he opens the door and turns on the light, fervently wishing he were escorting her to a lavish hotel suite.

Clara steps over the threshold. "It's not crummy at all. I think it's . . . cozy. And . . . charming."

He follows her gaze, trying to see the apartment through her eyes, wishing he had at least bothered to make his bed before he left this morning to catch that early train to the city.

Then again, the unmade bed conjures alluring images of Clara lying naked in the tangle of sheets and blankets . . .

Jed blinks away that forbidden image, feeling his face grow hot when he catches her watching him intently.

She hurriedly flicks her eyes away—right to the bed.

And somehow, he finds himself wondering if she can possibly be thinking the same risqué thoughts that are tormenting him.

He swallows hard, and it sounds like a strangled gulp in the still room. "Here, let me help you take off your . . . coat."

Clara nods, steps closer to him. His hands tremble at her nearness as she turns her shoulder to shrug out of the coat. Though she has worn it mere minutes, her clean scent wafts from the coarse woolen fabric as he takes it, and it's all he can do not to bury his face in it—or in her.

He blindly drapes the coat over the nearest chair and follows it with his own, and then strips off his suit jacket and loosens his tie. He is filled with an absurd longing to help her right out of her clothes, as well.

If only he didn't know about the lacy, racy lingerie that lies beneath that sedate, snug-fitting dress of hers.

Stop thinking about that! She's a lady. Be a gentleman, for Pete's sake.

All right, then. What would a gentleman do?

"Do you want—" He breaks off, clears his throat, wishing he didn't sound so darned hoarse.

Clara is looking at him, waiting—still standing close enough to touch.

Why doesn't she step back, away from him?

His whole body is clenched with the effort to ignore the attraction sizzling between them. His dangerously deviant fingers are confined safely into fists in his pockets, his eyes unaccountably fixated on her petal pink lips untainted by cosmetic stain.

Doesn't she realize how hard it is for him to maintain his willpower when she's this near?

Maybe she does realize, he thinks, spotting a telltale glint in her eyes.

Maybe she's trying to tell him something.

For that matter, *he* was trying to tell *her* something. Or ask her something. What was it?

He sorts through his muddled brain in an attempt to recover the train of thought. "Ah, Clara, do you want—"

"You to kiss me?" she cuts in boldly. "Yes."

Kiss her?

He wasn't going to ask her anything of the kind, but the banal offer of a glass of water has been instantly erased from his tongue.

"You have no idea how mortified I am that I just said that," she confesses on a nervous laugh.

"You have no idea how glad I am that you did," he returns as he wraps his arms around her. "Or how happy I am to oblige that request."

"I should probably stop you . . . shouldn't I?"

"No," he says, "you definitely shouldn't."

He pulls her close, enveloping her against the length of his body, his hands coasting down the warm planes of her bare arms.

Slowly, savoring this extraordinary turn of events, he lowers his face over hers, looking into her eyes until she closes them with an expectant shiver of a sigh. Only then does he allow his mouth to touch hers.

Desire roars to life within him as he revels in the silken nudity of her lips. He pulls her closer still, holding her fast against his body swollen with raw craving. He deepens the kiss and she responds with a quivering moan, her tongue receiving his in a swift, swirling duet.

Coherent thought has been obliterated; Jed is utterly intoxicated, his senses encompassed by the wondrous creature in his arms. His hands swoop up over the crest of her shoulders and the slope of her warm neck before he entangles his fingers in her soft tumble of hair.

She seems to melt against him, deliciously pliant and soft where he is rigid with urgent need.

He tears his lips from hers to blaze the searing trail his hands took, pressing hot kisses against her shoulders and her neck before nuzzling the delicate, subtly perfumed hollow beneath her ear.

With a soft moan, she takes a step backward, and then another, hauling him with her . . . *toward the bed,* he realizes in wonder.

"Clara, are you sure?" Jed asks, as she sinks onto the mattress and pulls him down on top of her, needing him against her, closer, even, than that.

"Yes."

"Is this your first time?"

No, she thinks as she shakes her head, her throat suddenly too clogged with emotion to speak. *This is my last.*

If not forever, her last for a long, long while. And certainly her last with him.

Propped with his elbows on either side of her head, he kisses her deeply.

"It's not too soon?" he asks, panting hot breath against her ear.

Too soon?

If he only knew that it's almost too late.

Too late for this . . . for them.

"Clara?"

"It's not too soon," she whispers, and he groans as she pulls his head downward to capture his mouth in another scalding kiss.

His warm hands tug her dress up over her hips, and she trembles, wondering if she should say something to warn him . . .

Before she can speak, he pulls her dress up over her head and instinctively, she knows it's okay. Somehow, she doesn't fear intimacy with him; she welcomes it.

His hands slip to her back and fumble with her bra band; he's looking for the clasp.

Steeling herself for whatever will come, she guides his fingers to the front, where it unfastens quickly—too quickly. He pushes the straps past her shoulders, edging the lacy cups aside, and she fights the urge to pull the sheet up to cover herself.

He looks up, into her eyes.

"What is this?" His fingers gently brush the thin strip of gauze high on her right breast. "Did somebody—did *he*—hurt you here?"

"No, Jed, there is no 'he.' I swear to you. You believe me, don't you?"

His blue eyes are troubled but, after a moment, he slowly nods. "But what happened to you?"

"I just . . . I had a medical procedure, but it's—it's fine now."

"What kind of—"

She cuts him off with a kiss. He groans deep in his throat when she untucks his shirt from the waist of his trousers, gliding her fingertips over bare skin and hard muscles. He lifts himself just long enough to shed his clothes.

Then she's naked in his arms, just as she imagined. She throws her head back as his fingertips, then his tongue, stroke first her left breast, then, ever so delicately, her wounded right. It is in the moment that he presses a gentle kiss on the bandage that she realizes she was wrong about her future.

Intimacy—with the right person—will be more profoundly meaningful than ever before.

But Jed is the right person, and Jed won't be in her life back home, after the surgery.

All they have is this one night. One perfect night. It will have to be enough to sustain her when he's gone.

Her gaze is locked on his in the moment their bodies join; she focuses on every detail of his face, imprinting it on her memory: the fine sheen of sweat covering his forehead, the ridge of razor stubble on his lower face, the way he bites his lower lip in pleasure as he slowly thrusts into her.

Heated friction builds to molten release; first her own, then, as the potent ripples subside within, Jed moans and begins to shudder. She clings to his shoulders, riding it out with him, her legs wrapped tightly around his waist.

At last, spent, he rolls onto his back, hauling her with him and cradling her against his heaving chest.

"I don't want to leave you tonight," he says raggedly when his breathing has finally slowed.

"Do you really have to?" she asks, even as she wants to beg him to forget about everything else—and promise that she'll do the same.

But she can't.

In the morning, before he awakens, she'll catch the first train out. What choice does she have? She's got an early location call tomorrow, a therapy appointment, responsibilities. She can't just abandon her own world for his. There are no guarantees that she can change anything if she stays.

"I'll spend the night here with you," he decides, stroking her hair. "They're probably all asleep in the house by now anyway."

"What if they're not?"

"It doesn't matter. I'm a grown man."

"But I don't want your family to think—"

"It doesn't matter *what* they think. Nothing else matters. I can't leave, Clara. There's no possible way I can drag myself away from you now."

"I feel the same way," she whispers.

And when the gray morning light seeps through the window to find her snuggled safely against a slumbering Jed, she is just as powerless to pull herself away.

Not just yet.

If she stays, there are no guarantees that she can save him . . .

But if she leaves, there is one: Jed will not only go to a certain death, but he'll face it believing she abandoned him.

So, for now, for just a little longer, her own world will have to wait.

But what about the scene she's supposed to be shooting this morning? What about her appointment with Karen tonight, and, in the next few days, with the doctors who are treating her breast cancer?

If you stay, you can't think about any of that, she warns herself.

If she stays, for as long as she stays, she'll have no choice but to put the future out of her head, no matter how hard it is.

She'll live in the here and now . . .

Because, with Jed, that might be all there is.

Might be?

Who are you kidding? That is *all there is.*

Even if she somehow saves his life, she can't spend it with him.

Nothing can change the fact that she's in mortal danger here. If she wants to survive her illness, she'll have to go back.

And when that happens, it will have to be enough just to know that Jed's life was spared.

Chapter 15

True to her vow, in the forty-eight hours since she decided to stay with Jed, Clara hasn't allowed herself to wonder for more than a passing moment what might be going on in her own life back home.

But those moments are harrowing. She can just imagine the chaos on the set when she failed to show up these last few days, not to mention her mother's panic if she realizes that not only has her daughter failed to return her phone calls, but has for all practical purposes fallen off the face of the earth.

Clara will just have to pick up the pieces when she returns.

For now, her every waking moment is encompassed by Jed Landry.

He's everything she hoped him to be, believed him to be . . .

Wanted him to be?

There it is: that last infinitesimal, nagging doubt that this . . . any of this . . . can possibly be happening at all.

What if she so intensely longed to escape her grim reality that her subconscious conjured all of this? Yes, she has repeatedly ruled that out since she got back here . . . but what if it was all just part of one long, incredibly detailed dream?

And if it is a dream . . .

Then, at any random moment, she might suddenly wake up . . .

And Jed will be lost to her forever.

That isn't going to happen, she tells herself, watching him sleep on the pillow beside her in the first hours of Saturday morning.

She reaches out and lays a hand on his muscular shoulder, just to be certain.

He's as solid and real as she is.

Of course he is.

For three nights now, they've shared his twin bed— and an insatiable appetite for each other.

After each long day working together at the five-and-dime and sharing family dinners in the Landrys' kitchen, Clara retires to the garage apartment and Jed goes through the motions of bedding down on his mother's sofa.

The hour or two she spends alone between the cold sheets waiting for him to come to her seem endless . . . but they have allowed her to come up with a plan to save Jed from his grim fate.

Rather, the first step in a potential plan. But it's crucial, because if it succeeds, she'll know whether her ultimate mission is even possible.

If it doesn't succeed . . .

If she discerns that saving Jed is out of the question . . .

Then she'll have no choice but to give up, go home, and save herself.

Either way, today is the day.

Saturday, December 6, 1941.

Something is different about today.

Jed can't help but notice that as he watches Clara efficiently wrap a customer's purchase in brown paper.

He can't put his finger on what it is, but there seems to be some kind of anticipatory energy hovering in the air.

"We'll need more string up here pretty soon, Jed," she calls, without looking up at him as she untwines a length from the spool on the counter.

"I'll grab one."

Clara is rapidly getting the hang of working here, he thinks as he heads for the back room. She fits as easily into the rhythm of his days as she has into his nights. Sometimes he feels as though she's always been here with him, a part of his life.

Yet other times, he battles the irrational fear that if he blinks, she'll be gone, as if she was never here at all.

Today, especially.

She seemed inordinately quiet all morning, and several times this afternoon, he's caught her glancing at the clock, almost as though she has to be somewhere.

Which is out of the question . . . isn't it?

He takes another spool of string from the shelf, remembering how he furtively watched her dress herself on this very spot just a few days ago.

Then, he was filled with suspicions.

How conveniently he's since cast them aside.

The few times he's brought up Clara's life in the city—the one she seemingly abandoned with ease— she shrugs off his questions with yes and no answers.

He does know, thanks to what little he's gotten out of her, that she's an actress, not surprising given her extraordinary beauty. She admitted to having done stage and screen, but she refuses to tell him the details. Is she being modest? Or evasive?

He also knows that she isn't particularly close to anyone back home—not on a daily basis, anyway.

"You mean, no one will miss you if you never go back to the city?" he asked just last night, only half teasingly.

"I have to, sooner or later," was her disconcerting reply, and she refused to elaborate—or meet his gaze.

Jed returns to the front of the store, whistling "I'll Be Home for Christmas." He hasn't been able to get the song out of his head and can't help but wonder why he has yet to hear it played on the radio.

The real radio—not Clara's strange, small music player.

At the register, he finds her handing the deftly wrapped package to her customer with a smile and a cheerful "Merry Christmas!"

But it's plain to see that her thoughts are somewhere else, particularly as the whistle of the daily southbound 3:27 train sounds in the distance.

Jed watches Clara turn toward the window, listening intently as the locomotive chugs into the depot.

There's a faraway look on her face, one that fills him with trepidation.

"Excuse me, Mr. Landry, do you have any cowboy comic books?"

He looks down to see little Jimmy Henderson, whose family lives across Chestnut Street.

One eye on Clara, who is drifting away from the counter, he says, "Sure, Jimmy, come with me."

When he returns to ring up Jimmy's Gene Autry comic, the train's rumble has faded into the distance and he finds Clara idly examining the broken snow globe again.

He's noticed, these last few days, that she seems to have developed some kind of fixation on the little angel with the wounded wing.

"See you later, Mr. Landry," Jimmy calls on his way out the door.

Jed waves, crossing over to where Clara is standing, gazing into the falling snow inside the glass orb.

"Are you all right?" he asks, keeping his voice low so that the browsing customers won't overhear.

She looks up in surprise. "I'm fine. Why?"

"I don't know . . . you seem . . . restless."

"Restless?" She sets the snow globe back on the table, watching the flakes settle in the bottom. "Maybe I am restless, a little bit. Do you mind if I . . . take a walk or something?"

"Right now?"

She shrugs, and he sees her glancing again at the clock.

He nods slowly. Reluctantly.

What else can he do?

"Go ahead," he tells her. "Just . . . promise me you won't disappear. All right?"

He expects her to smile.

She doesn't.

A chill of foreboding slips down his spine at her solemn expression as she says, "I promise I won't disappear, Jed. I wouldn't leave you again without saying good-bye."

Watching her head to the stockroom where she left her coat, he only wishes she hadn't tacked on those last three words.

For the first time since she arrived, Clara finds herself out on the street without Jed by her side . . . and all too aware that with public solitude, here, comes a familiar vulnerability.

But nobody seems to be paying much attention to

her as she scurries along Main Street, quite at home now in the forties' wardrobe gleaned from her suitcase. She only wishes Lisa had paid more attention to sizes when she was filling it with vintage items from wardrobe. Some of the clothes are much too large for Clara, others too snug.

Of course, the contents of the suitcase weren't meant to be worn. And whenever Clara opens the lid to rummage through the garments, she can't help but feel momentary guilt for leaving the production in the lurch.

Now, however, her mind is firmly on the task immediately before her.

The air is bitingly clear, but blue black clouds are gathering above the wooded hills in the west. Glenhaven Park's business district is teeming with activity. In the slushy street, enormous cars rumble along, trailing exhaust, occasionally sounding their distinct *ah-oogah* horns. The sidewalks are filled with pedestrians: uniformed soldiers on leave, busy Christmas shoppers, loitering teenagers, bell-ringing Salvation Army Santas, gaggles of children toting dangling ice skates, headed for the frozen pond in the park across the way.

Clara savors the small-town atmosphere as she weaves her way along the snow-scraped sidewalk, marveling that she feels almost at home here after just a few days.

If only . . .

Stop that!

No use in *if onlies*; she can't stay here under any circumstances.

In fact, if today proves that Jed is doomed regardless of her intervention in the past, she should leave right away, before she falls even more deeply in . . .

Stop that! she scolds herself again.

You don't love Jed. You can't possibly love someone after only a few days together . . .

Or can you?

It feels like love.

But even if what she feels for Jed is authentic, what does it matter?

It can't last, Clara reminds herself as she turns down Oak Street.

The long block is lined by two-story Victorian homes with tall old trees overshadowing small front yards. At the end, she can see the looming three-story brick rectangle that is Glenhaven Park Hospital.

But she isn't going that far; the house she seeks turns up in the middle of the block. The black 59 above the metal mailbox matches the address scribbled on a slip of paper in her pocket. She found it last night when, under the pretext of visiting the powder room during supper, she snuck a peek at the Landrys' *Glenhaven Park Telephone Directory.*

The festive evergreen wreath on the front door seems incongruous with the missing shutters, peeling paint, and straggly shrubs. The front walk could stand to be shoveled, as could the wooden steps that creak under Clara's weight as she ascends to the porch. Somebody must have made a haphazard attempt to clear a narrow path at one point, but fresh snow has since fallen and hardened to a bulky crust.

As Clara rings the bell, she again rehearses what she's going to say.

Her carefully prepared speech might very well be met with suspicion. It certainly would be in her own day and age.

But she's noticed that things are different in 1941. People are more trusting of strangers . . .

Unless they think the stranger might be involved in

espionage, she thinks ruefully, remembering Jed's initial assumption about her.

The door opens, and an elderly woman looks out in confusion and surprise.

"Yes? May I help you?"

"Hello, my name is Clara McCallum. I'm new in town, staying with the Landry family over on Chestnut Street. I'm going door to door to see if anyone would like me to run holiday errands . . . you know, like grocery shopping, that sort of thing."

The old woman raises a white eyebrow. "I wish I could hire you, dear, because there are quite a few things on my shopping list and I hate to go out when it's so cold. But I'm a widow, and I'm afraid I just can't afford—"

"Oh, I don't want to be paid," Clara hurriedly assures her. "I'm doing this strictly in the holiday spirit. Really, whatever you need from the store, I'll be glad to pick up for you."

Minnie Bouvier's face lights up. "Well, bless your heart. I'll get my list."

"Jed, I've got to talk to you."

He looks up to see Arnold Wilkens striding toward the cash register, his wrathful expression barely contained beyond thick lenses.

Thanks to a temporary lull in business, Jed can do nothing but fold his arms and wait for the storm to erupt.

"Jed," Arnold growls, fists clenched, ears bright red beneath his crew cut. "I can't believe this."

"What's going on, Arnold?"

"*Crazy Maisie?*"

"I beg your pardon?"

"You told the entire town that I call my wife Crazy Maisie!"

"Not the entire town. Just Pete Kavinski," Jed concedes.

"Just Pete Kavinski, who then told the entire town." Jed shrugs helplessly. "I'm sorry, Arnold, I didn't mean to—"

"Jed, do you know what kind of hell I've lived through these past few days since this got back to her? She won't let me leave her, even for a few minutes."

"Is she still constantly thinking she's in labor?"

"Not only that, but now she's got it in her head that if I go anywhere, I'll never come back to her."

Jed briefly considers telling Arnold he wouldn't blame him if he did just that.

Thinking better of it, he simply points out, "Well, you're gone now."

"Only because Maisie finally fell asleep. I figured she would sooner or later . . . no human can go days and days, ranting and raving, pacing and complaining, without sleep. I'm telling you, Jed, she's—"

"Crazy?" Jed asks mildly when Arnold breaks off.

"You said it. Not me. And you've got to tell her that, Jed. Tell her you're the one who made up that nickname. She doesn't believe me."

"I will, Arnold. I promise, the next time I see—"

"No, now. You've got to come with me right now and tell her. And we don't have much time. She won't stay asleep for very long." Arnold looks around furtively, as though he half expects his wife to bluster into the store at any moment.

"I can't leave right now, Arnold. I'm alone here."

"Yeah? What happened to your new clerk?"

"She's . . . out. How did you know I have a new clerk?"

"In this town? Do you really have to ask?" Arnold leans closer and says in a low voice, "It's her, isn't it. The spy."

"She isn't a spy."

"Then who is she? And why was she carrying that transmitter?"

"It was a regular radio . . . sort of."

"Sort of?"

"It plays records, only they aren't records, and—say, have you heard that new song by Frank Sinatra yet?"

"Who's he?"

Jed shrugs. "Some kid from Jersey who sings with Tommy Dorsey. He has this song, 'I'll Be Home for Christmas,' that I can't get out of my head. Clara played it on her music machine, and—"

"Clara? So you really think that's her name?"

"I know it is."

"How do you know?"

"Because she told me."

Jed hates the skeptical gleam in Arnold's eyes—hates even more that it's suddenly reflected somewhere deep inside of him.

That's just because she isn't here.

When she's with him, he trusts her implicitly. All he has to do is look at her and he knows she's telling the truth . . .

Except she really hasn't told him much of anything at all.

Not about her life, anyway.

But what does that matter?

"Jed, just watch yourself, okay?" Arnold says, clapping a heavy hand on Jed's upper arm. "Don't let some bit of fluff do you in."

"For crying out loud, Arnold . . . she isn't a bit of fluff."

"Right. And Maisie isn't crazy."

With that, Arnold strides toward the door, calling, "Don't forget to come on over to my place to talk to her later, Jed. I'm counting on you."

Jed gives him a two-fingered salute. Then he crosses to the plate glass window to watch Arnold climb into his blue Packard and drive away.

Scanning the street, hoping to catch sight of Clara on her way back here, he almost thinks he glimpses her disappearing into Ferguson's Grocery down the block. But he probably just imagined that.

After all, when you want something badly enough, Jed thinks, turning away from the window, *you can talk yourself into seeing just about anything.*

"Will that be all, ma'am?" asks the aproned grocer as Clara sets her purchases on the counter.

Despite having all but memorized the list, she peruses Minnie Bouvier's spidery handwriting one more time, to be sure she hasn't forgotten anything. In addition to eggs, baking powder, and molasses are the spices: cinnamon, nutmeg, mace, allspice.

"Mice got into my spice cabinet and I had to throw away every last spice I keep on hand," Minnie confided as she handed Clara her shopping list. "I just hope I'm not forgetting anything. I have the feeling that I am, but I can't figure out what it is."

"Why don't you check the recipe?" Clara suggested uneasily.

"Oh, I keep my recipes in here." Minnie tapped her white head. "But I suppose that doesn't seem like the safest place these days. My memory isn't what it used to be—unless, of course, I'm thinking about my dear Homer. There's nothing about him that isn't as fresh in my mind as if it happened just today."

"Homer is your husband?"

Minnie nodded. "We were married almost seventy years."

"*Seventy* years?"

"I wasn't even fifteen yet when we wed back in sixty-nine . . ."

Sixty-nine . . . she means 1869. Clara was incredulous.

"My papa told me that I was too young to know what I wanted. But I did. I wanted Homer. And I had him for all those years . . . someday soon, we'll be together again."

Minnie's faded gray eyes twinkled in her weathered face as she carefully counted and recounted two precious dollar bills and two quarters into Clara's hand, saying, "I'm giving you a little extra, to keep for yourself."

"No, I can't do that, Mrs. Bouvier. This is my pleasure."

"You're an angel, my dear," the woman responded. "A beautiful dark-haired Christmas angel."

Now, as the grocer rings up Minnie's purchases, Clara recalls what she said about being with Homer again.

It was exactly the same with her own grandfather, talking about his beloved Irene.

What if . . . ?

No! Don't go there, Clara, she warns herself.

But she can't seem to keep the dark thought from breaking through.

What if you aren't meant to save Jed . . . or survive your cancer?

Are they meant to be together in some other world . . .

Or perhaps, in some other lifetime?

But that won't be enough. Not for me. I'm not an old woman. I want to live my life, the one I have. I want to be Clara. I want to get married, and have children . . .

No, she isn't ready to die.

Not even to be with Jed.

"That will be two dollars and twenty-three cents, young lady." The grocer's chipper tone cuts into her thoughts.

As Clara counts out Minnie's money, she wishes she could use her own cash instead. But it's as useless here in 1941 as counterfeit bills would be. Yes, the quarters at least look almost the same at a glance, but the last thing she needs is to arouse suspicion with dated currency from the future.

"You must be doing some Christmas baking," the store owner comments, packing Clara's groceries into a paper sack.

"I am," Clara agrees, because it's the simplest explanation.

A female customer steps in from the street with a gust of frigid air. She's stylish in a sweeping fur coat and a wide-brimmed hat cocked at an angle. Her lipstick is deep crimson, and Clara can smell her floral perfume from several yards away.

"Hello, Mr. Ferguson," she calls from behind a curtain of wavy blond hair that curiously shrouds one half of her face.

"Hi there, Betty. Cold out there?"

"It is, but this new fur coat is keeping me toasty warm. Do you like it? It's Manchurian wolf!"

"Very nice. Is it snowing out there yet?"

"Not yet, and I don't think it's going to."

Oh, but you're wrong about that, Clara tells the new-comer silently as the storekeeper hands over the sack containing Minnie's groceries. *It's going to snow.*

Oh, and by the way, tomorrow at this time, America will be at war, and nothing in your world is ever going to be the same.

Clara trudges to the door, her steps heavy with the weight of her own useless precognition.

Useless . . .

Unless it turns out she can alter the past after all.

And I'll know very soon . . .

She quickens her pace, opening the door as the store owner asks the other woman, "What can I help you find today, Betty?"

Betty?

Clara suddenly remembers the giggling woman she heard Drew Becker talking to in his apartment the other night. Oddly—at least in the twenty-first century—her name was Betty, too.

"Just some nice sweet apples. I'm going to bake one of my famous pies for a very lucky fella."

"That lucky fella wouldn't happen to be Jed Landry, would it?"

Clara stops cold, one foot out the door, her hand frozen on the knob behind her.

The blonde giggles. "How did you guess?"

"This is a small town, Betty. Don't you think I don't know who's keeping company with whom."

Another giggle, followed by a pointed, pouty, "Brrrr."

"Say, miss," Mr. Ferguson calls in Clara's direction, "could you please close the door? You're letting in the chill."

Yes, and she's taking it with her, too. Numb to the

bone, she walks dejectedly toward Minnie Bouvier's house.

It never occurred to her until this very second that Jed might fall in love with somebody else after she leaves Glenhaven Park . . .

Or that he might very well have been—*keeping company*—with other girls before she got here. *Of course he was. He's a red-blooded man.*

Clara is desperately jealous of the fur-clad, pie-baking blonde—even as she reminds herself that her feeling is utterly irrational.

Jed's life will go on when she's gone . . . isn't that the point?

Doesn't she want him to live happily ever after—the key word being *live*—even if it can't be with her?

Of course she does.

It just hurts, knowing that she can't have him.

Knowing that she's saving his life to be shared with some other girl, perhaps old one-eyed Betty . . .

If I can save him at all.

She quickens her pace toward Minnie Bouvier's house, anxious to deliver the groceries . . . and, in doing so, avert the tragic accident that was to occur at dusk on the corner of Oak and Main.

Because if the past can be altered and Minnie Bouvier survives . . .

Then she'll know Jed Landry can, too.

Chapter 16

Peering out into the street as he turns over the CLOSED sign in the front window, Jed sees a swirl of snowflakes in the overhead streetlight's yellow glow.

"Please have snow . . . and mistletoe . . ." he sings softly. *"And presents . . . under the tree."*

"On the tree," Clara musically amends.

He turns to see her standing behind him, wearing her coat and hat and offering his.

"On the tree?" Jed echoes, taking them from her. "That doesn't make any sense. How can presents be on the tree?"

She shrugs, smiling as she pulls on her red mittens. "Don't blame me. I didn't write the lyrics."

"No, I know. The thing is . . ."

"What?" she asks reluctantly, as though she senses a sticky question coming her way.

"Why hasn't that song been on the radio yet? It's Christmastime. And it's a swell song. I don't understand why I haven't heard it anywhere but on your music machine . . . and nobody else has ever heard of it, either."

"Nobody else?" A shadow crosses her face. "As in . . . who?"

"Never mind. It's not important. Say, I had that flat fixed on the DeSoto yesterday, remember?" He settles his fedora on his head and buttons his coat. "How about if I take you out for dinner tonight instead of eating with the family? And afterward, we can go dancing at a nightclub. I bet you can do a mean Lindy Hop."

"I don't know, Jed . . . I'm not really in the mood for dancing. I think I'd rather spend a quiet evening alone with you."

"Being alone with you always sounds good, but I feel bad, never taking you out on the town." He opens the door for her and they step out into the falling snow.

"I don't need to go out on the town, Jed," she says, her breath puffing frosty white in the air between them.

"I know you don't *need* to," he says, reaching into his pocket for the list of things his mother asked him to pick up at the store when she called earlier, "but I thought you might *want* to."

"No. I just want to be with you."

About to lock the door, he looks up at her, uneasy at the note of desolation in her voice.

"What's wrong, Clara?"

"Nothing. What's that in your hand?"

He hands her the shopping list and sticks the key into the lock. "I guess Doris got to my mother, because she called and said she's going to make fruitcakes after all. These are the ingredients she needs. We can stop at Ferguson's, they're still open."

Clara holds the paper up in the glow from the streetlight, reading it. "Cinnamon, mace, allspice . . . Is she using Minnie Bouvier's recipe?"

"Yes . . . how did you know?"

"I just remembered. *Nutmeg, ground cloves*—" Clara stops short. Then she fumbles in her coat pocket, pulling out a wrinkled piece of paper.

"What's wrong?" Jed asks, watching her hurriedly

comparing his mother's list to what appears to be another list.

"Ground cloves," she murmurs, almost in . . . dread?

But that doesn't make sense.

"Clara, what—"

"That's what Minnie forgot! Ground cloves."

Before he can ask her what she's talking about, he hears the roar of a car engine, rapidly approaching from a distance.

Both he and Clara turn to see headlights coming down Main Street.

"Say, that's Arnold Wilkens's Packard," Jed notices as the car passes, wondering why his friend doesn't slow down or wave. Maybe he's still sore at Jed for not coming over yet to clear things up with Maisie.

"Packard?" Clara echoes.

"Say, he's got Maisie with him . . . I wonder if she could really be in labor this time!"

"Oh, no," Clara murmurs. "No!"

Startled, he looks at her and sees that she's gaping at the car in horror.

"What's wrong?" he asks, wondering if she's somehow, somewhere, had a brush with the notorious Crazy Maisie.

"Stop!" Clara screeches at the top of her lungs. "No, stop!"

In disbelief, Jed watches her running away, frantically chasing Arnold's car down Main Street.

Jed quickly turns the key in the lock and takes off after Clara, bewildered.

In the distance, he sees the Packard's red taillights disappearing around the corner of Oak Street.

Then, a sickening squeal of brakes.

*　　*　　*

"I brought you some hot tea."

Huddled on the bed, knees to chest, a blanket wrapped around her shoulders, Clara looks up dully.

Jed steps into the apartment with a tray and sets it on the table.

"At least, it was hot when I left the kitchen a minute ago. Doris insisted on making you some toast, too. With marmalade."

Minnie Bouvier's marmalade, no doubt.

"She wanted to come up and see you but I told her you weren't feeling well. I promised her she can come up later. She's worried you won't be able to go with us in the morning to chop down the Christmas tree."

Clara is silent, brooding.

"Come on, Clara. This will help."

She shakes her head bleakly.

Nothing will help.

A few hours ago, Minnie Bouvier, on her way to the store to pick up the ground cloves she forgot, was struck by Arnold Wilkens's Packard as he rushed his laboring wife, Maisie, to the hospital.

"I'm sure Minnie is going to be just fine," Jed says, sitting on the bed beside her. "We can even go over to the hospital in the morning to visit her."

Clara closes her eyes to shut out the image of the sweet little old lady lying crumpled and bleeding in the snowy road.

It was Jed who heroically covered her in his own coat and knelt beside Minnie, holding her hand.

"I'll get to the hospital and send help," Arnold Wilkens said helplessly, as his wife wailed and writhed in the Packard's front seat.

"Hurry, Arnold," Jed replied, focused on the injured woman. "Hang on, Minnie. Just don't go to sleep."

Minnie's eyes rolled, and her gaze seemed to settle on Clara, standing a few feet away.

"Angel," she whispered, smiling faintly, and her eyelids fluttered closed.

"You're seeing an angel? Minnie, come on, hang in there. Open your eyes." Somehow, Jed managed to keep her conscious until the ambulance arrived.

It probably didn't take long—the hospital was a stone's throw from the accident scene.

But to Clara, standing by helplessly in the blowing snow, the wait was interminable.

She wanted to do something, but she was too numb with horror to move or speak.

Several neighbors ventured out of their houses to survey the horrific scene, including a woman named Lorraine. Clara overheard her telling someone that Minnie had just minutes ago asked to borrow cloves from her and, when Lorraine said she didn't have any, decided she'd have to go buy them.

"I told her not to go," Lorraine said desolately, "but she wanted to get those fruitcakes made tonight."

Even after Minnie had been borne away on a stretcher, Clara was rooted to the spot, staring at the crimson stain in the snow.

And it wasn't Minnie's blood she was seeing.

It was Jed's.

"Clara . . ." Back in the garage apartment, he slips his arms around her. "Look at me."

She opens her eyes. "Don't, Jed."

"Don't what?"

Don't stare into my eyes that way . . .

Don't make me love you . . .

Don't die.

"I need to ask you something," Jed says slowly. "Right before the accident, you said something about

Minnie forgetting ground cloves. Lorraine said she had tried to borrow cloves and that was what she was going out to buy. Then, when Arnold drove by, you almost seemed as if . . ."

He trails off and looks at her, shaking his head.

"As if what?" she whispers.

"As if you knew what was going to happen."

Clara takes a deep breath.

I have to at least try, just one more time.

"That's because I did know, Jed."

Clara's words wash over Jed like a cold wave, leaving him sputtering, "But . . . that's . . . that's impossible."

"Nothing is impossible, Jed," she replies, wearing a cryptic expression. "If anyone is proof of that, I am."

Wondering what she means by that, exactly, he points out, "Seeing the future is impossible, unless you're . . . some kind of gypsy fortune-teller, maybe. Or . . . I don't know . . . *God*. And no offense, but I don't think you're either."

She doesn't even smile at his lame attempt at humor.

He watches her brow furrow as her front teeth settle over the lower corner of her mouth. Clearly, she's wrestling with something.

For a moment, the only sound in the room is the rattling windowpane and a faint creaking sound as the wind gusts outside.

Then Clara says softly, "The details aren't important. What is important is that you're willing to believe me, Jed—even if what I'm telling you sounds like the most bizarre thing you've ever heard. Are you?"

"Am I . . . ?"

"Willing to believe me."

"Oh. I . . . I don't know."

He knows what he heard, what he saw earlier, on the street outside the store. He didn't imagine Clara's inexplicable mention of Minnie, and cloves, nor her panicky reaction to Arnold's car as it passed.

Still . . .

"You're telling me you can see the future?"

"I'm telling you that I'm *from* the future."

He stares at her for a long moment. Then he bursts out laughing. "You don't look much like Buck Rogers."

"I'm not kidding, Jed."

"Neither am I. You don't even have a space suit." His mirth fades as he sees that she's deadly serious.

He reaches out and brushes her hair back from her forehead, revealing the yellowish gray bruise still visible above her brow.

"You're thinking I'm delusional." She pulls back. "Aren't you? You're thinking that this bump on my head has me imagining all sorts of things. You know what? I thought so, too, at first. I even thought I was imagining you."

"I'm real," he says gently, dropping his hand from her head to her shoulder.

"I know you are. And you've got to believe that I'm real, too, Jed. Because you might look back on this at some point and decide that I wasn't."

"Look back?" Dread seeps in. "Clara—"

"I'm going to tell you something that you have to believe, and you have to remember. Even after I'm gone."

"No!" he says sharply. "You can't go. I need—"

"I have to go back home," she cuts in, and he knew somewhere deep inside it would come down to this.

"I don't want to . . . believe me, Jed, I want nothing more than to stay here with you, forever."

"Then stay. Forever. We'll be together, right here . . . or we can get a real house! I'm making over two thousand dollars a year, Clara! We can get married, and—"

"Stop it, Jed! We can't get married, and I can't stay." She's sobbing now.

He opens his mouth to comfort her, to remind her that even if she does have to go back sooner or later, the city isn't on another planet; they'll still see each other as much as they can, until they can work it out so that they can be together all the—

She stops him before he can open his mouth, laying a fingertip against his lips. "Shhh, just listen. I knew Minnie Bouvier was going to be killed tonight, just like I know—"

"Killed? She wasn't killed, Clara. She was alive. She's in the hospital. I'm sure she's going to be just—"

"She's going to die, Jed. And . . . and *so are you.*"

Clara watches Jed's mouth drop open in shock. *Oh, no, I shouldn't have blurted it out like that.* But she had to get his full attention. *And you certainly have it now.*

He seems incapable of speaking . . . and she feels the same way. But she knows she has to keep talking—has to make him understand.

"If you enlist in the army and go off to fight in the war in Europe, Jed," she says, choosing her words more carefully this time, "you aren't going to come home. You're going to be killed."

Relief swoops over his face, and he lets out a nervous laugh. "Is that what all this fuss is about? That's what every gal says when her fella goes into the army. Listen, now that I have you, the last thing I want to do is enlist, so don't—"

"You say that now," Clara cuts in. "But you won't feel the same tomorrow."

He frowns. "Sure I will."

"No, Jed, tomorrow we're going to be at war. You have to believe me. The Japanese are going to attack Pearl Harbor."

"How's that?"

"Pearl Harbor. The Japanese are going to attack—"

"What is Pearl Harbor? And where is it?"

"It's a military base, it's somewhere in Hawaii, and hundreds of people are going to die, and I need to warn the president, or the police, or . . . or someone . . ."

"Clara, you can't do anything of the kind."

"But maybe I can save—"

"Do you remember what happened in the store the other day, when Pete was there? I barely managed to convince him that you're not some kind of spy. You can't go running around now, calling the police or the government and making dire predictions about imminent military attacks. They'll want to know how you know. And you'll tell them . . . ?"

"It doesn't matter, because I'm right. They'll see when everything I tell them comes true tomorrow."

"Which is when they'll arrest you on suspicion of treason."

She falls silent. He's right.

"But, Jed, you have to believe me about Pearl Harbor. You do, don't you?"

He rakes a hand through his hair. "I don't know what to believe."

"Listen to me. After the attack, FDR is going to

declare war, Jed. And he's going to make a speech on the radio and say that December 7, 1941, is a day that will live in infamy. That's tomorrow."

"Tomorrow," he echoes flatly.

Clearly, he has no idea what to make of any of this.

"You'll just have to wait and see."

"So let me just make sure I've got it straight. The Japs are going to attack tomorrow"—he begins to tick off items on his fingers—"and we're going to war, and Minnie Bouvier is going to die. Is that it?"

"It?"

"Those are your predictions? All for tomorrow?"

"Yes. Oh, and your friend Arnold's wife is going to have a baby boy," she remembers, "and they're going to name him Denton."

Jed throws his head back and laughs. "No, see, now I know you're joking around. The Wilkens baby is going to be a girl called Daisy."

"What makes you think that?"

"Maisie said so, and Maisie is never wrong. Anyway, what kind of a name is Denton?"

"Jed . . . " Clara swallows hard. "Please . . . if everything I've said comes true tomorrow, will you believe me then?"

"Believe that you can see the future? I guess I'll have to . . . if everything you say comes true."

She exhales in relief, ignoring the dubious look on his face. Once he has proof that she knows what she's talking about, he'll agree not to enlist. He has to.

She refuses to believe that she's powerless to change his destiny.

Maybe she just couldn't save Minnie because she left too much to chance. She probably should have come right out and told the old woman not to go out tonight, no matter what.

Yes, and would she have obeyed?

I could have made sure that she did. I could have come right out and told her that if she left the house, she was going to die.

Well, with Jed, she's already been straightforward.

Too straightforward, judging by the worried gaze he's fixed on her.

"What are you thinking about?" he asks.

"Poor Minnie."

"She's going to pull through, Clara. You'll see. That's what the ambulance driver said to her."

"He was just trying to keep her calm. You don't really think he'd tell her she wasn't going to make it, do you?"

"No," he admits, "I don't. But even if Minnie doesn't pull through, Clara . . . she's in her eighties. She's lived a long life, and she's been lonely without her husband. He was all she—"

He breaks off as somewhere beyond the cozy little room, a board creaks.

"Is that you, Doris?" Jed calls, looking toward the door.

No reply.

He stands and strides over, opening the door with a flourish. "Gotcha!"

Clara watches him stick his head out into the darkness of the garage.

"Huh. No Doris. Must have been the wind," he says, and closes the door. He locks it, then turns to look at Clara.

"Tomorrow is a long ways away," he comments.

Clara shrugs, knowing it's going to come all too soon—and when it does, she won't be the only one wishing the clock could be turned back.

"What are we going to do in the meantime?" Jed

asks slyly, returning to the bed and draping his arms around her.

Clara's heart quickens despite her somber mood. "I don't know . . ."

Jed kisses her, lightly. "Say," he says against her mouth, "I've got an idea . . ."

And for a little while longer, at least, there is nothing but the here and now.

Chapter 17

"Jed?"

Pounding footsteps up the stairs, an urgent knock at the door.

"Jed!"

"What is it?" he calls, hurrying over, legs weak with apprehension. "What's wrong?"

He opens the door to find his kid sister standing on the top step, bundled in a black woolen coat, a thick yellow muffler, and an old velvet hat of Penny's that ties with frayed ribbons beneath her chin.

"Come on, let's go get the tree!"

He groans. "Hold your horses, Doris! I thought something terrible happened."

Yes, thanks to Clara and her dire predictions for today.

"The only terrible thing that's happened," his impetuous sister informs him, "is that you're not keeping your promise."

"What promise is that?"

"The one where you said we'd go get the tree first thing."

"And we will, just as soon as Clara is ready."

"But that won't be first thing. That's more like *last* thing."

He sighs.

Doris has been pestering him since six, when she descended on him as he slept on the sofa. Of course, she didn't know that he had arrived in the house less than a half hour before, having spent the better part of the night in his own bed with Clara.

He didn't want to leave her.

He never wants to leave her . . . but he especially didn't last night. Not after the way she acted, the strange things she said.

Does she honestly think she can see into the future?

Can she see into the future?

He would almost believe it, based on her actions just before Minnie's accident . . .

If it weren't impossible.

Nothing is impossible, Jed. If anyone is proof of that, I am.

What did she mean by that?

"Come on, Jed," his sister pesters.

"Doris . . . be patient."

"I am being patient. You said to give you fifteen minutes."

"That was five minutes ago, toots. Why don't you go read the Sunday funnies or something?"

"I already did. Twice. There's a new one today— *John Carter of Mars*. Now come on!"

"It's okay, let's go, Jed." Clara has come up behind him.

Doris's eyes widen. "What kind of coat is that?"

He turns to see that Clara is wearing her puffy red parka again, with the red knit hat and mittens. And the dungarees she had on that first day, plus her white rubber shoes.

"If we're going out into the woods," Clara says simply, "I want to make sure I'm warm."

Jed notices uneasily that she isn't looking at him.

Well, Doris is the one who asked the question . . .

But it's almost as though Clara is avoiding eye contact with him.

Or is he just paranoid today?

I am, thanks to her.

Today is Sunday, December 7. The day Clara claims will live on in infamy . . . to quote the president's mythical speech.

Well, it's already midmorning, and there's been no word of an attack yet. When Jed asked Clara what time she thought the Japs were going to start dropping bombs on Hawaii, she said she wasn't sure.

So here he is, unable to shake the feeling that something is about to happen. Something awful.

But it has nothing to do with the war or Minnie Bouvier . . .

No, it's Clara. He's going to lose Clara.

He still doesn't know why, or when, exactly . . .

But she's going to go. She told him.

So? You'll see each other again. And she can move up here, or eventually, after Gilbert comes back, you can move down there . . .

But what if she goes, and he never sees her again?

Oh, come on, what are you thinking, Jed? You aren't going to just let her . . . go.

But what if . . .

What if it isn't up to him?

It won't be.

It wasn't with Carol, and it won't be with Clara, either. Somehow, he knows that.

Somehow, he's certain that this time, when Clara leaves, she'll have no intention of finding her way back to him. Ever.

And you know this based on what? he asks himself angrily. *An irrational hunch? A groundless fear?*

He isn't sure what's driving his pessimism.

But now, seeing Clara standing there wearing the same clothes she had on when she got here on Wednesday, his dismal state of mind isn't exactly eased.

"Come *on*," Doris prods again, though she's still looking over Clara's clothing with an inquisitive eye.

"Just let me get the keys and my coat, and then I have to go downstairs and look for Pop's axe."

"I already found it in the garage, Jed, see?" She swings it up to eye level.

"Jeepers creepers, Doris!" Jed grabs the handle to steady it in her hands. "Give that to me."

"Why do you get to carry it?"

"Because I'm the grown-up."

"Well, so am I." Doris sticks out her tongue at him. "Oh, and by the way, Mother wants you to take her to the hospital later to visit Mrs. Bouvier."

Jed looks at Clara, who refuses to look back.

"Has Mother heard anything about her this morning?" he anxiously asks his sister.

"No, that's why she wants to go. She called the hospital but they wouldn't give out any information over the phone. Now she's worried."

A chill slips over Jed. "Maybe we should stop there ourselves, then, on the way to get the tree."

"No!" his sister and Clara protest in unison.

He glances from one to the other in surprise.

Clara shakes her head slightly at him. *She doesn't want to bring Doris to the hospital,* Jed realizes, *because she's afraid something's happened to Minnie.*

"Children aren't allowed in the hospital," Doris informs him.

"Oh?—Well, I thought you were a grown-up."

"I *am* a grown-up. Except sometimes, I'm a child."

"Only when it suits you, though," Clara says with a grin. "Right?"

"Right," is Doris's cheerful reply.

Jed rolls his eyes.

"Let's go get the tree. *Oh, Christmas tree, oh, Christmas tree . . .*"

"Must you sing that *again*?" Jed grumbles at his sister as they all head down the steep steps.

"It's my favorite Christmas carol."

"Then we'll teach you a new one, and that can be your favorite instead. Listen: *I'll . . . be home . . . for Christmas,*" Jed sings, then breaks off to coax with forced enthusiasm, "Come on, Clara, let's make it a duet."

"*You . . . can plan . . . on me.*"

But he can tell her heart isn't in it either, and her thoughts are a million miles from here.

You're slipping away, Clara . . . and I have no idea how to bring you back.

For a few hours, at least, Clara was almost able to forget the harsh reality of today.

Tromping through the hushed, alabaster-carpeted woods north of town, singing Christmas carols with Jed and his sister, she temporarily relinquished the burden of knowing what's coming, locally, globally— and being powerless to do anything about it.

Now, however, as Jed pulls the DeSoto into the driveway back on Chestnut Street, toxic trepidation is once again corroding her from within.

Even so, she clings to a shimmer of hope.

Maybe Jed was right about Minnie Bouvier pulling through after all. Maybe she didn't die. Maybe—

"Look, there's Mother," Doris announces. "What is she doing out there? She must have been watching for us."

Yes, Lois Landry is stepping out onto the back stoop wearing a thin housedress, heedless of the flurries in the air.

Clara doesn't dare look over at Jed, beside her in the front seat. But she can feel the tension that suddenly clenches his body as profoundly as it does her own.

Something is wrong.

"Mother, look at the tree!" Doris bounds out of the car, gesturing at the evergreen lashed to the roof. "We got the biggest, best one ever!"

"Doris, go right inside," her mother commands, anxiously twisting the dish towel in her hands. "It's snowing."

"But don't you want to see—"

"*Now,* Doris."

"All right . . . I'll go up to the attic and find all the tree lights and decorations." She disappears into the house before anyone can protest.

Jed is already out of the car and opening Clara's door. His cold hand shakes as he takes hers to help her out, his gaze focused on his mother's distressed face.

"What is it?" he asks her as he and Clara hurry toward her.

"Sarah Wenick was just here—she came right over from the hospital. Minnie Bouvier passed away this morning."

Jed can't breathe, much less speak.

He feels Clara's hand tighten in his own.

"That poor old woman," his mother goes on. "What a terrible way to die. All alone, and she had to be so frightened—"

"No . . ." Jed recovers his voice. "She saw an angel,

Mother. When I was with her right after the accident. I'll bet she wasn't alone when she died."

Hearing a sniffle, he looks at Clara and is stunned to see tears running down her cheeks. But . . . why?

She doesn't even know the old woman.

Or does she?

Again, he realizes that Clara McCallum is purely an enigma, perhaps more so now than ever before.

Because she knew. Somehow, she knew Minnie wasn't going to make it.

Still, Jed supposes, it could have been a lucky—or rather, unlucky—guess.

"Mother," he asks, his eyes still focused on Clara's impermeable expression, "has there been any news today? About the war?"

His mother shakes her head distractedly.

If she hasn't heard anything, then nothing has happened. His grandparents will have had the radio on; they always listen to the string quartet on Sundays after church.

"Leave the tree for now. Come inside." Mother holds the door open for them.

Stepping into the kitchen, they're greeted by a scorched smell, and something bubbling over.

"Oh, no, my stew!" Lois cries out.

"Here, let me help you." Clara takes off her mittens and tosses them onto the counter.

Something clatters to the linoleum.

"You dropped these." Jed stoops to retrieve her key ring and hands it to her, along with the folded bills she's been carrying for days, unable to spend them here.

"Thanks." She hastily shoves the keys and money into her back pocket, then grabs a pair of crocheted pot holders.

"I'll be right back." Jed ignores the questioning look Clara shoots over her shoulder at him. "I've got to make a call."

From the next room, he can hear the radio playing. He recognizes the jaunty tone of his sisters' favorite program, *Swing and Sway with Sammy Kaye*.

Sure enough, Jed can see when he steps into the front hall that Penny and Mary Ann are sprawled on the floor in front of the radio reading the Sunday funnies, swinging their ankles in time to the music. His grandparents are dozing nearby.

"Did you get the tree, Jed?" Penny asks, looking up.

"Sure did."

"Goody! Where is it?"

"Outside," he tells Mary Ann as he lifts the telephone receiver. "I'll set it up later."

"How may I direct your call?" the switchboard operator asks in his ear.

"Glenhaven Park Memorial Hospital, please," Jed says tightly.

Sensing that she's being watched, Clara looks up from mopping up the mess on the stove top to see Jed in the doorway.

"Mother, you've had such a difficult day, why don't you go upstairs and lie down for a little while?" he suggests.

Glimpsing the grim look on his face, Clara offers, "I'll finish cleaning this and keep an eye on the stew for you, Mrs. Landry."

Jed's mother doesn't argue. Clara sees him tenderly pat her on the shoulder as she passes by.

He takes such good care of her, Clara notices, not for the first time. *Of all of them.* Jed is the man of the house, dutifully filling his father's place at the expense of his own dreams.

He told Clara about Boston, and his scholarship to Harvard Law. He admitted that it wasn't easy to turn his back on all of that when he lost his father.

"But a man does what needs to be done," he said simply.

Those words sent a chill down Clara's spine. Was that why he enlisted in the army?

The stair treads creak as Lois ascends to the second floor.

Still wearing her red hat and coat, Clara crosses to the sink. She can feel Jed watching her intently as she turns on the water and begins to rinse and wring the dishrag with shaking hands.

Why won't he just say something—anything?

Careful . . . maybe you don't want to hear what he has to say, she warns herself.

Finally, she turns off the water, drapes the rag over the faucet, and meets his gaze head-on.

"What?" she asks heavily.

"Arnold and Maisie had a boy."

Clara's breath catches in her throat.

She knew it, of course . . . but hearing it aloud, accompanied by the almost accusatory look on Jed's face, is overwhelming.

Jed goes on in a monotone, walking slowly toward her. "Arnold hadn't even bothered to think of any names in advance. They were positive it was going to be a girl. So positive that right now, the poor kid is wearing pink booties. Arnold had to pluck a boy's name out of thin air before Maisie went back on their deal to let him name it. The baby looked like he had a dent in his head, Arnold said . . . so that's his name."

"What is?" Clara's voice is barely audible, even to her own ears.

"Dent-in . . . Denton." Jed comes to a halt a foot away. "It's Denton Wilkens. But you already knew that, didn't you."

"Jed—"

"How could you have known? These people are strangers to you, Clara . . . aren't they? The Wilkenses, and Minnie . . ."

She remains silent. What can she possibly say now that she hasn't already?

Only this time, he'll believe you, she reminds herself. *This time, he won't shrug off your warnings . . .*

But what does that matter?

Minnie is dead.

Jed—

No. I can't just let him die, too, without trying one last time.

"Jed, you have to listen to me." She takes hold of his upper arms, pleading with him. "It doesn't matter how I knew. What matters is that I did know. About the Wilkens baby, about Minnie . . . and I know about you."

"What about me?"

"I already told you, unless you do something to change your destiny, you're going to—"

Her words are curtailed by an urgent, ear-piercing screech from the next room.

"Jed, come quick!" one of his sisters hollers.

He turns on his heel and bolts, with Clara on his heels.

Both Penny and Mary Ann are on their feet, staring at the radio.

"What's going on?" Jed's grandmother demands

sleepily as her husband makes his way over as quickly as his old legs can carry him.

Wide-eyed, Mary Ann says, "We just heard—"

"Shhh!" Penny jabs her. "Listen!"

"—from the air," an excited radio announcer is exclaiming in fast-paced staccato cadence. "I'll repeat that. President Roosevelt says that the Japanese have attacked Pearl Harbor in Hawaii from the air. This bulletin came to you from the NBC newsroom in New York."

Jed whirls on Clara, eyes blazing with . . .

Not anger. Nor is it accusation.

No, she thinks wildly, burned by his gaze, *it's . . .*

Sheer terror.

Overcome, Clara flees, hurtling herself toward the front door.

"Where are you going?" Jed calls as she throws it open, dashing out into the gently falling snow.

She doesn't know where she's going—knows only that she has to get away from that look in his eyes, and the horrific news of an attack she couldn't prevent, and everything else that's coming . . .

Particularly, the biggest tragedy of all; one that will further shatter the fragile lives in that house . . .

Not to mention my own life.

"Clara, wait!"

The Landrys' front door slams hard; Jed is chasing after her.

A few yards down the deserted block, sliding on the slick sidewalk despite her rubber soles, she gives up.

Panting hard, she stands absolutely still, head tilted back to the white heavens, feathery crystals alighting on her face to melt and run like tears.

It's like being inside a snow globe, she thinks, watching the swirling flakes come down. *And I'm the lonely little angel, with a broken heart instead of a broken wing.*

Then Jed is on her, grabbing hold of her shoulders, turning her toward him. "Where are you going?"

She can't answer, and not just because she doesn't know.

"I don't know what's going on here, but this is scaring the hell out of me. Forgive my language," he tacks on, ever the gentleman, even in crisis. "I just—"

"No, I know," Clara cuts in, finding a voice that sounds little like her own. "I'm afraid, too."

He pulls her close against him and she fights the urge to bury her head on his shoulder and cry.

"But listen," he says, "I keep thinking we're probably safe here, unless the Japs are—"

"No, Jed . . . I mean I'm afraid for us . . . for you."

He looks at her for a minute. "So we—I—don't have a chance. Is that what you're saying?"

"*We* don't have a chance, but you do, Jed. All you have to do is—"

"What do you mean *we don't have a chance*? How can you know that?"

"The same way I knew everything else. And because . . . I can't stay here with you. I have to go back."

"I'll go with you. Wherever you're going."

"You can't."

Or . . .

Can he?

What if—can he travel to the future with her?

Why not? If she could leap through time to his world, and back again, why can't he?

But he's already shaking his head. "You're right. I can't. Not yet, anyhow. I have to stay here with Mother and the girls and Grandma and Granddad. I can't go back on that vow . . . not even for you, Clara."

"I understand," she says softly. "I wouldn't expect you to."

"But you can stay. You said yourself that there's nobody in your life—"

"There are plenty of people in my life. I have parents, and friends, and—"

"But nobody in your life who cares about you the way I do—or who is counting on you the way my family needs me. Or is there?"

She shakes her head slowly. "No. It's nothing like that."

"Then what is it? Why can't you stay? Or at least wait until June, when my brother can take over here and I can go with you?"

She closes her eyes. "I'm sick, Jed."

"Are you going to faint? Here, lean on me."

"No, I mean . . ." *God, this is hard.* "I'm *really* sick. I have cancer."

The word drops like a bomb between them; she can feel him recoil even as one of his hands tightens on her arm and the other settles on the front of her coat, high above her right breast.

"That's what this is," he says, referring to the scar beneath the layers of clothing and gauze. "Isn't it?"

"Yes. And if I don't go back home," she forces herself to continue, struggling to keep the quaver from her voice, "I'll die."

"No! You won't die. I won't let you die, Clara. I'll take care of you." His voice is hoarse. "I'll help you. I'll—"

"There's nothing you can do here . . . now. There's a treatment, and I can only get it back . . . home."

"And it will save you?"

"Yes."

"So . . . after you get it . . . then you can come back."

The possibility flares before her, only to be extinguished almost immediately.

Even if she goes into remission, her disease can come back at any time . . . with a vengeance. And if it does, and spreads . . .

Well, even modern medicine is no guarantee. But at least she'll be monitored closely for the rest of her life, with ready access to every new drug that comes along.

"We'll both just have to do what we have to do, until we can settle down together for good," Jed goes on. "As my friend Arnold always says, sometimes the longest way round is the nearest way home."

"Jed!" a voice shouts, and they both look up.

A woman is leaning out the front door of the house next door to the Landrys, waving her arms. "Have you heard? The Japs attacked Hawaii."

"Yes, I've heard, Mrs. Wenick," Jed calls distractedly as his neighbor shields her eyes with a hand and looks up at the sky, as if fighter planes might appear at any moment.

Unnerved, Clara experiences a sudden, sickening flashback to September 11, 2001, in Manhattan. This is the same for Jed, and his family, and his neighbors . . . but not for Clara.

Would I rather be in their shoes, shocked and petrified, with no idea what catastrophic thing might happen from one minute to the next . . . ?

Or in mine, knowing how it's going to turn out . . . all of it. For better and for worse.

"I don't know what we're going to do," Mrs. Wenick is fretting in a high-pitched voice. "Next thing you know, the Nazis will be invading New York."

"That's not going to happen," Jed assures her. Then, shooting a glance at Clara, he mutters, "Is it?"

She shakes her head, thankful that she paid more attention in history class than she did in physics.

"You should go be with your mother, Jed." Mrs. Wenick sends a pointedly disapproving look toward Clara. "I'm sure Lois is frightened."

"I'm going in now, Mrs. Wenick," he responds with a wave.

After another worried glance at the sky, his neighbor retreats into her house, firmly closing the door behind her.

Before Clara can speak, Jed picks up where they left off.

"You'll go back home for now, Clara," he says logically, as though he has it all worked out, "and see your doctor, and do whatever it is that you have to do. We'll see each other every chance we get—I'll come down every Sunday when the store is closed, and you'll come up as often as you can, and—"

"I can't. I'm having cancer treatment, Jed. I can't come and go like some kind of . . . commuter."

He pauses. "When it's over, then. You'll come back here to stay, as soon as you're finished with your treatment."

"No. It isn't like that," she tells Jed. "I can't just *come back.*"

"Why not? Manhattan isn't on another planet, for Pete's sake."

"It might as well be, for me."

"You're not making any sense."

She thrusts her fingers into her snow-dampened hair

beneath the red hat. "I know, and I don't think I can make any sense, because if I told you the whole truth, I would be asking you to accept the impossible. Or at least, what *you* believe is impossible—not that I'd blame you for that."

"Try me."

"I already did. Last night. And you didn't believe me."

"So try me again. You said a lot of things last night."

"It was all true."

"But maybe I wasn't paying enough attention. And that was before . . . *today* happened."

"All right. Why do you think I knew in advance about everything that was going to happen today?"

"I've been thinking about it," he says, "and I keep remembering what I learned back in Sunday school, and . . . I think I understand. I think—you must be some kind of . . . prophet. Is that it? If that's the case . . . I can believe in that."

"Because you learned about it in Sunday school."

He nods.

Part of her wants to let him take whatever explanation he's willing to accept, and run with it.

But she can't. After all they've been through together, all the suspicion and the questions she hasn't been able to answer for him, she owes him the whole truth.

Whether or not he buys it is up to him.

But he deserves it.

"I'm not a prophet, Jed . . . and I'm not a gypsy fortune-teller. It's nothing like that."

"Then . . . what?"

"I'm not seeing the future . . . I'm just reciting the past."

"I don't understand."

"The things I've told you about have already happened. This very moment has already happened, sixty-five years ago. Which I know doesn't make any sense, even to me, but . . . look, I don't just live in Manhattan, forty-something miles away. I live in 2006. Sixty-five years away."

"2006," he echoes, not getting it.

"That's the *year*. In the next century. The future. I live in the future, and somehow I got back here, to you."

She waits for him to laugh, or keel over in shock, or something . . .

But he doesn't make a sound, doesn't move a muscle . . .

Other than his eyes.

And his eyes shift to her forehead, searching for the bump.

Her head injury, he's thinking, will explain everything. Maybe he'll even convince himself that it left her some kind of soothsayer, the way a lightning strike can leave a person with heightened sensitivity . . . or so she's read.

"Let's get you inside," Jed says. "You've been dealing with this illness on your own, and now the whole world is upside down with the war. No wonder you—"

He breaks off.

"What?" she asks, needing to hear him say it.

"Nothing." He won't look her in the eye.

That's when she realizes that no matter what she says or does in an effort to convince him, he's not going to believe her.

It's simply too far-fetched.

She turns away from him, suffocating in disappointment.

"Clara, come on."

"I have to go. But I'm begging you one last time, Jed . . . don't fight in this war. If you go, you'll never come home."

"And I'm begging you one last time, Clara . . . don't leave me. If you don't leave me, I—I promise you I'll stay right here."

For one wild moment, she actually considers it; considers sacrificing her own life for his.

Because if she stays, she knows she'll be able to keep him safe . . .

Or does she?

So it is possible, she hears herself asking Mr. Kershaw, *to go back in time and, maybe, change something that was supposed to happen? You know . . . save somebody's life?*

Ah, the classic paradox. That scenario would seemingly violate the law of quantum mechanics that says that what you do in the present is an inevitable product of the past.

Didn't Clara just prove, in her supreme effort to save Minnie Bouvier, that it can't be done?

"I have to go. There's a train—the 3:27—"

"No, Clara . . ."

"Don't touch me," she says sharply, flinching beneath his fingertips as they come to rest on her shoulders. "You have to let me go."

"I don't think I can."

She utters the only thing she can think of that will make him release his literal, and figurative, grip on her.

"If you don't let me go, Jed, and do what I have to do . . . I'll die."

He swallows hard.

Then, lifting his hands from her shoulders, he says softly, "Okay."

She closes her eyes hard, hot tears streaming from her lashes, her whole body quaking with the effort to contain a monstrous sob.

"But look at me, Clara." He's standing close, so close that his breath warms her ear. "Just turn around and look at me."

She does, and wishes she hadn't. His face is etched in pain.

"I'm going to promise you something. Do you hear me? Are you listening?"

She nods bleakly.

"I'm going to find my way to you somehow." Jed's voice is ragged. "No matter what. No matter where you're really going or why you don't want to tell me."

I did tell you, Jed. I told you the truth. You just didn't believe me . . . and I can't blame you for that.

But she doesn't say any of that. Words—hers, anyway—are futile now.

And so are his, because nothing he says can possibly change things.

Yet he goes on doggedly, "I swear I'm going to find you, wherever you are. And we'll be together again. Someday. No matter how long it takes. I promise you that, Clara. Because . . . I love you."

Those three words spill unexpectedly from his lips to light the shadowy depths of her soul where she banished her feelings for him, certain that what she felt couldn't possibly be love. Instead of withering there, that emotion took root, nourished by each hour, each moment, she spent with Jed. Now it stirs to life, entwining verdant tendrils around her heart as she looks into his eyes.

"I love you, too, Jed," she whispers, and hope, vibrant as the first bud of spring, unfurls within her.

"Don't forget me."

"I couldn't possibly forget you."

But you're going to forget me, she tells him silently. *A girl named Betty is probably baking you an apple pie at this very moment, and I bet you'll fall in love with her. With her, or somebody else.*

And I hope you do. I hope you fall in love, and live happily ever after.

Just . . .

Live.

Jed leans in and kisses her, tenderly . . . one last time.

"Jed! Clara!"

It's his mother, standing on the doorstep, waving them in.

"Don't you know what's going on?" she calls. Like Mrs. Wenick, Lois Landry looks ominously upward as if to ascertain that snow is the only thing falling from the sky.

"Poor Mother. She's going to be a wreck over this."

"I know. And about Minnie. Go help her."

"What about you?"

"I'm going to walk away now, Jed," she tells him softly.

"Now? Just like that?"

She nods.

"Jed! Clara!"

"Coming, Mother, just—go inside. You'll catch a chill." He waits until she obliges, then hurriedly tells Clara, "Just wait awhile, and I'll take you to the train when things calm down."

"No, I've got to go now. And I want to walk. The snow is beautiful."

"Then at least . . . I'll walk with you."

"Your mother needs you, Jed. Your family is upset. You've got to go back. And I've got to go."

"But . . . what about your things? Your suitcase? Your purse? Your little music player?"

"Keep it. All of it." Seeing the look on his face, she adds, if only to temper the ache, "For now."

"But . . . I had a gift for you. For Christmas."

For some reason, it's the word *Christmas* that brings tears to her eyes again.

"What is it?" she asks desolately, remembering the painful holiday that lies ahead for her.

"Do you want me to tell you?"

"Yes."

Otherwise, I'll never know, and I'll always wonder.

"It was the snow globe," Jed tells her. "The one with the dark-haired angel whose wing is broken."

"I would have liked to have had that." She smiles sadly.

"Then come to the store with me and I'll give it to you."

She shakes her head, knowing that she doesn't dare spend another minute with him. If she does, she'll never leave.

He casts an anxious look over his shoulder at his house, as though weighing his options.

Then, realizing he has none, he tells Clara, "Okay, then. I'll just . . . I'll give it to you the next time I see you. Look for me, Clara . . . because I'm going to find you. I promise."

Chapter 18

It isn't until Clara steps off the overcrowded subway train at Union Square, head bent to shield her raw, red-rimmed eyes from the world, that she realizes it's rush hour—a weekday.

What day is this, even?

Quick mental math tells her that it must be Thursday. Thursday evening. She's been gone five whole days . . . and God only knows what has transpired in her absence.

Well, at least she made it back. When the train had almost reached Grand Central and she was still firmly ensconced in the past, she began to feel anxious.

What if she was trapped in 1941? Her hand kept straying to the cancerous lump on her breast, poised to consume her without the proper medical intervention.

And what about her mother, who must be worried sick? And her father, and her cousins, and Jesus and Michael, and the movie—

The train entered a tunnel, the lights flickered, and everything went black for just a moment. And when daylight reappeared and the lights came on again . . .

She was back in the present.

That was when she started to cry. From grief, from relief . . . and she hasn't stopped since.

Now she covers the couple of blocks to her apartment swiftly, her eyes still swimming in tears and her thoughts consumed by Jed.

Will there ever be another moment when he isn't there, haunting her?

Saying goodbye to him was by far the most anguishing thing she's ever had to do . . .

But she had no choice.

They simply weren't meant to be.

Arriving on West Eleventh Street, she spots Ray's Pizza on the corner like a beacon.

Almost home.

That's good.

No, really . . . it is.

Right. That's why she's crying so hard she can barely see. She blows her nose on the already sodden wad of tissue she took from the bathroom in Grand Central.

Then she toils on.

Only when she reaches her building does it occur to her that she doesn't have a plan.

She didn't think things through before she left her world behind, and she hasn't thought things through upon her return.

What is she going to tell people? They'll want to know where she's been.

You'll just have to wing it, she decides, slowly climbing the steps.

She robotically fishes her keys from her back pocket and fits one into the lock on the door, then turns it. She opens the door cautiously, half-expecting to see Mr. Kobayashi lying in wait.

But the entry hall is deserted, and she can hear the faint sound of a wailing siren, screaming brakes, and chase music coming from his apartment below.

She smiles and sniffles . . . then stops short, remembering something.

Hurriedly patting her jacket pockets, she notes that they're flatter than they should be.

Yes, of course. That's because she left her mittens on the counter in the Landrys' kitchen . . .

And Jed returned them to me.

Stunned, she realizes he must have come here, must have given the painstakingly wrapped package to Mr. Kobayashi when he was a little boy. Of course, because he knew that one day, Clara's path would cross his—and that the mittens were special to her. That she'd want them back.

But I want you back, too, Jed.

Tears spring to her eyes again, and she brushes them away, emotionally spent.

She pulls herself together and climbs the stairs slowly.

Passing Drew Becker's closed door, she remembers their conversation on the stoop . . . was it only last week? How can that be?

It seems like . . .

Sixty-five years ago.

Wearily, she ascends the last flight to her door.

There's a sticky yellow Post-it note stuck to the door.

Fuzz were here. They're coming back with search warrant. Everyone worried. Where are you? Let me know if you get back. —Mr. K.

Fuzz. He means police. Her initial dismay is trailed by a glimmer of amusement. Having real live cops here must have made his day.

So who called them?

It had to be her mother. She must be frantic by now.

What am I going to tell her?

Not the truth—that's for sure.

She quickly unlocks the door and steps into the dark apartment. She flips a light switch and notices that there's a white envelope at her feet; somebody must have shoved it under the door.

Picking it up, she crosses to the phone and dials into her voice mail.

You have thirty . . . eight . . . new . . . messages.

No surprise there. Rather than listen to them, she begins to scroll through her caller ID log, which only keeps the last twenty incoming numbers on record. It looks like most of them occurred yesterday and today, and the majority are from her mother and father, plus a couple each from Michael, Jesus, and Jason.

First things first.

Clara dials her mother's number in Florida.

No answer.

She tries her stepfather's cell phone.

Bingo.

"Clara! Jeanette, it's Clara!" he shouts frantically. "Where are you? Are you all—?"

"Where are you? Are you all right?" her mother screams in her ear, having snatched the phone away from Stan.

"I'm fine, Mom." Her voice breaks unexpectedly.

I want my mommy . . . Oh, Mommy . . .

Suddenly, Clara is swamped in an unfamiliar childhood memory so vivid she wraps her arms around herself and shudders. She can vividly recall a long-ago night when she had a nasty stomach bug. She was really young; it was long before Daddy left, long before Jeanette became skittish and dependent. Maybe,

Clara realizes now, the changes in her mother that came after the divorce distorted—or obliterated—certain memories of their early years. Tender memories of a time when Jeanette was undisputedly the mother, and Clara the child.

Now she remembers how all night, that night, her mother sat on Clara's bed. She stroked her sweaty forehead and promised her that everything was going to be all right in the morning. That she'd wake up feeling fine, and her mother would still be right there, holding her tight.

And I did . . . and she was.

"Where are you, honey?" Jeanette is sobbing now . . . and so is Clara. "What happened to you?"

"Nothing, I'm . . . I'm home." She wipes her eyes with the back of her hand—a futile gesture. The floodgates have reopened and the tears are going to keep coming.

If only Clara were a little girl this time, and her mother really could make it all better.

"She's fine, she's home," her mother is telling Stan.

"Where are you guys, Mom?" Clara hates the plaintive tone in her own voice, but can't help it.

She's been stoic for too many days, faced her illness alone for long enough. Now, without Jed by her side—and shouldering the added burden of grief—Clara's strength is giving out.

"We're home."

"Home where? I just tried you, and there was no answer."

"Home in New York, where did you think?"

Clara's leaden heart lifts, just a little.

Her mother is here in New York.

Thank God.

I need you, Mom . . .

"When did you get back here?"

"This morning. Hang on a minute." Her mother covers the receiver but Clara can hear a muffled, "Take the phone, Stan . . . yes . . . because I feel like I'm going to pass out."

"Mom!" Tormented by her conscience, Clara wonders how she could have been so selfish. Had she allowed herself more than a passing thought of the life she so abruptly abandoned, she would never have put her mother through this hell.

"Oh, God, Mommy, I'm so sorry . . ."

"She'll be okay." Her stepfather is back on the line, but his reassuring words can't begin to assuage Clara's guilt.

"Are you sure?"

"I'm positive, she'll be fine, now that she knows you're safe, anyway. It's just been a rough couple of days."

"I can just imagine," Clara murmurs.

"Where have you been? Your mother's been trying to call you for days at home and on your cell. By Tuesday she was so frantic she called the police. But they said they had to wait forty-eight hours before they could open a missing persons case."

"I'm so sorry," Clara repeats, wedging a fist into her hair, pulling so hard her scalp hurts. "I got a note from my landlord saying the police had been here."

"Oh, him?" Stan sounds slightly disdainful. "He wouldn't even let us into your apartment this afternoon. He said it wasn't legal."

"Well . . . it probably isn't." Clara can just imagine her mother barging into the building in a frenzy, demanding access to her daughter's apartment.

"Ask her where she's been, Stan," her mother is commanding in the background.

Before her stepfather can oblige, Clara tells him, "I went away for a few days, that's all. I just had to get out of here. I know it was really irresponsible and I never meant to worry you and Mom and—and did she tell my father?"

"Of course she told him. Listen, your mother already has her coat on . . . we're coming right over."

"Now? But—"

"Do you really think I can stop her? She needs to see you for herself and make sure you're really okay."

I'm not okay.

And it's time to tell Mom the truth and hope she can handle it.

After all I've put her through, she deserves to know.

About the cancer. Not, of course, about Jed.

Clara will never tell another soul about that.

Oh, Jed . . . I miss you so much.

If only . . .

Can there possibly be a chance that he listened to her, that he survived the war after all?

No. Don't tease yourself like that.

What was that rule of quantum physics?

What you do in the present is an inevitable product of the past.

Meaning what's happened has happened. It can't be changed.

Clara shakes her head, crying all over again. What an emotional wreck she is.

If only I could see Jed again, one last time . . .

Why? an inner voice demands. *Would that be enough?*

Could you handle one more goodbye?

The answer to that question is abundantly clear.

No. You could barely handle the first goodbye. Look at you.

It's better, then, to leave Jed in the past, where he belongs. Better to always cherish the memories, and the red mittens he returned to her, and focus now on the challenge just ahead of her.

"Clara, do you want us to bring you anything?" her mother is asking in her ear, having grabbed the phone back from Stan again.

"Like what?"

"I don't know . . . milk? Bread?"

Milk. Bread. Oh, Mom.

"No." Clara smiles through her tears. "Just . . . come."

"I'm coming. I love you, honey."

"I love you, too."

She ends the call, then buries her head in her hands and lets out a shuddering sigh.

She should probably get in touch with her father now . . . and Mr. Kobayashi . . . and, probably, the police before they barge in with a search warrant . . .

And then there's the movie . . . she's got to call Denton right away.

Denton . . . Dent-in . . .

She smiles again, faintly, wishing for a fleeting moment she had stuck around 1941 just long enough to catch a glimpse of the new Wilkens baby.

Right now the poor kid is wearing pink booties . . .

My father always said it takes a real man to wear pink . . .

Her smile fades as she remembers Jed's ravaged expression in the very last moment before she turned her back and walked away.

Her eyes are hot with tears all over again; she bows her head and a fat, salty drop lands on the envelope in her hand.

The envelope . . .

She forgot all about it.

Turning it over, she sees that her name is written on the front in red ink.

Sliding a finger beneath the flap, she cautiously rips it open.

Inside are a long cardboard rectangle and a note, also scrawled in red: *See you there! Love, Santa.*

Heart pounding, she realizes that she's holding one ticket to *The Nutcracker* for December 24 . . . Christmas Eve.

Two hours later, she walks her mother and stepfather back down the two flights of stairs, her mother clinging to Clara's hand so tightly that her rings are quite possibly drawing blood in Clara's palm.

Naturally, Jeanette won't be going back to Florida anytime soon. She intends to see her daughter through every step on this journey—and Clara isn't about to argue, grateful to have her mother here and know she doesn't have to go it alone.

"Tomorrow," Jeanette promises, as they reach the front entry, "I'll bring you some flaxseed oil, Siberian ginseng, and wild yam. Oh, and chocolate."

"Chocolate? What does that do?" Clara asks, her head still reeling from her mother's whirlwind course in holistic healing.

"It tastes good and makes you happy."

Clara smiles as her mother wraps her in a surprisingly comforting embrace and a pungent cloud of aromatherapy oil.

"You're going to be fine, honey." Jeanette's green eyes, precisely the shade of Clara's own, are suspiciously bright. "You'll see."

"I know I'm going to be fine."

But Mom doesn't, she realizes, seeing her mother's lip tremble slightly as she pulls away. *She's going to go home and cry her heart out to Stan.*

Maybe that's okay.

Because she's channeled her maternal love into being strong for Clara, and eventually, that might give her inner strength for herself. Perhaps, when she sees that Clara is going to survive, she'll stop living every moment of her own life in fear.

"Just don't go running off again like you did," Stan tells Clara, taking his turn to put his short arms around her and pull her to his portly chest. "You gave us all a real scare."

"I know, and I'm so sorry. I guess I just . . . panicked."

"That's understandable after what you had been through."

Clara can only hope that Denton Wilkens will be as empathetic as her stepfather is.

Below, a door opens and Clara hears Mr. Kobayashi calling, "Hello up there?"

She crosses to the rail and pokes her head over. "Hi, Mr. Kobayashi."

"You're back!"

"I am. I just went away for a few days." She wants to ask him about the man who left the package for her all those years ago, but she can't with her mother and Stan here.

"The fuzz was here!" he announces. "And that little old lady came back looking for you."

"Little old lady! I'm not even gray!" Jeanette pats her brunette bob indignantly, and looks over the railing. "Hello? I'm Clara's mother."

"Not you," he says. "You're not a little old lady."

"I would hope not," Jeanette mutters under her breath.

"I mean the little old lady who was here before," Mr. Kobayashi tells Clara. "She came back today, a little while ago. Wanted to see you."

"Who is he talking about, Clara?"

"It's nothing, Mom. Just some soap fan who wants my autograph." To Mr. Kobayashi, she says, "Thank you for taking care of things for me."

"The fuzz are coming back with a search warrant."

"No, my stepfather already called them and told them it's okay."

Clearly, Mr. Kobayashi is disappointed to hear that news. He must have been looking forward to participating in a good old-fashioned missing persons investigation.

"Now when are you meeting with the surgeon?" her mother asks Clara after the super has returned to his apartment. She pulls a date book from her oversized purse and begins rifling through it, saying, "I want to be there."

"I'll let you know when it is," Clara promises, noticing that her mother's hands are trembling as she turns the pages. "I missed the appointment this week, Mom, so I'll have to reschedule. You don't have to be there."

"Clara! Why would you say that? Of course I'm going to be there. For all of it. I'm your mother."

She nods, her throat clogged by emotion again.

"I just hope this lapse doesn't mean they have to put off the surgery, honey. We want you all better by Christmas."

All better. She makes it sounds so simple.

But if the surgery does go off as planned, Clara should at least be up and about in time to celebrate Christmas after all . . .

And just in time to show up at *The Nutcracker* ballet to meet her secret Santa.

*   *   *

Alone again at last in her apartment, quantum physics be damned, Clara turns on her computer and signs onto the Internet.

Because she can't shake the nagging, irrational hope . . . and because she can't handle the knowing . . . but not *knowing*.

You've got mail, a disembodied electronic voice informs her.

"Yeah," she mutters, "I'll bet I do."

Ignoring the full mailbox icon, she opens a search engine and quickly types in *Glenhaven Gazette Archives, July 15, 1944.*

"Please," she whispers, waiting for the screen to load.

And then it does . . .

And then she *knows.*

ANOTHER LOCAL MAN CONFIRMED LOST IN EUROPE

A telegram from the War Department last night officially brought to ten the number of local men casualties in the first wave of the Allied invasion at Normandy on June 6. Previously reported missing in action, Sergeant Jed Landry of 21 Chestnut Street, son of Mrs. Lois Landry and the late . . .

So.

Quantum physics reigns after all.

You can't change the past.

No, you can only visit it, and helplessly watch it unfold, because destiny is destiny . . .

And Jed Landry's was to die on a European battlefield.

*   *   *

Denton Wilkens's New York office is in a converted warehouse on Gansevoort Street.

By day, this is the Meatpacking District—by night, the city's most fashionable neighborhood.

Clara's appointment with her director is right on the cusp, at five thirty on Friday evening.

As she crosses the uneven cobblestones toward the building's entrance, a truck at the curb is being loaded with animal carcasses from a wholesale meat company while a sidewalk menu placard is set in front of a trendy restaurant next door.

A few hours from now, designer heels, as opposed to bloodstained aprons, will be the neighborhood's required accessory.

The security guard in the lobby doesn't give Clara a second glance, ask for ID, or bother to read her name as she signs in. He simply hands over a visitor's badge, barks, "Fourth floor," and goes back to reading his *New York Post*.

Riding up in a large, drafty, and disconcertingly wobbly elevator, she realizes her palms are sweaty.

This isn't going to be fun.

No, but I'll go with K.T.'s advice and let Denton do all the talking.

"Just be prepared . . . He'll be sympathetic to your illness," the second assistant director said, "but he's not going to overlook the fact that you just cost the production a helluva lot of money by just not showing up on the set the past few days."

Just not showing up.

She was tempted to tell K.T.—and everyone else connected to the film—that she was in the hospital, or something equally dire.

But she couldn't bring herself to lie.

So she gave them all a form of the truth: said she was overwhelmed, and had to get away for a few days.

"I realize that it was irresponsible, and I'm so sorry."

How many times has she uttered those words in the last twenty-four hours?

Minutes later she repeats them, verbatim, to Denton Wilkens, who sits with his hands steepled beneath his chin. He's wearing a bright pink cashmere crewneck.

My father always said it takes a real man to wear pink.

"I know it doesn't help," she adds, as unnerved by the echo in her head as she is by his silent gaze from behind thick glasses. "But it's all I can say. That, and—"

She takes a deep breath.

"I need to drop out of the film."

Denton doesn't appear nearly as surprised by her announcement as Clara herself is.

But the moment the words have left her tongue, she feels a surge of relief.

Yes.

Yes!

This the right thing to do.

"Is this strictly because of your illness?" Denton asks. "Because we'll work to accommodate your surgery and treatment schedule, if you can give us your wholehearted commitment for the remainder of the production."

She's already shaking her head. "That wouldn't be fair to you. I don't know how I'm going to feel after the surgery, or what the treatment is going to do to me, physically . . ."

But I do know that I can't possibly learn to forget Jed Landry if I have to step into 1940s Glenhaven Park day after day for the next few months and go

*through the motions of falling in love with him all
over again.*

It's hard enough as it is. She's spent the past twenty-
four hours in a futile effort to reconcile her miraculous
ability to breach time with the fact that Jed died
anyway.

It just doesn't make sense.

If she couldn't change his destiny, what was the purpose in any of it? Why did she find her way back to
him, fall in love with him, if not to save him?

Perhaps she'll never know.

What she does know is that she can't bear to continue her role as the love of his life. Not even with a
fake Jed Landry on a fake vintage set.

"You'll have to recast the role," she tells Denton
firmly, her mind made up.

"This isn't the way I would have chosen to resolve
this, Clara. You were a perfect Violet."

"Thank you. And I'm sorry I didn't figure this out
sooner, before I put everyone through all those days
of chaos."

Denton shrugs. "Sometimes the longest way round
is the nearest way home."

Clara's heart skips a beat. "What . . . what did
you say?"

"Didn't you ever hear that expression?"

*Yes, more recently—and longer ago—than you can
ever imagine.*

"It was a favorite saying of my father's," Denton
informs her. "He had a lot of them, but that was his
favorite. In fact, my mother had it etched on his grave-
stone when he passed away a few years ago."

Overwhelmed by the sudden connection, once
again, to the past and Jed, Clara can only offer a trem-
ulous smile.

* * *

"Welcome back," Karen Vinton greets Clara at her office on Saturday morning. She clasps one of Clara's cold hands in both her warm ones. "I've been really concerned about you."

"I—thank you. I'm, um, sorry I blew off my Monday appointment, and I'll absolutely pay for your wasted time, and—"

"No need to do that. I just sat here knitting and hoping you were going to show. When you didn't, I assumed you got hung up at work."

Clara just nods, unwilling to dispute that . . . just yet, anyway.

"So it was no big deal and thanks to you, I almost finished the scarf I'm knitting my girlfriend for Christmas."

"I'm . . . glad."

"And I'm glad you made this appointment," Karen goes on, gesturing at a chair, as she closes the office door behind Clara.

I'm trapped, she thinks irrationally . . . as if she truly had any intention of fleeing.

All right . . . the notion *did* occur to her.

But she won't do that.

You really can't, she reminds herself, still standing, looking again at the closed door.

Karen follows her gaze. "A little nervous about being here today, huh?"

"Maybe just a little."

"That's all right. Have a seat. We'll go slowly. You take the lead, okay?"

"Okay."

Clara reluctantly sits. And waits.

"Why don't you fill me in," Karen suggests after a moment of silence.

"Fill you in on . . . ?"

Karen shrugs, sitting across from her. "Whatever it is that you need to talk about."

Clara still can't seem to say anything.

"You made the appointment," the therapist reminds her gently. "You must need to talk."

"I just . . . I don't even know where to start."

"Well, what's been going on since we last saw each other? It's been over a week."

Clara shrugs.

"Something must have happened, Clara."

"A lot of things happened," she agrees.

"Like . . . ?"

Let's see . . . I traveled back in time again, fell madly in love, relived Pearl Harbor Day, realized I couldn't save Jed's life after all, told him goodbye forever, traveled back to the present, reconciled with my mother, told her I have cancer, quit my job . . .

And here I am.

"You know, I probably shouldn't even be here," she tells Karen, shifting her weight self-consciously.

"You thought you should when you made the appointment. What's on your mind?"

"Right this second?"

"Right this second."

"Well . . . my surgery, for one thing . . . it's next week."

"How do you feel about it?"

"Afraid. Whenever I think about it I wish I could just run away again."

"Again?"

Clara hedges. "I sort of . . . did. Already. Last weekend."

"Was it like before?" Karen flips through her notes. "You'd had an episode . . ."

"No, it wasn't like that." *Because this time I knew it wasn't a dream, or some kind of psychotic fantasy.*

"How was it, then?"

"I just took a few days to . . . you know. Sort of . . . hide."

"From anyone in particular?"

"From the world, pretty much. I just know that I didn't want to deal with anything here."

"Here? You mean New York?"

Clara hesitates.

No. You can't tell her. She'll never believe you, or she'll think it was some kind of fugue, or fantasy—

And it wasn't.

It was real.

Jed was real.

At least she has that; she'll always have it, in her memory and in her heart, where it counts.

"Yes," she tells Karen, still waiting patiently, as always. "I mean New York."

"And where did you go?"

"Just upstate." *Just.*

"Alone?"

"Yes."

"What did you do there?"

"Just . . . not much. You know. Thought about things."

"About your illness?"

Clara nods.

"And did it help?"

"I don't know. I guess."

All these questions are starting to rankle. But she supposes that's the whole point . . . for Karen to get her to examine her feelings.

And when she does . . .

"I'm definitely going to beat this," she finds herself blurting. "I'm not going to just give in and . . . die."

"Of course you aren't. Was there really ever any doubt in your mind?"

She shrugs. "My grandmother died of breast cancer. It happens. But it isn't going to happen to me. I want to have a life."

Even without Jed. That's why I'm back here. I have to go on; I have to survive. It's what he would want. I know it is.

It isn't until Karen hands her a box of tissues that Clara realizes tears are streaming down her cheeks.

"Do you think," she asks, and pauses to blow her nose and wipe her eyes, "that everything happens for a reason?"

"Is that what *you* believe?"

"I want to, but . . ."

But why did I fall in love with Jed if I was only meant to lose him?

The troubling thought refuses to fade.

"Sometimes," Karen tells her, giving her a tight, welcome hug, "we can't see things clearly as they're unfolding. We're too caught up in the emotion."

"But hindsight is twenty-twenty?"

The therapist smiles. "Something like that."

Maybe, then, in time it will make sense . . .

Or Jed will somehow find me again, like he promised.

After all, nothing is impossible . . . right?

Again, she thinks of her secret Santa, and that single ticket to *The Nutcracker* on Christmas Eve.

What if . . . ?

No, Clara. Don't get your hopes up.

Some things really are impossible.

Chapter 19

"How are you feeling today, Clara?" asks Dr. Bronstein, the surgeon, as he walks briskly into her hospital room carrying a folder and a clipboard. Clara likes him; he's down-to-earth. He communicates with her on a human level rather than on a more formal doctor-patient one, as the oncologist does.

"I feel great today," she tells him—almost wholeheartedly.

Yes, the surgical site is sore despite the pain medication, and she's still feeling the aftereffects of the anesthesia.

And yes, she's frightened of what he's going to say now about what he found when he went in during the operation.

But at least that part is behind her.

"Do you think you can prescribe something stronger for her pain, Dr. Bronstein?" Clara's mother asks, seated in the bedside chair where she set up camp almost two full days ago.

"Are you in a lot of discomfort, Clara?"

"She is," Jeanette answers for Clara, who shoots her a look. Jeanette responds with a shrug, saying simply, "You can't fool me. A mother can tell when her child is hurting."

Dr. Bronstein scribbles something. "I'll take care of that."

Then he looks up and, in his straightforward way, says, "Well, I've got some very good news for you, Clara."

All the oxygen seems to gush out of her at those words, leaving her breathless, speechless.

"I can bore you with all kinds of medical terms and details, and trust me, I will at some point, but what I would really be saying is this: the margins are clear and the cancer hasn't spread."

At Clara's side, Jeanette makes a choking, sobbing sound and presses her hand to her lips.

"You mean . . . " Clara breaks off, clears her throat, tries to digest the wonderful news. "I'm going to be all right? I'm not dying?"

Dr. Bronstein smiles. "You are absolutely not dying. Although if you eat the so-called minestrone soup they're serving for lunch here today, you might feel like you are. I just tasted it and . . ." He makes a face and a thumbs-down sign at her.

Clara laughs out loud. "I'll pass on that. When can I go home?"

"Tomorrow, I think, if you feel up to it. Just rest now, and let the nurses—and your mom, of course—take care of you. Sound good?"

"Sounds great," Clara says sincerely, leaning her head back against the pillow in sheer relief.

Dr. Bronstein makes more notes. "Dr. Hunter will meet with you later to discuss his recommendations for further treatment and I'll check in on you again in the morning."

"Thank you," Clara murmurs, tilting her face toward the window beside the bed.

Outside, above the gray skyline, she can see a slice of clear blue December sky.

You'll come back here to stay, as soon as you're finished with your treatment.

She shakes her head, pushing Jed's words away.

Even if she did find her way back to him, he wouldn't be there for long.

"All right, then, Clara, I'm going to leave you now. Congratulations."

She turns back toward Dr. Bronstein and manages to smile. "I don't know how to thank you."

"You don't have to. Those happy tears in your eyes speak volumes."

She doesn't have the heart to tell him that they aren't happy tears at all.

Clara winces as she lifts her arm to pull the black velvet dress over her head.

It's been a week now, but the site of her lumpectomy is still sore, and it's likely to be for quite some time.

Every day, though, she feels a little less discomfort . . . and a little more optimism. All right—infinitely more optimism.

In part because Dr. Hunter, the oncologist, decided chemotherapy will be unnecessary. After a round of radiation treatments, mostly as a safeguard, Clara should be able to put this whole experience behind her . . .

Or so the medical team claims.

She can't imagine ever feeling entirely safe in her own skin again, and she'll be ultravigilant . . . as will her doctors.

But she isn't going to die young of breast cancer, as her grandmother did. She's going to have a life.

And for tonight—and tomorrow—especially, she's

going to forget about everything in it that's the least bit disturbing—Jed Landry included.

If that's even possible. Jed has been on her mind every moment of every day, haunting her dreams whenever she's asleep.

But those are just dreams.

So very different from her actual time with Jed . . .

And that, she remains certain, wasn't a dream.

She still hasn't come any closer to understanding why it all happened. In fact, the more time that passes, the more perplexed she feels.

But you're going to put that aside for now.

This is Christmas Eve, and somebody is meeting her at *The Nutcracker* ballet.

Her heart races every time she wonders who it might be.

It isn't going to be Jed, she reminds herself sternly. *You do know that . . . don't you?*

Of course she does. She just needs a reality check every so often, that's all.

She leans toward the mirror above her dresser, carefully clipping dangling diamond drops to her earlobes.

The earrings belonged to her grandmother, Irene— a wedding day gift from her loving husband. Grandpa gave them to Clara one Christmas long ago.

You look so much like her, Clara-belle, she hears him saying as she inspects her reflection.

Something flutters in the corner of her eye and she turns her head quickly to catch it . . . but the spot is empty.

"Grandpa . . . is that you?" she asks, standing absolutely still, listening . . . for his voice?

All she can hear is a steady drip from the bathroom sink, and, beyond the window, traffic on the avenue, and a car alarm howling in the distance.

Her grandfather isn't here. If he were, he'd let her know somehow.

No, but he and her grandmother might be out there somewhere, like she told Jason that time.

Maybe they were both reborn as babies right now, and they're going to grow up and find each other and fall in love all over again.

Comforted by the thought, Clara smiles. Of course, if they have found their way back to earth, Grandpa and Grandma would have no memory of their identities in their past lives.

The books she read made it pretty clear that without professional hypnotic past-life regression, most people have no idea that they are, indeed, reincarnated souls. But once in a while, a person can have a flash of inexplicable memory that might really be a glimpse into his or her own past . . . as somebody else. And some souls are irrevocably linked through the ages, destined to be reborn and find each other over and over again . . .

Maybe Clara's grandparents are like that. Maybe that romance, nipped so cruelly in the bud by untimely death, will have a chance to play itself out someday.

Yes, and maybe Jed—

The buzz of the bell downstairs shatters the hush as well as the beginnings of that unbidden thought.

Clara hurries to the security panel by the door, unnerved. She thought she was meeting her secret Santa at the ballet, but maybe he's picking her up here.

She presses the intercom button.

"Who is it?" she asks, and braces herself for the reply.

"It's me," a familiar voice answers. "Can I come up?"

She closes her eyes briefly, and releases the lock on the door.

Come on, Clara. You knew it wasn't going to turn out to be Jed.

Still . . .

Jason?

Yes, Jason.

Maybe she should have expected this. After all, he's called a few times this month, most recently leaving one message on her voice mail while she was hospitalized and another here with her mother afterward.

Plus, he would have been able to access the building using his key . . .

Then again, the whole secret Santa thing seems too . . . whimsical . . . for Jason's romantic style. Doesn't it?

Yes, definitely.

Well, maybe he's trying to show me that he's changed, she tells herself.

And if he has . . .

Do I want to give him another chance?

Honestly, now that she's about to come face-to-face with her ex-fiancé, she has no idea how she feels. Everything is happening so quickly . . .

Too quickly . . .

And it's not what I expected . . . or wanted.

Jittery, she opens the door and waits, listening to his footsteps coming up the stairs.

Maybe things will be different this time around, she tells herself halfheartedly.

Maybe we're meant to be together . . .

Still, what about Jed?

The stubborn thought comes out of nowhere.

What *about* Jed? Jed died. He isn't coming back . . .

No matter what he promised.

Unless . . .

Well, what if she mistook Jed's voice just now for Jason's?

What if he somehow—

Then Jason comes into view, looking exactly the same as he always did: clean-cut, freshly shaven, wearing a suit and dark wool overcoat and shiny black shoes.

And Clara instinctively reacts with the same sense of affection—but not attraction—as she always did.

"Hi." Jason looks uncharacteristically nervous.

"Hi," she responds quietly, trying to quell the crushing wave of disappointment.

She almost let herself believe . . .

But that was ludicrous.

Of course it wasn't going to be Jed.

Jed died. He isn't coming back to you, no matter what he promised.

When will you believe that?

Maybe never, she tells herself desolately.

"These are for you." Jason hands her a vase containing a big bouquet of red roses and Christmas greens.

"Thank you—they're beautiful." She sets the vase on the table beside the door.

"How are you feeling? Your mother answered when I called the other day and said you were sleeping and you'd just had surgery . . . ? She didn't want to give me the details. Said you'd have to tell me yourself. What's that all about?"

"I'll explain everything on the way. Just let me get my coat."

"Coat? Where are you going?"

"To the ballet . . . with you . . ." She frowns, watching his expression. "Aren't I?"

"The ballet?"

"*The Nutcracker*," she clarifies, wondering if maybe he didn't realize it was a ballet when he bought the tickets.

"*The Nutcracker* . . . with me?" he asks cluelessly, and all at once, she realizes . . .

He doesn't know what I'm talking about!

"I'm sorry, I got confused for a minute," she tells Jason, giddily relieved that he isn't her secret Santa after all. Not that she believes for one second that it still might be Jed, but . . .

Well, maybe just for one second.

"What are you talking about, Clara?"

"*I'm* the one who's going to *The Nutcracker*, and you're here because . . ."

"I want to talk to you about something and I thought you needed to hear it in person."

"On Christmas Eve?" Dear God, is he going to propose again?

"It's the only time I could squeeze it in . . . the market's going crazy and I've been working like a dog all week."

She nods knowingly. So what else is new?

"You, uh, might want to sit down for this, Clara."

"I can't sit down . . ." She checks her watch. "I've got to get uptown. What is it?"

"It's . . . Clara, I'm getting married."

Her jaw drops.

"Her name is Anne," he rushes on nervously, "and she's a terrific girl. She's an investment banker, and she lives on the Upper East Side, and . . . you'd like her, and I told her she'd like you, too. She knows all

about you, about us . . . She's the one who showed
me that article about you in *Entertainment Weekly,*
even . . . she saw it at the gym . . ."

Of course. Clara just knew Jason wouldn't have
picked up that magazine on his own.

"Hey . . . I'm really happy for you." She wraps him
in a heartfelt hug.

"You are?"

"Why wouldn't I be? You deserve to be happy, and
she sounds right for you." An investment banker from
the Upper East Side. Yes, perfect.

"I was afraid you'd be upset." Jason seems almost
disappointed that she isn't. "You know . . . it's so
soon after we broke up and everything. But when I
met Anne, it was . . . well, I guess I fell in love at
first sight, as they say. Who knew that was possible?"

I did.

Aloud she says, "That's great. And I wish you the
best, Jason. Really."

"Well, what about you? Are you seeing someone,
too? Is that who you're rushing off to go to the ballet with?"

Maybe.

Stop that! Of course not.

You're going to the ballet with . . . with . . .

Santa.

Right. Whoever that is.

"Clara?" Jason prods, and she merely shrugs.

"You don't want to tell me about him, huh? Fair
enough. Oh, here's the key to the apartment, by the
way . . . I never did return it." Jason removes it from
his pocket and hands it to her.

"And you didn't . . ."

"What?"

"You haven't used it lately . . . have you?" she asks,

just to rule out the remote possibility that he might be her secret Santa after all, even if he's in love with another woman.

"Used it for what?"

"Never mind."

Secret Santa really isn't his style.

So . . . whose style is it?

"Come on, Jason, you can walk me to a cab." She pushes her feet into black velvet pumps and slips into her dress coat.

For a moment, she toys with the black leather gloves she finds in the pockets.

Then she tosses them aside and pulls on her red mittens instead, slipping her *Nutcracker* ticket into one of them.

"All set," she tells Jason, her heart fluttering in anticipation of whoever she might find waiting for her at the ballet.

"Are you alone, ma'am?" a uniformed usher asks, as Clara stands at the top of the aisle above her section, holding her ticket and scanning the rows below.

"No . . . I mean, I don't think so, but . . . I'm, uh, meeting someone here."

And I have no idea who it is, or whether he's already here, or even whether he really is a he.

For all she knows, it might be her mother.

No, she was in Florida when the gifts arrived.

Well, her father, then. Or one of her cousins, or a friend, or Mr. Kobayashi, even . . .

But not Jed.

It can't be Jed.

"May I show you to your seat? The ballet is about to start."

Yes, it is, because she spent the last half hour milling around in the crowded lobby, searching for a familiar face. She just didn't know whose.

The usher leads the way down front, then hands her a program and gestures at two empty seats in the center of the row.

Clara thanks him and makes her way across several pairs of knees, feeling conspicuous to be here alone. She's grateful when the lights dim just as she slips into one of the empty seats; the buzzing audience promptly falls silent in rapt anticipation.

As the orchestra's opening notes fill the great hall, a melancholy feeling settles over Clara. She isn't just thinking of her grandfather, who sat beside her here for so many years . . .

No, she's mainly thinking of Jed.

Look for me, Clara . . . because I'm going to find you. I promise.

Those were his last words to her . . .

Right, so somehow, you expected to walk into the concert hall tonight and see him standing there, waiting for you?

Yes, maybe she did.

Maybe, she thought, he had found some way to slip forward through time the way she slipped back . . .

But that isn't going to happen.

It can't happen, because Jed died.

Nothing can change that now.

He died, and you have to move on . . .

"Excuse me," a voice whispers above her in the dark.

Clara looks up, startled, to see a crouched male form trying to sneak past her knees.

She twists in her seat to let him past . . . even as she realizes there's only one empty seat in the row . . . and it's the one beside hers.

Sure enough, he settles into it.

"Hey, Merry Christmas," he whispers, grinning at her in the dim glow of bluish light from the stage.

Shocked, she finds herself face-to-face with her neighbor, Drew Becker.

"There's one thing I still don't get," Clara says, as they stroll along their own quiet block munching Ray's Pizza slices in the glow of streetlights and colored Christmas lights and blue Hanukkah lights.

"What's that?" Drew asks, hot cheese stringing from his mouth to his hand.

"*Why* you did it."

"I told you . . . you said that you were spending Christmas alone, just like me . . . and I could tell you weren't any happier about it than I was. Plus, you looked like you needed some serious cheering up."

"I did." But of course she isn't going to tell him exactly why.

Not yet, anyway.

Maybe not ever.

After all, it's not as though they're going to be seeing each other again . . . as anything other than neighbors. He did a nice, platonic thing for her, to be . . . platonically neighborly. Right.

"Plus," he says, casting a sidelong glance at her, "I wanted to ask you out . . . but something tells me that if I had, you would have said no."

"Probably." She laughs, even as something unexpectedly stirs inside her.

"Probably?"

"Okay, I definitely would have said no."

"Why?"

"A lot of reasons."

"But you're out with me now . . . and it isn't so bad, is it?"

"No," she agrees with a smile, "it isn't. Except . . . what about your girlfriend?"

"My what?"

"Betty," she reminds him.

He just looks at her.

He's wondering how I know. He probably thinks I've been spying on him.

Embarrassed, she admits, "I heard you talking to her one night from the hallway."

"I don't think so. I don't have a girlfriend named Betty."

"What's her name, then? Maybe it just sounded like Betty. Is it Betsy, maybe, or . . . Hettie?"

"Hettie?" he echoes. "Wasn't she the heroine of *The Scarlet Letter*?"

"That was Hester." Clara declines to tell him she once played the role in a short-lived off-Broadway version of the story. He hasn't asked her about her work, and she isn't about to get into that.

Especially now that she's officially unemployed.

And really, what business is it of his, as a platonic neighbor?

"So I take it your girlfriend isn't Hettie? What, then . . . Letty?" At his dubious look, she laughs and says, "Come on . . . It was hard to hear, exactly, with the music playing."

"What music?"

"Perry Como," she recalls with humiliating ease.

Finishing his pizza, Drew wipes his hands with a napkin and stashes it in his pocket. "*When* did you say this was?"

She didn't. She frowns, wishing he would just tell her what his girlfriend's name is and stop making her feel so foolish.

"It was a Saturday night," she reluctantly tells him, realizing he's not going to move on until she gives up more detail. Which, of course, she recalls. "It was a few weeks ago. At the beginning of December."

He's nodding. "That's what I thought. I stayed home that night. *Alone.*"

"Are you sure?"

"Positive. I haven't had a date since I moved here, until tonight."

A date? He thinks this is a *date*?

But . . .

Well . . .

Is it?

And how does Clara feel if it is?

Not bad.

Maybe even . . . pretty good.

"I remember that night," Drew tells her. "I was watching an old movie on TV and burning a CD to send out with my Christmas cards."

At her surprised look, he explains, "I'm a multitasker, and I'd seen that movie a zillion times so I didn't have to pay close attention."

"No, I'm just surprised . . . you send Christmas cards? With homemade CDs in them?"

"It's kind of a tradition . . . I do it every year. Cheesy, I know."

Not cheesy at all, she thinks, struck by the notion of a single guy going to all that trouble.

"But . . . what about Betty, then?"

"Betty . . ." He appears to be trying to place the name. Then, all at once, he breaks out laughing. "Clara, that was Rosemary Clooney!"

"What . . . ?"

"Her character in *White Christmas.* That was the

movie I was watching while I was burning that CD. Rosemary Clooney played Betty. You're not jealous of her, now . . . are you?"

Her face is flaming as she shakes her head, aware that this changes everything . . .

And nothing at all, she tells herself firmly. *You can't go falling for Drew Becker just because he doesn't have a girlfriend and he did a really sweet thing for you.*

At the moment, she can't remember *why* she can't . . . but she just can't.

Definitely not.

"My only regret," he is saying, "is that I didn't make a dinner reservation for us after the ballet. What was I thinking?"

"Oh, pizza is fine. I love Ray's. Ray's is my favorite." She's talking too fast, chattering because she's nervous. What if he tries to kiss her?

Her cheeks grow hot at the mere notion.

She discreetly tosses her unfinished pizza crust into a garbage can as they pass and pulls her red mittens on again with jittery fingers.

"This is your first year in New York," she goes on hurriedly, grateful for the relative darkness. "You couldn't know that every decent restaurant that isn't closed on Christmas Eve would be jammed, right?"

"Well, at least we got to see the ballet."

She smiles. The ballet. It was magical, as always. Even without her grandfather at her side.

After all, it's Christmas Eve.

"That reminds me . . ." Drew pulls two ticket stubs from his pocket. He wound up with hers when they left their seats during intermission. "Do you want to keep this for your scrapbook?"

Her jaw drops. Can he possibly know that she has

saved every *Nutcracker* ticket stub in a scrapbook, or was it a lucky guess?

"Here." Drew reaches for her hand.

For a moment, Clara thinks—hopefully—that he's holding it.

But he isn't. He's tucking the ticket stub into her mitten . . .

Almost as if he knows that she has a habit of keeping things there, instead of in her pockets.

When he lets go, she feels a quick stab of regret, wishing he would hold her hand. For real.

"Actually . . ." Clara manages to get a grip on her thoughts, and her speech, at last. "That's the other thing I was wondering . . . how did you know?"

"Know what?"

"About me, and . . ."

The tickets in my scrapbook? And stashing things in my mittens? And . . .

"*The Nutcracker*?" is all she manages to say. "I mean . . . I used to see it every year, with my grandfather . . . and I really missed doing that now that he's gone."

"I'm sorry . . . and I actually didn't know about you and *The Nutcracker*. In fact, I'm not exactly a ballet buff. *Not* that I didn't thoroughly enjoy it," he assures her with a smile. "My mother once dragged me to it, and I knew the girl in the story's name was Clara, like yours . . . and I wanted to do something to make your Christmas Eve special, since you were going to be all alone . . . I guess something just told me this would be a good idea."

Something . . . or maybe someone, Clara thinks, tilting her head to the heavens.

Nice work, Grandpa, she tells the star-studded midnight sky.

In that moment, church bells begin to peal down the block, drowning out the ever-present city score of traffic and distant sirens.

" 'Hark the Herald Angels Sing,' " Clara murmurs, recognizing the clanging melody as they climb the steps to their building.

Humming along, Drew unlocks the door and holds it open for her.

"Do you want to come up for coffee?" she hears herself offering unexpectedly. "Or . . . eggnog? My mother brought me some yesterday . . . although I think it's organic soy."

He laughs. "That would be great. But . . . I thought you said your mother was out of town for Christmas."

"Oh, she was . . . but she came back."

Something flickers in his brown eyes. "So you're not going to be alone tomorrow?"

"No, I . . . no."

Her mother is cooking a Christmas goose with all the trimmings, and asked several friends and some of Stan's relatives to join them.

Invite whoever you want. The more the merrier, she told Clara.

Now, looking at Drew, she wonders whether she should ask him to come.

But that seems a little presumptuous . . . doesn't it?

What if he gets the wrong idea? Or, more embarrassingly, thinks *she* has the wrong idea? What if her family gets the wrong idea?

No, organic soy eggnog after an evening at the ballet is one thing.

Spending an entire holiday together would be quite another.

I'll just leave it at this, she tells herself as she opens the door to her apartment and ushers him in.

After all, he isn't Jed.
And if I can't have Jed . . .
I don't really want anybody.

On Christmas morning, Clara awakens early to pale winter sun slanting in the window and church bells ringing once again.

This time, it's "Joy to the World"; she hums and gurgles along as she brushes her teeth.

In the kitchen, she puts on a pot of coffee and washes the two white-film-covered glasses in the sink.

Drew lingered well into the wee hours. Somehow, there was a tremendous amount of conversational ground to cover.

No, he isn't Jed. But he's a good guy who managed to salvage what might have been a lonely Christmas Eve.

When he left at last, it was with a kiss on the cheek and a warm, "Merry Christmas. I guess I'll see you around."

She couldn't help but be disappointed.

Not that she wanted him to take her into his arms and ravish her . . .

No, not at all.

Still, if he had mentioned anything specific about getting together again, she would have invited him to come to her mother's today.

Oh, well.

She puts on the Bing Crosby CD he gave her and settles in the living room to wrap her gifts. Freed from her film production schedule, she managed to go Christmas shopping after all. Her heart wasn't really in it, thanks to her lingering grief for Jed and anxiety over the looming surgery. But at least she picked out special gifts for everyone on her list.

She's folding a cashmere sweater for Stan into a boxed layer of tissue when the door buzzes unexpectedly.

It's Drew is her first thought, and her pulse quickens in reaction.

Then she realizes that Drew wouldn't buzz from outside. He'd just come up and knock.

"Yes?" she calls into the speaker panel by the door.

"Clara McCallum?" a strange female voice crackles over the intercom.

"Yes?"

"May I come up? I have something for you."

"Who are you?"

There's a pause.

Then comes the name that steals Clara's breath away in a gasp.

"Doris Landry."

Opening the door with a violently trembling hand, Clara can hear her visitor in the vestibule two flights below.

She's an old woman now, her muddled brain realizes, trying to reconcile the painstaking footsteps with the memory of the young girl scampering up the steep steps to her big brother's apartment.

Yes, Doris would have to be closing in on eighty . . .

The stark realization washes over her like the first big wave of an incoming tide, followed directly by another: *It was her!*

The old woman who's been here, looking for Clara . . .

It wasn't an autograph-seeking soap opera fanatic.

No, it was, incredibly, Jed's kid sister.

Hearing a thump and a grunt from below, Clara calls, "Are you all right?"

"I . . . not really," is the warbled reply.

Clara leaps into motion. Flipping the brass security hook outside the jamb, she closes the door against it so she won't be locked out.

Then she flies down the stairs in her bathrobe, calling, "I'm coming, Doris . . . hang on!"

She stops short on the second floor landing, caught entirely off guard by the sight below.

A stooped, white-haired figure in a baggy coat, stockings, and black oxfords is at the base of the stairs, struggling to lift a large, familiar suitcase onto the second step.

Can it really be . . . ?

The woman looks up apologetically. "I guess I might need a little help."

Yes. It is.

Her face is a network of wrinkles; her hair is a mass of white waves . . . but behind her wire-rimmed glasses, a pair of bright blue eyes twinkle up at Clara, taking her breath away.

Jed's blue eyes, alive again.

Clara rushes to her, enveloping Doris with a hug and a sob.

"Well, my goodness, take it easy there," Doris exclaims, her face muffled against Clara's robe. "These old bones are pretty brittle, you don't want to snap one on me."

"I'm so sorry . . ." Finally getting hold of her emotions, Clara releases her visitor. "You just . . . surprised me."

"At least this time you're talking to me," Doris replies in her sassy, straightforward way with just a hint of old-lady quaver in her voice. "You could have saved me a lot of trouble if you hadn't been so skittish the night I called to you from my car."

"I'm sorry . . . I had no idea—"

"Oh, ish kabibble, relax. I'm just breaking your chops." Doris's grin is hauntingly familiar. "Just give me a hand with this darned bag of yours, will you? It weighs a ton and a half."

Clara hoists it, wincing only slightly at the pain in her surgical site. Step by step, she and Doris climb to the third floor.

Clara's mind is racing with questions, but she doesn't even know where to start.

Reaching her apartment, she holds the door open and offers, "Have a seat . . . Doris."

I still can't believe this. Can it really be her?

Of course it can.

Clara herself perceived back in 1941 that Doris would be an old lady by now. It's just a little shocking to come face-to-face with the evidence.

"Nice place," Doris pronounces, looking around with approval. "Spacious. I've got a two-bedroom up in the Bronx. Rent-controlled."

"That's nice."

"It is nice. I could have moved to fancier digs after I made all that money in the stock market a few years back, thanks to you."

"Thanks to me?"

"*Apple,*" Doris says mysteriously, and reaches into her pocket. She holds up Clara's iPod with a grin. "When the computer age dawned, I realized right away what was going on with that little Apple you had left behind. So I bought into Mac stock, big, first chance I got."

Clara bursts out laughing. "That's wonderful."

"It is. I'm a rich old broad . . . but like I said, I'm not moving. Too many memories where I am. I've been there since the day I came home from my honeymoon over fifty years ago."

"You're married?"

"Widowed, now." Doris sinks into the couch, noting Clara's expression. "Oh, don't be sad for me. We had a good, long life together. And a bonus: three great kids who take care of their mother."

Three kids . . . Jed's nieces and nephews. But he never would have known them.

Tears spring to Clara's eyes.

"You're thinking about my brother, aren't you?" Doris's voice is laced with uncharacteristic tenderness. She pats the cushion beside her. "Come here."

Clara sits beside her, and in a peculiar turning of the tables, Doris puts a comforting, motherly arm around her.

"You know about Jed, of course."

Clara manages only to nod.

"It's been a long time, for me. Of course I still feel sad when I think about him, but . . . it does get easier with time. I know the pain is fresh for you."

"Yes." She clears her throat. "I just thought . . . I mean, I hoped . . . he wouldn't go after all."

"We all did. He enlisted the summer after Gilbert came back . . . but only after trying to find you for months."

"He promised me he would." Clara's voice is choked with emotion. "He told me he was going to find me, no matter what. And I tried to tell him it was impossible . . ."

Even though I had already told him nothing is impossible.

That's why she's had herself believing, all this time, that Jed was going to find his way back to her somehow. Even now. Even last night . . .

Until it turned out to be Drew.

"Well," Doris is saying, "In the end, when Jed couldn't find you anywhere . . . not even a trace or a hint that you had ever existed . . . I think he finally believed you."

"Believed me?" Clara wonders how much Doris knows.

But then, she *must* know.

She's here, isn't she?

"I heard what you told him that night . . . the night before Pearl Harbor, and . . . everything. I was right there, of course . . . lurking outside the door, eavesdropping. I was a sneaky little stinker back then; what can I say?"

"So . . . you knew? About me? About what I was trying to tell him?"

Doris nods. "I heard everything you said. And I, of course, bought every word of it. I was just a kid. Logic didn't matter to me. It made my brother even more cool, in my eyes, that his new girlfriend was a time traveler from the future."

Clara can't help but laugh.

Doris does, too. Then she adds, "Even now that I'm all grown up, I don't find it all that hard to believe. I've seen a lot of miracles in my lifetime. Just not the one or two that I wanted the most."

Clara's smile is swept away on a wave of renewed grief for Jed. "So your brother only enlisted when he gave up looking for me?"

"Yes, but don't blame yourself. It was what he had to do. It was just who he was. Things were different back then. There was such a sense of patriotic duty—"

"Yes; but I had warned him that if he went, he wouldn't come home."

"He knew that. But it didn't make a difference. Maybe in part because . . ."

"Because?" Clara prods when Doris trails off.

But she knows the rest.

Because you left him. Because there was no one to come home to.

"You can't blame yourself," Doris repeats firmly.

"Did you ever tell Jed that you knew about me?"

"Before he left, I admitted that I had been eavesdropping and I knew. He seemed relieved. That was when he asked me to find you someday . . . and give you your things. As proof. In case you doubted that any of it had really happened."

"I don't doubt it . . . not anymore. I know it was real . . . and I'm so glad you came."

"I just wish I could have gotten to you sooner. But of course, I had to wait . . . more than sixty years, until after you had been there and back. Otherwise, you would have thought I was just some nutty old broad. But I found you years ago, you know."

"You did?"

"Sure. I've watched you grow up, you know. I've been in the audience at every Broadway opening . . . I even got hooked on that damned soap opera because of you."

Clara laughs through her tears.

"You've done beautifully, and you're going to be around for awhile to make it all last. Your best years are still ahead of you," Doris tells her firmly.

"How do you know?"

"I've been around long enough to be able to sense these things. I knew, deep down, that my brother wasn't coming home from Europe . . . and that my son was, from Vietnam. I even knew that my Henry

was going to pull through when his appendix burst on
our tenth wedding anniversary . . . even though the
doctors warned me that he might not make it."

"I'm glad they were wrong."

"Oh, I knew they were. Just as I know that you,
my dear, are going to survive, like I said. Some day
you're going to be a little old lady, like me . . . hard
as it might be to believe. You've got a good long
lifetime ahead of you and my brother would have
wanted you to live it to the fullest . . . even without
him."

Clara nods, knowing it's true . . . because she felt
the same way about Jed.

"Thank you, Doris." Clara hugs her, hard. "You'll
never know what this means to me. I'm so sorry I was
so evasive."

"Oh, that's all right. When you wouldn't see me
before, I figured I might as well wait until today, so
it would be . . . a Christmas gift from Jed."

Maybe, Clara thinks, *that's what he meant when he
promised to find me no matter what.*

It might not be what she had in mind, but it will
have to be enough.

Enough to last, as Doris said, a good long lifetime.

"One more thing," the old woman says, reaching
into her handbag.

She takes out a yellowed envelope and wordlessly
offers it to Clara.

"What . . . what is this?"

"It's a letter from Jed. For you."

> *July 4, 1942*
> *Dearest Clara,*
> *If you're reading this letter, I've probably been
> gone a long time; otherwise I'll be telling you all*

this myself. But Doris promised to find you and deliver this, and your Christmas present, if I can't do it in person, and Landrys always keep their promises. She's probably an old lady by now— imagine that!—and you're probably sore at me, wondering why I didn't listen to your warnings.

Well, today is Independence Day . . . not just on the calendar. In my heart, as well. I'm setting both of us free . . . but only for now. And only because I've spent more than six months trying to find you. I've looked everywhere, even though I realized quite awhile back that it's not going to happen. Not in this lifetime or in this world, anyway.

I don't know how you managed to do what you did, but I do believe you. This letter is proof of that. Yes, I believe what you told me about where you're from, and I believe what you told me about nothing being impossible.

So that's why I'm not giving up, Clara. Ever. I always keep my promises and you can rest assured that I will come back to you someday, somehow.

I want you to know that I understand why you left, just as I hope you understand why I have to enlist despite your warnings. It's just that I can't sit here waiting for you to come back when I realize now that it's never going to happen. I can't spend day after day just waiting for the war to end, or waiting to be drafted, or waiting for some other girl to come along and make me forget you (because that sure isn't going to happen). There are some things a fella just has to do in this life if he has an ounce of integrity in his blood. I do, and I've got no choice. If I come home, I'll keep trying to find you every day for the rest of my life. And if I don't come home . . . I'll find you anyway, maybe more easily, from wherever I am.

I guess all that's left to say is that I love you, Clara . . . only you. Forever. Don't wait for me; just look for me. Live your life, and be happy, and fall in love and get married and have lots of babies. Just don't ever stop looking for me, because someday I'll be there, like I promised. Maybe not in the way either of us would have wanted, or in the way you'd expect. But you'll know it's me. I'll make sure of it.

Yours always,

Jed

P.S. You left behind the mittens your grand-mother made for you. I brought them to your address the day after you left—I don't know, maybe I was somehow still thinking I was actually going to find you there. But of course I didn't, so I gave them to Isamu for safekeeping. I told him that someday you were going to show up, and when you did, he needed to give you the package. He promised, no questions asked. What a swell kid!

A good long cry, Clara realizes, wiping her eyes on a lace-edged handkerchief that once belonged to her grandmother Irene, *can be good for the soul.*

Sitting on her bed clutching Jed's letter after reading and rereading it repeatedly, surrounded by the contents of her suitcase and purse, she marvels at the musty smell. She just saw this stuff a few weeks ago . . . yet it's been put away for sixty-five years.

A paradox she'll never understand, perhaps not

even with help from Mr. Kershaw, should she ever choose to share any of this with him.

Doris told her that her belongings were stored in a far corner of the Landrys' attic, where they remained long after Lois Landry passed away in the 1960s.

Jed had left her a package for Clara, too, along with the letter.

"It was a square box, kind of heavy, wrapped in Christmas paper. Do you know how many times over the years I was tempted to open it and see what was in it? But I'm afraid it must have eventually gotten mixed up with the stuff Gilbert sold to an antique dealer when he cleaned out the attic after Mother died, because I never saw it again after that. I'm so sorry."

"It's all right." Suspecting what might have been in the package, Clara tried not to let her disappointment show. At least she has the mittens. And as much as she would have liked to have had the angel snow globe Jed wanted to give her that last day, she'll have to be content with just the letter. And Jed's words, she knows, will go a long way to sustain her through her grief.

Doris told her that Gilbert and his wife lived on at 21 Chestnut Street and raised their family there, eventually selling the house and retiring to Florida to be near their only daughter. Jed's spirited younger brother, whom Clara heard so much about but never met, passed away in Tampa a few years ago, a multimillionaire.

Mary Ann, too, is gone, but she left behind a husband, two children and seven grandchildren. Penny, once a tragic war widow whose husband was shot down in the South Pacific, went on to remarry and have two more children. She and her husband live not far from Doris.

"I'd love to have you see her again, but she has a bad heart . . . I'm afraid she'd keel over at the sight of you."

Clara laughed and promised to come visit Doris after the holidays, and Doris left her with a warm hug and shared tears.

For Clara, they have yet to subside.

At least she now has the proof to dispel any lingering doubt . . . not that she has any.

And she even has her iPod back . . . though it needs to be charged, of course.

Doris told her the battery ran out soon after she left. "Jed thought he broke the darned thing, of course," she said with a laugh. "He kept playing that one song over and over and he was sure he'd worn it out."

"Which song?" Clara asked, though she knew very well what Doris meant.

" 'I'll Be Home For Christmas.' You know, you were a little ahead of your time. It wasn't a hit record until 1943. My brother was overseas by then. I've always wondered how Jed reacted when he first heard it—and it was Bing Crosby and not Frank Sinatra singing it."

Now, still clutching Jed's letter, Clara returns to the living room. At the stereo, she trades the Bing Crosby CD for the Frank Sinatra one she downloaded onto her iPod last year.

She presses the SEEK button until the familiar opening strains fill the room.

Raising the volume, she stands, eyes closed, letter pressed to her heart, tears streaming down her face.

Caught up in memories of Jed, and what might have

been, she doesn't realize someone is knocking at the door even after she's subconsciously heard the sharp rapping a few times.

Wiping her eyes on the sleeve of her robe, she hurries to open the door.

Drew Becker is standing there, wearing an overcoat, his cheeks ruddy with the cold.

"Merry Christmas." He's somewhat breathless. "Good, you're still here."

"I'm still here . . ." And she must look a sight. She's been crying; her hand strays to her hair, uncombed since she rolled out of bed a few hours ago.

Yet nonetheless, despite the emotional upheaval over Jed, she finds herself glad to see Drew. More than glad, really.

Admit it. You are *attracted to him. And maybe he* is *your type.*

"I know you have to go to your mother's," he says hurriedly, "but I just wanted to stop by to say merry Christmas . . . and to give you this."

He thrusts a gift-wrapped box into her hands.

"What . . . ?"

"Open it. I went out for a long walk and to get the paper this morning, and . . . I found this antique store. More of a used junk store, really. But it was open, and I was cold . . . so I went in. When I spotted this on the shelf, I knew I had to get it for you."

"What is it?" Clara asks, looking down at the weighty square box.

"You'll see. Go on, open it." Clearly, he's anxious.

She tears the paper off carefully.

The box is plain cardboard—no hint to its contents.

In the background, Frank is singing about presents on the tree, and Clara swallows hard over a lump in her throat, remembering . . .

Then she opens the box lid . . .

And there it is.

A snow globe.

The snow globe.

Stunned, she lifts it out.

It can't be . . .

But it is. The exact one.

A dark-haired little angel with a broken wing tip smiles at her from behind a faint crack in the curved glass.

She looks up at Drew, speechless.

"For your collection," he says, gesturing at the mantel.

She told him about the dark-haired angels last night. She told him a lot of things . . .

But not, of course, about Jed.

Or . . . *this*.

How could he have known?

He couldn't have. There's no way on earth . . .

On earth.

She stares at the snow globe, her hands shaking so violently that the angel is lost in a blizzard of glittery white flakes.

"I can't believe . . . I can't believe you found this . . ."

"I can't either, actually. I was just walking kind of aimlessly, but something just told me to go into that store, and when I saw this . . . well, it was actually kind of strange. For a second there I almost thought you might already have it, because I definitely felt like I remembered it. You know . . . like I had seen it before."

"I . . . I don't already have it."

"Good. Oh, and it's musical, see?" Drew takes it from her and winds the key on the bottom.

Tinkling notes spill forth to mingle with Frank, in the background, singing about snow and mistletoe.

So caught up in shock is Clara that she doesn't immediately realize that the music box melody is, incredibly, the same as the one playing on her stereo.

"But . . . it's supposed to be 'Hark the Herald Angels Sing,' " she tells Drew in amazement.

"Are you sure you don't already have one like this?"

"No, it's just . . . the song. I thought it would be . . . different."

He just looks at her. "It's 'I'll Be Home For Christmas,' don't you hear it?"

"Yes . . . I do. I hear it."

And in her mind, Clara hears something else.

Just don't ever stop looking for me, because someday I'll be there, like I promised. Maybe not in the way either of us would have wanted, or in the way you'd expect. But you'll know it's me. I'll make sure of it.

Clara shakes her head, laughing and crying at once.

"Are you all right?" Drew asks, eyes wide.

"I'm fine . . ."

"Are you sure?"

"Positive. I'm just a little emotional. You know . . . because it's Christmas."

Drew watches her with uncertainty for a moment, then shrugs.

"Hey, you know what I've always wondered about this song?" he asks, changing the subject. "Why do they say presents *on* the tree instead of *under* the tree? That doesn't make any sense. How can presents be *on* the tree?"

Clara reaches out to take his hand. His fingers wrap around hers; she instantly feels warm, and safe, and a spark of something . . . familiar.

"Listen, what are you doing today?" Clara asks Drew Becker, and he grins.

"Oh, my schedule is wide open . . . why?" he asks with a wink.

A *wink*.

And in the background, the song concludes at last with a fervent, *"If only . . . in my dreams . . ."*

CLASSIC WINTER ROMANCE
TO READ BY THE FIRE